Peter Tremayne is the fiction pseu[...]
Ellis, a well-known authority on [...]
utilised his knowledge of the Brehon law system and seventh-century Irish society to create a new concept in detective fiction.

An international Sister Fidelma Society has been established, with a journal entitled *The Brehon* appearing three times yearly. Details can be obtained either by writing to the Society at 1643-B Savannah Highway, Suite 396, Charleston, SC 29407, USA, or by logging on to the society website at www.sisterfidelma.com.

Praise for the widely acclaimed Sister Fidelma mysteries:

'The Sister Fidelma books give the readers a rattling good yarn. But more than that, they bring vividly and viscerally to life the fascinating lost world of the Celtic Irish. I put down *The Spider's Web* with a sense of satisfaction at a good story well told, but also speculating on what modern life might have been like had that civilisation survived'
Ronan Bennett

'This masterly storytelling from an author who breathes fascinating life into the world he is writing about' *Belfast Telegraph*

'Rich helpings of evil and tension with lively and varied characters' *Historical Novels Review*

'The detail of the books is fascinating, giving us a vivid picture of everyday life at this time . . . the most detailed and vivid recreations of ancient Ireland' *Irish Examiner*

'A brilliant and beguiling heroine. Immensely appealing' *Publishers Weekly*

the dove of death

peter Tremayne

headline

First published in 2009 by
HEADLINE PUBLISHING GROUP

First published in paperback in 2010 by
HEADLINE PUBLISHING GROUP

2

Cataloguing in Publication Data is available from the British Library

ISBN 978 0 7553 5762 8 (B Format)
ISBN 978 0 7553 4724 7 (A Format)

Typeset in Times New Roman PS by Palimpsest Book Production Limited,
Grangemouth, Stirlingshire

Printed and bound in Great Britain by
Clays Ltd, St Ives plc

Headline's policy is to use papers that are natural, renewable and recyclable products
and made from wood grown in sustainable forests. The logging and manufacturing
processes are expected to conform to the environmental regulations of the
country of origin.

HEADLINE PUBLISHING GROUP
An Hachette UK Company
338 Euston Road
London NW1 3BH

www.headline.co.uk
www.hachette.co.uk

For my old friend Professor Per Denez, who first suggested that Fidelma visit Brittany; for Bernez ar Nail, for his advice and guidance; for Yves Borius, former mayor of Sarzhav (Sarzeau) near Brilhag and Conseil Général du Morbihan; for Hervé Latimier and Jean-Michel Mahé, for their translations of Fidelma into Breton; for Marie-Claude and Claud David for their hospitality and, indeed, for all my many Breton friends.

Gant ar spi e c'hello pobl Vreizh adkemer un deiz he flas e-touez pobloù ar bed gant he yezh hag he sevenadur. 'With the hope that the ancient Breton nation, its language and culture, takes its place once more among the nations of the world.'

Dat veniam corvis, vexat censura columbas.
The censor (magistrate) forgives the crows but blames the doves.

Juvenal, 1st – 2nd century AD

Non semper ea sunt quae videntur.
Things are not always what they appear to be.

Phaedrus, *c.* 15 BC – *c.* AD 50

PRINCIPAL CHARACTERS

Sister Fidelma of Cashel, a *dálaigh* or advocate of the law courts of seventh-century Ireland
Brother Eadulf of Seaxmund's Ham in the land of the South Folk, her companion

On the Barnacle Goose
Bressal of Cashel, Fidelma's cousin and envoy of her brother Colgú, King of Muman
Murchad, the captain
Gurvan, the mate
Wenbrit, the cabin boy
Hoel, a crewman

On the island of Hoedig
Brother Metellus, a Roman cleric
Lowenen, the chieftain
Onenn, his wife

On the Rhuis Peninsula

Abbot Maelcar of the abbey of the Blessed Gildas
Brother Ebolbain, his scribe
Aourken, a widow
Berran, a drover
Biscam, a merchant
Barbatil, Argantken's father
Coric, his companion

At the fortress of Brilhag
Macliau, son of the *mac'htiern* (lord) of Brilhag
Argantken, Macliau's mistress
Trifina, Macliau's sister
Iuna, stewardess of the household
Bleidbara, commander of the guard at Brilhag
Boric, his deputy and a tracker
Iarnbud, a *bretat*, or judge to the *mac'htiern* of Brilhag

Riwanon, wife of Alain the Tall, King of the Bretons
Budic, commander of her bodyguard
Ceingar, her female attendant

Alain Hir (the Tall), King of the Bretons
Canao, the *mac'htiern*, Lord of Brilhag

Kaourentin, a *bretat* or judge of Bro-Gernev

At Govihan
Heraclius, an apothecary from Constantinopolis

Koulm ar Maro, 'The Dove of Death'

hISTORICAL NOTE

The events in this story occur during the summer of ad 670 and follow those described in The Council of the Cursed. Fidelma and Eadulf are returning after their adventure at the Council of Autun in the land of the Burgunds via the seaport of Naoned (Nantes) in what had been called Armorica – 'the land before the sea'. The sea route home would bring them along the south coast of the peninsula before turning north, avoiding the Roches de Penmarc'h, and turning north-west across the Baie d'Audierne and on to Ireland.

Armorica had now become known as 'Little Britain' (Brittany). Its original Gaulish Celtic population had been re-inforced by waves of British Celtic refugees during the fifth, sixth and seventh centuries. These Britons were seeking asylum from the invading Anglo-Saxons, who were then carving out their kingdoms in southern Britain – kingdoms that were eventually to unite in the tenth century as Angle-land or England.

As St Gildas (*d.* AD 570), one of the British refugees, wrote in *De Excidio et Conquestu Britanniae* (*On the Ruin and Conquest of Britain*), the British Celts were being either massacred or forced to flee across the seas from the *'ferocissimi Saxones'*.

The British refugees brought to Armorica their dialect of Celtic, which was not too different from the native Gaulish language, and are today called Bretons. I have used this name to make them more easily distinguished from the original Britons.

In Fidelma's time the great Breton abbeys were centres of Celtic learning and literacy. The first surviving Breton language manuscript dates from the eighth century AD and is a century older than the oldest text in French. This is the *Leiden Mss Vossianus* held in Leyden in the Netherlands. It is a treatise on biology written by Breton scholars and unique among early medieval Celtic manuscripts for containing Celtic words in a medical context. It was in the eighth century also that it became possible to distinguish Breton from Cornish and from Welsh. Prior to this, the three languages were indistinguishable, not yet having developed as dialects of their British (Celtic) parent. This is why, in this story, Fidelma and Eadulf, who have some knowledge of the language of the Britons, sometimes find it hard to understand Breton.

There was also a great deal written in Latin by Breton religious. Texts of some forty saints' lives are known from the seventh to fourteenth centuries. There is also a *Libri Romanorum et Francorum*, which is actually a collection of laws pertaining to Brittany. At one time, scholars wrongly ascribed it as *'Kanones Wallici'* (Welsh Canons), but it is now thought to have been composed in Brittany in the sixth century. It survives only in a ninth-century copy.

Brittany at the time of this story was divided into several petty kingdoms, each giving allegiance to one overall ruler acknowledged as King of the Bretons. Because of the destruction of records and confusion of dating, the precise dates of reigns can never be asserted with absolute certainty. However, it is certain that Alain Hir (the Tall) ruled at this time.

Of the main Breton territories, by AD 670, Domnonia, in the

north, had become dominant and Alain Hir had descended from its ruling house. Domnonia had united with the southern lands of Bro-Erech, which became renamed Bro-Waroch in honour of one of its most famous rulers. There was also the south-west kingdom of Bro-Gernev (Kernev) later called in French Cornouaille. Gradlon ap Alain ruled it at this time. To the north-west of the peninsula was Bro-Leon, whose last King, Ausoch, had died around AD 590 and so this small kingdom had become a fiefdom. There was also the semi-independent territory of Pou-Kaer or Poher, which was eventually united with Cornouaille.

One can see, in the evidence of these place-names, some of the origins of the British refugees. Domnonia was settled by refugees from Dumnonia in southern Britain, the origin of the modern English county called Devon. Kernev or Cornouaille in Brittany is the same as Kernow or Cornwall in Britain.

For those of a technical questioning mind, I have accepted the chronology of St Theophanes Confessor (c. AD 758–818), the Byzantine aristocrat, ascetic monk and historian, when he refers to the invention of *pyr thalassion* (sea- or liquid fire) being in use just before AD 670. He points out that the invention of what we now call 'Greek Fire' was made by Callinicus, an architect and refugee from Heliopolis in Phoenice (the modern Becaa Valley in Lebanon). Callinicus had fled to Constantinople as a refugee after the Islamic conquest of the area. This *pyr thalassion* was difficult to extinguish – indeed, water served to spread the flames. Even as late as the tenth century, Emperor Constantine VII Porphyrogenitus cautioned his son, in *De Administrando Imperio*, not to give three things to a foreigner – a crown, the hand of a royal princess, and the secret of 'liquid fire'.

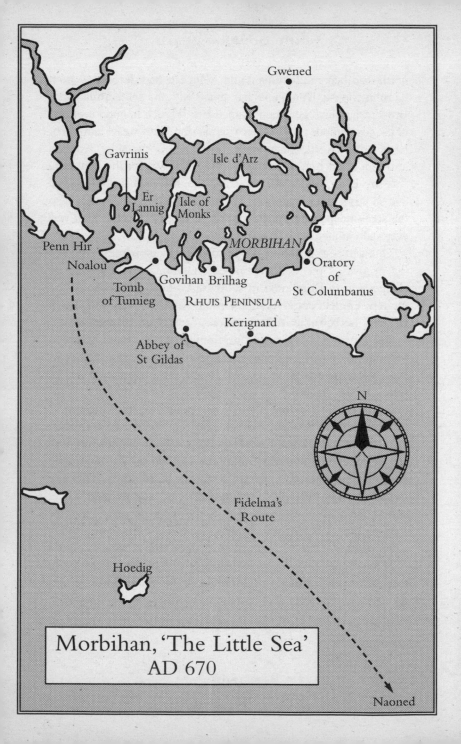

Morbihan, 'The Little Sea'
AD 670

CHAPTER ONE

F idelma of Cashel leaned easily against the taffrail at
the stern of the merchant ship, watching the receding
coastline.

'It is good to be heading home, Cousin,' smiled the tall
man with red hair who stood by her side. He could have been
Fidelma's brother, so alike were they. He was about her age,
in his late twenties, with pleasant features – although his jaw
was more aggressive than hers, square and jutting so that the
eye noticed it first rather than the humorous features and
sparkling grey-green eyes. His clothing was well cut and he
could have been mistaken for a wealthy merchant. However,
his muscular figure gave him the appearance of a warrior.

Fidelma turned her head slightly towards him.

'It would be a lie if I denied it, Cousin Bressal. I have been
absent from my brother's kingdom for far too long. God willing,
we will have an agreeable voyage ahead back to Aird Mhór.'

Bressal, Prince of the Eóghanacht of Cashel, nodded
solemnly.

'The weather is set fair, and although the winds are not strong, at least they are blowing from the south. When our captain changes tack, the wind will be against our backs the whole way.'

Fidelma turned back to the vanishing coastline. There was, indeed, a slight wind from the south and the day seemed fine and warm, although the sunshine was hazy. The sturdy trading vessel – the *Gé Ghúirainn*, the *Barnacle Goose* – was half a day out from the coastal salt marshes of Gwenrann and, for the moment, driving into the prevailing wind.

Bressal glanced up at the sails. 'Our good captain, Murchad, will be turning to catch the wind soon,' he observed. 'But I understand that you know him and this ship very well?'

'I was amazed when I found the *Barnacle Goose* harboured in Naoned when we arrived,' conceded Fidelma. 'I spent many days on this ship when Murchad took a group of pilgrims from Aird Mhór to the holy shrine of the Blessed James in Galicia.'

Bressal's smile broadened. 'I cannot see you in the role of a pilgrim, Fidelma. I have never understood why you entered the religious in the first place.'

Fidelma was not annoyed by her cousin's remarks. They had grown up together and knew one another as friends as well as family. Fidelma shrugged, for she had asked herself a similar question many times.

'It was our cousin Abbot Laisran who persuaded me to do so. I had qualified at the law school of Moram at Tara and did not know what to do to progress in life.'

'But you had qualified as an *anruth*, one degree below the

highest the law school could bestow. Why didn't you continue and become an *ollamh*, a professor of the law? I always thought that with your ambition you would do so. You could have become Brehon to the King.'

Fidelma grimaced. 'I didn't want it said that I owed my career to my family. Nor did I want to be tied down.'

'I would have thought that entering Bridget's abbey at Cill Dara was exactly that – being tied down with rules and restrictions.'

'I didn't know it then,' Fidelma said defensively. 'The abbey wanted someone trained in law. Well, you have heard why I left Cill Dara and, to be honest, I have not joined any institution since then. Instead, I have willingly served my brother, the King, whenever he needed me.'

'Eadulf told me that you had come several days' journey downriver from the land of the Burgunds.'

'We were attending a Council at Autun with some of the bishops and abbots of Éireann. We left Abbot Ségdae of Imleach and the others still in discussion there. Our services were no longer needed and so we determined to return to the coast and find a ship to take us home.'

It had been a surprise to Fidelma to arrive at the busy port of Naoned and find, almost among the first people that she saw, her own Cousin Bressal striding along the wooden quays. He told her that her brother, King Colgú, had sent him to the salt marshes of Gwenrann to negotiate a trading treaty with Alain Hir, the King of the Bretons, to take cargoes of salt back to Muman. Salt was highly prized in the Five Kingdoms of Éireann, so prized that the laws warned that everyone desired it and some might stop at nothing to get it. The salt of Gwenrann – the name, as it had been explained to Fidelma, meant the 'white land' for that is what the great salt marshes looked like – had been renowned from time beyond memory, and was much valued.

It was even more of a surprise for Fidelma to find that the ship her cousin had made his voyage on was the *Barnacle Goose*, in which she had had one of her most dangerous adventures. It was purely by chance that the ship had moored in the port of Naoned. The salt pans of Gwenrann lay westward along the coast, and the cargo holds of the vessel had already been filled with the sacks of salt wrested from the sea. Bressal had found that King Alain Hir had gone to his fortress at Naoned, and protocol had dictated that Bressal should take the time before his voyage home to give his thanks and farewells to the Breton King. The treaty was not merely for one cargo of salt but for ensuring a continuance of trade between the ports of Muman and 'Little Britain'.

'It was a lucky thing that we had to come to Naoned,' Bressal said, echoing her unspoken thoughts as she contemplated the coincidence, 'otherwise we would have missed each other entirely. Ah!'

The exclamation was uttered in response to a shout. It came from a sturdy, thickset man with greying hair and weather-beaten features. He could not be mistaken for anything other than the sailor he was. Murchad, the captain of the *Barnacle Goose*, was in his late forties, with a prominent nose which accentuated the close set of his sea-grey eyes. Their forbidding aspect was offset by a twinkling, almost hidden humour.

As Bressal had earlier guessed, members of the crew were now springing to the sheets, hauling on the ropes while the mate, Gurvan, threw his weight on the great tiller, helped by another crewman, causing the ship to begin its turn so that the wind was at its back. For some moments, Fidelma and Bressal clung to the taffrail to steady themselves as the deck rose and the masts above them swayed, the sails cracking as the winds caught them. Then all was silent and the ship seemed to be gliding calmly over the blue waters again.

Murchad walked across the deck to speak with Gurvan and obviously checked the direction of the vessel. Then he turned with a friendly smile to Fidelma and her companion and went below.

'A man of few words,' smiled Bressal.

'But a good seaman,' replied Fidelma. 'You know that you are in safe hands when Murchad is in charge. I have seen him handle storms and an attack by pirates as if they were ordinary occurrences.'

'Having sailed with him from Aird Mhór, I have no doubts of it,' rejoined her cousin. 'Still, I shan't be sorry to set foot ashore again. I am happier on land than I am at sea.' He paused and looked around. 'Speaking of which . . . I have not seen your husband Eadulf since we raised sail.'

Fidelma's expression was one of amusement although, examined closely, there was some concern there too.

'He is below. I am afraid that Eadulf is not a born sailor. Murchad has already warned him that the worst thing to do is to go below when you feel nausea. Better to be on deck and concentrate your gaze on the horizon. Alas, Eadulf was not receptive to advice. I don't doubt that he is suffering the consequences.'

Bressal smiled in sympathy. 'He is a good man in spite of—' He suddenly hesitated and flushed.

'In spite of being a Saxon?' Fidelma turned to him, her eyes bright. There was no bitterness in her voice.

Bressal shrugged. 'One hears so many bad tales about the Saxons, Cousin. One naturally asks: if those tales are true, how can a man of such worth as Eadulf come from such a people?'

'There is good and bad in all people, Cousin,' Fidelma rebuked mildly.

'I am not denying it,' Bressal agreed. 'Though you must admit that there was great consternation from certain quarters when you announced that you were marrying him.'

'Mainly protests from people who wish to bring in the ideas of those esoteric fanatics who want all members of the religious to follow this concept of celibacy.'

'Those do not count for much,' dismissed Bressal. 'I was thinking of some of our own people, the nobles who felt that you should marry a prince of the Five Kingdoms and not a Saxon stranger.'

Fidelma's eyes flashed dangerously for a moment. 'And were you of that number?' she asked.

Bressal grinned in amusement. 'I had not met Eadulf then.'

'And now that you have?' she pressed.

'I realise that people cannot make judgements until they know the individual. Eadulf is now one of us. I will stand with him and draw my sword to defend his rights.'

The ship suddenly lurched as a rogue wave hit against its side. Fidelma staggered a moment, then she turned, laughing at her cousin who was also trying to balance.

'I don't think Eadulf will be in the mood to stand with anyone at the moment,' she observed dryly. She looked up at the sails. They were not filling as she had expected. The southerly winds were mild, which made the ship's progress very slow. Gurvan, the mate, saw her gaze and called across to her.

'Typical summer winds here, lady,' he offered. 'Mild and slow. That was just a freak wave, as we call them. But once we get through the Treizh an Tagnouz Passage we ought to pick up a stronger wind. That won't be too long now. By tomorrow we'll be making good time, you'll see.'

Fidelma acknowledged his encouragement with a wave of her hand.

'We came through this Tagnouz Passage on our voyage here,' commented Bressal. 'It means "nasty" in the local language. It runs between some islands and the main coast but it is quite a wide one. You can barely see land on either side.'

'I was meaning to ask, why did my brother choose you as his envoy on this trip?' she asked curiously.

'Mainly because I speak the language of the Britons which is similar to those of the people of this land. Remember, I spent some time in Dyfed at the court of Gwlyddien after you had rendered him great service when you were there.'

'And was the King of this land easy to negotiate with?'

'Alain Hir? He is pleasant enough. His people seem to

have many ways that are similar to our lifestyle. But, like most kings, envy, greed and intrigue surround him. I'll tell you about a rumour I heard . . .'

'Would you care for a meal, lady?' interrupted a shrill voice. Wenbrit, the young cabin boy whom she had befriended on the pilgrim voyage, had come on deck. 'The sun is beyond its zenith, and I have some dried meats and cheeses in the cabin and a flagon of the local cider to wash it down with.'

Fidelma smiled softly at the young boy. 'I think I am hungry,' she confessed. 'Have you called Eadulf?'

'I did ask, but he simply threw something at me and turned over in his bunk.' The boy chuckled mischievously.

'Then we should leave him to his agonies,' said Bressal. 'Let's go and eat, Cousin.'

It felt strange for Fidelma to be eating with her cousin in the main cabin of the *Barnacle Goose*. It was a long time since she had regularly eaten there, but then it had been filled with the many pilgrims from the great abbey of Magh Bile en route to the Holy Shrine of Blessed James. Now there was only her Cousin Bressal, herself and Eadulf who were passengers on the ship. The rest of the vessel, apart from the crew's quarters, had been given over to the storage of salt, packed in great sacks.

Being on board, for Fidelma, was like being among old friends. She was even delighted to see the large male black cat sitting regarding her solemnly with bright green eyes from the top of a cupboard. Luchtigern – 'the Mouse Lord', as he was called – had actually saved her life during the voyage to the Shrine of Blessed James. Now the animal seemed to recognise her and leaped down, gave a soft 'miaow' and strode with almost aristocratic poise across to her, rubbing himself against her leg. She bent down to stroke the sleek black fur. On the back of its head she felt a hard lump in its fur.

Wenbrit, who was setting the plates, noticed her frown. 'Something wrong, lady?' he asked.

'Luchtigern seems to have a lump on the back of his head,' she said. She did not like to see animals ill or in discomfort.

The cat, having allowed itself to be petted for a moment or two, now turned and then, with a shake of its body implying its independence, moved off on some unknown errand.

'Don't worry, lady.' Wenbrit made a reassuring gesture. 'It is just a piece of pitch that has become entangled in his fur. I am going to cut it out later.'

Fidelma knew that pitch, a resin drawn from pinewood, was used to waterproof sails and even the hulls of ships, as well as domestic jars and pots. It was a viscous black liquid that stuck and formed a hard surface or lumps. However, Luchtigern did not seem to mind the sticky lump on the back of his head.

Fidelma recalled how she had discussed with Wenbrit the reason why the animal was called 'the Mouse Lord', for there had been a legendary cat who dwelled in the Caves of Dunmore in Éireann who had defeated all the warriors of the King of Laigin. They had wanted it killed, but 'the Mouse Lord' was far too wily for the warriors. Fidelma smiled at the memory, and recalled how Luchtigern had saved her life by warning her of an assassin's approach.

Fidelma was looking forward to their arrival in her brother's capital of Cashel. She longed to see her young son, Alchú, and had begun to regret missing so much time in his company. She should have been watching him develop from baby to young boyhood. But then, she had chosen the career of law and, as sister to the King, she had duties and obligations to fulfil. Yet she hoped that there would be no other demands on her time for the foreseeable future. She and Eadulf deserved a rest after all their travels on behalf of her brother. Fidelma shook herself subconsciously as she realised that regret could easily turn to resentment.

Her mind shifted to her husband.

Poor Eadulf. He was lying prone in their cabin, the same cabin that she had occupied on the pilgrim voyage, and was probably feeling that death would be a worthwhile alternative to the voyage home. He was not a good sailor at the best of times. Even though the weather was clement, he had begun to feel queasy almost as soon as they had left the mouth of the great River Liger, down which they had travelled from Nebirnum, on their return to Naoned from their perilous quest at the Council of Autun. That had truly been a council of the cursed. Once out of the Liger they had swung northward along what was called 'the Wild Coast'. It was then that Eadulf had to take to his bunk.

Wenbrit brought them bread, still fresh, for he had purchased it just before they had hoisted sail, and some cold meats with a jug of cider.

'To a good voyage,' toasted Bressal, raising his mug.

'To a quick one,' replied Fidelma.

'You are thinking of little Alchú,' observed her cousin.

She nodded wistfully.

'Have no fear for him,' her cousin replied. 'It was only a few weeks ago I saw him, just before I left Cashel. Muirgen and Nessán take great care of him, as if he were their own child. They seem to have no regrets about quitting their shepherd's life at Gabhlán to come and serve you as nurse and . . .'

He hesitated for a moment, trying to find the right word. The word he chose was *cobairech*, which meant an assistant or helper. Indeed, while Muirgen had adapted well to being a nurse within the great palace of Cashel, her husband Nessán had been a shepherd all his life in the western mountains. His role, therefore, was mainly to look after the livestock at the palace and assist when needed. Since the kidnapping of Alchú by Uaman, Lord of the Passes of Sliabh Mis, the infamous leper, the couple had been fiercely devoted to the welfare of the child and to Fidelma and Eadulf.

Sometimes it worried Fidelma. She tried to hide her concern that her role as a *dálaigh*, an advocate of the Laws of the Fénechus, often conflicted with the time she should have spent as a mother in her son's company. Even Eadulf had raised complaints from time to time. In the last six months the couple had been summoned to Tara to investigate the death of the High King himself. Barely had they returned to Cashel when Abbot Ségdae of Imleach, the principal abbey of the Kingdom of Muman, had requested her presence at the major Church Council that was to meet in the city of Autun in the land of Burgundia. It was a council whose decision might have a great impact on the rites and theology of the Church in the Five Kingdoms. Now, after so long, it would be good to be home in Cashel.

She realised that Bressal was regarding her worried expression with some sympathy.

'Cousin, you have no need to worry about the welfare of your child,' he repeated.

'It is a mother's privilege,' she replied simply, as she returned to her meal. After a swallow of the cider, she asked: 'And what news from Tara? Sechnassach was a wise man, well praised by the bards and the people. His assassination has truly disrupted the peace of the Five Kingdoms.'

Bressal toyed with his food for a moment, as if in thought.

'His death was certainly a great blow to the unity of the kingdoms,' he agreed. 'Thanks to your intervention, however, civil war was averted when you revealed the culprit.'

'But what of the new High King – Cenn Fáelad the son of Blathmaic. Is he as wise as his brother, Sechnassach? How is he regarded by the people?'

'There are many rumours . . .' began Bressal.

Fidelma frowned impatiently. 'What rumours?'

'As you know, Cenn Fáelad is of the southern Uí Néill, of the line of the Síl nÁedo Sláine. The family are always quarrelling amongst themselves. Sechnassach was able to overcome petty squabbles by diplomacy. Cenn Fáelad seems to lack that touch. But many believe that he should not have been elected to the High Kingship.'

'I presume that his *derbhfine* met – at least three generations in accordance with the law? Was not Cenn Fáelad legally nominated and elected?' Fidelma sniffed in disapproval.

'So I understand, but I am told that his Cousin Finsnechta Fledach, the son of Dúnchad, who was brother to Cenn Fáelad's father, has raised objections. He feels that he should have been elevated to the High Kingship.'

'The decision of the *derbhfine* must be respected under law,' Fidelma pointed out.

'Cenn Fáelad has tried to win his cousin over by appointing him lord of Brega in the Middle Kingdom.'

'And Finsnechta is still not satisfied?'

'The rumour is that he is trying to persuade the chiefs and provincial kings to rally to his cause to challenge his cousin. One rumour says that Finsnechta has sailed to Iona to seek the support of Abbot Adomnán.'

Fidelma looked grave. 'So there are troubled times ahead?'

'Your brother is determined to keep Muman out of the affair, for he sees it as an internal struggle between the Uí Néill only.'

'A difficult path to tread, especially if the legitimate High King calls upon my brother for support, which he is entitled to do.'

'It is a weakness of our kingship,' sighed Bressal. 'We have councils who nominate and elect our kings and thereafter have arguments on whether the decision was right or wrong. Our friends, the Saxons, simply say the eldest son of a king should inherit, no matter if they are good or bad, and if that King can keep the office by means of his sword, then he keeps it.'

'*Violentia praecedit jus,*' muttered Fidelma. Might before right. 'It is not a good system.'

They finished their meal and Fidelma went to look in on Eadulf in the cabin. He was lying on the bunk, groaning a little in his sleep, but at least he was sleeping. Fidelma smiled before gently closing the cabin door and returning on deck to join her cousin.

The late afternoon had turned darker although the sun was still shining through the uniform grey layer of clouds covering the whole sky like ground glass. She also noticed that the wind had dropped – no, not dropped, but had veered around so that it was blowing against them now.

Gurvan greeted them, still at his place at the tiller.

'A troubled sky,' he muttered. 'But no matter. We might have a storm – some lightning but without thunder. You can always read the signs in the sky.'

'Will it delay our journey?' asked Fidelma anxiously.

'Bless you, not at all,' replied Gurvan. 'A few days of unsettled weather is to be expected at this time of year. Good days are sometimes followed by rain. It can be very change-able. Once beyond those islands,' he thrust out a hand to indicate their direction, 'through the passage that I mentioned, it should be fair sailing. The wind will turn again soon, have no worry.'

To the south lay the blurred outline of an island which Gurvan now identified as Hoedig, which he confided meant 'duckling', and before them was a great mass called Houad, the duck, towards which the ship tacked its way. The passage would bring them between these southern islands and the thrusting headland called Beg Kongell.

As Gurvan was explaining all this to Fidelma, his eyes

suddenly narrowed. Almost at the same time, a voice called down from the masthead.

'Sail ho! Dead ahead!'

Fidelma turned to see what had been spotted beyond the rising and falling of the high bow of the *Barnacle Goose*. She could only just make out the tiny speck on the horizon: as it grew closer, she saw that it was a vessel under full sail, moving rapidly with the changed wind behind it.

'Call the captain,' Gurvan shouted to one of the crew.

'Is something wrong?' asked Fidelma.

'That's no merchant vessel,' replied the mate. 'It's a fast-trimmed ship and heading this way.'

Murchad, followed by Bressal, appeared on deck. He sprang up the rigging and peered towards the vessel. His expression became worried.

'She's a fighting ship, right enough,' he called down to Gurvan. He glanced up at the sails and then back to the oncoming vessel. 'She has the wind behind her and she's bearing down on us.' His comment was a statement of the obvious but no one spoke for a moment. Then he snapped: 'Prepare to go about – let's get the wind behind us. I'll head for the shelter of Hoedig.' The island was visible nearby.

Gurvan was already shouting the necessary orders to the crew.

'Is it serious, Captain?' Bressal asked quietly.

The skipper of the *Barnacle Goose* considered a moment before he spoke.

'The trade routes along the coast contain rich pickings for anyone who has no scruples about how they make a living.

When you see a fast warship approaching in these waters, then it's better to be safe than sorry. So we *take* it as serious but *hope* it is not.'

Bressal muttered something and hurried below.

The attention of the crew was now focused on turning the ship into the wind while, remorselessly, the sleek-built war vessel seemed to be straining, sails taut so that it was almost heeling over, bearing towards them, growing larger and larger. Fidelma grabbed at the railing as the *Barnacle Goose* began to turn, the deck shifting alarmingly beneath her feet, the oncoming vessel now behind them.

She saw Wenbrit, the cabin boy, poking his head above the hatch.

'Wenbrit,' she called, 'make Brother Eadulf aware of what is happening and get him on deck. Don't take *no* for an answer!'

The boy raised a hand to his forehead and disappeared below.

Almost at once, her Cousin Bressal reappeared. He had strapped on his war helmet and his sword and fighting knife, but she noticed that he held in his right hand the white hazel wand of office that denoted his status as a *techtaire*, an envoy of his King. He took his place by Murchad.

'Are your crew armed, Captain?' he asked.

Murchad pulled a face. 'We are a merchant vessel; certainly we are not armed to fight that sort of warship,' he answered, jerking his head towards the still-closing vessel.

'But if they try to board us, we must put up a resistance,' insisted Bressal.

'What if they mean us no harm?' Fidelma wanted to know. 'We are only assuming the ship has hostile intentions. It might be a war vessel of the King of the Bretons. Anyway, you are a *techtaire*, an ambassador of our King, and this ship is under your protection.'

This time it was Murchad who shook his head.

'Let us hope that whoever is the captain of that ship has respect for that protection. There is no flag at her mast, no symbol or insignia on her sails. And now I can see bowmen lined up along her side with their weapons ready. She'll be level with us in a moment.'

'Do you mean that it is a pirate ship?' Bressal enquired grimly. The term he used was *spúinneadair-mara* – sea plunderer.

'Pirates?'

The sharp question had come from Eadulf who, looking a ghastly pale colour, had scrambled on deck and stood swaying, clutching a rail to retain his balance.

In answer to the question, Fidelma simply gestured towards the pursuing vessel.

'If we can't fight her, Captain, what is your intention?' demanded Bressal, ignoring him.

'We can't fight her,' Murchad said. 'We can't even outrun her now. With those sails, she has the advantage of speed on us.'

'Then what?'

'I'll try to get into the harbour of Argol that's abeam of us on Hoedig. Perhaps if we are sheltered there, they will think twice about trying to board us. The people there might help.'

But Murchad had barely issued the order to Gurvan, at the helm, when there was a sudden whistling sound, and Gurvan gave a cry. They turned, staring with shock as they realised an arrow had struck the mate, piercing his neck. Blood was pouring from the wound and from his open mouth. He sank to the deck, letting the tiller swing idle.

One of the crewmen, Hoel was the first to recover – perhaps an automatic gesture from his training as a seaman. He leaped to the tiller and steadied it.

A voice called across the water in the language of the Bretons: 'Heave to, or more of you will die!'

Murchad was well acquainted with the language and hesitated a moment before he gave the orders to start hauling down the sails. He looked apologetically at Bressal.

'We won't make it. Their bowmen can easily pick us off before we reach the safety of the island.'

Fidelma had hurried to the side of the fallen mate but she did not even have to feel for his pulse to see that Gurvan was beyond help. By the time she returned to Eadulf's side, the attacking ship had closed, grappling irons were being thrown across, and men armed with swords were hauling themselves on board the *Barnacle Goose*.

The scene seemed unreal as the men swarmed through the ship, rounding up the crew. The only person armed had been Bressal, and now his weapons were taken from him. The young warrior stood, looking forlorn, his shoulders hunched, for he would have preferred to put up some resistance.

With the vessels tied to one another by the grapples, a

lithe boyish figure suddenly swung on board. The figure presented a strange sight to Fidelma, for it was clad from head to toe in white, from leather boots and trousers to a billowing shirt and small cape. But what was curious was the white headdress that hid every feature in the manner of a mask. A workmanlike short sword and dagger were slung from the belt of the newcomer.

The figure came forward to where Murchad and Bressal stood. Fidelma and Eadulf were standing a little apart.

The attackers, while watchful of Murchad's crew, seemed to stiffen respectfully in the presence of the newcomer, who was clearly in command.

The figure had halted before Murchad with hands on hips. Even though Murchad was burly and towered over this slight figure in white, yet it was the latter that seemed more threatening.

'What is the name of your ship?' snapped the white-clothed figure. The voice was barely broken and the language again was the local one.

'*Gé Ghúirainn* – the *Barnacle Goose*,' replied Murchad sullenly.

'Ah, *Iwerzhoniz*!'

Fidelma recognised this Breton word for 'Irish'.

'What cargo?' came the second sharp question.

'Salt from Gwenrann.'

'*Holen? Mat!*' The figure grunted in satisfaction. 'You have a choice, *Iwerzhonad*. You and your crew can sail this ship to where I and my men direct, or you can die now.'

The voice sounded so matter-of-fact that they had to think

of the meaning of the words for a moment or two before they understood them.

Bressal flushed and stepped forward before Murchad.

'I am Bressal of Cashel, envoy from King Colgú to Alain, King of the Bretons. See – this is my wand of office. This ship and its cargo are under the protection of the treaty agreed between them. I demand—'

Bressal broke off in mid-sentence.

Fidelma saw him bend forward as if he had received a punch in the solar plexus. Then her cousin seemed to slip to the deck on his knees and topple sideways. It was then she realised, with horror, that the figure was holding a blood-stained knife in its hand.

'You are wrong,' came the mocking voice. 'The ship and its cargo are under *my* protection.'

For a moment there was silence. The disbelief, the shock, was on the face of every member of the crew. The person of a *techtaire*, an envoy, was sacred and inviolable throughout the lands, and treated with respect even by the bitterest of enemies. The white wand of office had fallen from Bressal's lifeless hand, the very hazel wand Fidelma's brother would have presented him with at the start of his journey from Cashel. Now it rolled across the deck to rest at her feet. For a moment, she stared down at it as if she scarcely believed what she had seen. Then she bent down and picked it up.

'This is murder,' she said simply.

The white-clothed figure turned its head towards her but Murchad now stepped forward a pace. His voice was raised in anger.

'This is an outrage. It is murder! It is—'

The knife swung again, thrusting up under the burly seaman's ribs, and Murchad, the captain, began to slowly sink to his knees before her.

'Kill those religious and any members of the crew who do not want to sail under me,' called the figure in white, swinging on its heel and walking back across the deck even before Murchad had measured his length beside Bressal. 'Quickly now, or the tide will be against us.'

CHAPTER TWO

&

It was Eadulf who moved next. Even as Fidelma stood looking
on aghast at the carnage that had taken place before her
eyes, unable to fully comprehend it, Eadulf seized her arm and
was hauling her to the rail of the ship. All feelings of nausea
had left his body through the shock of what had happened. An
arrow splintered the wood of the rail by the side of them.

'Jump and swim!' yelled Eadulf. 'Swim for your life!'

He almost threw Fidelma over the side of the vessel and
a moment later followed her. They both hit the water within
seconds of each other, the first impact knocking the breath
from their bodies.

As Eadulf surfaced he heard shouting that was faint to his
ears, and was aware of splashes around him. Arrows! They
were being fired out from the ship. He glanced around and
saw Fidelma had surfaced nearby.

'Strike out for the island!' he cried. 'Try to keep underwater as much as you can until we are away from the ship.'

He knew that she had heard him but she did not waste

22

precious breath or time to acknowledge. She dived just as several more missiles fell about them. Somehow she had kept a tight hold of the hazel wand and as she struggled beneath the waves she managed to thrust it into the girdle at her waist. Eadulf knew their attempt at escape was probably futile. But faced with immediate death there was no other choice he could think of. It was only a matter of time before the pirates would launch one of the small boats and row after them and they, swimming in their encumbering clothes, would easily be overtaken long before they reached the distant island. In fact, the clothes were weighing them down so much that they were hardly moving at all.

He noticed that in her frustration Fidelma was trying to pull her robe off. She was a brilliant swimmer, he knew. She and her brother Colgú had swum as soon as they could take their first footsteps, in the rushing waters of the 'sister river' – the Suir, which ran near to Cashel. She was a better swimmer than Eadulf, but the sodden clothing acted in the same way as if her limbs were bound.

Eadulf heard a shout and glanced back at the *Barnacle Goose*. His fears were correct, for he could see a small boat being lowered from the side of the ship and three men were clambering down into it. He presumed they would be armed. The shore of the island was too far away. He closed his eyes in anguish for a moment and then a curious anger rose in him as he thought how stupid it was, that his life, Fidelma's life, could end in such a fashion.

Fidelma suddenly shouted to him above the splashing of the water. He could not hear what she said. Was it a warning?

He turned on his back and saw, bearing down on him, the sleek, dark outline of a small sailing craft. There was only one man in it, crouching at the stern. Eadulf was about to dive away, when he saw that the man was clad in the robes of a religious. He was leaning forward, one hand outstretched, the other on the tiller. Automatically, Eadulf reached out, missed the hand but managed to grab on to the stern of the vessel, which dragged him along, slowing its pace.

The man turned, let go of the tiller, grabbed Eadulf by the shoulders of his robe and literally heaved him into the bottom of the craft. In slowing the tiny vessel down by his weight hanging onto the stern, with the man leaving the tiller, the little boat jibed and lost way. It had allowed Fidelma to swim the few strokes that brought her to the bows of the vessel and she tried to clamber over. The man left Eadulf gasping in the bottom of the boat and moved forward to haul her on board.

Without another word, he glanced to where the three pirates were pulling away from the sides of the *Barnacle Goose* in their direction.

He muttered something, grabbed the sheets controlling his single sail, seizing the tiller again and moving to find the wind. He seemed to be an expert, for only a moment passed before the wind filled out his sail again. The breeze now carried the small craft along, like a feather across the little waves, the bow wave rippling behind it like a silvery furrow.

Fidelma and Eadulf had managed to struggle into sitting positions and glance towards the disappearing outline of the *Barnacle Goose* and the ship that had attacked her.

'I presume from the manner of your dress you are religious?' the man at the tiller said in Latin.

Fidelma spoke in affirmation in the same language. Their rescuer was middle-aged, his face weather-beaten, and he had black hair, dark eyes and a suntanned skin. He looked more like a sailor than the religious his robes and the crucifix, hanging around his neck, proclaimed him to be. He wore the tonsure of St Peter. While his tone was light, his expression was anxious and he kept turning to look at the ships behind them.

'We thank you for your timely rescue, Brother,' Eadulf said, coughing a little to clear the tang of brine from his throat.

The man grimaced. 'Your thanks may be a little premature. You are not out of danger yet – we are still being followed. If the black ship decides to send more warriors after you, then we may be in trouble, for we are simple fisherfolk and our little island is not large enough to hide you in for any length of time.'

Fidelma raised her head to gaze behind them. The rowing boat from the *Barnacle Goose* was still coming in their direction.

'What do you intend to do?' she asked their rescuer.

'I intend to offer you what assistance I can. I was on the headland when I saw that your vessel was being attacked. Then I saw two figures leap overboard and the flurry of arrows being loosed. I put out in my own small craft to see what I could do. Who are you?'

'I am Fidelma of Cashel, and this is Brother Eadulf.'

The man noted the manner of her introduction, as he replied, 'I am Metellus, Brother Metellus of the community of Lokentaz, the abbey of Gildas of Rhuis. It is on the mainland, but I am serving the little fishing community on Hoedig, which is the island to which we are now heading.'

'Is there a strong community there?' demanded Eadulf. 'Men who can help us against these pirates?'

Metellus shook his head. 'I told you, my friend, we are simple fisherfolk. We have no warriors, just stout fishermen, their wives and children. Enough for three men, if that is all they send after you, but against armed men from a warship . . . well. However, we'll do our best. I know a spot near the Menhir of the Virgin where you may hide.'

'Menhir?' queried Eadulf.

'A tall standing stone set up by the ancients which has been consecrated for the faith, for it was an old custom to go and offer prayers by it.'

They turned to the approaching island, growing large before them. It was mainly low-lying with little sandy beaches, and the waters had turned almost turquoise as they came close inshore. They could see the stretches of green growth on land, sprinkled with little yellow flowers, and here and there were tiny habitations of grey granite.

'It looks fairly large to me,' offered Eadulf.

'No more than a kilometre across and twice that or a little more long, my friend. If those on that ship yonder really want to make a search for you – then, as I say, there is hardly anywhere to hide.'

They were pulling into a bay and Brother Metellus stood

up to lower the sail. A small crowd of men, women and children of every age, were crowding curiously on the wooden quay to greet them. They had apparently seen what had taken place.

An elderly man addressed Brother Metellus by name from the shore and an exchange of words followed which was too rapid for Fidelma or Eadulf to understand. Willing hands helped them out as Brother Metellus secured the boat.

'Come – we must not delay,' he said urgently. 'Let us find you a safe place to hide.'

'But what of our pursuers? Can't we make a defence now?' demanded Fidelma, glancing seaward to where the rowers were still some distance out to sea.

'And bring the crew of that raider down on us? No, we'll have to find some other way of dealing with them,' Brother Metellus replied grimly, as he began to usher them through the collection of buildings that formed the main dwelling-places of the islanders near the harbour.

They had not proceeded far when they were halted by sounds echoing across the water.

It was a series of blasts on a trumpet or horn of some type.

Brother Metellus halted, turning with a frown. Then with astonishing dexterity, he scrambled onto a granite wall to give him a higher elevation and looked seaward.

'What is it?' asked Eadulf.

'Your pursuers have halted, and . . . yes, they are turning back to the ships. The horn must have sounded some signal to recall them.' He raised his face to the sky and let the wind blow across his features. 'The wind is changing, and the tide.

I think the captain must be calling the men back for the vessels to take advantage of it.'

'Is there a place where we can see what is happening?' asked Fidelma, her voice quiet and without emotion, although Eadulf could see that her features were still filled with shock from the experience of seeing the callous murder of her cousin and Murchad the captain.

'Come with me,' Brother Metellus said, jumping lightly down from the stone wall. 'The island is pretty low-lying, therefore it is hard to get a good elevation from which to see. However . . .' He pointed to a small building, which had a second storey and looked out of place among the other buildings of the island. 'We use it as a chapel and we are trying to construct a little tower on top,' he explained.

They entered and followed Brother Metellus, scrambling up a rough wooden ladder to the top of the unfinished tower. It did not give them a great commanding view of the sea. However, they could make out the bay and beyond it, just visible to the naked eye, the black dot on the waters that was the rowing boat, heading back to the dark outlines of the ships. There was the familiar shape of the *Barnacle Goose* and the darker silhouette behind of the ship that had attacked it. They still seemed to be linked together. Then, as they watched, it seemed the attacking vessel shuddered. It was an optical illusion produced as the sails were being set and the ship began to move slowly away from the side of its victim. The rowers had reached the side of the *Barnacle Goose*. Fidelma presumed that they had boarded and the rowing boat was being hauled up. Then the sails were billowing and the ship was turning after the sleek lines of its attacker.

'They are leaving,' muttered Brother Metellus, in satisfaction. 'Heading north-west. You are safe for the time being.'

'Safe!' The word was uttered by Fidelma with bitter irony.

At Brother Metellus' raised eyebrows, Eadulf explained: 'The captain of our vessel and some of her crew were slaughtered, and Fidelma's own cousin, Bressal of Cashel, and envoy to your King, Alain Hir, was slain – even showing his wand of office. This is bad, indeed.'

For a moment, Brother Metellus contemplated this. Then he gave a deep sigh.

'Before anything else, I suggest you come with me so that we may provide you with dry clothes and something to drink to get the taste of seawater out of your mouths. Then we will talk more of this. As you say, it is a grievous crime to kill the envoy of a king.'

Outside the chapel they found one of the fishermen who spoke rapidly in the local dialect. Brother Metellus replied and the man turned and hurried off.

'Our friend had come to report that the men had given up the pursuit and the ships had sailed,' he explained. Then he pointed to a nearby building. 'This is where I make my simple home. Come in and welcome. I will try to find some dry clothing for you.'

It was a while before they were dried, and changed into comfortable clothing, brought to them by a homely woman called Onenn. Fidelma would have liked to wash the salt water from her hair, but that would have been too much to ask their host.

They now sat with Brother Metellus in his small stone cabin, together with an elderly man called Lowenen, who was introduced as the chieftain of the island community. Lowenen had a craggy seaman's face, almost as if it were carved from the granite rock of the island. The sea-green eyes were piercing under heavy eyebrows, but his face was compassionate, expressing sympathy and gentle humour.

As they told their story, Brother Metellus acted as interpreter for Lowenen who spoke no other language than the island dialect. Although Fidelma and Eadulf had some knowledge of the language of the Britons, this local dialect was difficult to follow. Words they thought they knew from their time among the Britons apparently did not mean the same.

'This is a crime indeed,' Brother Metellus muttered after a moment's reflection when they had finished telling the full story of the attack. 'You have no idea of the identity of this vessel that attacked you? The captain of it did not identify himself?'

Fidelma shook her head. 'There was no name on the ship that we could see but then, I suppose, we weren't looking for a name in the moment of attack. I seem to recall it had a white flag at its mast.'

'I noticed that there was an emblem on the white flag,' Eadulf put in, 'but I could not make it out. However, there was a small carving on the bow of the vessel. A bird of some sort. I thought it was a dove.'

Only Fidelma noticed a curious expression cross Brother Metellus' face but it was gone in an instant.

'You must be mistaken, my friend,' he said quickly. 'If a

warship carves a bird on it as a symbol, it is usually a bird of prey.'

Eadulf reluctantly agreed, but said, 'It is strange, on reflection. It looked like a dove to me. But perhaps the person who carved the bird was not so talented as he thought.'

'And did you notice anything about the captain of this vessel?'

'Only that he appeared to be a young man,' Fidelma replied thoughtfully. 'But he was shrouded from head to foot in white so that his face was not to be seen.'

'White!' exclaimed Brother Metellus. 'A curious choice for a sea captain and a pirate. White is the colour of light and sanctity, and yet you say this man was a ruthless killer and hid himself under this shroud of white? And he was a young man?'

'He was slightly built with a high-pitched voice. But for all his apparent youth he was vicious, nonetheless. It was he who killed my cousin as well as Murchad the captain,' Fidelma confirmed. Then she paused and added quietly, 'And he shall answer for those crimes.'

'Is anything known of piracy in these waters?' Eadulf asked hurriedly, to cover the uneasy silence that followed Fidelma's statement, which had been delivered in a tone of cold hatred. He had never heard her speak in such chilling tones.

Brother Metellus interpreted Lowenen's response to the question.

'Alas, these waters have often seen bloodshed. It is not far from here that the galleys of the Romans did battle with our fleet.'

'Your fleet?' queried Eadulf in surprise, envisaging a battle between Roman galleys and the fishing boats of the island.

'The fleet of the Veneti who were the greatest mariners of this land,' the old man replied proudly. 'They sailed with over two hundred ships against the Roman commander. The battle lasted a full day before a disappearing wind becalmed our ships and allowed the Romans to destroy them. After that, all Gaul fell to the Romans. A sad day when the Veneti were defeated.'

The old man sighed deeply, as if contemplating something that had occurred but yesterday. Fidelma noticed there was an air of embarrassment as Brother Metellus interpreted these words; some reluctance in his delivery.

'That was many centuries ago, my friend,' Eadulf pointed out to the elderly chieftain, having realised that he was talking about the time when Julius Caesar had conquered Gaul.

'You are right,' the chieftain replied with a shrug. 'But, as I say, such bloody events have been frequent here. It is not long since we had Saxon raiders attacking this very island.'

It was Eadulf's turn to look uncomfortable. 'But we are talking of pirates and in recent times,' he pressed. 'We are looking for some means to identify our attacker.'

Lowenen shrugged. 'The great port of Naoned lies not far to the east of us on the mainland. It is a rich port. Merchants grow wealthy on the trade through that one port alone. Therefore, it is logical that it provides bait that will attract the rats. The Franks cast envious eyes at the town and it is already under pressure from Frankish raids and settlements. When I was young, I sailed there. The Frankish borders of

Neustria had not then approached within three days' ride of Naoned. Now I am told that the Frankish marcher lords claim territory within a quarter of a day's ride of the port. Their raids are not infrequent. Yes, raiders and pirates are not unknown in these waters, although I have not heard any stories of this black ship with its captain dressed all in white, such as you have described.'

Brother Metellus was looking at Fidelma. His eyes were troubled.

'There is vengeance on your face, Fidelma of Cashel,' he observed softly.

Fidelma's brows came together, and reading the danger signs, Eadulf jumped in with: 'Fidelma is highly regarded as a *dálaigh*, an advocate of the courts of the Five Kingdoms of Éireann, my friend. She is consulted frequently by kings and abbots. Even now we were on our way back to the Kingdom of Muman after attending a Council in Burgundia to advise the prelates there in law at their request. It is not vengeance you will observe, but a desire for justice.'

But Brother Metellus did not seem impressed. 'Sometimes justice can be used to mean vengeance,' he said.

Fidelma's lips thinned in annoyance. 'I took an oath to uphold the law and to bring to justice those who transgress it. It is true that this act of cold-blooded murder was against my own cousin, Bressal of Cashel, and against my friend, Murchad of Aird Mhór, but it is still justice, not vengeance, that cries out for this captain and his crew to be tracked down.'

Brother Metellus shrugged as if he would dismiss the matter from his mind.

'Surely, Brother Metellus, your people have a similar law system to that used in the Five Kingdoms of Éireann?' Eadulf asked. 'Therefore, if the murderer is caught, would they not be brought before that same justice?'

'I am not a Breton,' the religious confessed, 'but I have no quarrel with law and justice. So long as it is clear that justice is the purpose of seeking the perpetrator of this act.'

Fidelma held his dark eyes steadily. There was a flicker of green fire in her own eyes.

'That is my purpose,' she said tightly. 'But if you are not a Breton, where are you from?'

'I was born and raised in Rome,' he replied.

Fidelma realised why there had been some reluctance to translate Lowenen's remarks.

'You are far from home,' Eadulf observed.

'This is my home now,' Brother Metellus said quietly. There was a pause, then he had a quick exchange with Lowenen.

'He wonders what you intend to do now,' translated Brother Metellus.

'There is nothing we can do,' Fidelma answered, 'until we find a way of reaching the mainland where we can find someone willing to transport us back to my brother's kingdom. But for now we are destitute, having nothing save a few personal items and the clothes that we have borrowed from you.'

'How far would this be to the nearest point on the mainland?' asked Eadulf.

'About twenty kilometres across the water, north from here, is the abbey of Gildas,' Brother Metellus replied at once.

'I am under the jurisdiction of the abbot there. Given a good wind, we would be able to make it in half a morning's sail. I have done it several times. So, if you trust yourself once more to my small boat, I can take you in the morning. As you see,' he gestured to the window, 'the sky is darkening already, so it is too late to commence the trip today.'

'I would not wish to burden you, Brother Metellus,' Fidelma replied. 'You have already done much for us. You have given us our lives when they might have been lost.' She was a little confused because she was sure that the image of the dove had some significance for him that he was not imparting to them, but he had saved them from capture and death, and she was very grateful for that.

'Is this not what we are in service to the Christ to do?' Brother Metellus said, brushing aside her thanks. 'Anyway, it is time that I visited the mainland again, for there are some supplies that I want from the abbey.'

He turned and rapidly addressed Lowenen again before continuing. 'As you can see, I do not have room to shelter you here for the night, but Lowenen's wife, Onenn, has a spare bed. It was her son's. He was drowned last year while fishing off Beg Lagad. I presume that you . . .' He broke off awkwardly.

'You may rest assured that we are husband and wife.' Eadulf supplied the answer to his unasked question with some stiffness. 'We are not of that sect who believe in the celibacy of all religious.'

'I thought as much,' agreed the Roman monk with a sigh. 'As for myself, I believe in the teachings of the Blessed

Benedict. Chastity is a declaration of our commitment to the Faith.' Then he looked closely at Fidelma. 'I noticed that you introduced yourself as Fidelma of Cashel rather than Sister Fidelma. And Brother Eadulf here says that you are an advocate of your law courts – can you be both things in your own land?'

Fidelma replied in a slightly defiant tone: 'I am sister to Colgú, King of Muman, whose capital is at Cashel. It is one of the lands that make up the Five Kingdoms of Éireann, the land of my people. It is the largest of the Five Kingdoms,' she added, almost proudly. From her past experience in Rome she had learned that it was best to maintain a slight arrogance with Romans. 'My first commitment is to serve the law and my people. In our land, one can also serve both and still be in the religious.'

Brother Metellus bowed his head, hiding an amused expression on his features.

'I am sure that I speak for our chieftain, Lowenen here, when I say that it is an honour to have you and Brother Eadulf as guests on this little island. Alas, I was but a poor shepherd on the slopes of Mount Sabatini until I decided to follow the path of Christ.'

Fidelma could not make up her mind whether the man was mocking her or not. Before she could decide, he had turned and translated to the old chieftain, who immediately rose and bowed to Fidelma, and spoke with some intensity.

'He says that he is more than honoured to welcome a princess to his humble island. Whatever he has, is yours.'

Fidelma inclined her head to the old man, saying, 'Tell

him he has already given us enough and it is we who are honoured.'

Brother Metellus now rose to his feet.

'There will be a feast tonight. Lowenen insists upon it. A feast to celebrate your coming to this island. It is the local custom of hospitality. But we will try to get away to the mainland just after first light. Go with Lowenen now and have some rest, and I will come to escort you to the feasting later.'

Although forewarned, when Brother Metellus came to collect them from the house of Lowenen and his wife, Onenn, neither Fidelma nor Eadulf were expecting the festivities that greeted them. They were led down a path between the stone cabins and onto a sandy strand where a large fire had been lit. In fact, there were several smaller fires along the shore. Beyond them the dark seas, now and then with a thin line of white showing where the waves were breaking, whispered and chattered over the rocks before sliding silently shoreward. Many people were crowded round the fires. Brother Metellus had told them that there were only about a hundred or so islanders, and it seemed every one of them was there.

'Remember that the lives of these people are harsh,' he explained, 'so they seize any opportunity to celebrate and make merry.'

A few men were playing instruments, providing a musical background for a young man who was singing and amusing some of the younger folk who clapped their hands to the rhythm. The instruments were similar to those that Fidelma had seen in her own land, although one man was playing a set of pipes which had a higher pitch than those native to Muman.

There was a smell of cooking permeating the area, and many pots were steaming on the small fires while on others, various types of fish were being roasted on sticks. Brother Metellus led them to a table, erected on the sandy shore, on which plates with various vegetables and salads were set out, beside jugs of what they quickly discovered was cider. They were seated next to Lowenen and his wife Onenn.

The feasting, the songs, the drinking and the merrymaking went on into the night. Eadulf could see that, although she did her best to disguise her feelings, Fidelma was still reeling from the shock of the death of her cousin and from the events that had occurred on the *Barnacle Goose*. He attempted to help her by taking much of the conversation on himself. Having studied herbs as part of a medical training, he was interested in some of the salad that was presented to him; it contained some silver-green leaves that gave it a very strong flavour. Brother Metellus told him that they were from a plant that grew all over the land, in dry sandy soil; its spiky leaves did not vanish with the seasons but kept evergreen. Only at the height of summer did it produce yellow flowers, from which the islanders often made an infusion to cleanse their stomachs. Not knowing the plant and never having seen it in his own land, nor in Éireann for that matter, Eadulf could not speculate on its properties.

After an interminable round of toasting and the consumption of much cider, for wine from the mainland was scarce, it was Brother Metellus who eventually rose and suggested that they ought to retire as they would have a taxing sea journey to the mainland at dawn.

To Eadulf, it seemed that Fidelma looked relieved and rose with alacrity. They walked slowly back to Lowenen's house where Brother Metellus left them, saying he would come for them just after first light. They retired to the tiny chamber they had been given by Onenn and her husband Lowenen. The noise of the music and the people still at the feasting came faintly to their ears as they prepared for bed. Fidelma sat on the side of the mattress, holding the white hazel wand of office that she had managed to save in their escape; her Cousin Bressal's wand of office as an envoy. She turned it over in her hands in moody contemplation and then placed it by the side of the bed.

'I think that symbol of the dove meant something to Brother Metellus,' she said to Eadulf without preamble.

When he expressed surprise, Fidelma described the expression that she had seen for a fleeting moment on the Roman's face.

'Are you sure?' asked Eadulf, not convinced.

'You realise that I cannot go back to Cashel until I have tracked down the murderer of my cousin and brought him to justice,' she said, not responding to his question. 'Nor can I abandon Murchad's crew on the *Barnacle Goose* – young Wenbrit and the others who have been taken as prisoners or worse.'

Eadulf regarded her solemnly. He had suspected the thoughts that had been passing through her mind.

'Do you not think it more important to get home – home to Alchú, our son, and to your brother, who has more power to pursue this matter? He could send a delegation, warriors, to the King of the Bretons and they would be better placed to track down these murderers.'

Fidelma shook her head firmly. Her features were controlled.

'I do not make this decision lightly. Of course it is important for us to return home to our son. We have been away too long. But you do not realise the shame that would be upon me if I went back without making any effort to find out who has done this terrible thing. The satirists would bring blotches to my face and, more importantly, to the face of my brother, the King. He could even be forced to abdicate. The line of our dynasty, the Eóghanacht, could be stigmatised for ever.'

Had Eadulf not spent years among the people of the Five Kingdoms, he would have considered the statement overly dramatic. However, he knew that it was a preoccupation among his wife's people that their honour, what they called *enech* or 'face', should in no way be besmirched. If they were dishonoured, it was believed that a poet could write a satire that would raise blotches on their face for everyone to see, revealing their dishonour. A satire could even cause people to die of their shame. Eadulf was sure that Fidelma did not believe in the supernatural powers of the poets but, before the coming of the New Faith, it was widely accepted and even now, while some referred to it with half-hearted humour, many people fully believed. Indeed, even the laws of which Fidelma was an advocate, dictated that the composing of a wrongful satire was worthy of fine and punishment. Likewise it was illegal to satirise a person after their death. But if the satire was truthful . . . a king or a noble had to tolerate satire or lose their honour price if they brought the poet to the court and the court found the poet's words to be truthful.

Wisely, Eadulf did not rebuke her on the matter of dishonour.

'So what do you intend?' he asked.

Fidelma gestured with a slight rise and fall of her shoulder. 'Someone around these shores must know about that ship that attacked us. When the time is right, I shall ask Brother Metellus what that dove means to him. Someone will know which direction the ships sailed, or where the *Barnacle Goose* was being led.'

'The sea is a big place.'

'We have searched bigger,' replied Fidelma. 'And we have been successful in our searches.'

Eadulf suppressed a sigh. He realised that no matter what obstacles he pointed out, Fidelma would have none of them. She had made up her mind on a course of action and she was going to take it – in spite of all the obvious difficulties.

'I presume your plan will be to make enquiries at the abbey of this Gildas when we reach the mainland tomorrow?'

Fidelma could hear the disapproval in his voice.

'That would be a logical assumption!' she retorted, turning her back on him as she lay down in the bed.

Eadulf said nothing for a moment or two. Then he shrugged and blew out the candle.

For some time he lay on his back, hands behind his head, listening to the distant sounds of the music and the voices from the beach where the feasting was continuing. Then sleep caught him unawares.

It was still dark when he opened his eyes again. No; not quite dark. There was a greying light, that curious pre-dawn twilight, filtering through the window and causing dark shadows in the room. He wondered what had awakened him at this hour. Fidelma lay beside him, still asleep. He could hear her breathing deeply and regularly. It was surely time to rise and get ready to leave with Brother Metellus . . . Then he suddenly noticed: the wind had changed. Last night, its sound had been soft, almost sibilant, but it was moaning now around the corners of the house, tearing at the sloping roof. Overnight, the soft summer breezes had changed into fierce gusting winds.

He knew that until the winds abated, they would be forced to remain on this island. He also knew that his wife would not be pleased.

CHAPTER THREE

❧

Fidelma looked out across the bay for the hundredth time since she had awoken. As Eadulf had predicted, her mood was not of the best at her confinement by the weather. Brother Metellus had called by after first light, but merely to confirm that they would not be able to sail until the weather lifted. As morning proceeded, it became clear that they would be unable to leave the island that day.

Their own clothing had been washed, dried and even mended where it had been torn during their escape and rescue. While Fidelma had managed to retain her *ciorbholg*, her comb bag carried by all women of her country, because it was attached to her girdle, a lot of the contents were missing. She had no mirror, the soap was ruined although the *phal* of a fragrance made from honeysuckle which she preferred to use, was intact. One of her emerald ear-clips was also missing, lost in the sea, as was her favourite gold-leaf brooch. Her marsupium, which contained many travelling items and coinage to purchase food and passage, had been in the cabin of the *Barnacle Goose*. As for Eadulf, he had rushed on deck when the attack began, straight from his bunk, with only his clothes. The pair of them were destitute and at the sufferance of strangers. However, they did not discuss the matter for, at the moment, there was no prospect of resolving the problem.

Fidelma, being an active person, had announced her intention of exploring the island to pass the time. Brother Metellus had offered to show them the points of interest. Yet by midday, buffeted by the winds, they had already exhausted such sights as there were to be seen. The island was so low-lying that Fidelma could imagine a single large wave engulfing it. The main habitations and harbour had been built around a wide bay. It was a spot called Argol – the place of danger – a name Eadulf thought odd for a harbour. The rest of the island was one of wild heath; the dunes, especially to the east, were covered with small yellow flowers emerging from spiky silver-green leaf foliage that had a distinct and pungent fragrance. Eadulf recognised this plant as the curious addition to the salad dishes served the previous evening. Among the dunes, there were also wild carnations and sand lilies. Fidelma, so used to great mountains, broad rivers and fertile plains, wondered aloud why anyone would settle in such a dull place. Then she apologised to Brother Metellus for questioning his choice of home.

'If the truth be known, it was not my choice,' he replied gravely. 'It is a long story.'

'We appear to have time on our hands,' Fidelma said with dry humour.

'Very well, I shall explain. When I felt the call to join the religious,' began Brother Metellus, 'I left my family on the slopes of Mount Sabatini, which is north of Rome, and joined the community at Subiaco, where Benedict, patriarch of all the monks of the western world, first settled away from the vices of Rome. He was a man of peace and moderation, albeit singular in purpose in teaching the truth of the Faith.'

'From Subiaco to here is quite a journey,' Eadulf interrupted.

'I grant you, it is a very long journey. I was five years studying in Subiaco before accepting the mission to bring the Rule of Benedict to the west, where I was told that the people had strange rituals and philosophies that were in conflict with those of Rome.'

'And you came here to enlighten us?' Fidelma's tone was ironical.

'I have spent ten years now in this land called Bro-Waroch, among the Bretons. I have succeeded in teaching little, I am afraid,' admitted Brother Metellus.

'But why come here, on this tiny island?' pressed Fidelma.

'I wandered the countryside, teaching and learning the language of the Bretons and the Franks. But a year ago I went to serve in the abbey of the Blessed Gildas. At first, all was well, for the Abbot Maelcar said he supported the Rule of Benedict. Then I dared question an interpretation of scripture and the Abbot suggested that I come to serve the isolated community here to reflect and learn humbleness.'

Fidelma's eyes narrowed a fraction. 'Why would you need to reflect and be humble, for questioning an interpretation of scripture?'

'For questioning the interpretation of Abbot Maelcar,' corrected Brother Metellus. 'He is old-fashioned, the son of a noble family from the Brekilien Forest.'

'I would venture that it was the Abbot who needed to learn humility,' she commented. 'One learns by asking questions, and both the questioner and the questioned can profit by the exchange.'

'That is not how the Abbot thinks. Anyway, it is a pleasant enough place to be . . . for a while.' Brother Metellus turned and pointed. 'We have reminders, too, that people have been living here from the time beyond time.'

They found themselves staring at a strange standing stone, a tall menhir that stood almost three times Fidelma's height.

'Local people call it the Virgin's Menhir, and a little way from here is a large cairn which marks the last resting-place of an important chieftain who died long before the Romans came to these lands. The islanders tell great tales of this champion.'

But even with these fascinating sights and stories, it was not long before the couple realised they had traversed the complete island and seen everything.

Fidelma was confirmed in her frustration that she was a prisoner on this small rock of an island. However, the keening wind, the gusting little white billows on the sea, with the heavy grey clouds and a mist that seemed to hang like a shroud above the waters, were evidence that there was nothing else to do. So they walked slowly back to the shelter of the homesteads.

A few people were outside tending the small patches where

fruit and vegetables grew, but not many. Most people were inside, for this was a fishing community and in such weather, no one could put out to sea. The boats were bobbing up and down, tied together, in the comparative shelter of the harbour.

Fidelma looked longingly towards the shrouded mainland.

'So who was this founder of the abbey to which you belong?' asked Eadulf of Brother Metellus by way of distraction.

'Gildas was his name. He was one of the Britons who fled from the Saxon invasions of his land, as did many of the ancestors of these people here,' replied Brother Metellus.

'I am aware that the ancestors of my people are but recently settled on that island,' Eadulf acknowledged.

'Let us go out of the wind and have a cider to keep the chill at bay,' Brother Metellus suggested tactfully.

Seated before the smouldering fire inside of Brother Metellus' cabin, with cider to drink, Eadulf prompted him: 'You were telling us of this man Gildas who founded the abbey you served in.'

'His story is set against the settlement of your ancestors on the island of Britain, and I would not wish to say anything you might take amiss,' Brother Metellus replied frankly.

'How can one take history amiss, unless it is contrary to truth?' queried Eadulf. 'You are a Roman. Surely, in your wandering through the lands that were once conquered and ruled by Roman armies, you have met with all sorts of stories. You will know that to shut your ears to people's views of the history of your ancestors is to blind yourself to truth and progress.'

Often, Fidelma reflected to herself, Eadulf would surprise her by his deep insight into the nature of people. She glanced at Brother Metellus. 'Tell us about this Gildas,' she invited. 'I think I might know of the man.'

Brother Metellus sat back, taking a sip of his drink first.

'He was born in the year when the great general of the Britons called Arthur defeated the Saxons at Badon Hill, on whose slopes nearly a thousand Saxon princes were said to have been slaughtered.'

Eadulf stirred uncomfortably but he had often heard the stories from his own people of how they wrested control of the lands from the Britons and slaughtered them. He could not protest at hearing the story as seen from another viewpoint.

'That was about a century and a half ago. Then there were two decades of peace between the two peoples before that black day at Camlann when Arthur was slain. After that, the Saxons began to move westward again and Gildas and many other refugees fled here. He took sanctuary on the sister island to this.'

'The sister island?' queried Fidelma, stirring herself from her thoughts about the sea raiders that had been occupying her all day. She tried to concentrate on the conversation.

'The island of Houad. It means "the duck" and this island is called "little duck". Houad is a slightly larger island than this, just to the north-west. Gildas lived and worked there until the Prince of Bro-Waroch invited him to cross to the mainland, to the Rhuis Peninsula, and establish a community there. It was there he wrote his famous work on the ruin and conquest of Britain.'

'*De Excidio et Conquestu Britanniae,*' muttered Fidelma, surprising both Eadulf and Brother Metellus. 'I have read it. There is a copy in the great *scriptorium* in the abbey at Menevia in Dyfed. I read it when I was there.' Then, glancing at Eadulf, she added: 'As I recall, he blamed several of the kings of the Britons and clergy for their squabbling which allowed the Saxons to conquer the country. Didn't Gildas believe that the Angles and Saxons were sent to Britain as instruments of God's wrath?'

'I also took the opportunity of reading that book while I was in the abbey,' Brother Metellus responded. 'It is obvious that you know the work, Fidelma of Cashel. It is true that after this general called Arthur was killed, there was no one strong enough to unite the Britons against the Saxons,' he conceded. 'They quarrelled among themselves. Gildas likened the Britons to the Israelites, God's chosen people, who lost their faith and so were to be punished by God. He called on the prophecies of Jeremiah to foretell a bleak outlook for his people unless the Britons turned aside from their immoral course. He was a man of asceticism and fervour. Of course, there are other great works of Gildas, which they have at the abbey – like his letters on pastoral questions and the reform of the Church and his work on penance . . . Your own Columbanus admired his work and spoke of him as Gildas Sapiens – Gildas the Wise.'

'So this Gildas founded an abbey here?' prompted Eadulf.

'On the peninsula called Rhuis.'

'And that is where he died?'

'No, he did not die there but decided, after a while, to

return to Houad. It is there that he died about a century ago. His body was taken back to the abbey and he is buried behind the high altar.'

'Is it a large abbey?'

'There are about fifty souls in the community.'

'Is it a *conhospitae*, a mixed house?'

Brother Metellus shook his head, slightly scandalised. 'I am told it used to be, but when Abbot Maelcar took over, he introduced the Rule of Benedict. When I joined the abbey, the community was all committed to a life of celibacy.'

'And this Abbot . . . Abbot Maelcar, you said?'

'Abbot Maelcar, indeed. He is a man of Bro-Waroch.'

'I know little of this land of Bro-Waroch,' Eadulf said, 'yet I am confused. Some seem to call it Bro-Erech and some Bro-Waroch. Which is the correct name, and is it a large kingdom?'

'From the time of King Alain's father it has been called Bro-Waroch and it is, indeed, a large kingdom. I heard its history from people as I travelled through it. The earliest settlers from Britain had to regain some of the territory to drive the Frankish incursions back to the east. They say it was Caradog Freichfras of Gwent who founded the kingdom.' Brother Metellus sniffed in disapproval before continuing. 'The people, being frontiersmen continually fighting for their existence against the Franks, became a tough and vicious lot. Harsh lives make harsh morals. So it was for the first century of its existence as a kingdom. That left its mark on the lines of the kings. Canao, for example, killed three of his brothers to claim the kingdom. I am told that he died sixty years ago.'

'What or who is this Waroch, then?'

'He was an earlier King than Canao. After Canao died, his one surviving brother, Macliau, became King – and when *he* died, his son, another Canao, became King. Then he died and Judicael of Domnonia claimed the kingdom. In fact, Judicael claimed kingship of all the Bretons and also descent from Waroch. So he named the kingdom as Bro-Waroch, the country of Waroch.'

'I thought Alain Hir was King of the Bretons?' Fidelma said.

'He is the son of Judicael,' Brother Metellus confirmed. 'Judicael died about ten years ago, but it was he who merged the two kingdoms of Domnonia and Bro-Warwoch into one.'

'You sound disapproving?'

'I am a Roman. It matters not to me the machinations of these kings. I care only for the souls of the people. Meanwhile I am content with the simple life I lead. Alain Hir is a good King, so far as kings go.'

Fidelma smiled slightly. 'If you have so little time for kings, perhaps you have little time for authority – hence your problem with your Abbot?'

'Not so.' Brother Metellus grimaced sourly. 'Kings are, perhaps, a necessary evil. Before my own people sank into the stupidity of emperors, they had a good system – *res publica*, "affairs of the public". Every year the people elected consuls from the Senate to rule them.'

'And who were the people who comprised the *comitia centuriata* who elected the consuls, my Roman friend?' Fidelma asked sweetly.

Brother Metellus stared at her in surprise. 'Why, the citizens of Rome.'

'But wealth governed a man's ability to be part of this Roman democracy,' countered Fidelma. 'As the vote had to be made in Rome itself, the rural people never had a chance to participate. What's more, the rich always voted first and separately – and as the declaration of the result was made on a simple majority as soon as the first section voted, the poor hardly ever voted at all. And consuls could only be chosen from the Senate, whose membership for life was already made from those patrician families. No citizen was free to address that assembly without the consent of the magistrates and tribunes, and they alone had the right to debate matters.'

Brother Metellus' surprise turned into an expression of amazement. Fidelma felt moved to explain.

'I spent a period in Rome and occupied my time – well, some of it, that is – in studying some of your legal texts, ancient as well as modern.'

'You are saying that you believe our imperial system was better?' queried the Roman.

'Not at all. In fact, there were faults with both systems. Who your father was and what wealth he had acquired should be no gauge of your own ability.'

'Yet you are the sister of a king,' Brother Metellus pointed out, meaningfully.

Fidelma shrugged as if it were of no consequence.

'Presumably you were the daughter of a king as well?' he pressed.

'It so happened that my father, Failbe Flann, *was* indeed a king. He died when I was a small child.'

'So your brother succeeded him? Where is the merit in that?'

She tried to explain. 'That is not how kings are chosen in my land. Our system also relies on who is most able in the family – man or woman – to be head of the family and assume the role of King. During a king's lifetime, the *derbhfine* of the family have to meet and elect from their number the successor. They could be sons, brothers or cousins. My brother was the fourth ruler since the death of our father, chosen only after thirty years had passed and he had grown to manhood. No one who is not of mature age and reason can be a king.'

'What happened to the others? Were they murdered by their successors?' There was almost a sneer in Brother Metellus' voice. 'That was usually how it happened among our emperors. That is why I believe in the old *res publica* system.'

'Death overtook them. The Yellow Plague caused much death in our lands.'

Brother Metellus was not convinced, scoffing, 'And you claim that even a woman could succeed to be head of the family in your land?'

'It is so.'

'It would not be allowed in Rome.'

'So I learned,' agreed Fidelma. 'In your republic, a man had complete control over his wife and family, like property. A woman could not conduct business but a man had to be guardian over her, although married women did not have to live in seclusion and could take meals with their families inside their houses.'

'And your ways are better?' challenged the Brother.

'Our ways are different,' conceded Fidelma, 'but, on balance, I would argue that life for our people is, in many ways, better. But each society has to develop according to their beliefs and conscience. My argument with Rome is that what is good for Rome is not good for the rest of the world, whether imposed by the military legions that dominate the world or by the Church in Rome that tries to tell people how to behave even in lands far distant, with different customs and ways of looking at the world.'

The monk frowned ominously. 'That sounds like heresy, Fidelma of Cashel.'

Eadulf grew suddenly nervous at his tone.

'The churches of Éireann and of the Britons have different ways of looking at things, Brother. You must know that,' he intervened, trying to mollify the Roman. 'It does not mean to say that they hold beliefs that are opposed to the orthodox doctrines of the Faith, or beliefs which have been specifically denounced by the Church.'

'Our Lord told Peter that *he* would be the one to found the Church. Peter came to Rome and was martyred there. So the Christian Church was founded in Rome. Rome is the centre of the Church and must be obeyed,' replied Brother Metellus stubbornly.

'That is not the way the churches of the east see things,' observed Fidelma quietly. 'Nor how the churches of the western islands see things. The Bishop of Rome is regarded as having a primacy of honour among the bishops of the faith, but *not* a primacy of power.'

Brother Metellus reddened in annoyance.

Eadulf glanced quickly at Fidelma and tried to indicate a warning. He knew that she loved discussion, intellectual argument, but if Brother Metellus was taking this as an insult to his beliefs, then Eadulf envisaged that they might be stuck on this island for a long while. However, Fidelma was oblivious to his attempt to calm matters. She was merely pleased to concentrate her mind away from the events of the last day.

'What I mean is that the Church of Constantinopolis claims the same apostolic succession, celebrates the same sacrament and follows almost the same theology. Its own Chief Bishop is called the Patriarch whose title is from the Greek *pater-archon* – the "father leader". That is almost the same title as given to the Bishop of Rome. He takes the name from the Greek *pápas*, or father, as well. Other places like Alexandria also have their Patriarchs who do not consider themselves under obligation to obey Rome. They believe in their independence. Are all the eastern churches in heresy?'

Brother Metellus thrust out his jaw pugnaciously. 'During the last hundred years, the Bishops of Rome excommunicated the patriarchs of Constantinopolis from the Faith,' he ground out. 'Indeed, they have excommunicated the patriarchs of Alexandria and Jerusalem.'

'And doubtless the patriarchs have done the same to the Bishop of Rome,' countered Fidelma in good humour. 'What does that mean? It shows they are all, sadly, too human.

Instead of sitting down to debate their differences and come to a resolution, they resort to rituals of the supernatural as a means of exerting their will.'

Brother Metellus stared at her in disbelief for a moment and then, to the surprise of both of them, he burst out laughing.

'I swear that I have not had a good discourse with a woman on the Faith in many years,' he finally said, wiping his eyes. 'You are truly learned, Fidelma of Cashel. I am glad I decided to fish you out of the sea . . . both of you, that is. I don't agree with you, but I enjoy discussion. May we have many more arguments.'

'Rather exchanges of ideas,' corrected Fidelma solemnly, 'for without exchanging ideas, how can there be any learning or progression?'

Brother Metellus glanced at the cloudy sky outside.

'It will soon be time for the evening meal,' he said. 'Then we'll see how the weather shapes for tomorrow. In the meantime, there are services to perform in my poor chapel. I would invite you to join me, unless your rituals would prevent you?'

Fidelma gave a small mischievous smile. 'There is little difference in intent, and while we prefer to conduct our services in the language of the sacred texts – which is Greek – when we were in Rome, I observed little for me to object to.'

'Then you are welcome to participate in the service with me.'

By evening, the wind was beginning to die away and the sea was changing colour once again, losing its white billows and becoming calmer.

When they gathered for the meal later, Brother Metellus greeted them with a warm smile as if the intensity of their discussion that afternoon had not existed.

'I think we will be able to set sail in the morning,' he said with satisfaction. 'We'll leave at first light as we originally intended to do this morning.'

This time the weather grew tranquil during the night.

The day dawned calm and warm, with the sun beating down from an almost cloudless sky. The few clouds that did drift high above were fluffy white balls, like the fruiting puffs of groundsel. What was more, there was a soft morning breeze blowing from the south.

With the single sail hoisted, it quickly filled and the small boat, with Brother Metellus at the tiller, was gliding swiftly out from the bay, leaving a small knot of islanders waving their goodbyes on the foreshore. The journey across the water to the mainland seemed swift, and so calm was the sea that even Eadulf did not have time to feel queasy. Brother Metellus was an excellent sailor, manoeuvring his sailing boat with consummate skill, shifting every time there was a subtle change in the wind to re-catch the force of it in his sail. Fidelma observed that the monk knew the waters well, for there was a series of rocky shoals through which he navigated with ease. They did not speak much during the short voyage over the distance that separated the island of the Little Duck from the low-lying stretch of land that Brother Metellus identified as the Rhuis peninsula.

Fidelma was aware of the sheer numbers of seabirds as they approached the coastline. The ringed plover, with their distinctive black ring and bright orange bill and legs, were heading along the shoreline in search of shellfish in the mudflats. High up, marked by their white crowns and under-parts, but dark brown upper feathers, two osprey wheeled, alternatively flapping and gliding, as they hunted for fish swimming near the surface. A sudden pause, as if they were hovering, and then with partly closed wings, the birds dived on their kill. Fidelma had seen osprey before, but it was always a spectacular sight, watching them make their kill. Even the gulls, emitting cries like souls in torment, seemed to avoid these hunters.

'The abbey is around that headland,' called Brother Metellus, pointing to a rocky headland with a large green mound. The area was covered with thickly growing wood-land. There seemed no place to effect a landing.

'Don't worry, we shall come into the west of that, where there is an open sandy beach,' Brother Metellus said, correctly guessing the thoughts that were passing through their minds.

Indeed, Fidelma had already spotted the sandy strip stretching to the north-west towards another rising headland, which she estimated must be five kilometres away.

'They call this the Great Mount and the one over there the Little Mount,' explained Brother Metellus.

There was a tide with them now as well as the wind, and they came swiftly onto the sandy beach among several other craft that were pulled up there. Fishermen and some women sat in little groups, some mending nets, while others were simply talking and cooking fish over open fires. Two of the fishermen came trotting down into the surf to help draw the small craft up onto the dry sand, and one courteously helped Fidelma out. Greetings were exchanged in the local language and then Brother Metellus led the couple from the beach and up a winding path through a very green and fertile area, most of which appeared thickly forested. Fidelma noticed it was filled with broadleaf trees, mainly thick oaks and beeches, with a few conifers sprinkled here and there when a thinning of the woodland provided space.

'There is good hunting here and the nobles of Bro-Waroch often come to hunt in this area. The peninsula is fertile with game and with wild boar,' Brother Metellus explained. Fidelma had the impression they were crossing back towards the large headland overlooking the sea. 'Beyond that rise to the north is the fortress of the *mac'htiern* of Brilhag.'

'Mac Hiern?' Fidelma tried to repeat the phonetics.

'*Mac'htiern*,' carefully repeated Brother Metellus. 'It is the title of the Lord of Brilhag, who is the ruler of this area.'

'Surely, then, he would be in a better position to help us than your Abbot?' Fidelma suggested.

Brother Metellus disagreed. 'Better that we firstly speak with Abbot Maelcar. He is strict about protocol and might take it amiss if we went directly to Lord Canao.'

While Fidelma had the impression that this was a hurried excuse, Eadulf saw nothing amiss.

'Canao?' queried Eadulf. 'You have mentioned that name before.'

'I did,' agreed Brother Metellus easily. 'The Lord of Brilhag is a descendant of the old rulers of Bro-Waroch, many of whom had that name.'

They emerged abruptly from the surrounding trees and bushes to find themselves faced with a stretch of cultivated fields. Fidelma and Eadulf saw that many of them contained vines. In the centre of these fields stood a group of low sandstone buildings that must constitute the Abbey of Gildas. The buildings were not impressive, even though the Abbey was, according to Brother Metellus, about one hundred years old. There were basically four separate buildings placed around a quadrangle. To one side was the chapel, identifiable by its architecture. It was fairly small, topped with the traditional cross of the churches of the western islands, a cross mainly contained within a circle. Two of the other buildings rose to three storeys in height while the fourth one on the last side of the square was a one-storey structure and quite ornate by comparison with its fellows. The square itself was given over to a herb garden, from which an assortment of scents assailed their nostrils. However, compared with those great buildings that Fidelma and Eadulf had seen in their travels, the whole complex of the abbey was modest.

There were a few religious about, some of whom greeted Brother Metellus by name, while others hurried by with faces averted from them as though shocked by the sight of Fidelma in their midst. Indeed, some stared, scandalised at a woman's presence in the abbey precincts. Brother Metellus ignored them and they followed him through the small entrance between the buildings into the quadrangle gardens.

'This is the Abbey of the Blessed Gildas,' Brother Metellus announced, unnecessarily, with a slight gesture of his hand as if to encompass the buildings around them. 'If you will wait here, in the herb garden, I will go and inform Abbot Maelcar of your presence.' He hesitated a moment and then explained awkwardly: 'As I have said, this abbey follows the celibacy rule and is for males only. It is not a mixed house.'

'Do not worry,' Fidelma replied, and Eadulf discerned her slightly mocking tone. 'We will await your Abbot here so as not to outrage the abbey's sense of propriety.'

There was a rough carved wooden bench nearby and Fidelma promptly seated herself on it. Brother Metellus hesitated a moment more before making his way to the single-storey building and disappearing inside. Eadulf gave a little sigh before going to sit by her.

'This is certainly no port where ships from any of the Five Kingdoms will put in,' he observed.

'Our intention is to be directed to such a port,' Fidelma replied. 'But first, I want to ask some questions of the Abbot.'

'You hope that he might have information about the ship that attacked us?'

'He may know something. I would like to get some information as to the identity of that murderous captain and his vessel before we return home.'

'Returning home is our main aim. Don't forget that we are destitute,' Eadulf reminded her.

'We will hope that the charity of these brethren will help us. Also, I still have one emerald ear-clip left. Perhaps we can barter the stone for food or other things.'

Eadulf was sceptical. 'I doubt that will take us far,' he said. 'I think it would be better to seek out this Lord Canao.

He might be able to guide us to King Alain, who would surely help us as Bressal negotiated the treaty with him?'

'Perhaps,' agreed Fidelma. 'But it is a long way back to Naoned, and that is where Bressal said he had last seen the King. Even so, I want to find out more about these pirates before we set out for Naoned again.'

Eadulf saw the set of Fidelma's jaw and realised it was not worth arguing. Once she had made up her mind, the only way to change it was persuasion by example.

'So far as I can see, we will have to go where the tide takes us at the moment until we can find a benefactor,' he said dourly.

Fidelma glanced towards the building into which Brother Metellus had disappeared. Her impatience was obvious to Eadulf and he was about to urge calm when a 'miaow' at his feet caused him to look down. A large black cat had appeared, its nose in the air sniffing gently. It moved immediately towards Fidelma and rubbed itself against her legs. She stared down at it and then a frown formed on her features. She bent down and ran a hand across the sleek black fur at the back of its neck. The animal gave another 'miaow', then turned and stalked off without haste among the bushes of the herb garden.

Fidelma turned to Eadulf with a curious expression. 'Did you see that?'

'The abbey seems to have a pet,' he replied with a smile.

'You didn't recognise it?' she pressed.

'Why should I?' Eadulf did not understand.

Fidelma ran a tongue nervously over her lips and glanced

quickly round, lowering her voice in an almost conspiratorial whisper.

'Because that animal was Luchtigern. That was the ship's cat, the cat from the *Barnacle Goose*.'

CHAPTER FOUR

◈

E adulf regarded her in astonishment for a moment, not sure whether she was joking or not.

'You must be wrong,' he said eventually. 'One black cat looks exactly like another.'

Fidelma shook her head determinedly. 'That is not so. Cats have individual looks and personalities just as we have. That was Luchtigern – I know it. But how came the cat here?'

'Are you saying that the cat escaped overboard and swam here?' Eadulf tried to joke.

'I am not stupid, Eadulf,' Fidelma said irritably. 'I tell you that it was Luchtigern. On the back of his head is a lump of pitch that is entangled with his hair. I felt it just now. I saw it on the ship and Wenbrit told me just before we were attacked that he was going to cut it off.'

Eadulf was silent for a moment. He knew that Fidelma would not be so intense if she was anything but sure and the evidence of the pitch was damning.

'But how . . . ?' he began.

'Don't ask me how it came here!' she snapped. 'Maybe the *Barnacle Goose* had to put into harbour here and the cat escaped.'

'There is no harbour near here,' protested Eadulf. 'You saw that the beaches are long and sloping. A ship would have to stand off some way out to sea, and no cat could swim that distance to shore.'

'Then we must examine the coast round here. If Luchtigern is here then so are those who have survived the attack on the *Barnacle Goose*. The animal could not have travelled far on its own.'

'Don't male cats wander?' hazarded Eadulf. 'The ship could be miles away.'

Fidelma's expression indicated what she thought of his comment. She glanced around with a frown.

'We'll have to be careful about what we say until we know who we can trust.'

'Surely we can trust Brother Metellus? After all, he saved us.'

'It's true that he saved us,' she agreed. 'But I am sure the dove emblem meant something to him when you mentioned it. Also, he did not seem keen about us going to see this local lord.'

There was no time to say any more because Brother Metellus had reappeared, in the company of an elderly man. The latter was stocky in appearance, with a fleshy moon face and red cheeks. His hair, while bearing the tonsure of Peter, was a silver-grey and with thick curls at its ends. The eyes were dark, and there was some unfathomable quality to them as if they were a mask rather than expressive of the personality of the man. He wore black robes and around his neck was a golden chain with a crucifix denoting that he held the rank of Abbot.

His lips parted in what was meant as a smile of welcome but his features held no warmth behind the greeting.

'*Pax vobiscum*. Greetings, my children. You are welcome to our little community.' He spoke in Latin.

'*Pax tecum*,' they replied almost in unison.

'Brother Metellus has told me of your adventure but, *Deo iuvante*, you have survived.'

'Indeed, with God's help,' muttered Eadulf.

'Brother Metellus also tells me that you have been rendered without means of support. You may be in luck – we are expecting a merchant, called Biscam, to arrive here shortly. Biscam comes regularly to our community and he will be returning to Naoned within a few days. I am sure that he would offer you his protection and a place among his wagons as far as the port. Brother Metellus tells me that ships from many quarters of the world use the port, including those from your own land. I am sure you will be able to find a safe passage back.'

The man spoke firmly as if there would be no questioning of what he had decided.

'You are most kind . . .' began Fidelma.

The Abbot barely heard her before cutting in: 'But until the merchant arrives . . . well, we must secure you some shelter. Beyond the abbey is a little village of fisherfolk.' He paused and made a curious gesture with a motion of his hand.

'You see, we are a community of monks, those who have taken vows of chastity in accordance with what we believe is the true path to God. There is no place, no facilities, for a woman here.'

'I was told that a local chieftain has his fortress nearby and perhaps, out of respect for my brother, the King of Muman, he might give us hospitality and ensure our safe passage home,' interposed Fidelma.

A frown of annoyance crossed Abbot Maelcar's features. He clearly did not like to have his own plans questioned.

'The Lord of Brilhag is not resident in his fortress. In fact, I believe he is presently in Naoned with the King. Best that you travel there as soon as Biscam, the merchant, departs.'

'I have no wish to impose on your community,' Fidelma said coldly.

'Neither shall you,' replied the Abbot with equanimity. 'Brother Metellus will take you to the village and arrange your beds and also meals. You have the freedom of all places except the abbey buildings themselves.' He paused and shrugged. 'The reasons for that are obvious. The harmony and peace of our community cannot be disturbed. While Brother . . . er, Eadulf,' he struggled with the unfamiliar name, 'can join us if he wishes, either at meals or services, we cannot extend such hospitality to you, Sister. Our rules are strict.'

'I will not bother you, Abbot,' Eadulf intervened quickly, before Fidelma had a chance to respond. There was irritation on her face and he knew her response would be critical. 'We will be content with whatever arrangements you suggest, and thank you for your generosity. Are we not like that traveller from Jerusalem to Jericho who was set upon by robbers and left destitute and for dead? And have you not come as the Samaritan did to take pity on us? For this much we applaud your beneficence, Father Abbot.'

Fidelma was puzzled for a moment because the speech was so unlike Eadulf. Then she realised that he was using gentle irony to deflect the Abbot's thoughts. Abbot Maelcar apparently did not hear any mockery in what was said but merely nodded seriously.

'Although I do not approve of the path you have taken, Brother Eadulf,' he glanced from Eadulf to Fidelma, 'we are Christians together and must fulfil the tenets of our Faith that are compassion and charity. It is God's will that soon all the churches of these western lands will come into accord with Rome and every abbey and monastery will adopt the Rule of the Blessed Benedict. Only a few days ago, I received news of the ordinances of the Council at Autun, which has ordained that this Rule of Benedict be adopted by every religious community. Any other course leads to profligacy and depravity. Unless our churches here abandon those ways, there is no reward in heaven.'

Fidelma swallowed hard but Eadulf nodded quickly.

'Each sheep comes to the shepherd in his own way,' he smiled easily. 'It may interest you to know that we were among the delegates to the Council of Autun.' He ignored Fidelma's frown of warning.

'Delegates?' The Abbot's eyes shot up on his forehead in surprise. 'It was a Council of bishops and abbots. Why would you be among the delegates?'

'Sister Fidelma was asked to act as legal adviser to the Abbot of Imleach, the premier bishop of her brother's kingdom,' Eadulf said.

For the first time during this conversation, Brother Metellus cleared his throat and bent in deferential manner towards the Abbot.

'Sister Fidelma is a legal advocate in her own land,' he began to explain.

'When is this merchant, Biscam, due to arrive here?' asked Fidelma, cutting in sharply, and determined to draw the conversation back to the immediate problem.

'Biscam? He should be here within the next day or two. He and his brothers have been trading with us for many years.'

'Then we shall trouble you no further, Abbot Maelcar.' Fidelma glanced about the abbey grounds as if noticing them for the first time and commented: 'You have a beautiful place here.'

The Abbot's eyes widened at the change of subject. 'It was a spot chosen by the Blessed Gildas,' he replied.

'Your herb garden is especially fragrant and well kept.'

'God blesses the hands of our brethren in their tending of the plants.'

'I saw that the abbey has a cat and I presume that you keep it to fend off the pests that sometimes dominate in a garden.'

This time Abbot Maelcar looked puzzled. 'The abbey does not have a cat,' he replied.

'No?' Fidelma feigned surprise. 'The abbey does not have a large black cat?'

'We have no cat at all.'

'But I saw it wandering through the gardens.'

'Then it must be one from the village. And now . . .' The Abbot left the sentence unfinished as a token of dismissal.

'Of course. Forgive me. We have kept you for too long from your duties.'

'We will doubtless meet again before you leave our community,' the Abbot said, before turning and walking back towards the single-storey building.

Brother Metellus had been standing in silence, his head bowed and his hands folded in front of him. He sighed and stirred as the Abbot left them.

'He has told me to look after you until the arrival of Biscam,' he explained in a resigned voice. 'I had been hoping to use this fair weather to get back to the island.'

Fidelma could not resist a quick smile at his grumbling.

'It seems that Abbot Maelcar is not the friendliest of people. There is something about his manner . . .' She ended with a shrug.

'He is convinced that the correct path to a communication with God is through vows of celibacy and in following the order of the Blessed Benedict. The rites and rituals of the churches of the Britons, and those in your own land, are anathema to him. You must make allowances.'

'We are indebted to him, and to you, for all you have done for us, Brother Metellus,' Eadulf said hurriedly, lest the man think they were ungrateful.

Brother Metellus did not reply except to indicate, with a movement of his head, the north of the quadrangle. 'The village lies beyond these woodlands.'

There was a small area of woodland between the abbey buildings and the small hamlet beyond. They stood overlooking the same sandy bay in which they had landed. It was a practical village and not a picturesque one. The squat buildings were ugly, functional and no more.

'Where are you taking us?' asked Fidelma, curiously.

'To the Widow Aourken,' he replied.

'And she is . . . ?' prompted Fidelma.

'An elderly widow woman. Her husband, I am told, was a fisherman. Now she lives alone and so has room in her house.'

'We would not like to give her trouble.'

'You will not. She often offers the hospitality of her home to wayfarers. I think you will like her for she is also a woman of strong opinions.'

If it were merely physical strength that he was referring to, then Brother Metellus' description seemed an accurate one. Aourken was almost as wide as she was tall. The broad arms were muscular and her shoulders could, in Eadulf's imagination, take a heavy sack on them without effort. Her hands were twice as big as his own and he felt that one of them could squeeze an apple into a pulp. Yet her face was kindly, the eyes slightly melancholy and of an indiscernible colour. The hair, which reached beyond her shoulders in ragged tails, was white, streaked here and there with dark grey. Her teeth were bad but she maintained a twisted smile that seemed to disguise them. She stood at the door of one of the single-storey stone buildings, hands on hips, watching their approach.

'Greetings, Brother Metellus.'

These were the only words that Fidelma understood as the woman spoke rapidly in her own language. The words were so accented that she lost track.

There was a quick exchange and then, to Fidelma's surprise, the woman turned to her and began to speak in Latin – hesitantly, it was true, but in a form that was quite literate.

'You are welcome here. You are both welcome here.'

'Thank you,' returned Fidelma at once. 'We do not wish to cause you any problems.'

'Brother Metellus has informed me of your situation. God be praised, that you have survived the ravages of those pirates.'

Fidelma looked interested. 'You have heard of them?'

The woman spread her large hands. 'On this coast, there are always tales of sea-raiders. But in recent times, some of the farms on this coast have been attacked by brigands landing from the sea.'

'You speak good Latin,' interposed Eadulf.

Aourken smiled her crooked smile. 'I served the Faith for many years. Then I met my late husband and he convinced me a better life was serving him. Well, we had a good time while it lasted. God's blessing was on us. Brother Metellus has told me your story and I will do my best to make you comfortable until Biscam, the merchant, arrives. My house is your house.'

'We are very grateful for your hospitality,' Fidelma said again.

'It is nothing. Come inside and I will show you where you will sleep, and perhaps you would care for something to eat and cider to drink? I am sure that Abbot Maelcar would not have offered you anything.'

'You seem to know the Abbot well?' Fidelma smiled.

'In our youth, we studied together. We had decided to join the community of Gildas together. It was then, as other religious houses still are, a community of men and women serving the Faith and raising their children to do so. I knew Maelcar when he first arrived here from Brekilien, before he started to read the works about Martin of Tours and hear the stories of the dedication of those religious out in the eastern deserts and other inaccessible places who became hermits and vowed celibacy. That was when he decided to follow their example.'

'The abbey is not exactly in an eastern desert,' pointed out Fidelma dryly. 'But I have heard of this place Brekilien. Where is it?'

'It is north of here and still within the kingdom. Brekilien is a great expanse of forest where Maelcar was raised and which he oft-times returns to. In fact, he is not long returned from some such a visit. Not that visits to his home do anything to sweeten his temper, but rather make his disposition worse. I understand he returned muttering about the loose morality of King Alain's court where a provincial servant could fornicate with the King's offspring.'

'So Abbot Maelcar likes the secluded religious life?'

Aourken gave her a knowing smile and shook her head.

'Not far from here is an island which is now called Enez ar Manac'h – the Island of Monks. Maelcar initially went there to live out the hermit's life. He did not remain there long, however, but came back to the abbey. He lived a pious life and the old Abbot made him his steward. The community thought well of him, and when the Abbot died, he was elected to the post. No sooner was he settled in that office than he expelled all the females from the abbey and told the members that they must take vows of celibacy and agree to follow the rule of Benedict. And that is how it is in the Abbey of Gildas today.'

Brother Metellus coughed nervously at this recital.

'I have some matters to attend to – items to be gathered for my eventual return to Hoedig,' he said apologetically. 'My friends, I will leave you in the hands of Aourken and return here later.'

As Brother Metellus left them, Aourken said, 'Poor Brother Metellus. He is a Roman, you know. Another of those who feels constrained to live an unnatural life as a statement of his Faith. Why did God make men and women if He wanted them to live as eunuchs?' She laughed at her own humour.

Fidelma and Eadulf were ushered inside the dark but homely stone cottage and shown a room to sleep and where they might wash. Within a short while they were seated on a wooden bench outside, for the afternoon was now warm. Aourken provided them with a pitcher of cider and bowls to drink it from as well as fresh bread, goat's cheese and some apples.

The woman came and sat with them on a stool by the door. She had placed a bag of wool before her and taken out a distaff and spindle. Helping herself to a handful of wool, she wound it loosely on the distaff; then, using her left hand, the material was gradually drawn onto the spindle, which was held in the right hand. She did it automatically, unconscious of her dexterity, and chatting all the while.

'I take the thread to my cousin who lives at that cottage at the end there,' she jerked her head to indicate the place. 'She will weave the thread into garments for me.'

'Do you keep your own sheep then?' asked Eadulf.

'Bless you, no. I keep goats. I exchange goat's cheese and milk for the wool.'

'It must be a hard life, without . . . without . . .' Eadulf became embarrassed.

'Without a man?' she queried. 'My husband was a good fisherman. He and two others were drowned in the entrance of the Morbihan, which means the Little Sea. The tide flows quickly there and sometimes it can be too quick for safety's sake. One of the fishing boats got into trouble. My husband and his friends went to its aid and their own boat was swept onto the rocks, smashed to firewood and they drowned. The sea is a hard taskmaster. Anyway, the other fisherfolk here see that I get a portion of their catch so that I want for nothing. In turn I supply them with my goat's cheese. That is our way.'

Fidelma nodded approval. 'It is also the way of my own people,' she said before adding: 'You have a comfortable place here.'

'We are sheltered here,' Aourken agreed.

'In my land, we keep many pets,' Fidelma began.

'My goats are my pets,' replied the woman.

'And cats?' asked Fidelma.

'Oh yes, there are several cats in the village.'

'I thought I saw a black cat earlier.'

Eadulf suddenly realised where her question was leading. Aourken looked baffled. 'I have never seen a black cat here because our people think them a symbol of bad luck. To be honest, most people believe they carry demons and have special supernatural abilities. Black cats aren't welcomed here. The old ones say that they are human beings, undergoing punishment for evil deeds.'

Fidelma was surprised. 'In my land, it is the very opposite – for the wives of fishermen keep black cats, especially while their husbands are at sea, because they believe they will prevent danger coming against them.'

Aourken was silent as she continued her work with distaff and spindle.

'Why are you interested in black cats?' she asked after a while.

'There was a black cat on the *Barnacle Goose*. It was rather a special cat.'

'Fidelma thought she saw it in the abbey grounds,' Eadulf said, only to receive a frown from Fidelma.

'I *did* see the cat,' she insisted. 'It is identifiable by a lump of pitch that was stuck to the back of its neck.'

'So, you think that this cat managed to get from the ship to here?' Aourken pursed her lips. 'Well, no large ships have anchored in this bay for as long as I recall.'

Fidelma shifted her weight on the bench and stared at the mug of cider in her hand thoughtfully for a moment or two.

'Is there anywhere along this coast where large ships can take refuge?' she asked outright. There was little use in being subtle. 'You mentioned raids against the farmsteads here.'

Aourken stopped her spinning for a moment and observed Fidelma with her keen eyes. She said nothing. Fidelma decided to be honest with the woman, for her personality invited trust.

'You see, it occurred to me that the vessel might have come from somewhere along this coast,' Fidelma continued. 'When we approached the coastline from the south, it looked fairly open and with no natural harbours. But I was wondering if there was anywhere that a raiding ship could hide. Somewhere it could take a captive ship. The cat must have managed to get ashore near here.'

Aourken shrugged. 'I am afraid that there are many such places,' she answered, as she resumed her task at the spindle.

Fidelma and Eadulf exchanged a glance.

'From what we saw, we thought the beaches were fairly shallow and open, and the rocky places do not indicate a sheltered harbour.'

'That is only along this southerly coast,' replied the woman. 'But we are on a small peninsula – it is like a finger that sticks out. At the base of the finger is the abbey; at the tip of the finger is Noalou, a headland. There is a sea channel between that and another headland, Penn hir. That's the very channel where my husband lost his life. *That* channel leads from the Great Sea into the Morbihan, an area surrounded by land all except that channel into it and rivers. And in the Little Sea there are countless islands where ships and men can hide for all eternity.'

Fidelma was frowning with concentration as she followed her description.

'But you said this channel was dangerous? Could a large vessel enter into it?'

'If it is crewed by good seamen and the vessel is sturdy enough. One can only enter in and go out when the tide is right.'

'The right tide?' Fidelma was trying to remember something. Then she envisaged the slight white-robed form. *'Quickly now, or the tide will be against us!'* Was that what the murderous captain meant? Had he been anxious to get through that particular channel?

'I should like to see this Morbihan,' she said.

'That is easy. All you need to do is take the westerly path towards Noalou. Before you reach it, there is a hill nearby, which we call Ar mont bihan, the Little Height, on which there stands a great stone place built by the ancients – the tomb of some great king, so the old ones say: Tumieg's tomb. If you stand there, you will have a view across the peninsula to the Little Sea, and will be able to observe its vastness and all the islands in it.'

'You said there are many islands?' queried Eadulf.

'Yes, indeed. I've heard it said there is one island for every day of the year. No one has ever counted them, though my husband once said that there are around a hundred, counting the lumps of rock that rise out of the sea.'

Eadulf suppressed a whistle of surprise. 'That is enough. Are they all large?'

'Many are large enough to be inhabited.'

'How far away is this height where we can view the Little Sea?' The question came from Fidelma.

'Five kilometres on a good path.'

Fidelma glanced up at the sky and Eadulf, seeing the

movement, said nervously: 'We would not have time to go there and return before nightfall.'

Aourken nodded sympathetically. 'Brother Eadulf is right. You would have no time now before nightfall. Anyway, if you were looking for a ship at anchor, then you have no chance at all because it would be dusk. Indeed, my dear, that ship could easily be hidden behind any one of the islands. Make no mistake; we are not talking about a lake. That is why we call it the Little Sea. From one side to the other is half the distance to Hoedig, where you came from, and far more than that wide. There are inlets and rivers – not to mention the islands. You could lose an entire fleet of warships there. This was the very heartland of the great Veneti who fought the Romans in the ancient times.'

'You seem to know it well?' Eadulf said.

'When I first went with my husband, I sailed with him through those waters,' she said. Then observing that her spindle was full, she placed it beside her and drew forth another one.

Fidelma glanced reluctantly at the sky again. 'Tomorrow, early, we shall walk to this place. The tomb of Tumieg, you say? We will examine this Little Sea for ourselves.'

'You are a strange lady, in truth,' Aourken commented. 'If it were me, I would be merely content that I had been preserved from the attack of these pirates and head for my home as quickly as I could. I would not wish to put myself in the way of encountering those evil people again.'

'I have a duty to the dead and to justice,' replied Fidelma simply. 'And if there is a chance that some of the crew of the vessel that we were on are still alive, then it is my duty also to effect the rescue.'

'Then God protect you in that desire,' the woman sighed. 'Ah, here is Brother Metellus coming back to join us.'

The stocky Roman came striding down the path to where they sat, and they saw he was smiling happily.

'Good news,' he greeted them, waving aside an offer of cider from Aourken. 'I came to tell you that there is word that Biscam, the merchant, and his brothers are close by. They should be at the abbey tomorrow before nightfall. They will stay with us no more than a day or so, which means I can soon head back to Hoedig and you can both be on your way to Naoned.'

'Good news, indeed,' Eadulf responded, but he was aware that Fidelma did not seem to share their enthusiasm.

'We've just been discussing the situation, Brother Metellus,' she said quietly. 'It seems there is a possibility that the ship that attacked us and captured the *Barnacle Goose* might be harboured in a place called the Little Sea.'

Brother Metellus was astonished. 'Morbihan!' he exclaimed. He glanced at Aourken. 'What makes you think so?'

'I was just telling them about the Little Sea.' The elderly woman shrugged. 'I made no other speculation.'

'Do not blame Aourken,' Fidelma said. 'Some instinct tells me that the attackers came from along this coast and took the *Barnacle Goose* back to their hiding-place. I have now learned there is an entrance here into an inner sea which is where the ship could have come from.'

Brother Metellus drew up a stool to sit down.

'Have you heard of such a vessel in those waters, Aourken?' he demanded of the woman as she continued to work with distaff and spindle.

'In truth, I have not, Brother,' she responded obediently. 'Although some of the farms have been raided by strangers and their barns burned and stock taken. No one knows where these raiders came from. But if they came from a ship that had somehow managed to hide in Morbihan, you could search for all eternity and not find it.'

'I agree,' Brother Metellus said heavily. 'I have seen the extent of Morbihan, the Little Sea. Even if you were given months and a fast sail boat, you could not hope to search it thoroughly.'

'I still intend to examine this place tomorrow morning from the mound you inform me of,' Fidelma set her features stubbornly.

'I told her of the grave of Tumieg,' explained Aourken.

Brother Metellus actually smiled.

'In that case, once you have seen the extent of the Morbihan, you will realise that what I say is correct. And by tomorrow evening, Biscam will be here and you will soon be able to start your journey home.'

CHAPTER FIVE

F idelma had risen early the next day and, with Eadulf, set off on the path that Aourken had pointed out. The journey had not been profitable other than providing them with some breathtaking views of the sea and countryside that surrounded them. They had seen no more of the black cat that Fidelma had identified as Luchtigern – the Mouse Lord – from the *Barnacle Goose*. Eadulf was still unsure whether Fidelma had correctly identified the animal or not. It seemed incredible that it had escaped from the ship. The fruitless walk to the grave of Tumieg and back had not put him in a good mood.

It was true that the walk around the sandy bay, keeping to the high ground above it, and then climbing to the ancient stone barrow, was pleasant enough in the sun. However, Eadulf was concerned at Fidelma's lack of interest at securing their immediate homeward passage and her idea that she could track down their attackers. Reaching the spot to which they had been directed, the highest point so far as they could see, they had been met with a spectacular view to the north of an inland sea dotted with a myriad of islands. So many that they seemed to merge into one another as if they were one mass of land. Only now and then did the passage of a small boat show the channels between the islands.

The main movement was the circling birds above – mallards, plovers and even teals – all combining the cacophony of their cries into a noisy concert of protest at human presence around the mound. Fidelma and Eadulf saw no sign of anyone on their journey there, nor as they stood looking across the strange seascape before them.

Fidelma stared hard at the islands, but there were no anchored ships that resembled either the *Barnacle Goose* or the sleek black ship that had attacked them. She was reluctant to drag herself away from the scene and it was Eadulf who finally voiced the conclusion.

'The old woman was right. Aourken told us that this Little Sea was so vast and thick with islands that, even if the *Barnacle Goose* had been brought there, we might not be able to find it if we scoured the area for months in a small boat.'

Fidelma sighed; the slump of her shoulders indicating resignation.

'Yet where did that cat come from?' she demanded.

Eadulf decided to take the question as rhetorical and refrained from answering.

She delayed a moment longer, sweeping the horizon with her keen eyes, before turning and suggesting that they begin their return journey. In other circumstances, Eadulf might have enjoyed the warmth and smells of the countryside, the gentle whispering of the nearby sea as it teased the coast. Even the crying birds, the multi-species, should have provided a distracting interest but failed in the circumstances.

The sun was past its zenith when they reached Aourken's stone cabin and found the woman taking fresh bread from her clay oven. She smiled at their arrival and immediately bustled about to provide them with bowls of fish soup and fresh bread.

'You saw the Little Sea?' asked the woman, after they were seated.

'It was everything you said it was,' Eadulf answered philosophically.

Aourken looked at Fidelma keenly. 'But you did not see what you were hoping to see?'

'I saw what you told me that I would see,' Fidelma admitted quietly. 'I saw little else.'

Aourken nodded thoughtfully. 'It is a beautiful place. But, I am thinking that you were not looking at the beauty.'

'You are right.'

'The sea and sadness go together,' reflected the old woman. 'Come, sit you down and eat. You have had a long walk.'

Fidelma sat down, feeling depressed. She had been hoping against hope that she would have been able to discover something that would lead her to an explanation of Luchtigern's strange appearance at the abbey. The only way that the animal could have arrived there was if the ship itself had put into some harbour close by. But why would he desert the ship which had always been his home? She knew a male cat was more likely to wander than a female, but a ship's cat was usually very territorial.

'If the pirates were hiding somewhere in Morbihan,' volunteered Aourken, 'as Brother Metellus said, there is hardly a chance at all of spotting them . . .' She paused as she was placing bread on the table and suddenly looked thoughtful. Fidelma caught her change of expression.

'You have thought of something?' she asked hopefully.

'If there is a sea-raider in these waters then perhaps our *mac'htiern* might have word of it.'

'The lord of this territory?' enquired Eadulf. 'This Lord Canao who has been mentioned?'

'Our chieftain, he occupies the *curule magistracies*.'

'But we were told he was not here but at Naoned,' Fidelma pointed out.

Aourken shrugged at the news. 'So he has not returned? I did not know. A pity. He is a good man and is patron of the abbey. I taught his daughters Latin grammar when they were young.' She sighed with nostalgic remembrance. 'That I do miss, although they were a handful. The younger daughter – well, she was his foster-daughter – was very ambitious and, alas, very arrogant.' The old woman smiled wistfully. 'She once told me that when she grew up, she would rule not only this peninsula but all of Bro-Waroch and every kingdom of the Bretons . . .'

Eadulf had been listening patiently. 'A shame if this Lord of Brilhag is in Naoned.'

'If anyone had knowledge it would have been him,' Aourken agreed. 'But perhaps his son, Macliau, might help. However, he is not half the man his father is. He indulges himself too much with wine and . . . well, with women.'

'We were not told he had a son. Where would we find him?'

'You would go to see him?' She was a little surprised.

'It is the only way to acquire information,' affirmed Fidelma.

'He dwells at his father's fortress of Brilhag, which is on the north coast of this peninsula. It, too, overlooks the Morbihan.'

'Perhaps we could start now and—'

But Fidelma did not have time to end her sentence before the sound of hurrying footfalls came to their ears. A moment later Brother Metellus appeared. He was breathing rapidly from his exertion and there was a thin film of sweat on his forehead. Something had clearly put him in a state of distress.

'What is it, Brother?' asked Aourken, rising to greet him.

Brother Metellus halted before them and tried to recover himself.

'I have news of Biscam and his brothers,' he said between gasps.

'He has arrived at the abbey?' Eadulf asked.

'He has not,' Brother Metellus replied hollowly, turning with a tragic face towards him. 'The news is terrible.'

'Perhaps you will be good enough to tell us what this news is. Where is this man Biscam?' Fidelma demanded.

'Dead, Sister,' replied Brother Metellus, turning back to her. 'He and his brothers were attacked and their donkeys and goods were stolen. It happened only a mile from the abbey.'

Brother Eadulf grimaced and said: 'That is indeed terrible.'

'I think,' intervened Fidelma gently, 'that Brother Metellus would not be telling us this news unless it held a deeper meaning for us.'

The monk nodded. 'One of Biscam's drivers managed to survive. He is badly wounded but somehow he was able to crawl to the abbey. I think it better if you come with me and hear what he has to say.'

'You make it sound intriguing, my friend, but as you'll recall, Abbot Maelcar made it quite clear that I was not welcome in the abbey.'

'Then let Brother Eadulf come with me, for this should be heard.'

Fidelma stood up abruptly. 'As you are so insistent, let us all go to see this man. If Abbot Maelcar is concerned that my presence will destroy the spirituality of his community, then I will stand aside and Eadulf may listen to what there is to say. Where is the man now?'

'There is a little house behind the chapel, set aside for the ailing sick of the community,' Brother Metellus said, looking relieved. 'Biscam's man is there.'

'You said that he is badly wounded,' Eadulf said. 'Has he been attended to?'

Brother Metellus nodded quickly. 'We have a good apothecary in the abbey and his wounds have been dressed and tended. But the man has lost a lot of blood.'

They excused themselves from Aourken's presence and followed Brother Metellus back to the abbey buildings.

'What is this man's name?' asked Fidelma as they hurried along the path.

'Berran. He worked for Biscam and his brothers.'

'You have intrigued me as to what Berran might say that is of such importance,' Fidelma said. 'Is this one of the raids on local farms that Aourken told us about?'

'I don't know. I had not heard of them until yesterday, for I have been on my island for quite a while.' Brother Metellus fell silent and so they followed him without any further questions back to the abbey. He led the way straight to a small building behind the chapel. It was a single room in which some wooden cots were placed, only one of which was occupied. A tall thin religious stood nearby administering some dark-coloured liquid. He looked up with a frown of disapproval as they entered.

'The man needs rest,' he admonished Brother Metellus in a whisper. 'Sleep is the great healer in such cases.' Then he seemed to notice Fidelma for the first time and his jaw slackened a little.

'Sister Fidelma is here with my authority, Brother,' Brother Metellus said quickly before he could raise another objection. Fidelma had looked quickly at the figure in the bed.

'Is the prognosis good?' she asked quietly.

'It is not a life-threatening wound, if that is what you mean,' the physician murmured. 'He has lost blood and has pain from the wound, but he is young, and youth and time will lead to a good recovery.'

'Has Abbot Maelcar been here to see him?' asked Brother Metellus.

'He has. The Abbot has just returned to his own chambers.'

'Good.' Brother Metellus ushered them to the bedside. They were surprised to see that the man who lay there was conscious; his eyes were focused on them, though it was plain to see that he was in some discomfort. 'Hello, Berran,' Brother Metellus spoke gently. 'This will not take but a moment. I just want you to repeat to Sister Fidelma here exactly what you told us about the attack.'

Berran was, indeed, a young man, but his face was lined and weather-beaten and also furrowed with deep lines of pain. The eyes were dark and almost fathomless as he turned towards her.

'We . . .' he licked a tongue over his parched lips. 'We were not far from the abbey. Biscam thought we should reach it by mid-morning. We had fifteen donkeys laden with goods and there were five of us – Biscam, his two brothers, my friend Brioc and myself. The journey from Naoned had been without incident . . .'

He blinked and paused.

'It all happened so suddenly. I felt a pain and was knocked over by a blow on the shoulder. It was an arrow. I fell to the ground and was aware of my comrades falling around me. I heard their cries of surprise and pain, then I passed out. The attackers must have thought I was dead like the others but when I woke up, the donkeys and their packs were gone and only the dead lay on the forest pathway. I saw Biscam, his brothers . . . all dead. Only I survived.'

'Tell the Sister what you saw before you passed out,' Brother Metellus urged.

'I saw the attackers emerging from the trees and bushes

that lined the path. They had their bows ready in their hands and swords as well . . .'

'And . . . ?' pressed Brother Metellus.

'Their leader . . .'

'Yes, their leader?' cajoled the Roman. 'Tell us of their leader.'

'He was dressed all in white and wore a mask. He was a thin man with a shrill voice.'

Fidelma exhaled softly and glanced at Eadulf. She turned back to the wounded man.

'Is there anything else you can tell us about this man?' she whispered.

Berran was obviously trying to recall. 'No,' he gasped. 'I was overcome with pain and passed out. In fact, I kept coming to and crawling along the path, knowing that I would eventually get to the abbey.'

Brother Metellus turned to Fidelma. 'You see why you had to hear this? The leader was dressed in white as you described.'

Fidelma nodded thoughtfully.

'Tell me, Berran, have you ever heard any rumours or stories about robbers in this area? Was this the first time you have been attacked in this fashion?'

The young man's lips twisted in a spasm of pain before he answered. 'I have heard nothing of merchants being attacked in this area of Bro-Waroch. There were stories of some attacks on farmsteads when we entered the peninsula two days ago. But there has never been any trouble before.'

'Forgive me asking you again, Berran, but can you tell us anything more about the identity of these attackers? Apart from their leader, a slim man clad in white, you say?'

'That is all I can recall.'

'And you have no idea of where they came fr—'

'Enough!' The voice at the door was harsh.

They swung round to see Abbot Maelcar gazing angrily from the doorway.

'Did I not make myself clear, Sister Fidelma?' His eyes narrowed on her. 'You are not welcome in the abbey precincts and certainly *not* in these buildings reserved for sick members of our community!'

Brother Metellus took a step forward. 'It is my fault, Father Abbot. The people who attacked Sister Fidelma and Brother Eadulf at sea are the same that attacked Biscam and his men. I felt that she should hear what Berran had to say.'

Abbot Maelcar sniffed disapprovingly. 'You dare disobey me? You knew my orders!'

'Isn't it more important to discover who these murderers are, than keep strictly to the rules of the community?' Brother Metellus asked defiantly.

Abbot Maelcar's features reddened. His eyes flashed with fury.

'You still defy me?' His voice rose sharply.

'Abbot Maelcar,' Fidelma spoke quietly. 'We are in the presence of a sick man in the infirmary. If you wish to raise your voice, then we should repair outside and away from this place.'

The Abbot's mouth opened in astonishment and he seemed at a loss for a moment at what he considered her impudence.

Eadulf knew that she was doing no more than obeying the law that appertained in her own land. The laws of how hospitals were run were very precise, and nothing that disturbed the peace of the patients was to be allowed within a certain area of the house where the sick were being nursed – no barking dogs or noisy people. He moved forward, slightly in front of Fidelma, facing the Abbot, and spoke softly but firmly.

'I suggest that we leave poor Berran in peace and continue this discussion outside. It is too important a matter to argue over the dogma of rules when lives are at stake.' He turned to the worried-looking physician attending him and smiled to indicate his thanks, although Eadulf felt that his anxiety was more for the wrath of the Abbot than care for his patient.

The Abbot turned on his heel. He was waiting for them outside, his expression angry.

'I defer only to the sick man,' he said, his tone harsh.

'That is all we were asking you to do,' replied Eadulf. Fidelma was surprised by his tone. He did not usually assume a belligerent manner. 'As to the matter in hand, this man had important information about the people who attacked and killed the merchant's company. From his description, it was the same thieves who attacked our ship and killed the Prince of Cashel, the cousin of the Lady Fidelma here.' For the first time Eadulf had abandoned the religious title to emphasise that she was sister of the King of Muman. Before Abbot Maelcar could reply, Eadulf continued: 'That means these murderers and robbers are based in this vicinity. And *that* means your abbey might be in danger from them.'

But Abbot Maelcar did not seem concerned.

'Nonsense. Why would they, whoever they are, attack this abbey?'

'There are many reasons why an abbey is attacked,' pointed out Brother Metellus. 'For the precious icons, the riches of the goods bestowed on them and offered in praise of the Christ.'

'No robber would dare attack the Abbey of Gildas,' snapped the Abbot.

'If they would dare attack and kill merchants bringing goods to the abbey and within proximity to the abbey, then why not attack the abbey itself?' Fidelma's voice was still soft but her delivery was studied. 'If they would dare attack a ship sailing under the protection of a King's envoy, why bother about a remote abbey? This matter should be brought to the attention of your lord, or his deputy, so that he may extend his hand in protection here in case of attack.'

'Nonsense!' Maelcar said irritably. 'How do we know that what this man,' he gestured to the infirmary, 'says is the truth? A wounded man comes to the abbey with a story that starts a panic – who knows what his motivations are?'

Fidelma considered him with surprise.

'I presume that you have already sent someone to the spot where this attack took place to ascertain the facts and see if there were other survivors too badly wounded to move?'

The Abbot raised his chin stubbornly.

'I am not to be panicked into any course of action until I know the facts.'

'You will not learn the facts by sitting here and quoting rules!' Fidelma admonished him. 'There might be wounded men out there dying for lack of attention. We must go to where this attack took place and discover the facts.'

'I know the place that Berran was speaking about,' said Brother Metellus. 'It's less than a kilometre east from here in a wooded area. It would be ideal for the sort of ambush that Berran spoke of.'

Abbot Maelcar was staring angrily at Brother Metellus.

'I forbid you to leave this abbey,' he said.

'You may forbid Brother Metellus but you will certainly not forbid us from proceeding,' Fidelma rapped out. 'As sister to the King of my land, whose cousin, his envoy, was murdered, I invoke my right to claim the hazel wand of office from him and track down his murderer.' As she spoke, Fidelma drew forth the hazel wand that she had been carrying in her girdle since she had picked it up from the deck where Bressal's lifeless hand had dropped it. 'I will appeal to the King of this land, who recognised the embassy of my cousin, and who was duty bound to protect him. I will assert my right. Now, if Brother Metellus will point us along the right path . . . ?'

Brother Metellus was gazing defiantly at the Abbot.

'Not only will I give you directions but I will take you there myself,' he said, addressing Fidelma while continuing to gaze at the Abbot.

Abbot Maelcar seemed shocked.

'Have you not learned humility yet, Brother Metellus?' he asked. 'Were you not sent to Hoedig to reflect and learn humility?'

'Humility has nothing to do with this matter,' Brother Metellus said.

'The first degree of humility is obedience without question,' returned the Abbot in a voice like thunder. 'Does not the Rule of the Blessed Benedict say that as soon as anything has been commanded by the Superior of the abbey, no delay in the execution of that order is permitted. The order must be obeyed as if God Himself had commanded it. You will obey me without question.'

'Obedience is never blind, Maelcar,' the Brother said quietly. 'Obedience requires the use of prudence in accepting rights and obligations. Decisions can only be made with knowledge, a free choice to do good and avoid evil. To ignore what has happened is to go down the path of evil and I will not tolerate it!'

'Not tolerate . . . !' exploded the Abbot, but Brother Metellus had turned to them and pointed the way.

'It will not take us long to follow the path.'

They left the red-faced Abbot opening and closing his mouth like a floundering fish and not knowing what to do.

With Brother Metellus leading the way, Fidelma and Eadulf fell in step behind him. They said nothing, merely exchanged a glance as the monk strode before them, the hunching of his shoulders and bent head showing the angry tension in his body. For some time they walked on in silence until, finally, Fidelma remarked: 'This will put you in bad standing in the Abbey.'

Brother Metellus looked sideways at her and his angry expression broadened into a smile.

'It puts me in bad standing with Abbot Maelcar and those sycophants who obey him without question. I am not of their number. I believe in rules, that the religious life should be bound by constraints and authority, and I believe that the true path of the religious should be a celibate one, free from carnal desire . . .' Then he shook his head. 'But I do not believe in blind obedience – obedience for the sake of obedience. If we pursue that path then we are denying God's greatest gift, denying what has made us in the image of Him – which is the right of making our own judgements.'

Fidelma regarded him with some approval.

'I agree that we must reflect and make our own choices, for obedience without question leads to abuse of the power of the person giving the orders,' she said gravely.

'While commending you on your stand, Brother,' Eadulf added, 'it does mean that your time at the Abbey of Gildas will not be a prolonged one.'

Brother Metellus replied with a thin smile, 'The best service that Abbot Maelcar did me was to send me to the little island of Hoedig. I shall return there and continue as before with or without that man's blessing.'

'You do not hold the Abbot in high esteem,' observed Eadulf.

Brother Metellus grunted sardonically. 'You have witnessed his fondness for exercising authority. If he were wise as well as authoritative, then his brethren would follow him more willingly.'

'So you think his reluctance to let us go to confirm what Berran has reported is due merely to his desire to exercise his authority?'

Brother Metellus appeared puzzled. 'What else could it be?'

'I just found his attitude strange, that's all,' Eadulf replied, and then lapsed into silence.

Fidelma considered the implication of Eadulf's comment. It was true that some people behaved in ways that were inexplicable to others because that was their character. Indeed, she found the Abbot to be a person who set her hackles rising. Could it be that there was more to it?

They moved on again in silence along a broad track away from the abbey. On both sides of the track, a thick forest of trees of various species stretched, making the route appear like a dark and sinister tunnel. It was quite warm and Fidelma and Eadulf spotted several plants and bushes that they were unfamiliar with. Brother Metellus saw Eadulf examining one of the flowering shrubs as they passed along.

'I think my ancestors must have brought that into this country,' he smiled. 'They called it *nardus* and to buy that bunch there would cost a month's income for a farm labourer.'

'Buy them?' Fidelma asked incredulously. 'Do people actually buy flowers?'

'Of course. Herbalists do,' replied the monk. 'And especially when the plants are rare.'

Eadulf sniffed at the fragrance of the plants, saying, 'I thought so – it is what you would call *labondur*,' he said to Fidelma. 'It has good healing qualities.'

'Lavender, indeed.' Brother Metellus nodded appreciatively. 'The local people use it to soothe and heal insect bites. The climate here is very warm, so that you will find an abundance of flowers and plants that I would not have expected to see so far north. I try to make notes of such things,' he added.

'You are a herbalist, an apothecary?' queried Eadulf, who

had studied the healing arts in the great medical school in Brefni, a petty kingdom north of Fidelma's own country.

Brother Metellus denied any medical interest.

'I used to collect and try to catalogue the plants, drawing their leaves and flowers as best I could and noting their healing qualities. But I have little time now to do so.'

'Then tell me what those flowers are.' Eadulf pointed to green shrubs with an amazing assortment of coloured flowers on them. 'I have not seen the like of these before. Those ones with flowers that are red, pink and crimson.'

Brother Metellus' smile was almost proprietorial.

'I think those are a long way from home. Maybe they were brought here by the legions or by merchants. Even I don't know their proper name. The various colours belong to different plants while the bushes they grow from remain evergreen. They are known as *ruz*, the local word for red.'

'And isn't that the name of this peninsula?' queried Eadulf.

'A similar sound, although I am not sure whether the name derives from the same word.'

They had proceeded some way down the track by this time and now Brother Metellus halted and turned, lowering his voice.

'Perhaps we should tread carefully from here on, as I believe we are not far from the spot where this attack took place. If the thieves are still in the area, it is best not to give them warning of our approach.'

They moved on in silence.

They had gone no more than 100 paces before Fidelma caught at Eadulf's arm and pointed while with her other hand she placed a finger to her lips. Eadulf saw at once what she meant and he similarly warned Brother Metellus. Ahead there were signs of bent grass and broken shrubbery, and then a man's body, stretched on the path, became visible. He lay sprawled on his face, two arrows protruding from his back. There was no doubt that he was dead.

They walked on further.

There were three more bodies lying along the path. Arrows indicated how two of the others were killed while the third man was covered in congealing blood, the result of several sword cuts.

They halted and stood still, listening.

The sounds of the woodland were still all-pervasive. The warning call of a merlin, the soft cooing of wood pigeons and the collared dove high in the conifer trees, joined with others too numerous to distinguish, all in one background noise. There were several rustles in the undergrowth, though none so clumsy and loud that it would foretell the careless foot of man.

Fidelma relaxed a little and nodded to Eadulf.

Watched by his companions, Eadulf swiftly went to each body and, bending down, felt for a pulse in the neck. Then he stood up and shook his head.

'They are all beyond help.'

Fidelma turned to Brother Metellus. 'Do you recognise them?'

'I do. The man with the arrows in his back is the merchant, Biscam. Those two are his brothers. I presume the other is the drover mentioned by Berran.'

Fidelma examined the trampled soil carefully. 'There are certainly signs that heavily loaded animals have been halted here and were startled.'

Brother Metellus looked at her in surprise. 'How do you tell, or is that deduced from Berran's description?'

Fidelma gave him a pitying look. She had been brought up from childhood to be aware of the signs of nature and man's disturbance of it. If one did not know such basic rules, one did not survive in the countryside for long.

'You see the hoofmarks of the animals? Even in the dry earth they are deep. That means that they were heavily loaded. And at this point there is a confusion of prints, as if the animals did not know which way to go and were stamping and trying to turn. There are signs of some horses, shod and quite clear.'

Fidelma walked carefully around the site looking at the marks on the ground.

'A few imprints of human feet, tramping over the hoofs of the beasts,' she said. Then she gave a soft exclamation. 'They were led in that direction! North, I think, through there,' she pointed. 'The path is quite clear. Come on, let us see where it leads.'

'Shouldn't we wait?' protested Eadulf nervously. 'They might still be close by.'

'I hope they are,' replied Fidelma grimly, turning and striding along the small path, following the tracks of the donkeys.

Eadulf hurried after her with an appealing glance at Brother Metellus, who sighed, and followed.

After a while, they burst out of the trees and undergrowth and were confronted by a little stream that gushed frothy white over a bed of shingle and large stones. Fidelma was staring at it in disgust.

'What is it?' demanded Brother Metellus.

Fidelma pointed as if the explanation was self-evident. 'They drove the animals into this stream.'

'So?'

'It means we cannot track them, for a stream with a stony bottom leaves no trace.'

'They would have to turn downstream if they wanted to go any way,' offered Brother Metellus. 'I know that upstream from here is a rocky hill and no way to pass round it. Not for donkeys.'

'And downstream? Where does that lead?'

'I think it flows into some marshland. There is an area that the local people avoid for there are mudflats in which a man can be swallowed up before he has time to cry for help. There are one or two such areas here, even quicksand. However, if they know the way and can follow the stream, they could come to the shore of Morbihan.'

Fidelma was thoughtful. 'In that case, these robbers might know the country well, or they do not know it at all.'

'I don't understand,' Brother Metellus replied with a frown.

It was Eadulf who answered him.

'If they took the donkeys and headed downstream to these marshes, they either did so knowingly or out of ignorance. If in ignorance, in so short a distance they would be in trouble and have returned. We would have encountered some signs.

If they had knowledge, they must have used it as a means to prevent any pursuit of them, using the marsh for protection. They could have reached the sea by now.'

Fidelma smiled her approval of his reasoning.

'Whatever the explanation,' she said, 'we will follow. But first, I want to examine the bodies of the merchants, which I have neglected to do.'

'What can you learn from them?' demanded Brother Metellus.

Fidelma did not bother to respond. Again it fell to Eadulf to explain.

'Much may be learned from a body, my friend,' he said confidently. He knew that Fidelma was skilled in such matters.

Back at the site of the attack, Fidelma examined each body, not to see the manner of how they met their deaths but to study the arrows.

'The arrows are practically all the same,' she said, after a short while. 'Now here is an interesting thing – the man who made these arrows uses goose feathers and cuts the three flights with a sharp knife. That is the sign of a fletcher who is an adept at his art. They are of a high standard and, indeed, the same hand made all these flights.'

'But does it help us?' asked Eadulf.

'Not of itself, but it may well be useful later.'

She had risen to her feet when Eadulf noticed that the man whom Brother Metellus had identified as the merchant Biscam was lying face down, one arm flung out before him, while the other arm was hidden underneath his body. He had apparently fallen on it. But Eadulf had noticed a wisp of white cloth poking out from underneath the body. He bent down and turned the corpse over on its back. It was only then that he saw that the arrows had not been the immediate cause of death. There was a cut mark in Biscam's chest, above the heart. Eadulf had seen enough sword wounds to know that the man had been stabbed with a broad-bladed weapon.

But it was not this that caused him to exclaim and Fidelma to follow his gaze to the body.

The man was clutching a strip of white silk in his hand. There were some marks on it as well as bloodstains.

He knelt down again and prised it loose from the dead hand.

'Could it be that he tore it from his assailant?' whispered Eadulf.

'Perhaps,' replied Fidelma. 'There is a curious patterning on this silk.'

Brother Metellus had moved forward to peer over her shoulder at it. He was frowning and there was something in his expression that caused Eadulf to ask: 'Do you recognise this?'

He held up the torn strip of silk in his hands. It was a curious outline of a dove. Brother Metellus gasped.

'What does that symbol mean?' demanded Eadulf. 'The same symbol was carved on the ship that attacked us.'

Brother Metellus ran his tongue around his dry lips but he said nothing.

'You recognise this image,' Fidelma said softly. 'Just as you recognised it when Eadulf described what he had seen carved on the ship's prow. The black pirate ship that attacked us.'

'What does it mean?' insisted Eadulf.

Brother Metellus blinked and said hoarsely, 'It is the image of a dove in flight.'

'We can see that,' Fidelma replied. 'And its meaning? To whom does it belong?'

The monk took a deep breath before turning to them both and saying, 'That is the emblem of Lord Canao, the *mac'htiern* of Brilhag.'

CHAPTER SIX

E adulf was staring in fascination at the image of the bird on the torn silk.

'That is an odd emblem for a chieftain to have,' Fidelma said.

Brother Metellus spread his hands in a strangely helpless gesture.

'It is the Lord Brilhag's standard,' he replied.

'Do the people here believe it is an oracular bird, as we do?' queried Fidelma. 'They made stone figures of doves and, before the coming of the Faith, they used to pray to them in healing shrines for good health. Our Church Fathers often associated themselves with the dove. Crimthann mac Fedilmid took the name Colmcille – Dove of the Church. It is a symbol of peace and harmony, but surely an odd image for a chieftain to carry as an emblem?'

Eadulf folded the silk into a tiny square and placed it in his leather marsupium. 'Does this mean that this Lord Canao is the leader of thieves and murderers?'

Brother Metellus was shocked.

'The *mac'htiern* of Brilhag is very respected,' he said immediately. 'He is a friend and adviser to the King Alain Hir, and would not demean himself by attacking unarmed merchants. Anyway, he is supposed to be in Naoned.'

'But I hear he has a son who is not as worthy as his father?' Fidelma said thoughtfully.

'I have met Macliau several times,' Brother Metellus admitted. 'He is a young, vain man who likes wine and women. I cannot see him leading such an attack as this.'

Fidelma was silent for a while and Eadulf knew not to interrupt her thoughts. Finally she drew herself up and glanced at them.

'Nevertheless, the emblem of this lord of Brilhag features both in the attack on the *Barnacle Goose* and now in this ambush of these poor merchants. I think we must go to Lord Canao's fortress to see if there is more that we can learn.'

'That might be dangerous,' Brother Metellus said immediately, 'especially if there is some involvement. Though I cannot believe it.'

'Eadulf and I must follow this path as it is the only lead we have to finding the killer of my cousin and my friend – not least the killer of all these poor people,' Fidelma said, and she gestured at the bodies around them. 'You can return to the abbey and report this before you return to your island.'

Brother Metellus shook his head.

'I cannot abandon you in this strange country. You will need someone to interpret and one who knows this land. If you go to Lord Canao's fortress, then I will come with you. Besides, I am as much intrigued by this mystery as you are.'

'You do not have to come with us,' Fidelma assured him. 'As you say, it may be a dangerous path.'

'I have made my decision,' the other replied stubbornly. 'If we set off now, it is not a great distance and we should be there well before the day begins to close in.'

'Then I thank you, Brother Metellus. Your help is appreciated. Let us go back to the stream and see if we can pick up the tracks again.'

They returned to the spot where the stolen pack animals had apparently entered the stream, and turned to follow its course. Indeed, it was not long before the woodland on either side thinned and they were in flat, muddy marshy grounds where walking was difficult. Several times they had to resort to using the stony bed of the stream itself as an easier way than along the marshy riverbanks. But after a while, even the stream turned into a boggy waste and they had to look for other areas of dry land to seek a passage.

Whatever path the thieves had taken, they could not find it and they lost all signs of the movement of the pack animals and the passage of those who had taken them. But by that time, Fidelma was aware of the salt tang of the sea in the air and the mournful cry of the gulls that meant they were near to the northern coast of the peninsula. Trees began to appear again as they left the low-lying marshes, and the land became firm underfoot once more. The woodland rose on hills that formed a ridge along the coast separating the sea from marshland. Beyond the trees they could hear the gentle lapping of waves on the shore.

It did not take long to get through the woodland and then they emerged on a hill overlooking a deep inlet. On the top of a headland to their left rose a large sandstone fortress.

'That is Brilhag,' muttered Brother Metellus.

The outer walls rose about four times the height of a tall warrior and there was a tall tower to the seaward side. Fidelma realised that the great expanse of water before them was the Morbihan, or Little Sea. Brilhag looked very alien to the type of fortresses Fidelma was familiar with: it must have originally been of Roman construction. The complex was quite substantial. She could make out two warriors standing outside the tall wooden gates, their slouched postures showing they were bored with their duties. Their heads were turned towards the sea below them and not inland where Fidelma and her companions had emerged from the woodland.

Fidelma suggested they move back to the shelter of the treeline.

'Well, there are no signs of the raiders' ship anchored in this inlet.' Eadulf pointed out the obvious. 'It would certainly be an excellent place though, to keep a ship secure from prying eyes.'

'There are other inlets and islands all along here,' Brother Metellus said. 'The ship could hide almost anywhere.'

'I'd like to see inside this fortress first,' Fidelma said.

'Impossible,' replied Brother Metellus. 'If you think that the Lord of Brilhag is behind the attack on your ship, then

the moment you approach the fortress, they will know why
you have come.'

'*Aut viam inveniam aut faciam,*' replied Fidelma confidently. 'I'll either find a way or make one.'

It was only when a voice close by shouted harshly that
they realised that they were being observed. They had been
so closely engaged in examining the fortress of Brilhag that
they had not seen the two men approaching until it was too
late. They swung round to see two warriors, for such they
proclaimed themselves by their long swords, which were
sheathed, and shields, although they wore no war helmets or
body armour. They were young and muscular men. One was
short and stocky but with pleasant, even features, dark hair
and eyes whose scrutiny seemed to indicate that he missed
nothing. He spoke again, sharply. It was obviously an enquiry
as to what they were doing in this place.

Brother Metellus took it on himself to answer and he was
sparing with the full truth of the matter as he afterwards
related the conversation in translation to his companions.

'I am Brother Metellus, from the abbey. I am showing my
companions, who are strangers to this place, our beautiful
country.'

The two men glanced at one another but did not look
reassured.

'I do not recognise you,' replied the spokesman suspiciously.
'You have a foreign accent.'

'One is not responsible for where one is born, my friend,'
replied Brother Metellus. 'Merely for how we live our lives.'

'Why are you spying on the *mac'htiern*'s fortress?'

'I am showing my companions the amazing view.'

Fidelma and Eadulf, with their limited knowledge of the language of the Britons, had been trying to follow the conversation.

'Tell him we are not spying on the fortress. We are simply strangers from the land of Hibernia,' Fidelma instructed Brother Metellus.

'We have never heard of it,' replied the warrior, still suspicious.

'It is the island called Iwerzhon,' explained Brother Metellus, substituting the local name for the Latin one.

The warrior's silent companion now spoke rapidly to him and he turned to Brother Metellus.

'It may be that Macliau will desire to meet your companions,' he announced. 'You will accompany us to ascertain his wishes.' And, as if in emphasis, he dropped a hand to his sword hilt.

Fidelma saw Eadulf tense and she surreptitiously shook her head.

'Tell them that we shall be delighted to accompany them,' she said to Brother Metellus, wondering if he was able to translate the humour correctly.

The warriors made no reply but the leader merely motioned with one arm in the direction of the fortress, indicating that they should precede him and his companion.

'*Óis carcre*,' muttered Eadulf in Fidelma's own language. 'We are prisoners.'

Fidelma smiled encouragingly at him.

'Well, I wanted to examine the fortress,' she said. 'These

warriors have made it easy for us to do so.' She noticed that the warriors were regarding them suspiciously and she glanced at Brother Metellus' gloomy features. As they walked along, she spoke to him loudly, wondering if the warriors knew Latin. 'As you have told us, Brother, this is a magnificent view and this sea ahead of us is what you called the Morbihan?'

Realising she was speaking for the warriors' benefit, the monk returned her smile, although with a little effort.

'Exactly so. Beyond this headland of Brilhag are many islands. It is a beautiful area.'

They came to the gates in the sandstone walls. The sentinels, on observing their approach, had straightened up and assumed more rigid postures. One of their warrior companions shouted an order and the gates were immediately opened.

'Inside!' he commanded and, with Brother Metellus leading the way, they entered into a courtyard where they were called upon to halt. The great gates slammed shut behind them.

Then a voice called from somewhere above them.

A young man was leaning out of a window of a large building that towered over the courtyard. They could see that he was a slightly built youth, with a mop of fair hair, pale, sunken cheeks and watery eyes that might be light blue.

'Why are these people here?' His voice was a high, nasal drawl. Then he recognised the Roman. 'Is that Brother Metellus?'

'It is I, Macliau,' confirmed the monk, stepping forward.

'Then do not stand on ceremony. Enter.' The young man glanced at the warriors. 'There is no need for an escort, Boric,' he said to the leading man and then disappeared from the window.

The dark warrior addressed as Boric stepped forward and opened the great door for the visitors with an apologetic look.

'All strangers must be regarded with suspicion until they are shown to be friends,' he said in Latin, which surprised them. So he had understood them the whole time.

'*Ad utrumque paratus*,' Fidelma smiled with the phrase given to one who is prepared for all eventualities.

The warrior actually grinned. '*Semper paratus*,' he answered. Always prepared.

They entered into the great hall of the fortress. Logs blazed in the large fireplaces at both ends of the chamber in spite of the summer weather. Tapestries of bright colours and with fascinating imagery, presumably from the myths, hung on most of the walls, and in between, at regular paces, were displayed ornate shields. A great woven carpet, of matching bright colours, spread across the central area of the floor, which was of stone flags. On this was a stout, carved oak table set ready for feasting with bowls of fruit on it. Around the table were several wooden chairs. More comfortable chairs were placed in front of the fires while other chairs seemed dotted at haphazard angles in various parts of the hall. Here and there was a polished wooden chest or small table, and strange-looking earthenware pots and a giant amphora balanced on a stand in one corner. There were several doors leading off the hall and at the end, to one side of the great fireplace, was a wooden stairway that apparently led to the upper chambers.

In front of the fire a small dog had been stretched. It now

arose and came trotting towards them. It had long hair, with a blue-grey coat and black ears and muzzle. The hair reached over the forehead and eyes, so that they were barely seen, and ended in a moderate beard below the muzzle. It was a hunting dog – Fidelma recognised the breed as one often used in the pursuit of badgers. The dog sniffed around them. The young man who had hailed them from the window was now descending the stairs with a smile of welcome on his face. The dog looked up at him with a soft whine, the tail wagged slightly and it trotted back to its place in front of the fire.

Eadulf muttered: 'Well, this young lord seems friendly enough.'

'This is Macliau, the son of Lord Canao, the *mac'htiern* of Brilhag,' replied Brother Metellus quietly.

'It is good to see you again, Brother Metellus,' greeted the young man slightly effusively. 'You do not often grace us with your presence. I thought you had been exiled to the island of the duckling for arguing with our good friend Abbot Maelcar.'

Brother Metellus returned the youth's cynical grin with a slight bow.

'I think that you will know how easy it is to argue with Abbot Maelcar,' he replied dryly. 'My companions are the Lady Fidelma from Hibernia and her husband Brother Eadulf, a Saxon.'

'You are all welcome to the house of Brilhag,' announced the young man in fluent Latin. 'I am Macliau and I greet you in the absence of my father, Lord Canao.'

He bowed his head to Fidelma and then acknowledged

Eadulf with a quick smile. Close up, Fidelma saw the flaw
in the young man's handsome features. There was something
dissipated about them. A weak jawline perhaps, and the eyes
were rheumy and cheeks too flushed.

A male attendant had entered and was now hovering
discreetly in the background, ready to obey Macliau's wishes.

'First, we have to perform the protocol of our house,' the
young man announced in a bored fashion. 'Do any of you
carry weapons?'

Eadulf could not disguise his surprised expression.

Macliau laughed outright at it.

'Do not be concerned. My father is a man of traditions.
There is a custom, a very ancient custom here, that no one
can enter the hall of the *mac'htiern* of Brilhag as a guest if
he is bearing weapons.' He moved to a door and, taking down
a key from a hook beside it, unlocked it. He threw open the
door and pointed inside. They saw a small armoury of swords,
spears, daggers and other instruments of war. 'All weapons
must be discarded by visitors and placed here. They are
returned when a person leaves the great hall.'

'It is also an ancient custom in my land,' Fidelma acknowledged. 'When people sit down to feast, it is the custom that
all weapons should be left outside the feasting hall. And
perhaps it is a good custom, too, for when one is drinking
and arguing, tempers can grow hot. In anger, one's impulse
might be to reach for a weapon.'

'Just so,' agreed the young man. 'My father insists on the
continuance of this custom and many have been the times
that he has beaten me for not observing it. So, even in his

absence, I follow the rule in case word gets back to him.' He stared with apparent distaste at the array of weapons stored there. 'Thankfully, I am no warrior. Fighting and bloodshed – I abhor them. There are better things to occupy one in life.'

Eadulf smiled in agreement, saying, 'We of the religious do not carry weapons but only a knife to cut our meat.'

'Then enter freely and receive the hospitality of the son of the *mac'htiern* of Brilhag,' replied the young man, finishing what was obviously the ritual. He shut the door and motioned them towards the fire in the great hearth at the far end of the chamber. 'May I offer you all refreshment?'

They chose cider, which was the main drink of the country, and Macliau relayed their wishes to the attendant who duly hurried away to fulfil them. He waved them to seats and, as he slouched into his own chair, the little dog rose and came forward to spread itself at his feet with a contented sigh.

'So what brings you to our shores, lady?' asked the young man, reaching down in an absent fashion to fondle the ears of the animal whose tail began to beat contentedly on the floor. 'It is not often that we see wandering religious, especially one who is referred to by a noble form of address. I am sure Brother Metellus, who is a stickler for protocol in such matters, did not make a slip of the tongue when he introduced you.'

Fidelma had made up her mind to stick to the truth. It was pointless to pretend otherwise. She told their story briefly and without mentioning the dove emblem that had brought them to Brilhag.

The young man seemed to accept the news of the attack on the merchants with equanimity.

'I knew Biscam,' he said. 'He often traded with us. You say that he and all his men are slain?'

Fidelma had neglected to mention the one survivor and did not enlighten him, merely saying: 'Biscam is dead and all his pack animals and goods have been stolen.'

'And the thieves? Do you know where they have gone?' demanded the young man.

'They have disappeared through the marshy area near here,' Fidelma replied.

The young man was silent for a moment and then shook his head sadly.

'I am afraid that during the last week we have begun to hear stories of several robberies, attacks on isolated farmsteads on this peninsula. It is said that the raiders come from a ship and each time grow bolder. My father is away at the court of King Alain and means to escort him and his entourage here. But he is not due to return for several days yet. I will send four of my men to retrieve the bodies and take them to the abbey. Doubtless, Abbot Maelcar will want to perform the obsequies over them.'

Brother Metellus expressed his approval.

'Your men should have a care, for we do not know whether the cut-throats have entirely left the area,' he advised.

'I fear there is little we can do to trace the thieves at this late hour. However, I will order Boric to keep a special watch.'

Fidelma was regarding Macliau thoughtfully.

'Did you say that your King is coming here?' she queried.

'King Alain,' the young man confirmed.

'Does he visit here often?'

Macliau shook his head. 'He comes as my father's guest to hunt. This area is famous for its deer and boar.'

'It could be dangerous for the King and his entourage with such murderers and thieves about,' Fidelma pointed out.

The young man gave a confident laugh.

'I think not, lady. Rather it would be more dangerous for the thieves once the King and my father arrive here, for they will come in the company of their warriors. Meanwhile, my own men are on the watch for these brigands – and when they catch them . . .' He made a sharp gesture with his hand.

'Even so, the Lady Fidelma is right. Forewarned is to be forearmed,' Brother Metellus said cautiously. 'Perhaps word should be sent to King Alain and your father?'

'I take your point, Brother Metellus. But I assure you that they have nothing to fear here. If these thieves and warriors have managed to sneak into my father's domain, then they will not like the reception my father shall give them.'

Just then, they heard voices beyond one of the doors. Macliau put his head to one side and grimaced. The dog raised his head and gave a little growl but did not move.

'I think this is my sister, returning.'

As he spoke, the door was thrown open and a girl entered. Even from across the shadowy great hall, Fidelma and Eadulf could see that she was the twin of Macliau. Behind her came a tall young man with fair hair. The girl flung off her cape in an almost petulant gesture and was about to speak when she saw the group by the fire.

'We have visitors who bring us worrying news,' announced Macliau. 'And we are in need of your skills, Bleidbara.'

He continued to speak in Latin and the girl responded in the same language.

'Worrying news?' she repeated, and her voice held the same high timbre as that of her brother. It was unattractive.

Fidelma and her companions rose from their chairs as the newcomers came forward. Macliau waved a hand in introduction.

'This is the Lady Fidelma, who is sister to a King of Hibernia; her companion is Brother Eadulf and, of course, you will remember Brother Metellus from the abbey. This is my sister, the Lady Trifina. And this is Bleidbara, who is the commander of my . . . my father's bodyguard.'

The young man inclined his head towards them in a brief gesture. He was quite handsome, Fidelma thought. His features were regular, and his bright blue eyes seemed to have a discerning and caring quality about them.

The girl regarded Fidelma with a suspicious gaze as she seated herself.

'You are a long way from home, lady,' she said. 'We heard no word of a ship from Hibernia putting in around our coasts. What brings you here?'

'Nothing that is of my choice,' responded Fidelma, feeling hostility in her tone.

'Indeed,' interposed Macliau, and quickly outlined the situation as they had told him.

'And this is the worrying news?' drawled the girl.

Again it fell to Macliau to tell her about the attack on the merchant Biscam and his men. He turned to Bleidbara: 'I was about to give orders to Boric to take some men and gather their bodies and transport them to the abbey.'

'I will instruct him now,' the young commander said grimly. Then he glanced to Trifina. 'Biscam, now. The attacks increase.'

'We need fear no attack by brigands here,' Trifina said. 'We have enough warriors to protect us. And our father should return within a few days.'

'I have already assured our friends of that.' Macliau wore a thin smile. 'And, indeed, I feel we should insist that they remain as our guests until he does, rather than face the hazards of a return to the abbey. These marauders may not be gone entirely,' he added, 'and we would not wish anything to happen to you.'

Eadulf felt an uncontrollable shiver on his spine. Was there some hidden meaning to the young man's words? He glanced at Fidelma in expectation that she would make the excuse of returning, but Fidelma remained calmly smiling.

'It is a tempting offer,' she replied. 'You may be aware that Abbot Maelcar seems to dislike the presence of women at the abbey and we have had to rely on the hospitality of a nearby village.'

Macliau chuckled. 'Then it is settled. I will hear no protests. You are the guests of the house of Brilhag. I know that Brother Metellus here has little love for the Abbot and I am sure he will accept our invitation as well.'

Brother Metellus inclined his head in polite acquiescence, saying, 'I have offered my services to my friends here as translator and guide until such time as they can find passage back to their own land of Hibernia.'

'And I am sure that will not be long, once my father has returned,' replied Macliau in good spirits.

'One thing,' Fidelma interrupted. 'We need to send a message back to Aourken, with whom we were staying, to inform her where we are.'

'Aourken?' Trifina frowned. 'I know the name. She used to teach me Latin grammar when I was young.'

It was Bleidbara, still waiting to be dismissed, who answered Fidelma.

'I will tell Boric that when he recovers the bodies of Biscam and his men, he should inform Aourken that you are guests at Brilhag. He can bring your belongings here.'

'They will not amount to much as we fled ship in nothing more than what we stood up in,' replied Eadulf.

'See that the old lady is well compensated for foregoing their company, Bleidbara,' added Macliau.

The young warrior raised a hand in salute and left.

Fidelma turned to Trifina, saying, 'This fortress stands, I believe, on the edge of what you call the Little Sea?'

'That is true,' replied the girl languidly.

'Do you not fear attack from the sea?'

The girl did not answer but Macliau roared with laughter. 'Impossible. It was a natural fortification for our ancestors, the Veneti, in ancient times.'

'Could not these brigands be hiding out on these islands? There is room for a ship to anchor by them.'

'Impossible!'

They all turned to Trifina with some surprise at the vehemence in her voice.

'Impossible, lady?' Fidelma said quietly. 'Why so?'

'We have a fortified dwelling on Govihan, the island of the smithy's forge,' Macliau explained hurriedly, glancing in annoyance at his sister. 'From there our men maintain a watch along this coast. We are seafarers ourselves and have our own ships. If there were any strange movements, our men would know and inform us. It is the duty of the Lord of Brilhag to offer protection to our people in this area.'

'I have just returned from Govihan,' Trifina added, as if to justify her vehemence. 'That is why I have said it is impossible.'

'Where is this island exactly?'

'Govihan?' asked the girl. 'It is the first large island off the headland here.'

Macliau suddenly stood up with a smile.

'Come,' he invited, 'it is still light. Let me take you up the tower and you can see it for yourself. The tower also provides a good view of the Little Sea. And you will see why we do not fear attack.'

Trifina spread herself on her chair with a yawn. 'I will remain here. I have had enough exercise today,' she drawled.

Just as they rose to follow him, a girl came down the stairway. She paused at the bottom, caught sight of Macliau and smiled happily before moving towards him. She was young and of a fleshy build. 'Voluptuous' was the word that came into Fidelma's mind; this was a girl who knew her ability to attract certain types of men and was not above using it. She had dark hair, brown eyes and rosy cheeks, and full red lips. Seeing Macliau, she moved seductively across the floor to him, showing off the whiteness of her teeth in a proprietorial smile. Her clothing seemed to match her personality; it was bright and verging on the gaudy.

For a moment, Macliau looked rather embarrassed. Then he introduced her.

'This is Argantken. She does not speak Latin, but there is little need for you to talk with her.'

He turned without further ado and addressed the girl in a sharp tone. She pouted and said something in reply, then with a frown of displeasure at the company, but still without acknowledging them, she left the room with the same flouncing motion as that with which she had entered it.

Eadulf looked at Brother Metellus but the monk's face was impassive.

'To the tower.' Macliau began to lead the way, with the little dog trotting close at his heels. They followed him to a door at the base of a square tower, then up a narrow wooden stairway swung around the inner wall, intricately worked in oak beams; every five metres or so, it supported a floor, each floor given over to stores of various kinds. The upper floor held implements of war, bows and stacks of arrows. Fidelma commented on the fact and bent to examine one of the sheaths of arrows that hung from the walls.

'I am glad to see you are prepared,' she said. 'You say that attack from the sea on your fortress is impossible. The sea is a good road to the world, but the traffic is not all outward-going. Sometimes the sea brings guests whom we do not want.'

Macliau shrugged. 'So it was in the time of our ancestors when it brought the fleet of Julius Caesar within sight of these very shores. Of late it has brought the warships of the Franks and even of the raiding Saxons to our southern coasts, but they have not infiltrated into the Morbihan. Brother Metellus, wasn't it your writer Seneca who underscored the lesson by saying that it will not always be summer?'

'*Non semper erit aesta*,' repeated Brother Metellus, solemnly nodding.

'We are prepared for winter. But these recent raiders obviously have no wish to attack those who can defend themselves – just harmless merchant ships and isolated travellers.'

They emerged at the top of the tower, some twenty metres above ground. It commanded a magnificent panoramic view in all directions, the hills and forests on the landward side, and the great inland sea to the north with its multitude of islands stretching away as far as the eye could see. Many of the islands appeared forested.

'There, that is Govihan,' said Macliau, pointing to a stretch of land beyond the headland. They had elevation enough to see that it was shaped like a kidney bean with a long strip of white sand on its eastern side and a little stretch of sand on the west. It was thickly wooded at the southern end and they could also see a tall wooden tower beyond. 'That is the watchtower which rises from the little fortified dwelling we have there. Rather, it is an ancient villa given by my father to Trifina as her own house. As you see, between this tower and that, there is little that can move in this part of Morbihan, without being noticed.'

Fidelma agreed that the towers did command a clear view of the area.

'But how would you warn one another of danger?' she asked.

'Watchfires,' replied the young man immediately. 'And, on a clear day, we can use our banners.' He pointed to the pole attached to the tower, from the top of which hung a large rectangle of white silk. Now and then the wind lifted it, fluttering in the breeze so that the image of it could be clearly seen. It was the same bird image as on the torn piece of silk that now reposed in Eadulf's marsupium.

Fidelma regarded it innocently. 'Surely that is a strange emblem to have on your banner? It looks like a dove.'

Macliau chuckled in amusement, which caused the little dog to glance up at his master and whine slightly.

'It is a dove indeed, and when I am head of this family, I shall have it changed back.'

'Changed back?' queried Fidelma.

'Our ancestors were of the Veneti, as I have said. We dominated the seas in all directions. Even the Romans praised our skills. Our emblem was the osprey, the great sea hunter, the eagle of the sea.'

His voice had risen with pride and for a moment or two Fidelma allowed him to contemplate some inner vision he seemed to be experiencing.

'That doesn't explain why your flag now bears a dove on it. It is a symbol of peace,' she prompted.

A bitter expression appeared on the young man's face.

'It became a symbol of my family's shame,' he muttered.

'Shame? I don't understand.'

'When my ancestor, Canao, who was the second of his name
to rule as King of Bro-Erech, was killed, Judicael of Domnonia
took over the kingdom. He claimed descent from another King
of this land called Waroch, and from then on we were told the
land would be called Bro-Waroch. It was Judicael who ordered
my family to surrender their battle-flag to him and to cease
using the image of the royal eagle of the seas. My family had
no choice, but in protest they adopted the image of the dove . . .
an image of humility and peace. One day, God willing, we will
demand our ancient rights again and—'

Macliau suddenly caught himself and smiled quickly,
saying in more moderate tones, 'We are petitioning King
Alain to allow us to claim some of our ancient rights again.'

'This Alain is a descendant of King Judicael who forced
your family to surrender, isn't he?' asked Eadulf.

'He is the son of Judicael,' replied Macliau quietly.

Eadulf exchanged a quick glance with Fidelma.

'Doesn't that make this claim an . . . er . . . uncomfortable
one for him?' he asked tactfully.

The young man realised what he was implying and said
immediately, 'Oh no. Alain Hir is our friend, for he was
brought up with my father and neither of them blames the
enmity of the past on each other. You will see – Alain will
finally return the rights that have been taken from us by the
greed and avarice of others.'

'It is good to hear you say so,' Brother Metellus said; he
had been silent until now. 'But he has surely been many years
as King. Why does the matter of rights arise now?'

Macliau glanced at him with irritation.

'There was much to be done before he could turn his attention to righting past wrongs done to the house of Brilhag,' he said defensively. 'The Franks are always attacking our eastern borders, and some of the western chieftains have been in rebellion against him. Anyway, the matter will soon be resolved.'

The little group stood in silence for a while, looking out on the seascape with the lowering sun sending long shadows across the islands.

'A beautiful spot,' murmured Fidelma. 'Strange that there can be evil and death in such a peaceful landscape.'

Macliau looked up at the sky. 'It grows late. The evening meal will be prepared soon. Perhaps you would like to retire to your rooms and refresh yourselves?'

It was when Fidelma and Eadulf were alone in their chamber, to which a fussy middle-aged female servant had shown them, bobbing and wringing her hands and enquiring every few minutes if all was in order, that Fidelma finally relaxed, throwing herself on the bed and staring up at the ceiling.

Eadulf stood looking at her with a worried frown.

'I know what you are thinking, Eadulf,' Fidelma said, not even looking at him.

'I am thinking that I feel like a fly who has voluntarily walked into a spider's web.'

She exhaled in a deep sigh.

'Sometimes one has to put oneself in danger's way, to discover the truth,' she said philosophically.

'I'd rather not do so. We should have—'

'Should have done – what?' Fidelma sat up, her voice tense. 'Sat still, praying for a ship to take us home? That will not help us find these killers.'

'But—' protested Eadulf.

'*Sedit qui timuit ne non succederet,*' she countered. He who feared that he would not succeed sat still and did nothing.

'That's unfair!' Eadulf said.

Fidelma had regretted her sharpness almost as soon as she uttered the phrase. She knew that her temper was never good at the best of times. She said contritely, 'You are right, Eadulf. I was unfair. But I mean to find these killers.'

'What I fear,' Eadulf's voice was low, 'is that we might well have found them already. There is one other thing that worries me, apart from the emblem on their flag . . .'

Fidelma looked at him with an enquiry on her face.

'Cast your mind back to the image of the commander of those sea-raiders. A lithe figure in white.'

'And? He was masked so he could not be recognised.'

'A lithe figure with a voice that was high-pitched. Our host, Macliau, fits that description.'

'It has not escaped my attention,' she said slowly. 'Also, you saw the arrows stacked in the tower? Goose feathers in three sections, the work of an expert fletcher.'

'And?' asked Eadulf.

'You forget so soon,' she admonished. 'I'd swear the hand that made them, also made the arrows that killed Biscam and his men.'

Eadulf was shocked. 'Then what are we doing here, accepting the hospitality of these people?' he wanted to know.

'Because there is no better way to resolve this mystery than being at the centre of it. We shall proceed, but *arrectis auribus* . . . with ears pricked up,' she smiled, adding the Latin expression to be on the alert.

chapter seven

~

Dusk was making their chamber gloomy by the time they had bathed and made themselves presentable for the evening meal. A servant – a slim, mournful-looking girl with dark hair and blue eyes – had been sent with a choice of more comfortable clothing for Fidelma and the compliments of Trifina. She had also brought candles of beeswax for illumination. Fidelma spent time putting the finishing touches to her toilette, for among her own people such matters were of importance, although Fidelma did not go so far as to paint her fingernails crimson, nor dye her eyebrows black or redden her cheeks with berries of the elder trees as many women of the Five Kingdoms did. She preferred to keep her long red hair flowing to her shoulders and not even plaited but simply well-combed.

While he waited for her to finish, Eadulf sat on the low windowsill, looking out across the shores and waters of the Morbihan. Now that the dusk had swept over the area he could see lights appearing across the waters, indicating where the myriad islands must be occupied. He also saw lights along the foreshore below the fortress, moving this way and that, which fascinated him for it was not indicative of dwellings but rather of people moving along the shore and even boats setting out to sea. Then, to his surprise, he saw a large dark outline of a ship moving slowly in the gloom. He could just make out its dark lines being towed by two small rowing boats. Then it stopped in the centre of the bay below.

Fidelma had finished combing her hair and he called her over to point this out.

'It is strange there is so much movement once darkness has fallen,' she agreed. 'This is a time when most people should be at the evening meal.'

'But the ship,' Eadulf said. 'Do you think it is . . . ?'

'If it is, we must be careful. We must not allow them to know that we suspect them.'

'Can we trust Brother Metellus?'

Before she could reply, the slim, mournful-looking servant returned to announce that Macliau and Trifina were ready to receive their guests for the meal.

Brother Metellus was already seated at the long wooden table in the great hall when Fidelma and Eadulf were shown in. The great hall was lit with ornate bronze oil lanterns, rather like the type called *lespaire* in Fidelma's own land. On the table were several candles that gave a warming glow.

Macliau came forward to greet them, appearing as charming as ever. His sister, Trifina, remained in her chair and gave them an expressionless smile of welcome. There were three other guests – two men and the voluptuous-looking

Argantken, still arrayed in colourful attire that was very distracting. Ignoring them, she sat eating from a bowl of nuts and swallowing large mouthfuls of what seemed to be white wine from a glass.

Of the two men, one was the tall, handsome-looking warrior called Bleidbara, the commander of the warriors at Brilhag. The second guest was a stranger to them. He was a tall, sallow-faced man of middle age clad in long woollen robes that had once been white but grown dull with age. His dark hair was streaked with grey; he wore it long, with a drooping moustache but was otherwise clean-shaven in the old Celtic fashion. A thin band of burnished copper encircled his head. Around his neck was a gold chain hung with an ancient symbol, a circular solar motif. His cheeks seemed pale and bloodless, in contrast to his thin red lips. In fact, it crossed Eadulf's mind that the man must have reddened them with berry juice. The dark eyes were restless, moving constantly while they held an unfathomable quality. His bland expression, on the other hand, seemed to hold no emotion.

Macliau introduced him. 'This is my father's *bretat*. Iarnbud.'

'*Bretat*?' The word seemed so similar to her own language that Fidelma hazarded a guess. 'Are you a judge, a *breitheamh*?'

Iarnbud, like many she had by now encountered, spoke Latin, although it was not the old literary language which she had been taught but a curious rolling dialect.

'Just so, lady. Exactly as you are, for I have been speaking to Brother Metellus as to who you are and how you came here.'

Macliau waved them to chairs at the table. He took the head of the table with his constant companion, the little dog, curled at his feet. They learned that the animal was named Albiorix, which brought a smile to Fidelma's face. When Eadulf later asked her what the joke was, she explained the name, that literally meant 'great king', was the name of a Gaulish god of war equated with the Roman Mars; a curious name for such a docile looking animal. Eadulf had responded that it probably had more to do with Macliau's character than that of the dog. Fidelma was seated on Macliau's left and Trifina on his right. Brother Metellus sat next to Fidelma, and the girl, Argantken, had already taken a seat at the bottom opposite Brother Eadulf, with Iarnbud seated between Eadulf and Trifina. At the end of the table, facing Macliau, was Bleidbara.

'It is good to meet with a Brehon of this land,' Fidelma opened as the wine was poured. It was a cold white wine from the country. 'Brother Metellus has obviously told you of the murder and thefts that have taken place. I am interested in your law here. How would you attend to this matter?'

The drawn eyebrows were raised but there was no other expression on the sallow face of the man called Iarnbud.

'Attend to it?'

'How would you set about tracking down these thieves and murderers?'

Iarnbud shook his head. 'That is not my task. It is only once they are caught that the culprits are brought before me and arraigned for judgement.'

'So who tracks them down and brings them before you?' pressed Fidelma.

'Those who charge them.'

Fidelma gave a puzzled shake of her head, saying, 'There is no office under your law that would be responsible to undertake an investigation to find out the culprits?'

Macliau intervened with a smile.

'That is the duty my father would assign to his warriors, such as Bleidbara there.' He indicated the young man.

Fidelma turned with a gaze of enquiry to the young man, who seemed to have developed a high colour on his cheeks. He made a dismissing gesture with his left hand.

'In truth, lady, I am trained in warfare and the command of men in battle. I can track men as well as animals. But unless they leave tracks for me to follow, I cannot find them.'

'There are tracks from the scene of the murders of the merchants,' Eadulf pointed out. 'Have you examined them?'

'I sent Boric, my best tracker, who is also my second-in-command, to examine the spot and retrieve the bodies,' Bleidbara replied. 'He is not back yet. But the sky was darkening and perhaps it was too late to see anything – there would be nothing to follow. Nonetheless, we will await his report. We are anxious to meet up with these brigands.'

Fidelma became aware that, as he spoke, Bleidbara seemed to concentrate his gaze on Trifina. His expression was one of almost dog-like devotion, his eyes never leaving her face as if ready to jump to her bidding. For her part, Trifina did not bother to glance at him once. Fidelma noted that the warrior was a personable young man with an affable smile and ready wit. She was just wondering what their relationship was when Trifina suddenly yawned, placed a hand over her mouth and murmured an apology to Macliau.

Her brother seemed to take the hint.

'Come, let us turn our minds to more pleasant matters.' He glanced towards Fidelma and Eadulf. 'We have prepared a special meal for you because you are strangers to our land.'

He signalled to a waiting attendant and, from a side door, others brought in flagons of cider and more of the local white wine. The mournful young servant girl now appeared and started to direct the attendants with some authority as they served the evening meal. Her whole attitude had changed from subservience to authority. Fidelma's quick eye caught the special attention that this girl seemed to be giving the commander of the guard, Bleidbara, while the young man still seemed to exhibit an unusual interest in Trifina. This body language at the table amused Fidelma, for it was clear that the young warrior was attracted by the daughter of the *mac'htiern* of Brilhag, while the servant girl was obviously attracted by *him*.

Bowls of steaming soup were placed before them and platters of freshly baked bread. Eadulf examined the soup, stirring it with a frown of curiosity.

'Local mussel soup with leeks and cream,' Macliau smiled as he explained.

Brother Metellus was already halfway through his bowl and he paused to wave his spoon in appreciation.

'Leeks were a favourite of the Emperor Nero,' he said

breezily. 'It is said that he was very partial to a soup made of leeks.'

The soup was followed by a dish of young eels, which they were told were seasoned with salt, and dressed in imported olive oil and vinegar. The eels were not to Fidelma's liking and she contented herself with nibbling on a piece of bread while the others finished. Then came the main course: rabbit cooked in cider accompanied by a dish of ceps – large fleshy mushrooms cooked in butter, mixed with shallots, wild garlic, herbs and some nuts that Eadulf could not place.

Brother Metellus helped him out. 'We called them *nux Gallica*, nuts of Gaul.'

'Ah, I think we call them foreign nuts – Welsh Nuts,' said Eadulf.

The walnuts certainly added to the flavour of the dish. And there was another vegetable dish that made Macliau smile as it was presented to them.

'This one I am sure that you will not have come across.'

Fidelma surveyed the dish before tasting it.

'I recognise what the Greeks call *katos*, the heart of the artichoke, which has long been known to our merchants importing them from the Mediterranean. I have also tasted this juice before . . . ah, it is lemons. I had them when I was in Rome. There is also sorrel mixed with it.'

Macliau looked disappointed. 'So you have been to Rome?' he asked, a little enviously.

'I have.'

'One day, I mean to travel there, for Brother Metellus has told me much about it. It sounds a great city,' Macliau continued.

'*Nullus est instar domus*,' Eadulf soliloquised softly. There is nothing like your own home.

Fidelma glanced at him thoughtfully. He was looking down at his plate, his mind apparently elsewhere. Although Eadulf had spent years in her own land, he was actually an Angle from Seaxmund's Ham in the land of the South Folk. He even made a joke of it when he was constantly referred to as a Saxon. Fidelma had made the assumption that he had accepted without question that he would remain happily at her brother's capital of Cashel, although there had been little time spent there due to the nature of the tasks she had been requested to do on behalf of her brother, the King. In fact, she had made only one journey with Eadulf to his home territory, when his friend Brother Botulf had been murdered at Aldred's Abbey. Was she assuming too much? And there was the matter of their son, Alchú. They had spent so little time with the child, having to leave him with his nurse Muirgen when they went on their journeys. Although Fidelma had a great sense of duty to her brother, the King, it had become a constant worry these days that the child would think that Muirgen was his mother rather than Fidelma.

At the bottom of the table to her left, she was aware of Argantken tucking into the food with gusto and hardly speaking to anyone. When she did, Fidelma tried to understand what she was saying but could barely make out one word in twenty. She felt sorry that the girl had no knowledge of Latin, which seemed to be the common language of the others at the table.

Then Fidelma realised someone was speaking to her. It was Iarnbud.

'I beg your pardon?' she said hastily.

'I was merely asking your frank opinion of Rome. Unlike Macliau, I have no wish to go there. Rome has caused many problems to my people.'

Brother Metellus grimaced wanly as Fidelma glanced at him.

'Don't worry,' he sighed. 'Iarnbud and I are old antagonists but our battles are merely verbal.'

Fidelma turned back to Iarnbud.

'I can understand your viewpoint, for I know some history of your people. But through Rome, the new Faith has been spread.'

Iarnbud sniffed to indicate he thought little of the idea.

'A good thing or a bad thing?' he asked, making clear that he thought the latter. 'Ask a lot of fishing folk hereabouts and they'll tell you they prefer to put their trust in the old gods of the sea when they set sail.'

Fidelma nodded politely, but did not reply; instead, she addressed Macliau.

'Speaking of fishing folk, this evening there seemed to be a lot of activity along the shore, below the fortress. Why is that?'

Macliau gazed at her in bewilderment. 'Activity?'

'People were gathering on the foreshore here with lighted torches, and there was a large ship being towed to anchor in the bay below.'

Eadulf tried to disguise his surprise that she had mentioned the matter so blatantly, having previously warned him to be careful. Her words seemed to create uneasiness at the table. Bleidbara glanced at Trifina, and this time she returned his look with a frown.

Macliau was hesitating. 'Activity? I did not . . .'

'I think you refer to my men, lady.' It was Bleidbara who spoke. 'They are taking supplies to my ship which has been guided here to a safe anchorage for the night. That is all.'

'Your ship?' queried Fidelma.

'As I have said, we are a seafaring people,' broke in Macliau. 'The ship is that of my father, Lord Canao. Bleidbara is her captain.'

'You will often see lights along the foreshore in this area. Fishing is often done at night.' It was Trifina who spoke. She had remained remarkably silent throughout the meal, sitting with her slightly bored expression, which Fidelma now realised was her standard facial cast 'Don't the people go fishing for carp at night?'

Fidelma smiled quickly. 'Forgive me, lady, but carp is usually found in fresh water. I presume your Morbihan is seawater?'

Trifina waved her hand as if to indicate the matter irrelevant. 'There are plenty of other fish to be found at night.'

Iarnbud's expression had become more serious, if such a feat were possible on his impenetrable features.

'Many things are found at night when fishermen leave their homes,' he stated.

'That sounds mysterious, my friend.' Fidelma turned to examine him.

'It is not meant to be so. It is just a statement of fact.'

'What sort of things?' Eadulf demanded.

Macliau joined in with a chuckle. 'Iarnbud is just jesting with you.'

'Indeed, I have spoken in jest.' The thin-faced man gave a parody of a smile. But there was no conviction in his voice and he looked away.

'Yet there is a meaning behind your jest, Iarnbud,' Fidelma challenged him. 'Perhaps you will share it with us?'

Iarnbud turned his sallow face to them with his thin red lips drawn back in a mirthless smile. For someone whose features were usually without emotion, it was like watching a mask being bent and altered into unusual shapes.

'All I mean is beware of this shore, lady. It is not a place to venture after nightfall.'

Fidelma regarded him with interest.

'*This* shore?' she asked, using his emphasis. 'Why would that be?'

'The fisherfolk around here will tell you,' the man replied, as if wanting to increase the air of mystery.

'I regret that I cannot wait to go out and find a fisherman,' Fidelma said coolly, 'so perhaps you will enlighten me – since I presume that you know the story?'

Iarnbud blinked at the forthrightness of her manner. He seemed to receive no help from Macliau or his sister Trifina.

'This is the haunted coast. Along these savage shores the souls of the dead wait for their transportation to the Otherworld,' he intoned solemnly.

While Eadulf shivered a little, Fidelma was doing her

best to suppress a smile that played at the corner of her mouth.

'And if we venture out at night we might encounter ghosts?' she added innocently.

'Since time began, the sea folk that dwell along this coast have known the route to the Otherworld,' Iarnbud replied. 'Fishermen recognise the day when they are marked to perform a sacred duty. At midnight, they will hear a knocking at their door and they must then go to the shore, where they will see strange boats awaiting them – and these boats are not their own but strange empty vessels. They must go aboard and loose the sails and, even if there is no wind, an inexplicable breath of air will come and they will be taken out to sea and along the coast to the west to the place we call *Bae an Anaon . . .*'

'The Bay of Souls,' interpreted Brother Metellus. 'I have heard it lies at the western end of Bro-Gernev, the kingdom that borders us to the west.'

'Indeed,' Iarnbud said. 'It is a desolate place where the lost city of Ker Ys sank beneath the waves when its King was cursed by the Abbot Winwaloe because of his allegiance to the Old Faith.'

Once again, Fidelma tried to hide her amusement at their solemn faces, saying simply, 'It seems that this Abbot was a powerful man if he was able to drown a city with a curse.'

Iarnbud sniffed in disapproval at her levity.

'He was the son of Fracan, a prince of Dumnonia in the Old Country who had to flee here to escape the Saxons. He founded a great abbey in Bro-Gernev called Landevenneg.'

'So what has this to do with the Bay of Souls?' Eadulf was touchy at yet another reference to his people.

Iarnbud smiled, almost maliciously this time.

'I say it to point out that it is a mysterious place, where there are mysterious currents beneath the waves and dark forces above them. The swell enters the bay with such mystical force that many avoid those brooding waters.'

'I don't understand the connection with warning us to avoid the shores here after nightfall.' Fidelma was growing tired of Iarnbud's tendency to the dramatic.

The sallow-faced man suddenly looked pained. 'I am coming to that,' he said.

'You were talking about the fishermen being drawn by some strange wind to this Bay of Souls,' prompted Brother Metellus with a grin at Fidelma.

Iarnbud compressed his lips for a moment in frustration at the loss of atmosphere the interruption in his story had made.

'As the fishermen approach the Bay of Souls, they hear muffled voices around them and their boats grow heavy; so heavy that a boat's gunwales sink to barely a finger's breadth above the waterline. Yet they see no one on their boats and their crafts are drawn westward at amazing speeds – so that within a short time they come to land. They come to a place where there should *be* no land, but they arrive at an island, and here their ships are halted, and soon the weight in the boats lightens as if they were empty, and as they lighten the boatmen say they hear a voice asking invisible people for their names, and the names are given – men, women and children, all who are dead souls, who have waited for the time when the gods of the dead will transport them to the Otherworld, to the Island of the Blessed. And then the wind comes up again and the boats go back, the fishermen disembark and return to their homes and the strange vessels vanish until the next time the fisherfolk of these shores are asked to transport the souls of the dead again.'

Iarnbud sat back with a deep sigh at the end of his narrative.

Eadulf snorted indignantly.

'It seems to me that the fishermen are superfluous in this story. If these dark forces supply the craft and the wind to take them to the Otherworld and back again, why are human fishermen needed to man their ships? These forces could do the job by their own powers.'

Iarnbud looked shocked.

'We have similar stories,' interposed Fidelma. 'Stories even the coming of the New Faith has not entirely eradicated from our land. To the west of my brother's kingdom is an island we called Tech Duinn, the House of Donn. Donn was our God of the Dead. It was an island where the souls of the dead had to assemble before they began their journey westward to the Otherworld.'

Iarnbud glanced at Bleidbara and shrugged as if he were disappointed. It was so slight that the motion of his shoulder was almost lost on Fidelma – but not quite. She turned to where Bleidbara had been sitting in silence during this whole conversation.

'You are a warrior, a practical man,' she said smoothly, 'and you say you command a ship. Do you believe in such tales?'

Bleidbara had been deep in thought and now he looked up.

'Tales?' He reflected hurriedly. 'I believe only in what I see, feel, hear and smell, lady.'

'Anyway,' she went on, 'it was a good story, well told, and these ancient beliefs are to be respected.'

She looked at Eadulf for support. He interpreted her expression correctly, for he nodded earnestly.

'That is so,' he agreed. 'For there is usually a reason behind an ancient tale. It is best to be sitting before a blazing hearth fire or, better yet, to be in a warm bed, rather than stalking the shores in the dead of night when the powers of the old gods are exalted.'

Brother Metellus regarded him in disgust.

'The old gods have only the power we give them,' he rebuked.

'As do the new gods,' Iarnbud rejoined quickly.

'Are you a believer in the old gods, then, Iarnbud?' asked Fidelma gently.

Iarnbud looked nervously at Macliau who pretended to be interested in his little dog, still stretched asleep at his feet.

'I am, as you have heard, *Bretat* to Canao, Lord of Brilhag. I am a keeper of the arcane knowledge of the people of this land.'

'That is not what I asked,' Fidelma responded gently. 'It just sounded as though you gave equal credence to the old gods as you do to the New Faith.'

The man pursed his lips in thought for a moment or two and then sighed.

'It would seem strange, lady, that the gods who the people

143

accepted at the time that was beyond time, and who were believed and worshipped for generation after generation for millennia, could suddenly lose their power and disappear in such a short space of time when some people turned to stories of other alien gods from the east.'

Brother Metellus did not seem outraged but he observed quietly: 'That is sacrilege.'

Iarnbud was unperturbed by his condemnation.

'You know from old, Brother Metellus, that I merely state what is logical. Many of our people still make offerings to the old gods and goddesses. They have proved their worth over the generations while the new deities have only just appeared in the land and need to demonstrate their greater power – if they have it.'

Macliau stirred and set down his wine and, as he had been doing throughout the evening, bent to caress the ears of his little dog Albiorix. It was obvious that he was fond of the animal.

'Is it not enough that when the New Faith entered our lands, it did so soon after the Roman legions?' he said vehemently. 'First the Roman legions came and slaughtered our people, and then the New Faith came and subverted the minds of those who remained, turning them away from their very roots.'

Fidelma and Eadulf stared at the young man in surprise. Fidelma was aware that he had been helping himself very liberally to the wine and she wondered if this had been the means of making him so outspoken.

Trifina surprised them even further by giving a peal of laughter.

'My brother likes to annoy people by being contrary,' she said. 'He says what he knows to be opposite to their views merely to provoke them.'

Macliau stared at his sister for a moment and Fidelma was sure that she gave him a warning signal. He turned back with a shrug.

'I do not believe it is a fault to stimulate conversation,' he explained grumpily. 'If we all sat around agreeing with each other, it would surely be a boring existence.'

'The way our great teachers provoked knowledge was taking an opposite view, to induce the student to bring forth argument,' confirmed Iarnbud.

'That was also the method in our land,' agreed Fidelma. 'But it sometimes gets in the way of the seeker after facts.'

Iarnbud leaned back in his chair and examined her quietly for a moment.

'Then the facts are simple. This New Faith is spreading through the land. The princes have seized upon it and great centres have been erected, like the abbey built here by Gildas. These new centres dominate the lives of the people. But the beliefs of a thousand years and more are hard to eradicate. The old gods and goddesses live on, and in the depths of the great forests north of here, they are still respected and worshipped. And even among those who follow the Christ, while they might genuflect before His symbols, in their minds they still respect the old gods and the customs of the ancestors.'

Eadulf stirred uneasily. He had been a youth brought up with the gods of the Saxons – Woden, Thunor, Tyr and Freya

– until a wandering monk from Hibernia had converted him to the New Faith. But still, in times of stress, it was the old gods that he mentally invoked. Iarnbud's comment was a telling one.

Iarnbud noticed his discomfort and smiled knowingly.

'I think you understand me well, Saxon,' he said, before turning to Fidelma. 'You have travelled on shipboard to this place, lady. Have you noticed the behaviour of seamen or the fisherfolk? Have they abandoned their faith in the protection of the old sea gods? They have not. They will give them their due, especially to the goddess of the moon who controls the seas. They will not even mention her true name once they set foot on shipboard for fear of her.'

Fidelma had to agree that among the fisherfolk of her own land, this was true, for there were many names by which the moon was called, and all were euphemisms for her proper name. Names such as 'The Brightness', 'The Radiance', 'The Queen of the Night' and 'The Fair Mare'. She shivered slightly. Was Iarnbud secretly laughing at her?

Eadulf was trying to disguise his irritation.

'What does it matter?' he said. 'Most people accept the Faith now.'

'The New Faith is but a veneer to disguise other true allegiance to the old ways.' Iarnbud turned to face him. 'When your Saxon hordes started to land on the island of Britain, the Britons had long converted to the New Faith and welcomed you at first with talk of peace and the rule of Thou Shalt Not Kill. Your people, crying upon your War God Woden, soon dissuaded them by eliminating them or driving them from the land.'

Eadulf's jaw tightened. 'I am not responsible for what my ancestors did,' he muttered. 'I live in the present.'

'And the Saxon kingdoms are now being converted to the New Faith,' pointed out Fidelma, coming to his defence.

Iarnbud laughed. 'Indeed, converted by those religious of Hibernia. Do you see any Britons converting the Saxons? The Britons have better sense. One day you Hibernians may regret it.'

Trifina suddenly stretched languorously and yawned.

'You will excuse me,' she said, rising to her feet. 'The hour grows late and I must retire.'

With a glance that embraced the company, she rose and left them.

Eadulf waited until she was ascending the stairs before he turned to Iarnbud.

'What do you mean,' he demanded angrily, 'that the Britons have better sense?'

'When the Bishop of Rome sent the Roman Augustine to Britain less than a hundred years ago, he decided to meet with the bishops of the Britons. He even chastised them for making no attempt to convert the Angles and Saxons to the New Faith before his coming. Augustine was an arrogant man who had swallowed the stories told him by the Saxons that the Britons were savages. So, when he met the bishops of the Britons, he pitched his camp on their borders and demanded that they come to him. When they did so, he remained seated, not even rising to greet his fellow bishops as was the custom, but launching into a tirade of criticism of their behaviour and rites and rituals. He ordered them to join him in converting the Saxons and accepting his church at the old capital of the British Cantii as their spiritual centre.'

Eadulf frowned. 'The Cantii?'

'The town or burgh, as you call it in your language, of the Cantii, Canterbury. Augustine was ignorant as well as arrogant. Did not the Britons have greater and older centres of their faith? There was Blessed Ninian's great abbey of *Candida Casa* in Strath-Clóta with its extensive library. And the Blessed Dewi's abbey of Menevia in Dyfed. Augustine was a brash upstart and the Britons were astounded at his behaviour. And when they refused to submit themselves to him, he lost his temper and in a rage told them that the Saxons would come and the Britons would suffer vengeance for refusing to meet his terms. On his return to his new Saxon flock, he even officially designated Athelberht, the King of Kent, as Bretwalda, ruler over all the Britons.' Iarnbud's voice was bitter. 'So the Britons continued to flee from the Saxon arrogance in search of new lands to dwell in freedom.'

At this point, Bleidbara rose abruptly.

'Forgive me. I have to be on board my ship early in the morning, for I have duties to attend to.' The warrior bade a good night to them all and left through the door that led to the kitchen quarters.

No sooner had he departed than the girl, Argantken, rose and said something in pointed tones to Macliau. As the young man stared at her, it was clear to Fidelma from the way his eyes took time to focus that he had indulged himself a little too freely with wine. When Macliau answered her, in a slightly slurred speech, Fidelma was surprised to see the girl flush and reply in petulant fashion, even stamping her foot. Macliau's face grew angry, his voice irate as he responded. The girl's mouth became a thin line and she stomped her way across the room and up the stairs.

Macliau glanced at the company with an imbecilic grin, which was obviously meant to be one of apology, but Brother Metellus was pretending not to notice that anything was amiss.

'We are all human beings,' the monk was now pointing out, continuing the discussion that had been raging. 'Augustine was a stranger in a strange land. He was a monk from the Caelian Hill in Rome, and had merely been wrongly advised as to the nature and history of the Britons.'

'So ignorance excuses all things? Do you Romans not have a saying – *ignorantia non excusat*?' Iarnbud riposted, picking up the thread again.

Macliau was chuckling and nodding approvingly.

'A point well made, Iarnbud. I swear that I enjoy your visits. At least we are not wanting in stimulus.'

Fidelma had raised her head with interest. 'So you do not reside in this fortress, Iarnbud?'

The *bretat* shook his head. 'It is my choice to live on my little boat among the islands. I prefer life under the open sky.'

'You have no fear of these thieves and murders?' Eadulf enquired.

'Fear?' The sallow-faced man smiled thinly. 'I fear only that the sky may fall and crush me, the sea may rise and drown me, or the earth may open and swallow me.'

Fidelma recognised the ancient ritual saying which meant that he feared nothing at all.

She glanced at Eadulf and raised a hand to her mouth as if to disguise a yawn. Eadulf took the hint and he rose, bowing slightly to Macliau.

'This has been a long day for us. We will retire, with your permission.'

Fidelma followed him, leaving Macliau, Brother Metellus and Iarnbud still in conversation.

Once in their chamber Eadulf showed his irritation.

'Well, I for one did not find Iarnbud's conversation stimulating but rather insulting,' he began, but Fidelma raised a finger to her lips.

'You cannot change history and so you cannot stop people from giving their views on it, Eadulf,' she admonished.

'And what about those silly ghost stories of fishermen transporting souls at night?'

'It is obvious that Iarnbud and, by logical deduction, Macliau and his sister do not want us investigating any strange lights along the shore at night. Their supernatural story was meant to frighten us. That is why I pretended to go along with it in the end, once I realised their intention.'

'So you don't believe in such phantoms as claimed by Iarnbud?' queried Eadulf.

'You should know me better by now,' she rebuked him. 'However, I have read Procopius.'

'Procopius?' Eadulf repeated.

'The Byzantine historian who wrote about the Gothic Wars as part of his *History of the Wars of Justinian*. Just over a hundred years ago he recounted this story of the transportation of souls, the belief of the people of this very area of

Gaul. I have heard the tale many times and yet we cannot go through life believing all the old folklore and legends.'

'If it was a story purposely told to stop us investigating what was happening on the shore, what do you intend?' Eadulf had gone to the window and was watching the area where they had previously seen the lights. There was no sign of any light or movement there now, although he could just make out pinpricks of light from the distant islands. The large ship was still a fairly discernible black shadow in the inlet below.

'It is too late now but I think we should go to the shore tomorrow and see if we can discover anything,' she said. 'Particularly, I would like to examine that ship to see if it is painted black and has a dove engraved on its bow.'

'I doubt we will see anything,' Eadulf said in resignation, returning to the bed. 'They have had plenty of warning to change things, having heard our story.'

'Yet why do so at all when they could simply silence us? The captain had no compunction about slaughtering Bressal or Murchad.' She was silent for a moment, and Eadulf knew she was mastering her emotions. Eventually she went on: 'I was trying to work out the relationship between Macliau and the girl Argantken. She is without finesse.'

'That one is easy enough,' shrugged Eadulf indifferently. 'She is his mistress.'

Fidelma's eyes widened. 'Would a chieftain's son bring his mistress into his father's house? She is lacking in grace and manners . . .'

'*De gustibus et coloribus non est disputandum,*' sighed

Eadulf. About tastes and colours there is no disputing, meaning it was better not to argue about matters of personal preference.

He was about to get into bed when through the window came the sound of raised voices, as if in argument. They were speaking in the language of the Bretons but their tones sounded familiar.

'There you are,' grinned Eadulf. 'I'll wager that is Macliau and Argantken.'

Fidelma swung out of the bed and went swiftly to listen at the window. The voices continued for a few moments and then suddenly ceased. She told Eadulf, 'If I took that wager, you would lose. That was Trifina, and I swear the second voice was that of Bleidbara.'

'And if that were so, what of it?' Eadulf enquired tiredly, lying down.

'Did you notice that Bleidbara seems to be enamoured with the lady Trifina, who studiously ignores him, but the girl with the dark hair who was serving us was making cow's eyes at him while he acted oblivious to her?'

Eadulf had not heard the expression 'cow's eyes' before but he got the idea.

'I wonder what they were arguing about?' mused Fidelma as she returned to the bed.

'Unrequited love?' yawned Eadulf. 'If the young man is enamoured of Trifina, then maybe he chose this moment to seek her out and make his protestation of love. And if she was not interested, she might well have stated it in strong terms. Is it really any of our concern?'

Fidelma pulled a face at him.

'I am not concerned at all. Mysteries interest me, that is all. Anyway, we've had a long day. We will talk about these things tomorrow.'

CHAPTER EIGHT

∽∾

Eadulf came awake with a start. The room was bathed in that cold light that marks the moments after an early-summer sunrise when the sun is still shrouded by cloud. He wondered what had disturbed him and then he heard a movement by the window. Fidelma was sitting there, wrapped in a cloak and staring out to sea. Eadulf eased himself up on the bed.

'What's wrong?' He found himself speaking in a whisper.

Fidelma glanced at him without moving from her perch on the sill.

'I've been sitting here watching since just before dawn. Sometimes, at that hour, people will move about thinking the world is asleep. I was hoping to see the ship and get some explanation for the lights last night.'

'Is it the same ship?' queried Eadulf, swinging from the bed.

Fidelma beckoned him. 'See for yourself.'

Eadulf hastened across the cold boards and stared out. The ship had gone. There was no sign of it.

'If you were here before dawn, then the ship sailed in the night,' he gasped. 'Bleidbara must have moved it immediately after the meal, warned by our conversation. Perhaps we should not have referred to it?' he added in mild rebuke.

'I feel that the answer to this mystery is out there – on one of those islands,' Fidelma continued, ignoring his censure. 'I can see no sign of the vessel at all.'

'The banner of a dove flies above this castle,' contradicted Eadulf. 'The answer must be *here*.'

'I was thinking that if the answer was that simple, then our presence should have concerned our hosts enough to attempt to be rid of us.'

Eadulf shivered a little and tried to put it down to the early-morning chill. He went to put on his sandals before returning to stare out at the seascape before him. There was a faint morning mist rising from the dark outlines of the islands dotting the waters of Morbihan. The sea was flat and calm, glinting now and then as the sun broke through the clouds. Visibility was fair but he could see no movement on the waters.

'We are not even sure that Bleidbara's ship is the sea-raider,' he said reasonably.

'It would be a coincidence if it were not,' Fidelma mused. 'It would explain how the ship's cat reached the abbey.' Observing her husband's hesitation, she went on: 'Let's consider this: our ship is attacked and you observe a carving of a dove, which is a strange emblem for a warship to have. It sails off, having taken our ship as a prize. We escape and eventually land here, where we come across the ship's cat, wandering wild. We find a merchant and his companions attacked, killed and robbed. One of the slain has a torn banner clutched in his hand that also bears the symbol of a dove. We are told that this symbol is the emblem of the lord of Brilhag. We are more or less taken prisoner by his warriors and brought inside this fortress where the same flag of these raiders flies above us. We see a warship anchored in the inlet below which is said to be in the service of this same lord and captained by the commander of his warriors, Bleidbara. There are strange lights along the shore and we are told some ancient legend which is meant to scare us from investigation. What is the logical deduction?'

Eadulf smiled wanly. 'You have always taught me that there can be more than one answer,' he pointed out.

A frown of irritation crossed Fidelma's brow, since she immediately admitted to herself that he was right. The logic *was* tenuous – and it was only the mystery of how Luchtigern, the cat, had come to the abbey that made her determined to follow that logic.

'Very well. If there is more than one logical interpretation of these facts, then it is the task of the *dálaigh* to investigate and discover which is the correct one,' she said at last.

Eadulf was about to respond when there was a knock on the door. It was the mournful girl who had been in charge of the servants during the night before.

'I beg your pardon,' she said, 'but I heard your voices and wondered whether I can be of assistance to you? I can order the preparation of your breakfast, if you wish.'

Automatically Fidelma replied that they would wash first and come down for breakfast later.

The girl inclined her head and was about to leave the chamber when a thought suddenly occurred to Fidelma.

'Wait,' she called. The girl turned expectantly back into the room. 'What is your function here?'

'I am the stewardess of this household, in charge of the running of its domestic affairs and of all the household attendants.'

'You speak excellent Latin,' Fidelma commented. 'What is your name?'

'Iuna, lady.' A faint smile hovered on the girl's lips but did not form completely. It was as if she had disciplined her features to remove all emotions from them. 'You are about to observe how can a mere servant be educated? This is Armorica, lady – although we now call it Little Britain by virtue of the refugees from Britain that have flocked to our shores during recent centuries.'

She seemed to offer it as an explanation. Eadulf remained puzzled and said so, and therefore the girl continued with further explanation.

'This was part of Gaul, conquered by the Romans, and it became a province of their empire centuries ago. Many of the great families were brought up for generations as bilingual, with Latin as well as their native tongue. You will even find that many of the Britons who came here were also adept in Latin, for Britain, too, was a province of Rome. So many people speak Latin quite naturally and as well as they speak their own language.'

'Ah,' smiled Eadulf, 'then it also explains why your Latin is so different from that which we were taught.'

Fidelma thought she should say something here in case the girl thought he was insulting her command of the language.

'My land, Hibernia, was never part of the Roman empire, and the Latin we have learned is from the texts, not the colloquial form that you speak as a living language. I have noticed that Iarnbud also speaks a Latin that does not derive from the ancient texts.'

The girl shrugged as if she was uninterested. However, Fidelma saw a glimmer of suspicion in her eyes.

'How long have you been in service here?' she asked.

'Most of my life,' the girl replied shortly. 'Now if there is anything you desire . . . ?'

'What are your bathing customs here?' Fidelma attempted to mollify her. 'We did not bathe last night and I should have asked but neglected to do so.'

'You have only to express your wishes, lady,' replied the girl. 'They will be fulfilled.'

As Eadulf knew, the people of Fidelma's land bathed daily, generally in the evening when, before the main meal, they had a full body wash in hot water. It was a custom Eadulf still found slightly alien, for he had grown up when a bath, apart from a swim in a local river, was very infrequent. Baths were attended with perfumes and soap called *sléic*. In the morning, it was the custom to wash only the face and hands and often in cold water. So Fidelma passed on her wants to the girl and was assured that bowls of water would be brought to them immediately, together with any toilet articles that might be wanted.

When they eventually came down into the great hall for breakfast, they found no one else there except the girl, Iuna, preparing the table.

'I believe that Macliau still sleeps as he was late to bed,' she explained when Fidelma asked where everyone was. 'Iarnbud left in the night. He never accepts the hospitality of the fortress but prefers to sleep on his small boat . . . if he ever sleeps.'

Fidelma's eyes narrowed at the comment. 'What do you mean?'

'The *bretat* is a strange man. He was raised in these islands,' the girl gestured with a hand. 'He sails the Morbihan at night when seamen fear to sail the dangerous waters. It is said that he is of the old religious and communes with the Otherworld. He wanders the woods and forests and islands almost as a recluse, and yet he appears here whenever lord Canao has need of him.'

'More superstition,' muttered Eadulf in the language of Éireann.

'And where is the lady Trifina?' asked Fidelma, ignoring the comment.

'She left the fortress before first light.'

Fidelma was surprised. 'Is that usual?' she asked.

'It is not my place to comment on what the Lady Trifina does,' replied the girl softly.

'Of course. And Brother Metellus?'

'He was late to bed as well. I believe that Macliau and Brother Metellus were slightly the worse for drink.' Iuna's voice was disapproving.

'And the girl, Argantken?'

'I have no idea where Macliau's guest is.' The voice this time held an obvious meaning. 'She is a local girl and may come or go as she pleases. Now, is there anything you desire for breakfast?'

Fidelma had the passing impression that it was Iuna who was in charge of them rather than being the servant fulfilling their wishes.

They chose a frugal breakfast of barley bread, some cheeses and cold spring water. And when they had finished, Fidelma asked: 'Will there be any objection to our leaving the fortress?'

The girl's eyes narrowed slightly.

'You are guests,' she replied. 'You are free to come and go as you will. But what should I tell lord Macliau and your companion, Brother Metellus, when they discover that you have gone?'

Fidelma was patient.

'I hope we shall return before they are even awake. It was my desire merely to take a stroll along the shoreline below us.'

'Then it might be advisable, lady, to take one of the guards for your protection.'

'We will be within sight of the fortress, just along the inlet below.'

The girl opened her mouth as if to protest and then seemed to realise it was not her place to do so.

'As it pleases you, lady,' she said tightly.

They left the great hall and walked down to the main gates that were opened, although two warriors stood guard by them.

One of the warriors greeted them and Fidelma responded before passing on. They were not questioned and no one objected to their passage, which Eadulf had been expecting, fully believing they were prisoners. Now he began to wonder whether his fears about Brilhag were valid. He silently followed Fidelma along a winding pathway that led across the headland to make a rapid descent to the shore.

The sun was higher now, and slightly behind them. The mist had cleared from the stretch of water before them, which was now reflecting the blue of the sky. The nearest islands stood out clearly, although they became hazier in the distance.

Halfway down the path, Fidelma glanced back across her shoulder towards the fortress. Then at the shoreline before them.

'This is where we saw those lights last night, along this stretch,' she said. Then she added quietly, 'Don't look round, but we are being followed.'

Eadulf stiffened a little. 'Followed? By whom? The guards did not seem to be interested in us.'

'I think it is Iarnbud. I am not too sure.'

Eadulf compressed his lips in annoyance. He had been about to dismiss his fears about their being prisoners and now they swam back into his mind again.

'Is it just he who is watching us?'

'Just he,' she replied, turning and moving quickly on, following the steep path as it wound down to the sandy shore. Then she halted. She had been expecting to find a line of fishermen's huts or other buildings from which the lights had emanated. There was nothing. Stepping onto the white sands of the beach, she looked up and down. There was nothing to be seen in either direction. Eadulf regarded her with a puzzled expression as she began to walk along the beach, eyes down, concentrating on the sand, going 100 metres or more before turning back and then walking the same distance in the opposite direction.

'What are you doing?' he asked.

'Does anything odd catch your attention?'

'Apart from our friend sitting on that hill watching us?' he replied.

Iarnbud was now sitting on a rock on the hill from which they had descended and trying to look inconspicuous.

'I mean about this place,' Fidelma replied.

Eadulf shrugged. 'What should catch my attention? It's just a normal sandy beach with nothing else.'

'Exactly. No fishermen's cabins, no sign of boats. And look at the sand. There are no footprints or signs of disturbance; it is as if nothing has been here.'

'Perhaps this was not the exact place where we saw the lights,' Eadulf suggested, as baffled as she was.

Fidelma jerked her head towards the distant fortress. 'Look again.'

Eadulf realised that this was the only shore that could be seen from the window of their chamber in the fortress. He looked about him more carefully, then shivered superstitiously as he remembered the story Iarnbud had told.

Knowing him of old, Fidelma reassured him. 'The intention of the story was to frighten us from investigating this beach. Look, Eadulf – they were so worried that they have

eliminated *all* traces of whatever activity has gone on here!
That confirms there is a mystery – and that mystery will lead
us to the sea raiders.'

'Eliminated all traces?' Eadulf was sceptical. 'You are
surely guessing.'

Fidelma controlled her irritation.

'After all this time,' she responded quietly, 'you should
know that when I am putting forward a hypothesis, I say that
I am doing so. When I make a statement of fact, then it is a
statement of fact. Look at this.'

She crossed the sand to the treeline and pointed. Following,
Eadulf looked at the object she had indicated. It was a short
branch of horse chestnut, snapped off but leaving its thick
foliage on it. It was only now that Eadulf realised what the
curious patterns across the dry, grainlike sand were.

'Someone used that branch to sweep away any marks in
the sand,' he noted.

'Just so. And don't pick that branch up in case our friend
on the hill sees that we have spotted it. We will walk along
the shore as far as that rocky outcrop there.'

Eadulf pulled a face but followed her, thinking out loud.

'There are, of course, several innocent reasons as to why
people should be loading boats by torchlight here. Bleidbara
said his men were taking supplies to the ship.'

'Of course,' agreed Fidelma in conciliatory fashion. 'This
is a natural landing-place by the fortress and, as Trifina said
last night, they have a similar dwelling on one of the islands.
Why shouldn't they be transporting things to and from and
at whatever time of the day or night they think fit? Bleidbara

was quite open about it, once he had permission from Trifina. You did not see the looks passed at the table last night?'

'No.' Eadulf glanced at her uneasily.

'So why did they alert our attention to the fact that they wanted to keep this hidden?' she went on. 'They surely cannot think we would be so stupid as not to see through all their storytelling?'

They walked along the beach deep in thought for a while. Fidelma suddenly halted.

The beach was intersected by a stream coming down through the woods from the hill behind the fortress before trickling across the sands to the sea. Beyond it was a large outcrop of rocks that acted as a natural breakwater and as a wall between the sandy shore and what lay on the far side of the rocks. Between the stream and the rocks the sand seemed to change its colour and texture a little. Eadulf knew that he had seen something similar before, but he could not remember where.

However, it was not this that had caught Fidelma's attention; she was staring at the rocks beyond.

'Look!' she said softly. 'There is the mast of a boat. Beyond those rocks must be the harbour for the fortress. I thought it odd that they would use an open beach without a jetty.'

Eadulf followed her gaze towards the sea end of the line of rocks. Indeed, there was a boat's mast poking above them. He estimated it was a small sailing craft. At the top of the mast was a strip of white silk. Although the emblem was not clear, for it hung limply as the morning breeze had dropped away, Eadulf was sure that it was the dove emblem of the *mac'htiern* of Brilhag.

'Come on,' Fidelma urged. 'Let's have a look at it. We can easily scramble over these rocks.'

The water from the stream trickling across the sands barely came over her insteps and she crossed it in two strides and went enthusiastically onward.

Eadulf was halfway across the stream close behind her when he suddenly recalled where he had seen the texture of the sand before.

'*Stop!*'

By the time his yell had resounded, she was up to her ankles in quicksand.

He came quickly up, searching the sands behind her, before he grabbed her and pulled her backwards. They tumbled down together into the cold water of the stream – but at least the stream was flowing across a thickly compacted, firm stretch of sand. Then they scrambled hastily to their feet and moved back to where they knew the sand was safe. Fidelma had lost her sandals in the quicksand; indeed, they had already vanished beneath it.

She stood looking at the innocent-looking expanse, breathing heavily.

'I'm sorry,' muttered Eadulf, trying to dislodge the clinging wet sand from his clothing. 'I should have realised it sooner. Remember the quicksand across the stretch of water to the fortress of Uallaman the Leper? It eventually killed him and could have killed many others. I knew I had seen such a texture of sand before; it is not the same as normal sand. There is something about it . . .'

'Well, thankfully you recognised it in time,' Fidelma interrupted. 'Had I been moving more quickly, then—'

'Hóigh!' They heard the voice faintly and glanced back. The familiar form of Brother Metellus was hurrying across the sands, waving at them.

Fidelma looked at Eadulf with a grim expression.

'I wonder if we have just found out the answer to our question?' she mused softly.

'The answer . . . ?' Eadulf's eyes widened as he took in what she meant. 'Do you think that we were intended to go into that quicksand?'

'It is a thought,' she said, and turned to face Brother Metellus who came panting up to them, red-faced and a trifle out of breath.

'Deo favente!' he gasped. 'I have caught you in time. Do you know that you were walking into an area of quicksand?'

Fidelma answered with an ironic smile. 'I am afraid that we have already learned that,' she said.

The monk glanced down at their soiled clothing and his mouth opened and for a moment he could say nothing. Then he stammered, 'Th-thank God you have been saved. How?'

Eadulf was watching Brother Metellus' face closely.

'By the grace of God,' he replied simply. 'But how came you here after us?'

Brother Metellus blinked. 'I was told by Iuna that you had gone walking on the shore alone.'

'Alone?' Eadulf jerked his head towards the hills. 'I thought Iarnbud was watching over us from a discreet distance.'

'Iarnbud? I saw no one on my way here. No, when I heard that you had set out for this shore I wondered if anyone had warned you of this area of quicksand. It is notorious among locals, and people avoid this side of the rockline between there and the stream.'

'That we can imagine. But we were *not* warned.'

'*I* came hurrying after you – to warn you.'

'Why were you so sure that we had come this way?'

Brother Metellus looked bewildered for a moment.

'There is only one strand where there is danger. This one. To get to the safer little harbour you have to leave the fortress through the kitchens and out a side door. But you came through the main gates. So I came here immediately and saw you from a distance. I shouted to warn you. Why do you ask these questions? Do you not believe me? Do you not trust me?'

Fidelma reached out a hand and laid it on the man's arm in reassurance.

'Forgive us. It was a close escape from danger and we are slightly distraught. But for your timely assistance, Brother Metellus, we are most grateful. And now, I'm afraid, we must return to the fortress and prevail upon our hosts for more clothing and footwear, for I am afraid I have lost my sandals and our clothes need washing.'

They turned together and began to walk slowly back along the beach.

'Were you looking for anything in particular?' Brother Metellus asked after a few moments, breaking the silence. 'You seemed interested in the lights on the foreshore last night.'

'What should we be looking for?' queried Fidelma innocently.

'Bleidbara explained that his men were taking supplies to his ship last night. I thought perhaps you took the opportunity to come to see. But I note that Bleidbara has already sailed.'

'Did you know that the Lord of Canao kept a ship?'

'Many of the lords around Morbihan have ships.' Brother Metellus smiled and shrugged. 'It is a tradition among the people whose ancestors were the Veneti.'

His words gave Fidelma food for thought.

There was no sign of Iarnbud as they returned up the hill towards the fortress. Nor was there any sign still of Macliau when they entered the great hall, but Iuna came forward, allowing her eyes to drop to Fidelma's bare feet and the dishevelled clothing.

'You have met with misfortune, lady.' Her voice was flat, unemotional.

Fidelma wondered for a moment if the girl was being sarcastic. Iuna's features were composed as if carved from wood.

'You did not warn us about the quicksand on the beach.' She made it into a statement and not an accusation.

'I did advise that you take a guard with you, lady, but you seemed adamant to proceed on your own. I had no means of knowing that you would take that path to that beach. It is not a place that leads anywhere.'

Fidelma realised it was pointless to pursue the matter.

'Well, Eadulf and I shall need new clothing and these should be cleaned.'

Iuna lowered her gaze a fraction. 'It shall be done, lady.'

It was only a short while before they both rejoined Brother Metellus in the great hall, by which time the youthful Macliau had risen and joined them, his ever-present dog Albiorix trotting closely at his heels. It was clear that he was suffering from his over-indulgence of alcohol on the previous evening. However, he greeted them warmly, as if relieved to see them both again.

'I was told that you nearly walked into the quicksand on the beach. It is a bad area indeed – you should have avoided it. Why did you leave the fortress without a guard?'

'We merely wanted to go for some exercise along the beach,' Fidelma replied. 'We were in sight of the fortress and thought no harm would have come to us.'

'Ah well, no matter. What is the ancient saying – *si finis bonus est, totum bonum erit* – if the end is good, everything will be good.' Macliau paused a moment and then said: 'Boric and his men have returned from the abbey. He tells me that he has seen Aourken and brought back your few belongings. Iuna will send them to your room. The bodies of Biscam and his men have been taken to the abbey and Abbot Maelcar has agreed to give them burial.'

'That is good,' Brother Metellus commented.

'But there is also bad news,' added Macliau. 'The survivor of the attack did not live the night. You did not tell us that there was a survivor?'

'The wound was a bad one but I did not think it life-threatening,' Eadulf blurted in surprise.

'We forgot about him,' Fidelma said quickly. 'Dead, you say?'

'The physician at the abbey told my men that his condition had been very bad,' continued Macliau. 'In fact, he said that there was no hope for him. He was surprised that the man survived long enough to get to the abbey.'

Eadulf's lips compressed in annoyance. That had certainly not been what the physician had told them when they had seen the man at the abbey. And Eadulf had not told anyone that he had spent some years at Ireland's foremost medical school of Tuam Brecain, studying the healing arts. He knew that the man should not have died. He glanced at Fidelma but saw the warning look in her eyes.

'So now we have no one who can identify the attackers,' Brother Metellus sighed, having also picked up the warning glance.

'And that is a pity,' Fidelma said heavily.

'Indeed,' agreed Macliau. 'Moreover, my warriors also tried to follow the tracks of Biscam's donkeys. They led into the marshy land before they disappeared.'

'Is it not worrying to you that your sister Trifina has left this fortress early this morning, apparently alone?' Fidelma suddenly asked.

Macliau chuckled and shook his head.

'My dear lady, my sister and I were born and grew up here. We know these woods like the backs of our hands. And no one would dare to challenge us in this, our own territory. Anyway, Trifina has probably gone back to our island of Govihan. She frequently goes there. And, wherever she goes, she takes a couple of warriors.'

'You have no worries about her safety in the circumstances?'

'When you are home in your brother's kingdom, does your brother come running after you, lady?' replied Macliau.

'If there were raiders wandering loose, he might well be worried,' Fidelma replied sharply.

'I think they will have fled back to their lair, having carried out such an attack. That might be anywhere.'

Fidelma sniffed. 'Perhaps. But it would be better to be certain.'

'Well, lady, it is a matter of speculation. I have no evidence to the contrary. Speculation without knowledge is pointless,' Macliau said glibly.

Fidelma coloured as the young man used a phrase she was fond of declaiming.

'Anyway, Argantken and I have arranged to go hunting,' he continued, still with an amused expression. 'So the hospitality of Brilhag is yours to do with as you see fit.'

The statement surprised both Fidelma and Eadulf. After his late night and heavy consumption of wine, they were amazed that the young man had been able to rise before noon. Seeing their expressions, he interpreted them as concern for his safety under the present conditions.

'You need have no care for me either,' he told them smugly. 'I shall have my warriors with me. I will return this evening but, meanwhile, this fortress may be considered your home. Ask of Iuna what you will, for she is in charge of the household.'

'I look forward to your safe return, Macliau,' Fidelma replied coolly.

It was Eadulf who thanked him for his continuing

hospitality, feeling that perhaps Fidelma had been a little too abrasive with the young lord. The latter merely nodded in acknowledgement, turned away and whistled – at which sound his little dog came bounding towards him.

Fidelma and Eadulf looked from one of the windows of the great hall and saw that horses were already saddled in the courtyard outside. Argantken was mounted and waiting for Macliau. Two warriors and two others, huntsmen by their attire, were also in attendance. When Macliau had joined them, the party set off through the gates, with Albiorix the dog yelping and scampering behind them.

After they had gone, Brother Metellus addressed Fidelma sternly.

'You made your disapproval of the conduct of Macliau very obvious. I feel it my duty to point out that you are here under the laws of hospitality, and that although you are honoured in your country of Hibernia, being the sister of a king, here you are a stranger in a strange land. Macliau is the son of the *mac'htiern* of Brilhag, a descendant of the rulers of Bro-Waroch, and he should be treated with all respect.'

Fidelma's eyes flashed warningly, which only Eadulf interpreted, and he spoke quickly before she did.

'You are right to point these things out, Brother Metellus, and we accept them. But these are trying circumstances and we should not have to repeat warnings of the dangers.'

Brother Metellus was also serious. 'I had some role in this matter, as I recall.'

At once, Fidelma was contrite.

'My apologies to you, Brother Metellus. You saved us from death. But do you not find it odd that the man we left, well on his way to recovery, was now said to be so ill that he did not survive the night?'

Brother Metellus hesitated a moment. Then he spoke quietly.

'I am not forgetting why we came to this fortress. I am not forgetting the banner that Biscam held in his lifeless hand – the banner that flies above this very place. But truly I cannot see what reason there would be for the family of Brilhag to be involved in either sea raiding or robbing merchants passing through their country. Having said that, I cannot deny the evidence of the banner.'

'For the moment, what we know about that banner must remain between us,' Eadulf advised.

'Do not worry,' returned Brother Melletus. 'I am as concerned about the truth of this as you are.'

'Then we are agreed,' Fidelma said. 'I will try to be more circumspect, but it is frustrating to feel that there is a mystery here and no path to follow to seek it out.'

'Let us consider this logically,' Brother Metellus invited. 'Why would the *mac'htiern* of Brilhag be behind these actions? Why would he turn sea raider or thief when he is lord of all on this peninsula and indeed, can claim authority throughout all of Bro-Waroch?'

'You ask good questions, Brother Metellus,' Fidelma replied. 'I cannot supply the answers to them yet. In those answers is the solution to the conundrum that faces us: whoever is behind these crimes does them under the banner of this fortress. Now you tell me why that is?'

But Brother Metellus was unable to offer an explanation, and as he struggled to do so, a faint trumpet sounded from beyond the gates.

'What does that signify?' asked Eadulf, as he saw Brother Metellus raise his head with a puzzled expression. 'Is Macliau in trouble?'

'It is a call to alert the guards of the approach of someone of importance.'

The trumpet sounded again, closer to the fortress, and they all went out together to watch the newcomers' arrival.

Several guards had now taken up positions. A line of horses was trotting along the track towards the open gates. Warriors rode the first two animals. The next carried a woman, who rode on her own. She was a tall, slim figure, richly clad. Behind her came another woman, then two more warriors, and finally two attendants who were holding the lead reins of two asses on which baggage was strapped.

The cavalcade entered the fortress and came to a halt before the steps leading to the doors of the great hall where Fidelma's little party stood.

One of the warriors, a good-looking young man, immediately leaped down from his horse and went over to the tall woman's mount, where he knelt, so that she could use his broad back as a step to alight. No one else moved as she did so. Then she walked slowly over to the steps where Fidelma, Eadulf and Brother Metellus stood. The young warrior came behind her, eyes narrowed as he held them in his keen gaze, his hand resting lightly on the hilt of his sword. They halted at the foot of the steps.

The woman was as tall as Fidelma; her hair was a honey colour, glinting with slight touches of red. Her headdress was fastened around her forehead by a circlet of gold with a gleaming sapphire stone in its centre. Her clothes and jewellery were equally rich, for she had pushed back her blue riding cloak, displaying her costume and jewellery. But it was not these accoutrements that drew Fidelma's attention. It was her unusual beauty.

The woman was younger than Fidelma and her heart-shaped face had a curious ethereal quality. And yet the firm chin spoke of authority and purpose. Her eyes were soft grey in colour; her red lips owed nothing to artifice.

At this moment of meeting, her grey eyes stared with curiosity into the fiery green of Fidelma's eyes. Then she spoke in the language of the country.

Brother Metellus coughed nervously, moved a step forward and said something quickly in response.

The grey eyes widened a fraction. The woman did not respond to Brother Metellus but continued to gaze thoughtfully at Fidelma. After this close scrutiny she then addressed her in Latin.

'I am Riwanon, wife to Alain, King of the Bretons. Why am I requested to speak to you in this language?'

CHAPTER NINE

B rother Metellus appeared to feel that he should make the explanations and introductions.

'It is because these strangers do not speak the language of this country, lady. This is the lady Fidelma of Muman in the land of Hibernia. Her companion is Brother Eadulf of Seaxmund's Ham in the land of the South Folk in the country of the Angles.'

The young woman's expression did not change, nor did her eyes drop from the steady gaze with which she held Fidelma's eyes.

'You and your companion are a long way from home, lady.' The comment seemed to Fidelma to be a standard opening.

There was an embarrassed cough from Riwanon's female companion, who was still sitting patiently on horseback, apparently awaiting permission to dismount. Riwanon glanced over her shoulder and then turned back, with an apologetic expression that encompassed the three of them.

'Until I am formally invited to enter, my attendants sit

outside awaiting my pleasure. Are my hosts inside? Why are they not here to invite me to cross their threshold?'

Fidelma immediately realised their bad manners in keeping the wife of the King standing on the steps. She stood back while Brother Metellus explained: 'Forgive us,' he said. 'The *mac'htiern* is not here, nor is his son, Macliau or his daughter, Trifina. We are guests, but alone here for the time being. So allow me to presume to invite you to enter in their absence, lady.'

'And your name?' asked Riwanon.

'Brother Metellus, lady.'

Riwanon frowned slightly, opened her mouth to say something and then changed her mind. She smiled quickly before passing inside, shadowed by the taciturn young warrior. The three followed her as the female attendant and the relieved escort began to dismount. The attendant hurried to her mistress's side while the warriors of the escort stretched themselves and chatted with the stable boys who arrived to attend to their wants.

Riwanon strode across the great hall, throwing off her riding cloak, which was deftly caught by her bodyguard, before she sank into a comfortable chair by the fire. The warrior took up a stand behind her.

'This is the commander of my personal guard, Budic of Domnonia,' Riwanon announced.

The young man jerked his head forward in a brief acknow-ledgement. He was handsome, of that there was little doubt. He possessed well-chiselled features, blue eyes and fair hair – and a slight quality of vanity, as if he seemed to know the attraction of his physical qualities. Fidelma took in the gold necklet and ornaments on his arms, and the rich red cloak he sported. Budic was obviously no ordinary young warrior – and then she realised that the introduction 'of Domnonia' meant he was of a noble family of that place.

Iuna had appeared and came forward to greet the newcomers. As she looked from Riwanon to the male warrior, Fidelma was sure that some form of recognition passed between Budic and Iuna, and a faint flush came to the girl's cheeks. Then she bowed slightly towards the new arrivals and apparently greeted them in the language of the Bretons.

Riwanon regarded her thoughtfully, as she had done Fidelma, before replying, and Fidelma heard her calling the girl by her name.

'I presume that you were not warned to expect our arrival?' Riwanon asked, lapsing back into Latin.

'Lord Canao has not returned, lady,' the stewardess said. 'We were expecting him to arrive in the company of King Alain. However, as no word has come, Macliau has gone hunting and the lady Trifina has retired to her villa for today. There is no one to greet you, save I.'

Riwanon's lips parted in a disappointed smile.

'Indeed? We have left my husband and Lord Canao of Brilhag about two or three days' ride from here, pursuing wild boar in the forest. That is not to my taste and so I came on here before them.'

Then, realising that they were all respectfully standing, she waved a hand indicating the chairs.

'You do not have to stand in my presence,' she conceded.

Then she turned to Iuna. 'I presume that you have rooms for my entourage and myself?'

'Of course, lady. I shall order it done. Your escort can be accommodated among our own guards.'

'Budic will be given accommodation close to mine – and my maid must have a room next to me.'

'It shall be done, lady.'

Riwanon turned to her female attendant. 'Make yourself useful, Ceingar. Go with this servant and ensure that the rooms are properly prepared.'

For an instant, Iuna stood still. Fidelma noticed an offended look on her face. Then she turned abruptly and, followed by the girl called Ceingar, went off. A moment later, when another attendant came in to serve refreshments, Riwanon noticed that the others had not accepted her invitation to be seated.

'Sit you down,' she repeated in Latin, seeming equally at home in that or her native language. 'Now, Fidelma – is that your name? Tell me who you are and what you are doing in this country. The Saxon, I see by his tonsure, is a religious but you were described as Fidelma of some place that I cannot pronounce, a place in Hibernia. I would like to know more of you.'

Brother Metellus stepped forward hurriedly. 'Fidelma is also of the religious in Hibernia,' he put in.

Fidelma glanced at him in irritation and nearly said that she could speak for herself. Riwanon caught the glance and smiled as she interpreted it correctly.

'Come, Sister Fidelma, and tell me what brings you to our part of the world.'

Fidelma briefly explained, leaving out many of the details, such as their suspicions about Brilhag.

During her recital, Budic stood behind Riwanon's chair, his eyes fixed thoughtfully on Fidelma. She found his appraisal slightly embarrassing, while Eadulf clearly found it annoying, for he grew restless.

'You must rank highly among the officials of the Hibernian churches to represent them at this Council of Autun,' Riwanon commented, for Fidelma had begun with their return from the great Council.

Fidelma corrected her.

'I am only an advocate of the laws of my land, and my knowledge of such law was sought by the abbots and bishops attending the Council. I do not hold high ecclesiastical office.'

It was then that Budic spoke for the first time, his Latin fluent. He had a pleasant baritone voice but it held a note of arrogance.

'Brother Metellus refers to you as "lady". That is an unusual title among members of the Faith, even in Hibernia, is it not?'

'My brother, Colgú, is King of Muman, which is the south-west kingdom of Hibernia.'

'Ah, then you are a princess of rank, Fidelma,' mused Riwanon. Then she went on, 'But those names . . . I seem to have heard of them somewhere before. And recently.'

Just then, Iuna re-entered with refreshments.

'Your attendant, Ceingar, has seen to the unpacking of your baggage and is preparing your bedchamber, lady. I presume that you and your entourage will be staying until the King arrives?' Her words were deferential, not so her tone.

'Your presumption is correct, Iuna.' Riwanon smiled as she spoke, but Fidelma sensed the antagonism between the stewardess and the newcomers. It was curious, but Iuna's attitude seemed to be less that of a servant and more that of someone of authority. However, she then proceeded to ensure that everyone had what refreshments were needed before leaving the hall.

Riwanon returned her gaze to Fidelma with a bright smile as if nothing was amiss.

'So, Fidelma of Hibernia, tell me something more of this curious adventure that has brought you here.'

'There is little more to say, lady,' Fidelma replied stiffly, 'except that I am determined to find these pirates who attacked our ship and killed my cousin. Bressal was envoy from my brother to your husband and had negotiated a trade treaty between our kingdom and this one.'

Riwanon suddenly started. Her eyes widened. 'Your cousin? *Bressal*?'

Fidelma, puzzled, affirmed it.

'What must I have been thinking of?' Riwanon sighed softly. 'That is why the names seem familiar. You should have reminded me, Budic,' she rebuked her bodyguard. 'I met your cousin twice, Fidelma, when he came to present himself to my husband, the King, and indeed, sought a trading treaty between your brother's kingdom and our land. He was given leave to take a cargo of salt from the salt marshes of Gwenrann. And, you say that it was his ship that was attacked and Bressal himself who was killed?'

'And the ship's captain, Murchad,' added Fidelma grimly,

'and at least two of his crew. All killed in cold blood, lady, by the leader of these sea raiders.'

'We are sisters in rank, Fidelma,' reproved the woman, in a friendly tone. 'You do not have to call me anything but Riwanon.'

'That I will do gladly,' Fidelma replied.

'You have my condolences,' Riwanon continued sadly. 'I can assure you that my husband will leave no stone unturned in a search for the culprits.'

'But it may be that they have fled from these waters,' pointed out Budic, without enthusiasm. 'Alas, we have a plague of sea raiders along these coasts. They are like buzzing insects feeding on our prosperous ports. The Franks not only press our eastern borders on land but they raid along our shores. And then there are Saxon pirates from the north . . .'

Budic paused and glanced slyly at Eadulf; Fidelma could tell that the words had been deliberately chosen to provoke. Eadulf, a red dash on his cheeks, appeared to be studying the floor industriously and was not rising to the bait.

'Eadulf is my husband and has long lived in my land and helped me with my duties,' Fidelma felt moved to explain. 'He is what is called a *gerefa* in his own land. A magistrate of the minor nobility of Seaxmund's Ham.'

Budic's grin broadened. He made to speak, but Riwanon cut in sharply. 'I hope Budic's words do not cause you offence, Eadulf of Seaxmund's Ham.'

'Lady, I am well aware that we are not all angels,' Eadulf replied. 'There is good and bad in all peoples.'

'Speaking of which,' Fidelma interrupted, wanting to return

to the subject of the pirates, for she felt that she should solicit the help of the Queen and, if possible, the King, 'I believe that these murderers may be of this country and *not* from elsewhere.'

'Why do you say that?' Riwanon's eyes narrowed slightly.

'I have some evidence which, alas, it might not be prudent for me to state publicly at this time. That is no disrespect to you, Riwanon, for you would be the first I should tell, were it discreet to do so. One piece of it I can state, and that is that we have cause to believe that the attack on those merchants carrying goods to the abbey of Gildas was carried out by the same brigands. The merchants were slain without mercy.'

'You believe the attacks were committed by the same people?' demanded Budic with a frown.

'I do.'

Riwanon suddenly smiled broadly, then confided, 'I have been bored these last few days. Hunting is not a pastime that appeals to me, though it is my husband's passion. But, good sister from Hibernia, I do think that you may stimulate my wits to wrestle with these mysteries. So you think these sea raiders are from Armorica? That they might even be in this territory?'

'I do, indeed.'

'Then, once you have entrusted us with your evidence, they shall be tracked down and be punished as they deserve. Budic, here, shall personally lead the search for them. And if there be want of a vessel to transport you back to your own land, and none suitable entering our ports, my husband shall fit out such a vessel to take you and your companion to Hibernia with our condolences and with all proper reparation to your brother.'

'You are too kind, Riwanon,' Fidelma replied, warming towards this woman who did not seem to stand behind rank or ceremony. She sensed a person of her own temperament and thoughts. 'Brother Metellus has served us well; not only do we owe him our lives but he has been invaluable as our guide and interpreter during this troubled time. I sense that his Abbot may chastise him for the service he has performed for us. The Abbot is a person of rigid ideas.'

'His Abbot? Do you mean Maelcar?' Riwanon seemed amused at something.

'It was Abbot Maelcar of whom I spoke,' agreed Fidelma. 'Then you know him, lady?'

'I shall make my wishes known to Maelcar,' she replied without answering. 'Rest assured you will have no problems from *him*. Have you been at the abbey long, Brother Metellus?'

Brother Metellus shook his head. 'My duties lay on the island of Hoedig where I was able to render these folk some service. It was my duty as a Brother in Christ to do what I could for these strangers, lady, so I brought them to the mainland.'

'You have done well, Brother. Not everyone recognises their duty, let alone fulfils it,' sighed Riwanon.

There came the sound of a brief trumpet call from the gates of the fortress and she glanced up.

'Ah, this may be our host Macliau or his sister Trifina returning.'

Brother Metellus, who knew something of the protocol, shook his head.

'It does not announce the arrival of one of such rank.' He rose and went to the door of the great hall and peered outside. They could hear his sharp intake of breath across the hall and he performed the sign of the cross. '*Lupus in fabula*,' he muttered. The wolf in the fable. Eadulf frowned, trying to understand the colloquialism and then realised that it would be translated in his tongue as: speak of the Devil and he will appear.

'What is it, Brother Metellus?' he asked.

'Abbot Maelcar. He comes in the company of another Brother.'

A moment later, the elderly Abbot was admitted into the great hall. His dark eyes swept the company, widening in puzzlement as they fell on Brother Metellus and then on Fidelma and Eadulf. Then his gaze came to rest on Riwanon and his expression changed to one of relief. He crossed to her quickly, halting with a slight bow.

'Sister, I am here.' He spoke in his native language but now Fidelma had enough familiarity to understand some simple phrases.

A look of irritation crossed the Queen's features.

'Abbot Maelcar,' she replied, but in Latin, 'I can observe the fact that you are here. We are in the company of those who better understand this language,' she added by way of rebuke. 'We shall continue to speak in it.'

'I came as soon as I could,' the Abbot continued.

'Indeed. And why would that be?'

There was no disguising the bewilderment that moulded the Abbot's dark features.

'I came in answer to the summons of your husband, the King.'

There was a silence.

'My husband is not here, Abbot Maelcar,' Riwanon finally said. 'He is still two or three days' ride from here and still pursuing the boar hunt with his companions. Who sent you such a summons?'

Abbot Maelcar spread his hands in a helpless gesture.

'I don't understand. A messenger came to the abbey of Gildas and told me that the King demanded my presence *at once* at the fortress of the *mac'htiern* of Brilhag. I came right away with my scribe, Brother Ebolbain, who waits outside until he is needed.'

Riwanon regarded him in equal bewilderment.

'Are you telling us that my husband is due here now? I can hardly believe he has interrupted his hunting to get here so quickly. When did this messenger arrive at your abbey?'

'Early this morning, for my companion and I have walked across the peninsula to this place. I was informed that the King was already here with his entourage and needed to speak with me urgently,' the abbot replied. He glared accusingly at Budic. 'You did not send a message from your father?'

'I am commander of my lady's bodyguard. I am not a messenger,' Budic answered him loftily.

'Excuse me,' Fidelma interrupted, not able to control her interest in this exchange, 'but when and by whom were you told this, Abbot Maelcar?'

The elderly Abbot glanced at her with an expression of disdain, and even seemed as if he were going to ignore her, when Riwanon leaned forward and spoke in a soft but deliberate tone. 'My sister from Hibernia asks a good question, Abbot. A reply is necessary from you.'

Abbot Maelcar flushed at the reproof.

'As I said, early this morning,' he replied with a surly tone and looking at the Queen instead of Fidelma, 'a messenger, presenting himself as being sent from King Alain, came to the abbey and gave me the impression that the King needed my urgent attendance. I had some religious offices to perform,' he half-shrugged, 'but as soon as these were fulfilled, Brother Ebolbain and I set out for this place.'

'And this messenger from the King, where is he?' pressed Fidelma. 'Did he accompany Ebolbain and yourself?'

Abbot Maelcar looked at Riwanon as if seeking her approval before he should answer. The glint in her eye told him that he should.

'The messenger came on here before us. Should he not be sent for, to explain this matter instead of people demanding answers of *me*?'

Riwanon glanced at Fidelma. 'Now here is a mystery, indeed, my sister,' she said softly.

Abbot Maelcar moved restlessly, unable to understand their curious behaviour.

'The messenger has not returned here because he was not sent from here,' Riwanon said patiently. 'The King, my husband, has not been here – nor do we expect him for several days.'

'Then why . . . ?' began the abbot hopelessly.

Riwanon chuckled softly.

'Was I not saying that I was bored? Now it seems that I have too much stimulation – not one, but several mysteries to set my wits racing. Fidelma, you say that it is your task in your own land of Hibernia to solve such conundrums? Then there are plenty here for you to take on.'

Fidelma's mind was turning over this latest twist.

'It may well be that this is part of the same mystery, Riwanon; the mystery that has led us along the path to this place,' she said. 'Who, if it were not your husband, would use his name to bring the Abbot here? And for what purpose? Is there some connection with the attack on the merchants?'

Riwanon glanced at Abbot Maelcar and extended her hand towards a chair.

'In expectation of answers to be gained at some time, perhaps the good Abbot should sit with us and be comfortable for a while. It would be fruitless for you, Abbot Maelcar, to return to your abbey before those answers are presented. I presume that your scribe . . . Brother Ebolbain? Yes, Brother Ebolbain, can be given hospitality among the servants?'

Iuna, who had emerged from the kitchens at the arrival of the Abbot, had been waiting discreetly in attendance. She now stepped forward.

'I will ensure that instructions are so given, lady, for the Brother to be fed and provided with a bed while awaiting the Abbot's pleasure. A bedchamber will be prepared for the Abbot as well.'

Abbot Maelcar absently glanced up at the girl and then, for a moment, his body seemed to tense. It seemed that only Fidelma noticed a strange expression cross his features.

He composed himself quickly, however, before she could identify it, and turned back to the Queen.

'There is no need to go to such trouble, lady. If we leave
now, we can still return to the abbey by nightfall.'

'Nonsense!' Riwanon replied. 'This mystery is too fascinating to let you return without its resolution.'

'But,' the Abbot protested, 'if the messenger was sent to
bring me on a fool's errand, perhaps it was done for a purpose?
Perhaps someone plans some mischief at the abbey in my
absence?'

'That is a good point,' conceded Brother Metellus, speaking
for the first time since the arrival of the Abbot. The latter
scowled at him; he had obviously not forgotten the manner
of their parting.

'There are several warriors here,' Fidelma pointed out.
'Perhaps some of them could be sent to the abbey to warn
the community and maintain a watch in case of anything
untoward occurring?'

'Excellent,' approved Riwanon. 'Then we shall relax and
enjoy the fire and the food, which I am sure this generous
fortress will provide, and Ceingar can indulge us by demon-
strating her talents upon the harp. Let us relax and leave it
to our good sister from Hibernia to fathom the mysteries of
this day.'

She turned, waved Budic to come forward and proceeded
to issue rapid instructions in her own language. After a few
moments, the warrior hurried away. Riwanon looked round
with satisfaction.

'I have commanded two of my warriors to set out for the

abbey in case of any problems. Budic will order the guards here to keep a careful watch on the roads in case my husband does decide to make a descent on this fortress – though, if I know him, he will be too intent on hunting his wild boar for a while yet.'

The Abbot sat down, but it was obvious that he was pre-occupied. Riwanon had to repeat a question before he realised he was being addressed.

'It is a few years since I visited the community of Gildas,' she said. 'My husband informs me that you have made some changes?'

The abbot looked at her blankly. 'Changes?'

'When I was there last, it was a *conhospitae*, in the old traditions of our people. Now I believe it is confined to males only and the Rule has been changed to that of the Roman religious Benedict. Is this so?'

The abbot frowned and his voice was defensive as he stated, 'It is done with my authority, lady. In such matters I follow the Father of our Faith and his Curia.'

'I would not question your authority, Maelcar. Once elected by your brethren, then you may run your community as you will – for as long as you have their support.' Riwanon seemed to smile mischievously.

Abbot Maelcar flushed in annoyance. The old system, which was also part of the tradition of Fidelma's land, was that abbots and bishops, like chieftains, were elected by their communities. They were constrained by an adherence to the laws to promote the welfare of their people. If they did not, they lost office. Obviously, Maelcar had been appointed Abbot by this method, but now it seemed he was imposing his own pro-Roman views on his community. Fidelma saw that Riwanon did not approve of it.

'If only males are allowed at your community now,' went on Riwanon, 'I was wondering what had happened to those women and their children who were part of that community?'

'They have gone safely to form their own communities,' the Abbot replied stiffly.

'I recall the kindness of Sister Aourken when I was small and was brought to the abbey by my father,' Riwanon murmured, speaking almost to herself. 'I wonder what became of her?'

'Aourken?' Fidelma repeated. 'I can report that she is well. She gave us hospitality when we came to Gildas, for the abbey could not provide it.'

'No women are allowed to stay within our community,' snapped Abbot Maelcar, as if his hospitality was being questioned.

Riwanon gazed sadly at him.

'Then times have changed, indeed,' she sighed, before turning to Fidelma. 'I am glad to hear that Aourken thrives. I must make a point of visiting her before I leave this area. So come, sister, let us draw closer to the fire and you may tell me what you know of the kindly Aourken.'

It was clear that Abbot Maelcar was not regarded highly by the Queen, and Fidelma could not condemn her for it. He was all the things that she held in contempt in a man of rank and one who proclaimed the Faith.

Riwanon's female attendant Ceingar had reappeared and

removed herself to a corner of the hall with Budic, and the pair were chatting gaily away, with now and then a peal of merry laughter. As Fidelma and Riwanon drew apart to talk pleasantly of various matters, Fidelma noticed that, while Eadulf and Brother Metellus sat with Abbot Maelcar as good manners dictated, their conversation was mainly with one another. However, the Abbot seemed to exclude himself and merely sat with a frown contemplating the space before him.

Once when Iuna entered to announce the readiness of the evening meal, Fidelma noticed the Abbot once more staring at the young woman with a curious look. When she returned to the kitchens, he rose and, muttering something about the privy, disappeared. Curiosity seized Fidelma as she noticed this and while Riwanon turned to speak to Eadulf, she rose and moved to the door and stealthily went through it. Along a darkened corridor she could hear raised voices. There was no mistaking the Abbot's heavy growl and the higher-pitched indignation of Iuna. Fidelma strained to hear what they were arguing about, but when the voices lowered she returned quickly to rejoin the others. A moment later, Abbot Maelcar returned, clearly upset and in an ill temper.

The evening passed without further incident, until Eadulf raised the question that had begun to worry him since darkness had descended across the fortress.

'Is it not strange that Macliau and Argantken have not returned from their hunting expedition? He said they would be back by evening.'

Brother Metellus rose from his place.

'Forgive me, lady,' he said to Riwanon. 'I will go to the gate and see if there is news of him.'

He was gone for a while and when he returned and resumed his seat, the others looked at him expectantly.

'Boric, who now commands the guard, tells me that they are not unduly worried,' he said. 'Macliau and Argantken left with four men, including his chief huntsman. Boric tells me that Macliau often does not return from the hunt until he has something worthy of returning *with* – and frequently stays out all night.'

Riwanon was frowning slightly. 'Boric? I thought Bleidbara was in command of the warriors at this fortress?'

'Bleidbara has gone as escort to Trifina, lady,' offered Iuna, who was attending them at the table. 'They have not returned yet. Perhaps they will not. Trifina often spends more time on the island of Govihan than in this fortress.'

Budic grinned, his expression full of some cynicism, which seemed to be habitual with him.

'It is a peculiar household where all the hosts vanish and no one is left to offer hospitality save the servants. Who is Argantken, by the way?'

'Just a local girl,' muttered Iuna resentfully.

This seemed to amuse Budic even more, but a sharp glance from Riwanon caused him to compose his features.

'Argantken did not strike me as the sort who took pleasure in staying out all night in pursuit of game,' Brother Metellus offered, but no one responded to his comment.

There was a sense of relief all round when the meal finished and it was announced that Riwanon would retire to her chamber. Now protocol allowed freedom for the rest of the company to disperse.

As Fidelma was climbing the stairway behind Eadulf, she caught a movement out of the corner of her eye: Iuna was clearing away the plates from the table in front of Budic. The warrior caught her wrist and Iuna looked down at him, shook her head and then motioned towards the kitchen and whispered something. Budic glanced around as if to be sure they had not been seen. Thankfully, he did not glance upwards and Fidelma hurried on.

Once Fidelma and Eadulf were in their own chamber, they could talk freely. Eadulf had felt inhibited about saying much in the presence of Riwanon, but now he was eager to ask questions. Fidelma could only agree with him that the absence of Macliau and Argantken, as well as Trifina and Bleidbara, was strange – as well as a breach of all the protocols surrounding hospitality.

'And what of Abbot Maelcar?' he demanded. 'In truth, I have not felt so uneasy in a place since I had the misfortune to stay at the abbey of Fearna.'

Fidelma shivered slightly at the memory of how Eadulf was nearly hanged by the evil Abbess Fainder.

'Someone wanted Abbot Maelcar to come here,' she deduced. 'Yes, I agree that coincidences can happen, but there are enough strange events occurring here that I feel they are happening for a purpose. *Omnia causa fiunt*, Eadulf. Everything happens for a reason. But we can only speculate after we have the information to do so. And that is the problem. We have no information.'

Eadulf was disappointed and said so.

Fidelma's thoughts were preoccupied with the curious behaviour of both Abbot Maelcar and Budic towards the girl Iuna. Both seemed to know her and both surreptitiously sought her out. One to quarrel and the other apparently to have a secret assignation. What was the meaning of it?

Fidelma gave a tired smile as she slid into bed.

'We can only see what tomorrow brings. Perhaps the mystery will soon be sorted. In the meantime, it is sleep we need more than conjecture.'

Fidelma came awake fretfully. Her mind was filled with images of the masked figure in white and that terrible moment when she saw her Cousin Bressal collapsing in his own blood on the deck of the *Barnacle Goose*. Yet other things, other images, crowded into her mind. She sat up in bed. The prone figure of Eadulf beside her was emitting deep, regular breaths and, for a moment, she was irritated that he was able to sleep so soundly. Then she gave an inward smile. He deserved rest. They had been through much recently.

She drew her tongue over her dry lips and realised just how parched she was. At the window, the racing clouds had passed across the bright orb of the moon and she saw the jug of water by the bed. She reached over – and found that it was empty. For a moment or two she entertained the thought of returning to sleep, but knew that her dry throat and the constant thoughts of the strange sea-raiders would keep her awake. There was no other course than to make her way down to the kitchens behind the great hall to see if she could find fresh water.

With a reluctant sigh, she swung out of the bed and drew on her robe, making her way over the cold wooden boards to find her shoes of soft leather. Then, glancing back into the gloomy half-light of the chamber, she drew open the door and passed quietly out into the corridor. In spite of her robe and the leather on her feet, the cold of the stone walls seemed to permeate her very being. The bright moon cast its light through the tall window at the end of the corridor, throwing eerie shadows.

Fidelma was moving quietly, keeping to the middle of the corridor to avoid the chests and standing vases that fringed the walls. Thus it was that when the figure seemed to leap from nowhere into her path, she had warning enough to move to avoid a collision.

The figure halted a moment and seemed to cower back. It was clear that whoever it was had not seen Fidelma's approach, but had come rushing from a side door, beyond which a flickering candlelight spread a little illumination.

It was Fidelma who recovered first and recognised the features distorted by the blending of the half-light.

'Iuna? I am sorry that I gave you a start.' She then became aware of the strange posture of the girl, her visible trembling. 'What is the matter?'

The girl did not respond but looked silently back into the room from which she had just come.

At first, Fidelma could see nothing; frowning, she walked into the room. A dancing light emanated from a candle on a table beside a bed. A figure lay on the bed, something projecting from its chest, around which spread a dark, shining substance. It was the handle of a knife.

Fidelma moved forward and looked down.

Abbot Maelcar, of the abbey of the Blessed Gildas, was dead. He had been stabbed through the heart.

CHAPTER TEN

꩜

A group of very worried people were huddled in the great hall as the grey light of dawn crept through the windows. Riwanon, attended by Ceingar, sat moodily before the smouldering wood fire, while a male servant tried to coax it into bright flames. Iuna stood sullenly to one side, still wearing a gown stained with the blood of the Abbot. Fidelma was standing opposite the Queen while Eadulf and Brother Metellus stood nervously by the table. Budic, fully dressed and looking relaxed and refreshed, was perched on the edge of the table, one leg swinging, wearing his perpetual grin. They had been in silence for some time while the male servant was attending to the fire. Finally, Riwanon let out a long sigh of impatience.

'That's enough!' she told him. 'We can attend to it ourselves. You may go.'

The man bobbed his head in acknowledgement and seemed glad to leave the room.

Riwanon gazed from Fidelma to Iuna and then back again.

'Well, my sister of Hibernia? What now? You told me yesterday that you were adept at making enquiries into unnatural deaths. I ask for your advice. In fact, I now commission you to investigate this murder and am resolved to abide by your finding. You have my word.'

'I thank you for the confidence you have shown me, lady,' Fidelma said. 'But I am a stranger in a strange land. I do not know your laws nor am I qualified to interpret them.'

'I do not ask you to do so,' Riwanon told her. 'I ask you to find out who is responsible for this crime and then we shall sort out the laws to apply.'

'Very well. Perhaps you will allow me to begin by ascertaining some facts?'

Riwanon made a quick gesture with her hand that implied consent, and said, 'It is better than we make ourselves comfortable, so you may all be seated. You as well, Iuna.'

The stewardess started nervously and then sank obediently into the nearest chair.

Everyone turned to look expectantly at Fidelma.

'Let me start with you, Iuna,' she began, not unkindly. 'You told me that you chanced by the Abbot's room and found him thus. How came you there at such an hour?'

There was a sound from Budic – a curious cynical grunt – and Riwanon glared at him. The warrior grimaced as if in apology and was quiet.

'It is my task to rise early and ensure that all is prepared for the day in this household,' Iuna stated. 'I have to see that the servants have brought water in, that it is ready to heat and that the fires have been rekindled, where they have been allowed to die during the night. I have to see there is enough fuel for the day. There are many things to be done.'

'That explains why you were up at such an hour, but not how you came to be in the Abbot's room.'

'My room is adjacent to the lady Trifina's room for, when she is staying here, I am appointed her personal attendant and I am so placed that she can call upon my services when she requires.'

'And Trifina's room is where?'

'At the far end of the corridor. I left my room and was making my way along the corridor . . .'

'Without a candle?' Fidelma asked sharply. 'You did not have one when I came upon you.'

'The candle in the Abbot's room was mine.'

'So what happened? Tell us in your own words. You came along the corridor . . .'

'As I was about to pass the Abbot's room I heard a noise, the sound of a groan. Believing the Abbot might be ill, I paused and knocked on the door. There was no response. I saw that it was slightly ajar and so I pushed it open.'

'Ajar?' Fidelma interjected. 'Not closed?'

'Ajar,' confirmed the girl.

'Continue.'

'I pushed it open and called to ask the Abbot if he was ailing or required anything. There was no response.'

'No groan?'

'No sound at all. I raised my candle and entered the room. I saw the Abbot lying still on the bed. I think I spoke again, asking if he was all right, but there was no reply. I moved across to the bed, put down my candle and bent over him. I felt something hard as I did so . . . it was the handle of the knife protruding from his chest. I felt blood on my dress. I turned and fled the room in panic . . .'

'And nearly collided with me,' Fidelma ended. 'Now tell me, you say that you heard him groan before you entered the room?'

'I did.'

'Perhaps it was his last dying breath,' offered Budic. His eyes were focused at some point on the ceiling and he did not see Fidelma's irritated glance at his interruption.

'One presumes,' she continued, 'with such a wound that it would have been the cause of an almost instantaneous death. However, you heard nothing else – no sound of anyone leaving the room by another exit? For surely the killer must have been in the room.'

'There is a window,' the girl replied quietly.

'So when you entered the room,' Fidelma went on, 'did you observe if the window was open?'

'No, but there is a sheer drop below it.'

'The door was ajar, you say. Had you seen any movement, anyone coming from the Abbot's room as you came along the corridor?'

The girl shook her head. 'I saw nothing else. I saw no one leave the room as I approached along the corridor.'

'Now this window in the room,' reflected Fidelma. 'I examined it. It was closed.'

'So we have a mystery again,' Riwanon intervened. 'How did this killer leave the bedside of the murdered Abbot? Could someone from the outside have entered the fortress?'

Fidelma gave a thin smile.

'I have already asked Boric, who I took the precaution of summoning through Iuna, to examine the area and grounds adjacent to see if there was any sign of any egress or exit.'

'And therefore . . . ?' came Riwanon's prompt.

'There is none. Whoever killed the Abbot knew the way in and out of his room. Also, they must have known which bedchamber he had been assigned.'

Iuna shifted nervously in her chair.

'Which means?' demanded Riwanon.

'The conclusion, according to Iuna's statement,' Fidelma went on, 'can only be that the killer left in the darkness moments before she came down the corridor. That someone has to have access to this fortress and know their way about this building, even to the location of the room where the Abbot was sleeping.'

'Supposing that it *was* the Abbot who was the intended victim . . .' Budic still had a trace of a smile on his face.

Fidelma turned to him with a raised eyebrow.

'Can you expound on that remark?' she asked.

'Perhaps this killer was not committing a premeditated murder. Perhaps they were merely a thief, a thief who wandered into a room by chance, woke the occupant by accident and struck out to silence him.'

'It is an interesting theory,' said Riwanon. 'Perhaps we should make a search for missing items?'

'I doubt whether anything is missing.' Fidelma's expression did not change. 'And it would still mean that the killer had knowledge enough to wander this place at night, knowing their way around. There is one other thing that we are already forgetting.'

'Which is?' Riwanon leaned eagerly forwards.

'The strange message that brought the Abbot here yesterday. It purported to be from your husband, Riwanon. Was that message designed to lure the Abbot here, to bring him to his death?'

'Lure?' Brother Metellus' brows were drawn together. 'You mean that the message was purposely sent to bring him here, for him to be killed? That sounds dramatic.'

'It is something to be considered,' Fidelma said calmly.

'But who could have done such a thing?'

'Isn't that what we are discussing?' Riwanon sighed impatiently. 'All I can say is that the message was *not* sent by my husband.'

'The point is,' Eadulf intervened, 'who would want to kill Abbot Maelcar?'

Brother Metellus could not restrain a chuckle, saying, 'He was not the most likeable of men. There are plenty who would not shed a tear at his demise.'

'According to what you have told us, Brother Metellus, that would include yourself?' Fidelma pointed out dryly.

His shoulders tensed for a moment before he relaxed with a rueful laugh.

'Just so, lady,' he conceded. 'As well as many members of the community at Gildas. And there are many more who are no longer of the community, those whom the abbot expelled when they did not agree with his new Rule, who would doubtless bear a grudge against him.'

Fidelma turned to Iuna. 'One more question: . . . how well did you know Abbot Maelcar?'

Iuna started. '*Know* him?'

'Abbot Maelcar did know you, didn't he?' she said, before the girl could deny it. 'I saw from his expression that he recognised you last night.'

The girl regained her composure quickly, saying, 'He has been to Brilhag several times to see Lord Canao. Of course, I know him.'

'He seemed to be arguing with you in the kitchen last night,' Fidelma said gently.

Iuna looked shocked for a second, and then sighed. 'He was remonstrating with me for not making Confession under his new religious rule.'

Fidelma saw the closed look on the girl's face and realised that pursuing things further at this stage would not help them make progress.

'I think we can allow you to go and change out of that bloodstained gown,' she said gently.

The girl rose, glanced at Riwanon, who nodded as if to confirm Fidelma's suggestion, and hurried off.

Fidelma turned to Brother Metellus. 'Do you know the scribe who accompanied the Abbot here?

'Brother Ebolbain? Not well at all. Only by sight.'

'Will you find him and bring him here? We should hear if he has anything to add to the reason why the Abbot came here.'

Brother Metellus left the great hall.

Fidelma went to the table where, at the beginning of the

gathering, she had placed something wrapped in a cloth. Now she carefully unwrapped it and held it up, so that Riwanon could see it.

'I wonder if you recognise this, lady?' she asked.

Riwanon frowned at the object.

'Why would I recognise it, apart from the fact that it's a knife?'

'Examine it,' invited Fidelma.

'It's a hunting knife.'

'Rather it is a dagger used in warfare,' Fidelma corrected. 'But what I wanted you to particularly notice, and express if it means anything to you, is the symbol engraved on the handpiece.'

Riwanon peered closer. 'It is an image of a bird, a dove. Oh, that is the symbol of the house of Brilhag.'

'And this was the knife that was embedded in the chest of the Abbot,' Fidelma explained solemnly.

Riwanon seemed unperturbed.

'Then it is a dagger that belongs to this household. It would probably mean that the killer grabbed the first item to hand to kill the Abbot. Ah, I see. That would mean that it was not a premeditated act.' She smiled. 'You see, I have observed our own advocates pleading in the courts and know some of the ways of their thinking.'

'Or it could mean that the killer was part of this household,' Fidelma corrected her. 'Thus they would have access to the Abbot's chamber. And who would leave a war dagger lying about? I noticed that Macliau, when he greeted us, was most particular about the placing of weapons in a room for safety. He told us that his people share an old custom with mine. No weapons were brought into the great hall but kept in that small room, over there.' She indicated the chamber at the end of the great hall, which Macliau had showed them.

'The custom is so strong that even your bodyguard, Budic, last night handed his weapons over. That means that the killer would have had to collect the dagger from that armoury, taking the key from its hook to unlock the door. I checked this morning. The door was still unlocked.'

'In which case it was a premeditated act,' Eadulf finished. 'And the dove . . .'

Fidelma frowned warningly at him as she said, 'Exactly. The dove is the symbol of this household.'

The door opened and Brother Metellus returned. Trailing in his wake was a small, balding man, peering nervously about him in shortsighted fashion. His eyes were large and round, almost owl-like.

'This is Brother Ebolbain,' announced Brother Metellus, adding: 'I have informed him what has happened.'

The little man nodded emphatically, moving his head up and down rapidly in a birdlike motion.

'The Abbot slain! Terrible! Terrible!' he muttered.

'Come forward, Brother Ebolbain,' instructed Fidelma, pointing to a spot before them. She re-wrapped the dagger and placed it back on the table. 'Do you know who that lady is?' She indicated Riwanon.

Brother Ebolbain continued the jerking of his head as he mumbled, 'Riwanon. The wife of our King, Alain Hir.'

'I am Fidelma of Hibernia and have been requested by

your Queen to ask some questions about the death of Abbot
Maelcar. Do you understand?'

Brother Ebolbain looked from Fidelma to Riwanon and
back again.

'I suppose so. I saw you outside the abbey infirmary when
you were there a few days ago.'

'So tell us, how did you and the Abbot come here?'

'We came by foot, Sister,' replied the monk ingenuously.

'I meant, what caused you to come here,' corrected Fidelma.

'The Abbot told me to do so.'

Budic, still seated on the table, sniggered.

'Did he explain why?' asked Fidelma patiently.

'Oh yes, he told me that the messenger had instructed him
to meet the King, your husband,' he turned to Riwanon, 'as
a matter of urgency.'

'Did you see this messenger?'

'Oh yes. He was in the Abbot's study when the Abbot
called me in.'

'Describe him.'

This instruction caused the scribe's eyebrows to raise. He
hesitated a moment.

'He was ordinary. A messenger – that's all. There was
nothing to mark him apart.'

'He wore no insignia, nothing to denote he was a King's
messenger, no sign that most heralds affect to show their
office?'

Brother Ebolbain shrugged. 'I suppose he must have shown
the Abbot some badge of his office. I did not see it. One
warrior looks much like another, to me.'

'So he was accoutred as a warrior? He carried shield and sword?' Fidelma said quickly.

'I suppose he did. I did not notice.' He thought a moment. 'Yes, he did have a shield.'

'Was there an emblem on it?'

'Probably. I can't recall. I know that, as I entered, the youth left and said he would precede us to this fortress. I have seen no sign of him among the warriors here. I have been told that the King and his escort are yet to arrive.'

'You said that the youth left. The messenger was young then?' Fidelma persisted in a calm voice.

'He was slightly built and did not have much stubble on his face. Thereby I presumed him to be a youth. In all honesty, I did not look closely at him, for the Abbot was then giving me instructions.'

'And these instructions were?'

'To accompany him here.'

'Did the Abbot say anything on your journey? Anything that would relate to the reason why the King had asked to meet him?'

The balding little man shook his head.

'Can you make a guess?'

'It is not my place to guess, lady.'

'Perhaps guess is the wrong word,' replied Fidelma patiently. 'Did you have any thoughts as to this matter?'

The scribe sniffed at the rewording of the question.

'It is my task to serve the Abbot and not to express my thoughts on the whys and wherefores of the orders he gives me.'

Eadulf suppressed a sound that was between a bark of laughter and a snort. Fidelma bit her own lip.

'It will be a sorry world when no one can express an opinion,' she sighed, 'or if no one even has an opinion.'

The elderly scribe flushed, stung by the rebuke.

'The Rule of the Blessed Benedict says that the first degree of humility is obedience without delay,' he snapped. 'It is the virtue of those who serve Christ and fear hell's damnation that as soon as anything has been ordered by the superior, the Abbot, it is received as a divine command and there should be no delay in executing it, for the obedience given to the Abbot is given to God.'

Fidelma regarded him sadly.

'So, if Abbot Maelcar had told you to go to a high cliff and jump off, you would have obeyed it as a divine command?'

Budic broke into a laugh as the scribe's brows came together in a puzzled expression.

'He would not have ordered it.'

'But if he had? You say that you must obey every superior of the Faith, whatever orders they give you?' pressed Fidelma.

'Indeed, you are right, for that is the Rule of Benedict. But in such a matter it cannot be taken so literally,' Brother Ebolbain replied stubbornly.

'Where in the Rule does it say that?' Fidelma responded sharply. 'Are you saying that, in spite of the Rule, you can pick and choose which ones to obey? We have recently been at the Council in Autun where this Rule has been debated. There is nowhere in the Rule that says that you can choose what orders you will obey.'

'You have clearly not read the Rule properly, Sister,' protested the scribe. 'There is such a Rule if the order is unreasonable.'

Fidelma eyes sparkled.

'I know the Rule well, for it has been my task to examine it to see if it is contrary to the laws of my people,' she told him. 'You are the one who misunderstands, Brother. What the Rule actually says is, if a Brother is given a difficult or impossible task he must receive the order with meekness and obedience. If the task is beyond his strength, he may go to the superior and submit his reasons for his inability to carry it out. And if the superior still insists on the order, the Brother must obey, relying only on the help of God. There is no choice, my friend. No choice. Blind obedience is an evil. *Caeci caecos ducentes!* The blind lead the blind.'

Even Eadulf stirred uneasily as her voice grew angry. He knew that Fidelma did not tolerate those who never questioned and went blindly through life obeying rules.

Brother Ebolbain stood stiffly before her.

'I have my beliefs,' he said slowly. 'My loyalty is to my Abbot.'

'And since he is dead? Then to whom?'

'Whoever is appointed his successor.'

She shook her head in frustration and dismissed him with a wave.

'Well, my sister from Hibernia, you seem to have strong views.' Riwanon was regarding her with amusement. 'Also, it seems that you have an adherence to the old beliefs of your people.'

'I dislike the idea that one should obey and not question, no matter how extreme the order. I especially dislike it in those who are presumably bestowed with intelligence. In them it is a sin worse than ignorance, for as we often preach, ignorance does not excuse one from responsibility. How can we do this if we teach them to obey without understanding?'

'You are angry, my sister.'

'Such things do anger me, Riwanon. Forgive me.'

'There is nothing to forgive, for I am in accord with you.' She paused a moment and then said: 'I suppose we must despatch Brother Ebolbain back to the abbey to inform the community there of what has happened. Perhaps some of the *mac'htiern*'s attendants can transport the body of the Abbot back to the abbey for the interment?'

Brother Metellus began to speak and then stopped.

Fidelma turned to look at him enquiringly. 'You have a thought, Brother Metellus?'

'I just wondered if I should return with Brother Ebolbain. I am a member of the community. If a new Abbot is to be chosen by the brethren, I would not like the decision to be made precipitately or without an opportunity to express my opinion.'

'Would they choose one so soon? Should not the obsequies for Abbot Maelcar be conducted first?' queried Eadulf.

Brother Metellus pulled a cynical face.

'Abbot Maelcar gathered around him some, like Brother Ebolbain, who might be panicked into a wrong choice.'

Riwanon now intervened.

'Brother Metellus is correct that he should return to the

abbey. To be honest, Brother Ebolbain does not seem a person who is able to present himself in a leadership role, and that is probably what is needed at this time. The community will be shocked and fearful. Brother Metellus here has the strength of character that is needed to guide them.' It was a statement without guile or any hint of flattery. 'I am sure that if a guide or interpreter are needed for you and Brother Eadulf, we can find someone to replace Brother Metellus in this role.'

Fidelma was, in fact, reluctant to see Brother Metellus leave, for his knowledge of the area was invaluable. But she found herself assenting. As most people seemed to speak a form of Latin as well as their own tongue, she was not worried on that account.

'You are right, Riwanon. I am too selfish in this matter. Of course, I agree that Brother Metellus should go to the abbey.'

Brother Metellus smiled at her and Eadulf.

'I will see you again soon. You will be waiting here for King Alain, no doubt. I may well return before his arrival.'

After he had left, Riwanon excused herself to accompany her female attendants in a walk in the grounds while Budic muttered something about attending to the horses and also left.

'What now?' Eadulf asked Fidelma.

'I am going to have a further word with Iuna,' she said and, as Eadulf made a movement to join her, she added: 'You stay here. I think she might be more amenable to my questions without a witness. I want to challenge her about the subject of that argument with Abbot Maelcar.'

'As you wish,' Eadulf replied. 'Though I cannot see her revealing anything more than she has already.'

'You do not know how revealing someone can be when they do not wish to answer questions,' Fidelma replied dryly, then turned and went through the door that led into the kitchens.

Eadulf lowered himself into one of the comfortable chairs by the fire with a deep sigh of relief. He turned matters over in his mind and came to the conclusion that, while he had been in worse situations, none had made him so uneasy. Was it being in an unfamiliar country whose language he did not speak, whose laws he did not know, which, combined with the mysteries with which they were faced, made things seem so malevolent and threatening? Sea-raiders . . . well, he certainly knew about them from the stories he had heard in Seaxmund's Ham, where he had been brought up. The sea was nearby – the very shores across which raiders had come to plunder or to settle since time began, including his own people only a few centuries before.

He was saddened for Fidelma's loss of her cousin and her friend Murchad, the captain of the *Barnacle Goose*. But such things happened. It was a part of life, and life was brutal. Attacks on merchants and their goods – that, too, he knew about. And the murder of abbots was not unknown: Eadulf had been with Fidelma enough times when they had to investigate the untimely deaths of prelates. So what was the cause of the dark threatening atmosphere that seemed to be oppressing him? He had just settled to his analysis when the door through which Fidelma had vanished a few moments before, burst open and she stood there, flushed and slightly breathless.

'Eadulf, come quickly.'

He sprang up and went towards her.

'What is it?' he demanded. 'What is the matter?'

'I have just seen Iuna in animated argument with Iarnbud and they have left the fortress,' she replied, motioning him to follow her. 'I want to know where they are going.'

'Iuna and the old pagan? I didn't think she liked the old man.'

'Come. They are moving so fast, they might disappear before we catch up with them.'

Eadulf did not protest further but ran with her through the kitchens, ignoring the puzzled glances of those servants who were busy about their duties, preparing the food for the day.

Fidelma led the way to some storage rooms and halted before a door.

'I could not find Iuna,' she explained, opening it, 'so I asked one of the kitchenmaids where she was and was told she was in here. When I came here, the door was open and I heard raised voices. She and Iarnbud were quarrelling. A door was slammed shut on the far side of the room. I waited a moment and went in. The door led out onto the cliffs, and the two of them were moving together down the path towards the shore. So I came back to find you.'

As she was speaking, she and Eadulf went through a storage area to another door. It was a sturdy one with bolts and chains on the interior which, of course, had not been secured.

This door, Eadulf found, as Fidelma had told him, opened

beyond the fortress walls to where a path led through an area of thick bushes and trees, steeply downward towards the shore of the Morbihan. It was a well-trodden path and they were able to move quickly down it. The salt tang of water was immediate, and within a few moments they had come to a small inlet surrounded by rocks where waves lapped noisily against them and where several wooden boats bumped against each other with a hollow thudding noise. Eadulf realised that the other side of the rocks to their right must be the stretch of sandy shore where Fidelma had nearly come to disaster in the quicksand.

Rocky steps had been carved on the more precipitous part of the incline that had ended in a natural harbour. There seemed no one in the vicinity.

Fidelma halted, peering around in frustration.

'This is a means of supplying the fortress from the sea,' Eadulf commented, 'but it presents a weak point in times of war.'

But Fidelma was not interested in his martial views. She was looking for some sign of Iuna and Iarnbud. Then she noticed a sail some way out on the glinting waters before them. It seemed to be heading in the direction of one of the islands.

'Can you see who is in that boat?' she demanded.

'It's too far away.'

'What was the island – the one where the boat is heading? Macliau or Trifina told us the name of it.'

'Govihan, I think. The island of the smith's forge, they said it meant.'

'That's it. It's where there is a fortified dwelling and watch-tower where Trifina prefers to spend her time. That's where Iuna and Iarnbud are heading. Come on, I believe some answers will be there.'

Eadulf's eyes widened in alarm. Fidelma was already descending the stone steps at a dangerous pace into the small harbour.

'Wait a moment . . .' he began.

She ignored his protests and seemed to be examining the remaining boats moored there. Two were small boats with oars but a third one held a mast and single sail.

'We'll take that one,' she said firmly. 'Come on.'

'But . . . but I hate sailing,' protested Eadulf.

Fidelma's brows drew together. 'I'll handle the sail. It doesn't require more than one person in this tiny skiff.'

'But we are stealing . . .'

'Borrowing,' she corrected.

'We ought . . .'

'Do I have to go alone?' she threatened.

Eadulf knew when he was beaten and, with a shrug of his shoulders, moved down the steps to join her. She had clambered into the small skiff and was untying the sail.

'Unfasten the rope there,' she instructed, 'and push us away from those other craft.'

He did so without further argument. There were two oars in the skiff as well, and while she made ready with the sail, he used one of them to push the boat away. He tried to guide them out into the mouth of the inlet. There was a wind blowing from shore which flapped at the sail, and now Fidelma hoisted it; it immediately filled with wind and a tremor went through the vessel as the offshore breeze caught it. It began to move, slowly at first.

'Quickly, come and sit here by the mast,' she instructed. 'Mind the boom.'

Eadulf moved with alacrity as the vessel began to gather speed across the wavelets. Fidelma went to the stern and took the tiller. She steered the vessel out into the open water.

'You do realise that we will be seen as soon we approach that island?' Eadulf fretted. 'Remember what Macliau said about the watchtower and having lookouts posted there?'

Fidelma had forgotten but did not say so.

'We will be careful,' she assured him. 'If we can find one link in this mystery then we will ask Riwanon for assistance.'

'Riwanon? So you think Macliau and his sister are involved?'

'It is their symbol that these brigands are using. It is logical to believe that they are involved.'

'This is true,' agreed Eadulf. 'Except that if they were, why didn't they make us prisoners or even kill us when we turned up at their fortress? The leader of the pirates certainly had no compunction about killing when he raided the *Barnacle Goose*.'

Fidelma compressed her lips for a moment.

'Yes. That is one thing that I cannot explain at the moment,' she agreed.

Eadulf twisted round to glance at the island ahead of them. When he had viewed it from the tower at Brilhag, it appeared small and compact. Now it grew larger as they approached it.

There seemed no sign of the other craft that Fidelma had presumed Iuna and Iarnbud were using. Indeed, they had probably made landfall on the island already. Eadulf hoped that Fidelma had thought matters through because, as soon as they approached the island, they would surely be spotted and if she were right, then they would have no excuse about disguising their suspicions of the guilt of the children of the Lord of Brilhag.

The island's southern end rose, inhospitable. Eadulf knew from his observation from the tower that to the east was a long sloping sandy shore while to the west there was a small strip of sand. Both provided easy landing-places, but either would be easily observable.

'Where are you going to land?' he asked nervously.

It was something that had just begun to bother Fidelma. She did not want to land observed, if possible. She actually hoped their crossing from the peninsula had not been seen or, at least, mistaken as a normal fisherman crossing the waters. But to land on either beach was to invite inspection from the inhabitants of the fortified dwelling on the island.

'The one place that won't be watched is the southern end of the island,' she said at last. 'We could bring the boat in unobserved under the high banks there and climb up to the treeline. Then we could see the lie of the land before committing ourselves.'

Eadulf's jaw tightened as he viewed the dark, high shore-line. 'Land *there*?'

'It is not that forbidding,' replied Fidelma calmly.

'There's white water there. Rocks.'

'Get into the bow and tell me if I come near anything. Use one of the oars to stand us off.'

Muttering under his breath, he turned and scrambled forward, dragging an oar with him.

They were closing fast – too fast, thought Eadulf.

'Left!' he shouted, waving his hand in that direction. 'Keep left!'

They were still a long way from the stony seashore when he realised that not only did the white water herald rocks poking above the sea, but there were also shadows of hidden rocks beneath the dark waters.

'It's too dangerous!' he protested. 'We should turn back.'

Even as he spoke he could see they had come in too close among these underwater rocks to turn with any degree of safety. There was a tidal current driving them towards the shore.

'Right!' he suddenly screamed. 'Bear right!'

He felt the boat begin to respond.

Thoughts raced through his mind. They were going too fast. They ought to take down the sail. But he was needed as lookout to shout warnings of the rocks, and Fidelma was needed at the tiller. It was too late to take the sail down and no one to do so anyway. And now they could not turn out of danger. There was still 100 metres to go before they reached the shore. It was just a matter of time when . . .

The impact knocked Eadulf forward over the bows and into the water. He felt his head bang against a rock and, for a moment, he was confused and dizzy. For a split second, before he was thus precipitated, he had been conscious of a

219

tearing sound, and had an image in his mind's eye of a sharp rock ripping into the wooden planking of the boat. Then he was struggling in the water, struggling for his life for the second time in recent days. The currents and eddies among the rocks were strong and pulled him this way and that. He reached out, trying to grasp a rock but they were all covered with slimy weeds and he could get no purchase. The waves smashing down from the swirling currents drove the breath from his body, and when he opened his mouth to inhale, seawater gushed into it and he swallowed automatically. He was choking. He had no breath and then suddenly everything was black. He felt a brief moment of regret; regret that life had to end in such a fashion.

CHAPTER ELEVEN

'I am sorry ... I am sorry ... I am sorry ...'

Fidelma's voice echoed as if in a cave far, far away. Eadulf found himself fighting against the black oppressive current, swimming badly upwards towards the light and suddenly ... His eyes snapped open. Fidelma was leaning over him, her hair and clothing soaked, water streaming down her face – mingling, it seemed, with tears. Her expression was tragic.

He started to cough and spit out seawater. The taste in his mouth was vile.

'I am sorry.' Her voice came again.

He sank back. 'It seems that we are making a habit of trying to drown one another,' he managed to croak, unable to control the timbre of his voice.

Her face above him broke into a smile of relief.

'Eadulf!' was all she said, and was unable to speak further for emotion.

Eadulf became aware that he was lying on grassy ground.

The crash of waves came at a distance. He was soaked through. His head ached and his throat was sore. The realisation came to him gradually that he must have been hauled from the water and carried to this spot. He looked at Fidelma and was about to form a question when he observed the shadows behind her. He tried to focus on them and after a moment they moulded into two grim-faced warriors whose swords, however, were sheathed.

Fidelma saw his glance.

'We were seen – these men came down to the shore and managed to save us.'

He became aware of another man kneeling by his head and proffering a goatskin water bag.

'Take a sip, swirl it round your mouth and then spit it out,' the man instructed. 'You have swallowed much seawater and 'tis better not to digest any more water until your mouth has been cleansed.'

Eadulf tried to raise himself on one elbow but his head started to swim.

'Better if I could spew it forth,' he replied, remembering the advice of the physicians under whom he had trained.

'We caused you to vomit on the seashore, otherwise . . .' The man did not finish.

Obediently Eadulf took a sip, tasting the cool fresh water in his mouth. It was hard not to swallow but he rinsed his mouth and spat the water out again.

The man took the goatskin bag and put back the stopper. Then he signalled to his men. They lifted Eadulf like a child between them.

'It is not far to my lady Trifina's dwelling,' the man said. 'Do you require assistance, lady?' This last enquiry was addressed to Fidelma.

Eadulf did not hear her answer but it must have been negative.

'It was lucky for you that we were at the southern point of the island,' the man said, as they began to move forward. Eadulf had the impression that he was young and swarthy. He was feeling light-headed again and wanted more than anything to close his eyes and sleep. However, he struggled to keep his senses attuned as he remembered their circumstances and realised that they might soon be in trouble.

'Is the lady Trifina in residence?' he heard Fidelma ask innocently.

'She is often at this island, which she regards as her home more than at her father's residence. Do you know the lady Trifina then?'

'We have met.' Fidelma's voice was solemn.

It seemed that Eadulf must have passed out then, for when he came to, he was inside a building and could feel the warmth and hear the crackle of a fire. A young man was bending over him and prodding him with firm but gentle fingers. Eadulf felt nauseous and his headache had not improved. He blinked and groaned but his eyelids felt like lead.

'He will be all right after a short rest, lady,' the young man said to someone behind him. He spoke in Latin.

'What on earth has happened?' The voice was familiar and it took him a moment or two before he identified it as that of Trifina.

'We were coming to pay a call on you and mistook a safe landing-place,' he heard Fidelma reply. Even through the fog of his mind, it did not sound convincing. 'We struck a submerged rock and our boat broke up. It was fortunate for us that these men saw the incident from the shore and effected a rescue. They saved our lives.'

'They will be rewarded,' responded Trifina distantly. 'But how did those at Brilhag let you come out here alone? Macliau knows how dangerous the waters around these islands can be, unless one has knowledge. I do not understand it.'

'Your brother is away hunting,' Fidelma said.

Trifina gave an exclamation of surprise.

'He left you and . . . ?' Then her tone became brisk. 'But we must get you dry, into warm clothes, and it looks as though your companion stands in need of some attention. Heraclius, my physician, will take care of him. If only Iuna were here,' she added absently.

'Iuna is not here?' Fidelma's ejaculation of surprise was apparent but then it seemed she controlled her astonishment. 'I thought I had heard that Iuna was coming to join you here,' she added.

'Indeed not,' responded Trifina. 'Why should she? I left her to attend to your wants at Brilhag.'

'I thought that she might have come bearing the news.' Was Fidelma searching for an excuse?

'News?' Trifina's tone was perplexed. 'What news?'

'Firstly, that Riwanon has arrived at Brilhag with her entourage.'

'Riwanon!' The voice had the tone of surprise but there was something not quite right to Fidelma's ears. A note of falseness. 'Then are you saying that King Alain and my father are at Brilhag?'

'They have not arrived yet,' Fidelma rejoined. 'Riwanon had left them hunting and came on by herself.'

'Then it is a good thing that Iuna is at my father's fortress. And my brother has decided to go hunting at this moment? For shame! No one there to welcome the Queen.'

'There is even more news, lady,' Fidelma said. She cleared her throat. 'Unwelcome news, I regret. Abbot Maelcar of the community of Gildas arrived at Brilhag . . . and was murdered last night, or rather, early this morning.'

There was a long silence.

'Are you jesting?' demanded Trifina. Yet again there was something unconvincing about her tone as though she were affecting surprise rather than truly being surprised.

'I do not jest about murder, lady,' Fidelma replied firmly.

'Let me get this right. You say that Abbot Maelcar was murdered while staying at my father's fortress at the same time as Riwanon arrived?'

'Indeed. It was to bring you these tidings that we came.'

Eadulf presumed that Fidelma considered herself to be merely twisting the facts to suit the moment, rather than telling an outright lie. Even in his befogged state of mind he could almost smile at the logic.

'We will talk more about this when you are dried and changed,' Trifina announced abruptly.

Eadulf was aware of instructions being issued but he still

could not open his eyes. A great lethargy seemed to overcome him and he slid into a gentle sleep.

Fidelma had followed Trifina's attendants, who carried Eadulf
between them through a light oakwood-panelled corridor then
up a broad stairway. They ascended without pausing and went
along another corridor to a comfortable chamber where a
wood fire was already crackling in the hearth. While Eadulf
was being bathed and placed in a warm bed, a female attendant invited Fidelma into a small adjoining chamber where a
tub of hot water had also been prepared for her and some
dry clothing had been brought. It did not take long before she
felt restored to her normal self, and one of the female servants
told her that the lady Trifina was now awaiting her with
refreshments.

She looked in on Eadulf before she left and saw that he
was sleeping fairly comfortably. The young physician, who
looked little more than a youth, stood respectfully by the
fire.

'I will stay with him for a while, lady,' he said. He spoke
in excellent Latin but she could not place his accent. 'The
water is out of his lungs but the immersion has disturbed
him; also he has a bad graze on the head, and so he desires
sleep above all things. I have seen this desire for sleep happen
before, when someone has been resuscitated after near-death
by drowning. A rest, and he will be well again. Have no
fear.'

'Trifina says you are a physician.' Fidelma gave the youth
a slow scrutiny.

'I am qualified in my own land in medical matters, lady.'

'What is your name?'

'Heraclius, lady.'

'I have heard that name before. And surely it is a Greek name?'

For a moment an expression of pride crossed the young man's features.

'I was born and educated in Constantinopolis.'

'Then I leave Eadulf in your hands, Heraclius. Be sure to send for me, if anything is amiss.'

'Have no worries, lady. He will be well soon.'

Fidelma turned and followed the waiting female attendant along the panelled corridor again to the stairway. The interior of the building was almost entirely of wood, with the exception of a stone tower and lower foundations. There were outer walls of sandstone which surrounded the large two-storey building. It was an impressive place and Fidelma had seen few buildings to compare with it. It was, in many respects, reminiscent of structures she had seen in Rome.

'This is a magnificent building,' she commented to the attendant. The girl bobbed nervously.

'Indeed, lady.'

'And old?'

'They say that a Roman governor, sent to rule over the Veneti many years ago, had it built as a summer palace.'

Fidelma congratulated herself. So that explained the similarity that she had felt between this villa and some of the buildings she had seen in Rome. However, Roman residences were not usually built with second storeys and watchtowers, so she presumed that much had been added to the building over the years. From the bottom of the stairway, the attendant led her along a corridor and through a door which entered on a typical Roman-style inner courtyard with what might once have been a fountain but which no longer gushed water. On the far side of this courtyard, the attendant opened a carved oak door and ushered Fidelma inside.

Trifina received her in a large chamber. A fire was blazing in the hearth at the far end and oak chairs were set on either side. There was a similarly ornate table laid with various dishes and jugs, and Trifina waved towards it.

'There is mulled wine or soup to choose from. Take what you will,' she invited. 'Something warm will help you recover from your ordeal.'

Fidelma took a goblet of mulled wine and went to the seat by the fire indicated by Trifina.

The daughter of the *mac'htiern* of Brilhag stretched herself in the second comfortable chair and examined Fidelma carefully from under lowered lids.

'You did not really make your journey here just to bring me news, did you?' she opened. It was not said as an accusation but a confident statement seeking an expected confirmation.

Fidelma decided to be honest.

'Not entirely,' she admitted. 'Although it is true that Riwanon has arrived and that Macliau is not at Brilhag. It is also true that Abbot Maelcar has been murdered.'

Trifina continued her close scrutiny but without expression.

'But that is not what brought you on your foolhardy voyage here, is it? Let us start, though, with the death of the Abbot. Who murdered him – and why?'

'We do not know. At the moment, the only suspect seems to be Iuna.'

Trifina's eyes widened in surprise.

'Iuna? Abbot Maelcar was not the friendliest of men and his attitude certainly made him many enemies locally. However, I can't believe . . . Iuna. Why?'

'I found her fleeing from Abbot Maelcar's bedchamber. She said that she had discovered the body a moment before. I do not think she told me the entire truth. Then I saw her leaving the fortress with Iarnbud in a small sailing boat. They were heading in this direction. Hence, Eadulf and I followed.'

At this, Trifina's expression turned to one of incredulity. 'Iarnbud and Iuna? You are mistaken.'

'I am not. Abbot Maelcar said that he had come to Brilhag in answer to a plea, which was purportedly sent by the King. But it was clear, at once, that no such message came from the King or your father, neither of whom had reached Brilhag at the time.'

'What are you saying?'

'I think Abbot Maelcar was purposely lured to Brilhag to meet his killer. The message was, as Riwanon said, a false one.'

Trifina's eyes narrowed slightly.

'And so you say that Iuna was the killer and somehow acting in concert with Iarnbud? I say you are mistaken. I know them both and well.'

'Someone who kills is always known by someone else,' Fidelma pointed out. 'Just how long has Iuna served you?'

Trifina considered the question a moment before she decided to answer.

'She came to be fostered by my father when she was seven years old.'

'Fostered?' The girl had used the Latin term *curare*. Fidelma wondered if it were the same system as the one that prevailed in her own land; the system called *altramm* which was so important to the society and the rearing of children. For when a child was seven years old, he or she could be sent to a family for education and rearing. The fosterage could be *altramm serce*, for affection, to families of equal rank in which no fee was paid. There was a second, less usual form, and that was fosterage for a fee. In both cases the foster family had to maintain the child according to the rank in which it was born. This was done under legal contract.

Fidelma tried to outline this to Trifina who, to her surprise, confirmed a fairly similar method among her people.

'A friend of my father in Brekilien who was also a distant relative sent Iuna to us. He was a noble who soon after lost his life defending the eastern borders against the Franks. Iuna's mother was killed at the same time. So we became her family.'

'Iuna has been raised as one of your family? Yet she says she is the house stewardess and acts as your servant.'

Trifina shrugged in a dismissive fashion.

'She can choose whatever title she is pleased to call herself. Her family being annihilated in a Frankish raid, she has remained with us. We continue to hold her in the affection of our family but she has decided to fulfil the position of . . .' she paused, trying to think of a correct word '. . . *quae res domesticas dispensat.*'

'A housekeeper,' supplied Fidelma.

'The steward of our household. She likes to be in charge of the domestic arrangements, although she can claim the privilege of rank within our family. But she has the temperament of a martyr. It is a role she seems to enjoy and, to be truthful, we welcome it, especially since my mother died of the Yellow Plague some six years ago. Iuna has complete freedom and can come and go as she pleases. In fact, she does. She has her own boat and is an expert at sailing.'

'I am sorry to hear that your mother succumbed to the plague.'

'I doubt if there is a family in all the world who was not touched in some way by the onslaught of that plague,' was all Trifina commented.

'Did Iuna know Abbot Maelcar well?'

Trifina actually smiled. 'Know him *well*? Our family are patrons of his community. We have all known him for several years. Since he took up the Rule of Benedict, my father is not pleased, for he supports the old ways. The Abbot is not originally from this area. In fact, he comes from Brekilien, which is where Iuna's family originally came from.'

'And Iarnbud? How does he get on with the Abbot?'

'You ask a lot of questions,' frowned Trifina.

'It is my task in life,' Fidelma replied defensively. 'I have mentioned before that I am an advocate of the laws of my own land, and my role—'

Trifina held up her hand for a moment.

'I have understood that. What I cannot understand is why you are asking your questions here – and of me. You have no authority in this kingdom.'

'Riwanon has asked me to discover who killed Abbot Maelcar.'

'That is a curious commission to give a stranger.' The girl's eyes narrowed suspiciously.

'It is not the first time that I have been employed by those not of my own country,' Fidelma said irritably. 'Saxons, Romans and Britons have all sought my services.'

'You would have been more competent for the task if you were able to speak our language.' Trifina sniffed a little in disapproval.

Fidelma flushed for, indeed, it was a weakness that she was well aware of.

There was an awkward silence before Trifina spoke again.

'So you claim that Iuna left Brilhag in a sailing boat with Iarnbud and they were heading in the direction of this island? Well, I find that hard to believe, and I can assure you that Iuna is not on this island to my knowledge.' Her words were spoken in a studied fashion and her eyes held those of Fidelma without fear or guile. She was either a good actress or she spoke the truth.

'You were about to answer my question about Iarnbud,' Fidelma pressed.

'Iarnbud is harmless,' replied Trifina. 'A crazy man of the woods but my father has known him ever since he was growing up. He is loyal to my family. For charity's sake, we ensure the man wants for nothing. He employs the fiction that he is my father's official *bretat* or judge, although I would not like to be judged by him.'

'In what way do you mean that?'

'His idea of judgement is to cut the wood to see if people are guilty or not.'

'Cut the wood?' Fidelma was puzzled.

'We call it *prenn dethin* . . . an ancient custom among people where pieces of a sacred tree are cut and these are tossed on the ground. Depending on the way they fall, the person is guilty or not. It is an ancient pagan custom that most people had given up long before Julius Caesar invaded our land.'

The idea reminded Fidelma of something she had heard.

'I think we had a similar custom in ancient times. It was called *crannacher* and means the same thing. From what I heard the other evening, when Iarnbud discoursed with Brother Metellus, he was very sharp of mind and knowledge.'

'Of course. Iarnbud is knowledgeable. But he is one who believes in the old ways, and his old ways stretch back to the dawn of time.'

'He lives on his boat amongst these islands?'

'He does. Why do you ask that?'

'I wondered where he would be going in his boat.'

Trifina frowned. 'I cannot see that this has anything to do with the Abbot.' Then she chuckled sourly. 'You think old Iarnbud persuaded Iuna to kill the Abbot in some dispute about Christianity and the Old Faith? I can tell you that you are wrong. Iarnbud needs people like Brother Metellus and

Abbot Maelcar so that he can expound on his criticisms of the New Faith and reinforce him in his own belief. He would not kill Abbot Maelcar.'

'One of the things I have learned in life is that, given the right circumstances, everyone is capable of killing someone,' replied Fidelma quietly.

Trifina shook her head in disagreement.

'Philosophically, you may be right. But practically, I doubt it. Anyway, you are claiming that Iuna and Iarnbud, after killing Abbot Maelcar, ran off . . . well, sailed off to one of these islands and that is why you pursued them? I don't believe it.'

'I am not interested in belief. Only in fact,' Fidelma responded. 'Do you have any ideas as to why Iuna and Iarnbud would have any serious business together?'

'So far as I know, Iuna doesn't like Iarnbud particularly. She tolerates him out of respect for our family.'

A memory came into Fidelma's mind.

'Are you the eldest daughter of the chieftain of Brilhag?'

'I am the *only* daughter of my father, Lord Canao,' replied Trifina sharply.

'You have had no younger sister?'

'Of course not. Why do you ask?'

'Aourken said that she taught Latin grammar to you and—'

'Oh, you mean Iuna – my foster sister.'

'Ah,' sighed Fidelma softly. Of course, that explained the reference to the younger sister. 'And is there any reason why Iarnbud would arrive at your father's fortress on the morning after Abbot Maelcar was murdered, seek out Iuna, why they were having an animated discussion and why they would leave without telling anyone, get in a boat and sail out in this direction?'

Trifina was silent, staring at the floor for a while.

'I have told you, Fidelma, that I cannot give you an answer. I could not even begin to *guess* at an answer. But I will say this: I can only admire your foolhardiness at taking a small sailing craft and following Iarnbud into these waters.'

'Foolhardiness?' Fidelma echoed.

'What else was it but foolish?' reproved Trifina. 'Do you realise how near death you and your Saxon friend came? You obviously took a sailboat without permission and blithely set out after them, sailing into waters you did not know. These are dangerous waters, dangerous rocks. Then you tried to land at the most perilous point of this island. If my men had not been watching you from the shore and reached you in time, you would both have drowned.'

Fidelma let the criticism pass over her with only a slight flush coming to her cheeks. She knew that the girl was right and she was aware that she had nearly been the instrument of Eadulf's death. She tried to disguise the shiver that passed through her frame at the thought. Trifina saw the movement, however, and was able to sense the cause of it. She smiled humourlessly that her words had had that effect.

'So long as you know and have learned the lesson,' she said with harsh satisfaction. 'But as for your question, I will reiterate once more . . . I cannot hazard a guess why Iuna and Iarnbud should behave in the manner you claim. Nor, indeed, has it been reported to me that they have arrived on this island.'

'I assume that you would know if they had?' Fidelma asked. 'There is nowhere that they could have landed, unknown to you?'

For a moment the girl's brows drew together in anger and then her face relaxed and she actually chuckled.

'You obviously tried to land without me knowing. You see what good that did? There is no way they could land here without being spotted by my men. Of that I am sure.'

'Where, then, *would* they be heading?'

'There are countless islands in the Little Sea. Take your pick.'

Fidelma was disappointed. 'There are no other islands that come to your mind where Iuna or Iarnbud might be making for – one in this direction?'

'There are other islands, mostly inhabited by fishing folk. I would not be so foolish as to give you a boat to pursue the useless and dangerous quest that I think you have in mind,' she added, correctly guessing the thought that had occurred to Fidelma.

Fidelma smiled tightly and rose.

'Then there is little I can do here. I will, with your permission, go to see how Eadulf is faring.'

'I am sending one of my men to Brilhag to inform them that you are both safe and well and with me. When your companion is recovered, then I will return you to Brilhag. In the meantime, accept the hospitality of this place.' She suddenly gazed wistfully around. 'It was my mother's favourite residence.'

She also rose and accompanied Fidelma to the door where an attendant waited to guide her back to the chamber where she had left Eadulf.

Fidelma found Eadulf sitting up, leaning against the pillow and looking pale and drawn. He managed to form an expression that was meant as a rueful grin. Someone had brought him a bowl of hot broth, which lay on the bedside but it was untouched.

'How do you feel?' she asked, coming to sit on the edge of the bed.

'As if I had nearly drowned,' responded Eadulf with dry humour.

'I am sorry,' she began contritely, but he reached out and caught her hand.

'I know. I heard you on the shore when they pulled me out.'

'I was doing what I thought was best.'

'*Audaces fortuna iuvat*,' he sighed. Fortune favours the daring. 'Sometimes it works, sometimes . . . Are we now in trouble?'

If the truth were known, Fidelma was still horrified that her stubborn attitude had nearly been the instrument of Eadulf's death. She discounted the fact that she, too, had nearly drowned. She had managed, however, to cling to a piece of intact boat until the warriors had effected their rescue. She tried to hide her emotions and turned to look at the broth. It was still warm.

'We are not,' she said shortly. 'And you have not eaten,'

she accused, changing the subject and picking up the bowl and spoon. She held the bowl before him. He grimaced. So she took the spoon and held it to his mouth as one would coax a child. He obeyed her unspoken order and opened his mouth to allow the warm liquid to trickle into it. As she fed him, she told him the gist of her conversation with Trifina.

'You believe that she is speaking the truth?' asked Eadulf.

Fidelma put down the empty bowl and spoon.

'As much as one can trust one's instincts,' she replied. 'Her surprise when I told her about Iuna and Iarnbud seemed genuine enough. How do you feel?'

'I can get up,' he said. 'The headache was the main thing and, thanks to the potions of a physician here, I feel much better.'

'Are you sure you feel able?'

'I hate lying abed, especially when there are things to be done,' he replied.

'Trifina has supplied us with dry clothes.' Fidelma gave a short laugh. 'This is getting to be a habit, borrowing clothes after being immersed in the sea.'

'Let's not make it a third time,' replied Eadulf with grave humour. 'My constitution will not stand it.'

Fidelma rose, went to the window of the chamber and peered out. From the position of the sun she concluded that she was looking eastward across a short sandy shoreline and a small stretch of water to another smaller island – and beyond that to various patches of rising land. This 'Little Sea', what the natives called the Morbihan, was filled with islands, and Iuna and Iarnbud could have gone to any one of them. But *why*? She sighed deeply in frustration.

Eadulf was pulling on the dry clothes, although not with the alacrity he usually displayed. He was still fairly weak.

'Have we reached another dead-end?' he asked.

'Not exactly,' she replied. 'Iuna and Iarnbud left together. There is a link there, and we must find it. While there is still plenty of light, I am going to see if I can explore the island a little. I think Trifina was being truthful with me, but it is always a wise precaution to make certain. It shouldn't take long to examine any bays and coves where Iuna and Iarnbud could hide.'

Eadulf gave a groan. 'To be honest, while I am better, I don't think I am up to exploring islands as yet.'

'Stay in the villa,' Fidelma suggested, looking sympathetic. 'I shan't go far on this small island.' And she left him, sitting by the fire that had been lit in the chamber.

There was no one about outside and so Fidelma made her way down the stairs to the ground floor again, and along the corridor into the small courtyard, which led to the room where she had seen Trifina. As she neared the door, she saw that it was ajar and she heard voices raised. Familiar voices. Even though the speakers were conversing in the language of the Bretons, she recognised the commanding tones of Trifina. She would have entered, had it not been for the second voice. She was almost sure of the identity of the speaker before she peered through the crack between the door and the doorjamb – it was Bleidbara, looking serious. It was clear that Trifina was giving him instructions. He seemed to be asking a question or two and nodding at the answers. Then, to Fidelma's surprise, the young man ended the conversation by leaning forward and kissing Trifina in a manner that bespoke a deeper intimacy than she had been led to believe. And what was more, Trifina responded with no less fervour.

Bleidbara was turning for the door when Fidelma realised she had to act. The only place of concealment was a small recess not far away. It would be useless if the warrior turned in her direction. Thankfully, he chose the opposite direction and vanished through a door at the far end of the corridor. Fidelma waited a moment, her mind already made up, and hurried after him.

The door gave access to a small ante-room leading into a tiny yard and then a pathway that wound down to the eastern shore of the island, a long strip of white sand in a curving bay.

The warrior moved quickly down this path, oblivious to Fidelma coming up behind him. At the bottom, on the shore, two men were awaiting him. Fidelma spotted them just before they glanced up to see Bleidbara coming towards them. She had already crouched down behind a bush before they did so. She could hear a cheery greeting and the warrior answering. Then she peered carefully around the bush. All three were walking across the sandy beach towards a small rowing boat, by which another man stood. Bleidbara and one other man climbed in while the remaining two men pushed it out into the water and scrambled in as it rose on the waves.

It was only then that Fidelma realised there was a large ship at anchor in the bay to which the men were now heading, two of them hauling at the oars as the boat bobbed its way over the waters. The ship was a large wooden sailing vessel.

It was painted black from bow to stern with the exception of the jutting spar and bow timber. These were a deep orange in colour that made the vessel appear very sinister. Fidelma's eyes rose to the white flag flying from the masthead – a large white flag with the image of a bird on it . . . the image of a dove.

She gave a sharp intake of breath and was about to move forward to gain a better view when she was aware of a soft footfall behind her.

She pivoted round, rising automatically.

Trifina was standing regarding her with an amused expression. Behind her stood one of her guards, his hand resting lightly on the hilt of his sword.

CHAPTER TWELVE

❧

Eadulf was feeling better. The young apothecary had been accurate in his prognosis. The shock of near death by drowning must have caused the reaction of the stupor that had come over him. Even his headache had gone, thanks to the potion that he had been given. He rose from the chair in front of the fire and took a swallow of water from the mug left on the table. The cold liquid refreshed his mouth, although he felt a distinct soreness in his chest and an ache in his stomach as if he had eaten bad food.

He had begun to feel frustrated by his inaction and moved to the window and gazed out on the western coastline of the island. The day seemed pleasant enough. In fact, there was little need of a fire at all for it was quite warm. He walked up and down for a few moments, realising that he was now in complete control of all his senses and movements.

Eadulf knew enough about the practice of the apothecary's art to be aware that a warming cordial would do better for his chest than sipping fresh water. Deciding to go in search of the young apothecary or of the kitchens of the villa where he could make his own soothing concoction, he left the room and walked down the corridor until he found the stairway to the floor below. A young girl was hard at work scrubbing the stairs. Her head was bent down to her work so she did not notice him until he reached the step above her.

When he asked where he might find the apothecary she started nervously.

He smiled reassuringly at her and asked again. It was clear that she did not understand Latin and he tried to drag from his memory a word from his sparse knowledge of the language of the Britons. No word came to mind.

'*Culina*,' he said again, using the Latin word for kitchen, and made motions implying drinking and eating.

The girl seemed to understand his mime and pointed down the stairs saying something in her language, repeating the word '*kegin*' several times.

Eadulf thanked her and moved past her down the stairway to the lower corridor. The girl had pointed almost directly under the stairs and Eadulf saw a doorway which led into an ante-room lined with shelves. Immediately his senses were bombarded with a mixture of aromas, sweet-smelling herbs and spices combined with dried meats that hung from metal hooks from the ceiling. The room was like a narrow corridor through which he passed quickly and, opening a door at the far end, he entered into a courtyard. In the covered area on one side were three great clay brick ovens and places where a fire could be lit in such a manner that a pot could be placed on an iron arm over the flames. Pots and pans hung along the wall behind the ovens. In the centre of the court-yard was a well, obviously the source of the fresh water for cooking.

There seemed no one about but this was clearly the kitchen area. He thought it strange that there was no one attending to the preparation of food in such a large villa as this. The rooms along this side of the courtyard consisted of various storerooms and a few that were clearly occupied by the kitchen workers as their personal quarters. He walked along, peering into each but there was no one around.

At the far corner, another open door led into what was clearly the dispensary. He was surprised that this was not closed and locked, but saw a key hanging from a hook just inside the door and presumed that the young apothecary had forgotten to lock up. Eadulf went in, examining the shelves. At one end there was a pile of moss in water, but a moss smelling strongly of the sea. Eadulf recognised it at once for it was a red alga that he knew was found along the western shores of Éireann among the sea-bathed rocks. That was just what he was looking for.

He reached forward and picked up some, smelling it to make sure it was the same plant.

'What do you want?'

The sharp voice caused him to start. The youthful apoth-ecary, who had attended him, was standing in the doorway. He was tall, with curly blue-black hair and dark eyes, with a swarthy face and a permanent furrow over his brows as though in constant thought.

'I am looking for something that will relieve the soreness

in the back of my throat and chest and the uncomfortable feeling in my stomach,' replied Eadulf, trying to remember his name. 'I think I have found it.'

The young man's frown deepened as he glanced at the plant Eadulf held.

'You appear to have a good knowledge of the healing qualities of plants and herbs,' he observed suspiciously.

Eadulf confessed that he had studied the art in Tuam Brecain, a great medical college of Éireann.

'I have not heard of it. However, you have picked a wise choice in *pioka ruz*,' the young man said, nodding to the moss he held. 'It should settle your ailment.'

Eadulf tried to repeat the name and added: 'It is called *carraigin* in the language of Hibernia.'

'It is a good demulcent,' confirmed the young man. 'You know how to use it?'

'If I can boil a little of the plant to produce a syrup . . . ?'

'There is no need. I was preparing such a mixture earlier this morning as it is also used to make sweet dishes. I make a jelly substance mixed with honey, which the lady Trifina especially likes. Come, I will give you some.'

The young man pointed to the bowl standing near to where Eadulf had picked up the moss. He took an empty dish and measured out several spoonfuls from the bowl.

'There now, it is a syrupy taste that coats the throat and will also make its way to your stomach. Perhaps you would like a spoonful of honey to sweeten the taste more?'

Eadulf shook his head as he tried an experimental spoonful. As the familiar taste of what he knew as *carraigin* made contact with his tongue, he swallowed and felt its comforting contact with his throat.

'What did you call this, my friend?' he asked.

'I know only the name in the language of the Bretons, which is *pioka ruz*. I hear that it is known by several other names in various parts of this country. It is a plant that is unknown in my land.'

'But it grows along these shores?'

'It does, indeed.'

Eadulf nodded appreciatively as he finished the bowl. 'Ah, that should settle my stomach.'

'You feel better?'

'Better than when I was lifted from the sea,' smiled Eadulf, trying to regain his sense of humour.

The young man nodded. 'It was the worst place on this island to attempt a landing.'

'My name is Eadulf, by the way.' Eadulf decided to change the subject and introduce himself.

'That I know,' responded the young man.

'And your name is . . . ? I think I heard it spoken but have forgotten.'

'Heraclius of Constantinopolis.'

'And you are Greek then?' Eadulf said. 'You are further from home than I am.'

'Indeed, I am,' Heraclius said dryly. 'My father, Callinicus, was of Heliopolis in the land of Phoenice. He had to flee from there before my birth when our armies were defeated at Yarmouk by Abu Ubaida ibn al-Jarral over thirty years ago.'

'Alas, I know nothing of these names nor of that part of
the world.'

'Abu Ubaida commanded the great Muslim army and after
our defeat at Yarmouk most of our people fled from Heliopolis
leaving behind much booty for him. My father went to
Constantinopolis to take service with the emperors of
Byzantium.'

'I have vaguely heard of these Muslims. When I was in
Rome, I was told about them raiding the coastal towns,' Eadulf
said. 'Was your father also an apothecary?'

The young man shook his head quickly.

'No. He was an architect. He built some of the great buildings for which Heliopolis had been famous.'

'But you became an apothecary?'

'I did.'

'How did you come here? It is a long way from your home.'

'I decided to leave Constantinopolis to seek my fortune
for there is a surfeit of apothecaries at home. I took ship
with a merchant and travelled through the Middle Sea to
Massilia. Finally, a year ago, I came to this country, this
land they called Bro-Waroch, and took service with the
noble family here. They appreciated my skills and so I stayed
here.'

'You are young to have made such a journey.'

The young man shrugged. 'I am five and twenty years,
but a youthful countenance is passed down in my family.
Callinicus appears to be more my brother in appearance than
my father.' Eadulf had placed the age of the apothecary at
around twenty years. Heraclius was examining him with

interest. 'Why did you give up the path to being a healer? You say that you have studied the art?'

'I studied only that I might be of some assistance to my brethren, but not to spend my time in a dispensary,' replied Eadulf.

'Ah, yes. I forget that you are a religious. You are the companion of this Hibernian lady . . .'

'She is my wife,' Eadulf corrected him.

'Ah.' Heraclius nodded. 'Then you do not follow this concept that all religious must be celibate and remain separate from one another, as does Abbot Maelcar? We, too, in the East, do not believe that all our religious should be celibate.'

'I once thought I should follow that path,' affirmed Eadulf. Then he frowned a little. 'So you know Abbot Maelcar?'

'While I prefer to follow my experiments here, I serve this family and often go to the mainland. I have met him and, I confess, I do not like him.'

Eadulf realised the passing of time and made a quick apology. 'I must now find Fidelma. Have you seen her?'

'I have not for a while. This part of the villa is usually the province of the attendants. I doubt she would come here.'

'I am surprised the kitchens are deserted.'

'Well, the villa is not expecting guests and so the lady Trifina has no need of many workers in her kitchens.'

'This villa is run very much in Roman style, isn't it?' queried Eadulf, interested in what he had seen.

The young man seemed diffident.

'I would not know,' he said. 'It seems a normal way of living to me.'

'Of course. You are Greek. This way of life is not usual in the far west.' Eadulf hesitated but he sensed the Greek was growing tired of his questions and so he decided not to press him further. 'Well, Heraclius of Constantinopolis, I thank you for your help. Indeed, I should probably thank you for my life.'

'The warriors who plucked you from the sea managed to make you vomit the seawater from your belly, otherwise you might have drowned. They should be thanked. I did but little.'

'In that case,' responded Eadulf, 'I shall thank you for that little you did do. What was the name of the warrior who saved me?'

'I am not sure. You will have to ask Bleidbara.' Heraclius turned away before he saw the surprise on Eadulf's features.

In deep thought, Eadulf left the apothecary and went out into the courtyard. Instead of exiting by the way he had come, he walked slowly around the far side of the rectangular court to examine the building which he realised was very Roman in structure and also old. Clearly, in the days of the empire of Rome this had been built to demonstrate the wealth of the owners. He also realised that this courtyard could not be the only one in the villa, for the main courtyard would be reserved for the convenience of Trifina and her guests. He wondered whether there was some way of reaching it without retracing his steps. There was a small door at the far side of the courtyard.

He tried the handle and found that it opened out onto a small and pleasant garden, filled with herbs and plants doubtless destined for the use of the cooks. It was walled and on the far side was yet another door. He crossed the garden and again he found that once the internal bolt had been withdrawn, the door opened easily. The first thing that struck him was the salt tang of the sea, and he found himself gazing across the open waters to the eastern side of the island. But he was distracted immediately by a stronger, more curious smell. He noticed a small stone-built hut standing a little way from the outer walls of the villa and the smell seemed to permeate this building. It contrasted strongly with the balmy sea air.

Curiosity compelled Eadulf to walk towards the grey stone building. Then he heard a cry, a shout as if of warning, from below. He glanced down and caught sight of a small craft almost below him. It was a small sailing dinghy with its sail furled and one person standing up in it, gazing upwards towards him.

Eadulf started, his eyes widening as he recognised the features of Iarnbud.

At that moment, he began diving into a dark whirlpool; he had a split second of consciousness before the dive began, when the thought registered that someone had hit him on the back of the head.

'Well, Sister Fidelma,' Trifina was saying slowly. 'You seem very interested in that ship?'

Fidelma's mind raced for a plausible reason as to why she should be hiding behind some bushes watching Bleidbara's departure. She decided that honesty was the best policy.

'I was wondering why a warship – for its lines proclaim

that it is no merchantman – should be anchored off this island,'
she said defensively.

Trifina gazed thoughtfully at her.

'The ship is called the *Morvran* and it is in the service of
my family,' she said. 'If you remember, it is the same ship
that Bleidbara informed you that he was captain of the other
night – the same ship that was anchored in the inlet below
Brilhag. When I need to come here, this is the ship that trans-
ports me. There is nothing sinister about it.'

'You did not tell me that Bleidbara was here,' Fidelma
remarked.

'Why should I need to? I did mention that I would send
one of my men back to Brilhag to inform them that you and
Eadulf were here on this island with me. I have sent Bleidbara.'

Fidelma did not respond, her mind rapidly turning over the
information.

Trifina saw her concentration.

'Shall I tell you what you are thinking, Fidelma of Hibernia?
You see the banner of my father that flies from the great
mast? It bears an emblem of a dove, doesn't it? I'll lay a
wager with you. When your own ship, the *Barnacle Goose*,
was attacked, my wager is that the attacker bore the same
emblem. You are now thinking that you have discovered the
ship that attacked you. Am I not right in this assumption?'

Fidelma had been so careful to withhold this important
information from Trifina or Macliau. Only Eadulf and Brother
Metellus knew about the dove emblem. Now, here was Trifina,
confronting her with the knowledge. She ran her tongue
around her lips.

'The thought did occur to me,' she admitted slowly. It was useless to deny it. 'Your wager was a safe one.'

An expression of satisfaction crossed Trifina's face.

'Take a good look at Bleidbara's ship,' she invited. Her voice was serious now. '*Is* it the same vessel as the one that attacked your ship?'

Fidelma turned back to see the vessel hoisting its sail and moving slowly southward along the coast. She had already realised that the colour was wrong. Although both ships were basically black in colour, the pirate ship certainly did not carry the strange orange bow that Bleidbara's ship had. Nor were the lines of the ships similar.

'Well?' demanded Trifina.

Fidelma sighed. 'The vessel is of different construction but it flies the same flag.'

'I think you should return to the villa now, Fidelma of Hibernia,' Trifina quietly ordered, indicating the path back. 'You are entering into matters that are not your concern.'

The warrior accompanying Trifina stood, his hand still on the hilt of his sword as if waiting for an order from the daughter of the *mac'htiern*.

Fidelma began to walk slowly back up the incline. Trifina fell in step behind her.

Eadulf was about to be hanged. He was being led down a line of cowled Brothers and Sisters of the Faith, preceded by a single Brother of the community bearing an ornate metal cross. They were all chanting in an eerie fashion that sent shivers down his spine. His hands were tied behind him and the procession moved inexorably towards the platform where a single rope seemed to hang in space, formed into a noose.

The face of Abbess Fainder suddenly floated before him.

'Abhor your sins, Eadulf of Seaxmund's Ham. Life for life, eye for eye, tooth for tooth, hand for hand, foot for foot . . . that is the law.'

He wanted to cry out – '*But you are dead! You do not exist!*'

The noose was about his neck.

'Let God's will be done!' shrieked the Abbess in his ear.

He started to scream. He was lying on damp earth. It was cold and wet against his cheek. It took him several moments to realise he was lying on the grass outside the villa on the island of Govihan. Without moving, or raising his head, he looked around. There was nothing in his area of vision and so he gently moved himself up into a sitting position and peered round again. He was alone, lying outside the still-open door that led from the villa's herb garden.

He raised a hand to the back of his head. It came away sticky and he saw that it was covered in blood. The area was tender and throbbing.

Remembrance came back to him in a moment.

He peered cautiously down to the sea. There was no sign of the small sailing boat nor of Iarnbud.

His next thought was to warn Fidelma, and he was about to get to his feet when he heard a movement through the door of the herb garden.

*   *   *

Fidelma returned slowly to the villa with Trifina, the watchful warrior following them at a distance. Trifina left her at the gates of the villa with a curt farewell; her bodyguard remained at the gates.

Frustrated, Fidelma had no alternative but to enter the main courtyard. As she did so, she caught sight of a man moving quickly through the far door. In that split second, she recognised the figure of Iarnbud. Then the door slammed. She paused only a second before she almost ran to the door and tried the handle – but it had been bolted from the other side.

Iarnbud! He was here in Trifina's villa, yet the daughter of the *mac'htiern* had denied any knowledge of Iuna or the pagan *bretat*.

She turned from the door and her frustration increased. But she had realised two things. One, that Trifina was a liar. And two, that there was a sinister mystery here in these beautiful islands of Morbihan.

Eadulf found himself once again looking into the eyes of Heraclius, who was staring at him in amazement.

He came forward immediately and held out a hand to raise Eadulf to his feet.

'Why, what has happened? Did you fall and hit your head?' he asked with concern.

Eadulf forced a grim smile, saying, 'It seems that my destiny is either to drown or be bludgeoned to death.'

'Bludgeoned?' queried the young man in astonishment.

'Someone hit me from behind.'

Heraclius looked around. 'There is no one around here.

You have not long left me. Are you sure you did not fall and hit your head?'

Eadulf groaned, reaching out and touching the back of his head again.

'It does not take long to strike a blow,' he said.

Heraclius was examining the wound.

'However you came by this, I must dress it. There is a small gash where the skin has opened and is bleeding, but it will heal swiftly. However, you will have bruising, and coming on top of the immersion in the sea, you should rest to prevent yourself from further harm. It is not wise to take a blow to the head so soon after the previous one.'

'I did not intentionally seek a further blow to the head,' Eadulf said bitterly. 'I don't suppose you saw anyone follow me out through the herb garden?'

The young man shook his head with a smile. 'I have only just come from there.'

'Why?' Eadulf asked.

'Why?' Heraclius repeated, not understanding.

'What brought you here?'

'I was looking for a herb, and when I entered the garden I saw this door open. I came out here and found you sitting on the ground. Why do you ask?'

Eadulf instinctively felt that the young apothecary was lying.

'And you saw no one else? You did not see any sign of a small sailboat down there?' He indicated the seashore below them.

'A sailboat? I have seen nothing, I assure you.'

'Very well, give me a hand back to your rooms and let us get this wound dressed. Then I must find Fidelma.'

'Where have you been?' was Fidelma's first question when Eadulf returned to the guest chamber. Her second question, on seeing his bandaged forehead, was: 'What has happened to you now?'

She had returned to the room and, having found it empty, was about to set out in search of him. Eadulf told her briefly of his adventure.

'So you saw Iarnbud too,' she breathed softly when he had finished.

He was surprised. 'You saw him as well?'

'Only for a second. He was in the villa and I just caught sight of him vanishing through a door. But when I tried to follow, the bolt had been secured on the other side.'

'If Iarnbud is here, that means Iuna is here.'

'That is logical. But Trifina does not want us to know that. Why?'

Eadulf grimaced. 'I would wager it has something to do with that stone building outside the wall of the villa. There was a strange smell hanging over that place, a smell that I can't quite identify.'

'You suspect that this apothecary, Heraclius, was the one who knocked you out?'

'I can't see who else it could have been.'

'Why would he do so?'

'To prevent me examining the interior of the hut or challenging Iarnbud.'

'You say that the door was closed. He could have simply asked you to leave, without knocking you out.'

'Perhaps.'

Fidelma hesitated a moment or two and then said: 'Well, let us both go and examine this place to satisfy our curiosity.'

'Heraclius might now be on his guard against me returning to the hut,' Eadulf said doubtfully.

'Or perhaps, having dealt with you – if it *was* he who knocked you out – he might be complacent that you would never return so quickly. Anyway, you say that the building is outside the villa on the eastern side of the wall?'

Eadulf nodded.

'Then if we leave the villa in some other spot and follow the walls round, we might approach it unseen rather than attempt to go through the kitchen area and the herb garden.'

They left the room and went down to the lower floor. It seemed deserted, but it was no use going through the main door, for there were bound to be guards outside. Fidelma strode determinedly along the lower corridor until she found a door that opened onto a veranda overlooking a garden with a surrounding high wall. The couple stood for a moment examining what must be the outer wall of the villa complex.

Eadulf touched her arm and silently pointed.

There was a small door in the wall.

She nodded and they forced themselves to stroll casually across the garden towards it, pretending to be deep in conversation. If they were seen, then they would not arouse immediate suspicion. The door proved to be so small, they had to bend to it. It was barred on the inner side and Eadulf found it easy to slide the wooden bar back and push the door outward. They slipped through it without trouble and Eadulf pushed the door back into place again.

For a moment or two they stood breathing quickly, waiting for some shout which would have announced they had been observed.

Keeping close to the wall, they moved within its shadow to the corner that marked the north-eastern end. There was still no one in sight and no one to challenge them. The sea before them was empty, apart from a few distant sails, faint outlines on the sparkling waters.

Once more they hurried along, towards the stone cabin that Eadulf had identified.

'This is it.' Eadulf felt relief as they came to the mysterious building. At least no one had spotted them so far.

The stone building seemed isolated.

The odour reached their nostrils at the same time.

'It seems like sulphur, but there is something different about it,' Fidelma mused thoughtfully.

Eadulf went forward and tried the handle.

'It's locked,' he announced, glancing downwards and finding an iron lock on the wooden door.

'Why are you surprised?' Fidelma muttered in vexation. 'If there is something in here which no one is permitted to see, then it would scarcely be left open.'

There was no sign of a key anywhere. Then Eadulf suddenly remembered the key hanging inside the door where Heraclius had his dispensary. An idea occurred to him.

'There was a key hanging in the apothecary's room. That might be the one to this door.'

Fidelma gestured impatiently. 'Then go and get it. You'll have to chance being seen in the kitchen area, after all.'

Eadulf hurried to the door of the walled herb garden. He was surprised to find that it had been left unsecured. He crossed the garden swiftly and slowly tried the handle of the inner door. Glancing into the courtyard beyond, he found it just as deserted as it was before. He shrugged at his luck. So he and Fidelma had made their circumnavigation of the villa for nothing. They could have come this quicker way.

It seemed that luck was with him all the way, for the kitchen area was devoid of movement and the apothecary's room was still open.

He almost grabbed the key that hung from the hook inside and, clutching it tightly, he broke into a trot as he hurried back and breathlessly rejoined Fidelma. She had taken the opportunity to rest and was sitting with her back against the stone hut, looking moodily out over the waters.

'Well?' she enquired.

'I have it,' muttered Eadulf, and quickly inserted the key into the lock. It fitted. In his nervousness it took him a few attempts to turn it but finally it clicked and he pushed the door open.

Fidelma had risen and was at his shoulder as he moved into the noxious-smelling single room of the building. Two windows let in a bright light from the sea and there was no need for an artificial light. Perhaps it was just as well, for the smell of sulphur was overpowering and Eadulf knew that

it could be flammable. The place was similar to an apothecary's shop, for there were various jars of strange-looking
concoctions on shelves around the room and a workbench.
And in one corner was a potter's wheel.

'Pottery? And why the sulphur, I wonder?' Eadulf mused.

Fidelma had picked up some branches of an evergreen
from a workbench and peered at it curiously.

'It looks as if someone has been extracting the resin from
this. What do you make of it, Eadulf?'

He shook his head. 'This is beyond me,' he admitted. 'And
– look!'

Near the potter's wheel, standing along the wall, was a line
of newly made pots. Except on closer inspection they were
not pots at all. They were round balls the size of a man's
head. There was neither hole nor means of ingress into them.
Eadulf bent down to pick one up and found that it was not
very heavy. The balls were obviously hollow, but there was
a strange imbalance to the one he was holding. He raised it
and jerked it from side to side.

'It is hollow but I think there is liquid inside,' he announced.

'Break one open and let us see,' advised Fidelma. 'Whoever
is mixing strange potions here, I wonder why he keeps it so
secret.'

Eadulf raised the ball in both hands, ready to smash it on
the ground.

'Stop!' cried a sharp voice. 'Stay absolutely still, if you
value your lives!'

CHAPTER THIRTEEN

The young apothecary, Heraclius, stood in the doorway. There was an expression akin to horror on his face.

Eadulf froze, the clay ball in his hands, staring at him in wonder. There was no doubting the intensity of fear in the young man's tone.

'What . . . ?' began Eadulf.

'Put it down on the floor and do it gently!' ordered Heraclius.

Eadulf slowly replaced the ball on the ground.

'Now step away from it,' instructed the young man, still tense.

As Eadulf did so, the young man exhaled in relief and seemed to relax his body. It lasted no more than a moment before a look of anger crossed his features.

'How *dare* you break into this hut!'

'We did not break in,' Fidelma corrected him pedantically. 'You will see that we opened the door and entered.'

'Having stolen the key from my dispensary,' Heraclius

replied, not misled by semantics. 'This is my personal domain and no one comes here but me.'

'You seem to have something to hide,' she replied, looking towards the clay balls.

'Only from prying eyes and idiots,' came the uncompromising response. 'You are not idiots so you must be spies. Spies of the *Koulm ar Maro*! Now you will come out – but make no attempt to escape. There are guards within call. We will go to see the lady Trifina.'

Fidelma exchanged a glance with Eadulf and then shrugged. They had no other choice.

They left the hut. Heraclius drew the door shut and turned the key in the lock. Making sure it was secure, he held the key firmly in his hand and motioned them back through the walled herb garden, then through the cooking area of the villa and into the main corridor, halting finally outside the room where Trifina had first received Fidelma. Heraclius addressed the warrior who stood on guard outside and the man knocked on the door. Heraclius disappeared inside.

The guard fixed them with a watchful glare, with his hand resting ready on his sword hilt.

'What now?' muttered Eadulf.

'Now we will have to see what Trifina has to say,' shrugged Fidelma. 'There is no other course.'

In fact, it was only moments before the door opened and the young apothecary motioned them inside.

Trifina stood in front of the fire with a frown of annoyance on her face. She said something to Heraclius who gave a short bow towards her and left the room, closing the door behind him.

Trifina went to a table and poured red wine into a glass. She gazed at it thoughtfully for a moment and then held it out towards Fidelma with a look of interrogation. Fidelma shook her head. Eadulf, when it was offered to him, moved forward and took the glass. His thought was that someone who offers you wine is not going to kill you – at least, not immediately. Trifina poured another glass for herself and sat down, indicating with her free hand the chairs before her. Fidelma sank into the seat while Eadulf, feeling like a naughty child summoned before its parent, nervously seated himself.

'So,' Trifina said at last, shaking her head sadly, 'what am I to do with you?'

'It is not for me to advise you, lady,' replied Fidelma softly.

Trifina actually chuckled. 'Indeed not. Yet you are wandering round my villa, prying into things. I thought I made it clear that you are in territory that does not concern you.'

Fidelma decided to be blunt.

'That depends what those things are. I told you that Riwanon asked me to investigate the mystery . . .'

'The mystery of Abbot Maelcar's death – which happened in Brilhag. Why are you really here?'

'The location where a murder is committed does not imply that the murderer is to be found on the same spot,' responded Fidelma.

'That may be true,' agreed Trifina, her voice tight. 'I presume that you suspect me of somehow engineering the

Abbot's fate, even though I was not at Brilhag when he was killed?'

'I do not accuse you. I simply do not like mysteries.'

'Did you expect to find a solution in the workshop of Heraclius, perhaps? Heraclius is our apothecary and he has full permission to pursue his experiments in pursuit of his understanding of herbs and medicines.'

'Earlier this afternoon I was seeking Fidelma,' Eadulf interrupted, feeling he should justify himself. 'By chance I happened to stroll through the walled garden and out to where this stone building is. I went quite innocently to examine it when I was knocked unconscious. Heraclius was nearby when I came to. I determined that Fidelma and I should investigate further.'

Trifina smiled cynically at him.

'You are a truly loyal soul, Eadulf. This lady was nearly responsible for causing your death a few hours ago. Yet you rise from your sickbed to go sleuthing for her. And now you are claiming that Heraclius knocked you on the head, to . . . what? To stop you seeing into his workshop? Couldn't he have asked you simply to leave?'

Eadulf thrust out his chin aggressively.

'I hadn't even seen inside it then. I was near it when I heard a shout and, looking below, I saw Iarnbud in a boat. That was when I was knocked on the head. Yet I am told you claim Iarnbud was not on this island.'

At the name of Iarnbud, Trifina set down her wine glass.

'You saw *Iarnbud*?' she demanded. A flush had come to her face.

'He was alone in the sailboat that Fidelma and I followed from Brilhag. However, there was no sign of Iuna in it.'

Fidelma's mouth tightened, and the line of Caesar as he crossed the Rubicon came into her mind. *Alea iacta est.* Truly, the die is cast. So she added: 'I too saw Iarnbud – in this villa. Do you still deny he and Iuna are here?'

Trifina sat back and regarded them both with a long scrutiny.

'I see.' The words were spoken almost as a whisper. 'So, Eadulf, you saw Iarnbud and, a moment later, you say that you were knocked out?'

'As I said, Heraclius was standing near me when I came to. I presumed that he had knocked me out rather than let me see what was in the hut. That's why I went back there with Fidelma.'

'Did Heraclius admit that he did so?' Trifina asked mildly.

'Would he admit it if he had done so?' Eadulf countered.

'As I have pointed out, if he wanted to prevent you, all he had to do was tell you not to go there. After all, the door was locked, wasn't it?'

Eadulf flushed, for it was almost word for word what Fidelma had remarked. He did not reply.

'Surely a locked door should have been enough to tell you that your attentions were not wanted there? The place is Heraclius' workshop where some of his mixtures might be dangerous if touched without supervision.'

'What of Iarnbud?' demanded Eadulf.

'Iarnbud,' repeated Trifina. There was a silence for a while before she spoke again, turning to Fidelma. 'You seem to take this commission seriously, Fidelma – the one from Riwanon to find Abbot Maelcar's assassin.'

'I take all commissions seriously. I am a *dálaigh* . . .' Fidelma searched for the right Latin word. 'I am a *jurisconsultus*, a lawyer. This is my job.'

'As I remarked before, I find it hard to accept that Riwanon would give such a task to a foreigner who does not speak our language or know our laws. But,' Trifina held up her hand as Fidelma was about to speak, 'I accept your word that this is what has been done. You seem also to believe that Abbot Maelcar's assassin is connected with the attack on your ship.'

'I do. And who or what is the *Koulm ar Maro* – and why would Heraclius conclude we are spies of whoever it is?'

There was another pause.

'I am going to be honest with you, Fidelma of Hibernia,' Trifina said slowly, after she had taken a sip or two of wine. Then she glanced at Eadulf. 'Honest with you both, that is.'

They waited patiently.

'I admit that Iarnbud was here, but deny that Iuna came with him. I was aware that about two weeks ago, a ship flying the emblem of our family, the flag of the *mac'htiern* of Brilhag, started to conduct raids around this coast. Each raid became more audacious than the last. Those who saw this ship not only reported that it flew the flag bearing the white dove emblem, but that on its prow it had carved in wood the figure of a dove.'

'That was the ship that attacked the *Barnacle Goose*,' Eadulf confirmed.

'Let me state clearly to you both, this ship is *not* under

the authority of my father nor of any member of my family. If you believe that we are involved with this sea raider, then you are mistaken.'

Fidelma looked deeply into the eyes of Trifina and was impressed with the frankness she saw there.

'Then why is there all this mystery?' she asked. 'Why do you behave as if you have something to hide?'

Trifina made a small cutting motion with her hand.

'Whoever is behind these attacks is using our emblem purposely to bring discredit upon my family. There can be no other explanation. Some of the merchants and farmers who have suffered losses from these pirates are already stirring the countryside against us, poisoning the people's minds against us.'

'And what have you done to counter these stories?' Eadulf asked.

'It was not until yesterday that I heard about the details of the attack on your ship – that a prince of your country was murdered and that you had escaped. I then heard of the slaughter of Biscam and his men and I realised that things were becoming serious. There had been no significant casualties until this time. But, for the last few days, we have been trying to track down this ship that we have named *Koulm ar Maro*, the Dove of Death. Our flag with the dove symbolises peace, but this dove brings only death and destruction. The more attacks it makes bearing our family's emblem, the more people suspect we are responsible.'

'And for what reason do you think the raiders are trying to impugn your family in this manner?' asked Fidelma. She suddenly realised that the name was close to her own language: *colm marbh* – the dove of death.

'So that we may be dispossessed of our lands and titles. There can be no other reason.'

'So the flag is deliberately flown or planted to mislead people. You used the term "we" when you mentioned that you have been trying to track down the raider. Who is "we"?'

'Bleidbara and I. Last night we decided to fit out the *Morvran* . . . It is really my father's ship, the name means the Cormorant, which was the warship that you saw. We have fitted her out to search the Morbihan, to find the sea raider.'

The cormorant, with its dark body and its yellow to orange bill, was exactly how the ship that Fidelma had seen a short while before had been painted.

'And the lights we saw on the shore below Brilhag the other night?' Eadulf asked.

'We told you the truth about it. Bleidbara and I came to the conclusion that this *Koulm ar Maro* must be hiding in these waters.'

'I see. Does your father approve of this?'

'My father has been away from Brilhag for several weeks in Naoned. He has probably not heard the news of the activities of the *Koulm ar Maro* yet. When he returns, he will be made aware by the growing hostility of the people here, and we must have a solution because he will be in the company of King Alain – and the people will exhort Alain to punish us for these attacks for which we are not responsible.'

'So it is only you, your brother and Bleidbara who know of this?' Fidelma asked.

To her surprise, Trifina shook her head. 'My brother Macliau does not know what Bleidbara and I are doing.'

'Why is that?' Fidelma asked sharply.

'Because Macliau cares for little outside of his hunting, drinking and his pursuit of women.' Trifina's voice had a disapproving tone.

'Argantken?'

'She is his current dalliance,' Trifina sniffed, making her disdain abundantly clear. 'Argantken is the daughter of a local farmer called Barbatil. Macliau would not have dared to bring her to my father's fortress had he been there.'

'So your brother . . . ?'

'Is a silly wastrel, indulged by my father after the death of my mother.' There was no vehemence in her tone. She stated her view as a simple fact. 'If there is justice, he will not succeed my father as the *mac'htiern*.'

'But you would be willing to put yourself forward to the office?' Fidelma suggested.

'In the old days, the women of our people could succeed if there were no suitable male of the family to do so. I am told in your country of Hibernia that this is still so. However, our people have become too Romanised. Five centuries of rule from Rome has all but destroyed our ancestral ways of life.'

Fidelma agreed that there was nothing to prevent women rising to such power among her people.

'So who else of your household is in this secret? Iuna?'

Trifina shook her head quickly, saying, 'Only Bleidbara and Iarnbud.'

'Iarnbud? You trust him in this matter?' Fidelma was surprised.

'He has supported our house since before I was born. He has the freedom to sail the waters of the Morbihan and to scour the forests around here, and thus is able to report on any gathering of warriors who might be connected with these raids.'

'So that was what he was doing on this island . . . coming to report to you. Then why did he bring Iuna with him?'

'He did not mention her when I saw him. Nor was there any sight of Iuna in his boat when he arrived.'

'You mentioned Iuna to him? I presume he is no longer here?'

'He sailed off not long ago, and I did not mention your claim to him because I felt you were mistaken. There is no way he would have allowed Iuna to know our plans.'

'Had he brought you any news?'

'Only about the arrival of Riwanon and the death of Abbot Maelcar.'

'And that is why you were not surprised when I gave you the news?'

Trifina nodded grudgingly. 'You have sharp eyes, Fidelma. That was indeed why,' she confirmed.

'But so far as you know, Iuna was not with him?'

'As I have said.'

'Iuna may be on this island.' Eadulf pointed out the obvious conclusion.

'Impossible! I trust Iarnbud entirely. But as you are not convinced, I will ask my guards to make a search.' Trifina called to the guard outside the door and when he entered, she issued the instructions.

'It is still difficult to see a reason why this *Koulm ar Maro* – we may as well use the name for the person behind the raiders as well as the ship – should be so set on bringing your family into disrepute – *and* by such extreme means.' Fidelma took up the theme that was worrying her once again.

'If we knew that, we might know who is behind this,' Trifina said simply.

'Then let us consider why your family might have incurred the wrath of someone to this extent. The *mac'htiern* of Brilhag is an ancient noble family of this area, so I am told. In fact, your father's ancestors were kings of this land not so long ago?'

'The emphasis is on "were",' replied Trifina. 'We are no threat to anyone now.'

'Brother Metellus spoke about your family, but I have forgotten the details. Tell me the situation so that I can understand it better.'

'This was once the kingdom of Bro-Erech, which used to be the largest of the kingdoms of this land of Armorica. That was the old Gaulish name, which meant "the land before the sea". That has now been displaced. Now it is called "Little Britain" because of the many settlements from Britain in these last two centuries.'

'That I have understood,' Fidelma said.

'There was Bro-Erech and then to the north of us was Domnonia and to the west was Bro-Gernev. There were smaller kingdoms such as Bro-Leon and also Pou-Kaer, but these are no more; both were absorbed many years ago. So now there are three large kingdoms.'

Fidelma acknowledged that she was still following.

'Domnonia, while not as large as Bro-Erech, became very influential and was bearing the brunt of attacks by the Franks and Saxons along the northern coast and eastern borders. Just before I was born, Domnonia was ruled by Judicael who defeated the Franks twice in great battles and even travelled to the court of the Frankish King Dagobert in Paris to conclude a treaty of peace. Judicael claimed to be King of all the Bretons. The scribes wrote that the terror of his name alone was sufficient to keep evil men from violence. Although he was said to be mighty and brave in battle, he eventually decided to follow the religious life and abdicated, retiring to an abbey in Brekilien.'

'Very well. But how does this tie in with your family and Bro-Erech?' Fidelma asked, slightly impatient.

'At the time when Judicael ruled in Domnonia, my family ruled here in Bro-Erech. Just before I was born, my great-grandfather Canao, the third of his name to rule here, died. It was then that Judicael claimed the kingship. He maintained that Waroch, the greatest of our Kings, was also his own ancestor and that Waroch's daughter, Trifina, after whom I take my name, was his own grandmother. There was a dispute and my grandfather, called Macliau, was defeated. Thus he and my father after him became only the lords of Brilhag.'

'Your brother mentioned this and explained the symbol of your flag. He also said that one day, he hoped to restore the family to their rightful place. Their place as kings – is that what he meant?'

Trifina laughed sardonically.

'That is vain talk. My brother is a fool and a dreamer. We must accept reality now. Canao, the last of our family to rule here, was not a nice man. In fact, by all accounts, he was mad. He killed three brothers to secure the throne. Our family are better off out of such politics.'

'Yet someone is bringing you back into that world,' Fidelma said thoughtfully.

'You mean that this is a way to discredit our family in case we ever made the claim against the King?'

'That might be a reasonable theory. What is your family's relationship with King Alain?'

'Alain is the son of Judicael but he succeeded to the kingship after his brother Urbien, who died of the Yellow Plague, so he was not involved in the struggle between my grandfather and his. My father is now a close friend of his. Alain is fair-minded and his rule brings prosperity to us all.'

'So you do not think there is a chance that he would be regarding your father or your family with suspicion?'

'I doubt it. As I said, he is a good friend to my father. Even if my brother's silly ideas were known to him, he would treat them with the contempt they deserve.'

'Nevertheless, in looking for motivation to back your theory that this *Koulm ar Maro* is trying to discredit your family, this seems to be the only area where we can find any plausible grounds.'

There was a sudden knock on the door and, at Trifina's summons, one of the guards opened it and spoke rapidly.

'A search of the villa and island has not revealed Iuna,' Trifina interpreted. 'I did not expect it to.'

'Then where did she disembark from Iarnbud's boat?' Fidelma began. 'We must find—'

Another warrior suddenly pushed his way unannounced into the room. He looked embarrassed as he saw Fidelma and Eadulf. Trifina seemed to recognise him for her features changed and she said something quickly. The man spoke at a breathless rate. Fidelma's ears were growing used to the sounds of the language. Now she was able to pick up the words *Koulm ar Maro* and then the name of Macliau.

Trifina went deathly white and half-rose before slumping back in her chair.

'What is it?' Fidelma demanded. 'What news has he brought?'

The girl turned anguished eyes on them.

'This man brings a message from Bleidbara – from Brilhag. He says that the local people claim to have caught the Dove of Death, the murderer, and are about to execute him.'

'Who is it?' demanded Fidelma.

'Macliau, my brother!'

CHAPTER FOURTEEN

❧

It did not take them long to return to Brilhag in the same fast skiff that had brought the messenger to Trifina. She, with Fidelma, Eadulf and three warriors, had immediately set out for the fortress on the peninsula of Rhuis. A worried-looking Bleidbara greeted them as they landed on the quay just below the fortress. He looked surprised for a moment at seeing Fidelma and Eadulf in the party.

Helping her from the boat, Bleidbara began to speak rapidly, but Trifina said something and he reverted to Latin.

'The message came from Brother Metellus just after I returned,' he said. 'Brother Metellus says that Macliau had reached the abbey with a mob on his heels crying for his blood. They would have killed him there and then, but Macliau pleaded for sanctuary. Brother Metellus, acting for the community, granted it.'

'A mob? Who constitutes this mob?' demanded Trifina.

'Local people, farmers, fishermen. They are led by Barbatil.'

Trifina recognised the name. 'The father of Argantken?'

'The same. The situation is that despite sanctuary having
been given, they have surrounded the abbey and are preparing
to attack to take Macliau away by force and kill him. The
monks are threatening them with damnation if they enter the
chapel where he has taken refuge. Such threats will not keep
their anger at bay for long, however.'

'And this mob are claiming Macliau is the Dove of Death
– the leader of the raiders? They are mad!' Trifina was angry.
'Very well. Raise your warriors and we will teach them a
lesson they won't forget!'

'I have already despatched a dozen warriors to the abbey
with Boric in command,' Bleidbara offered. 'I had told them
to defend Macliau and the monks, but only if their lives are
in jeopardy.'

Fidelma reached forward and caught the girl's arm.

'Calm yourself,' she admonished. 'Let us establish the
facts. I agree we must stop this mob from visiting harm on
Macliau, but we know how people are able to blame Brilhag
for these attacks. In no way should you bring force to bear
against these people until we have a chance to reason with
them.'

Bleidbara added: 'We need to keep warriors here in case
this is a trick to make us leave Brilhag unguarded and Riwanon
unprotected.'

'I am not concerned with Riwanon's safety but that of
my brother,' snapped Trifina. She thought for a moment.
'We will take these men,' she pointed to the warriors who
had accompanied her from Govihan, 'and ride for the
abbey.'

'Can you give Eadulf and me horses?' asked Fidelma. 'We need to come with you.'

Eadulf gave an inward groan. The idea of confronting an angry mob with a few warriors and two women was not his idea of being prudent.

As they made their way into the fortress, Bleidbara was already shouting orders for horses to be saddled. Budic agreed to command the warriors remaining in Brilhag.

It was as they were riding out of the gates of the fortress that something made Fidelma glance back over her shoulder. Standing on the steps before the great hall, watching their departure, was Iuna. For a moment, Fidelma contemplated reining in her horse and turning back to question the girl, but she was swept along in the group of riders, whose priority was to get to the abbey. The mystery of Iuna would have to wait.

The ride to the abbey of the Blessed Gildas was accomplished at breakneck speed. Bleidbara and a warrior led the way, Trifina and Fidelma came next, then Eadulf, with two warriors behind him. The pace of Eadulf's mount was thus forced by those in front and behind, so that Eadulf, as bad a horseman as he was a sailor, simply clung to his mount and hoped for the best. His headache had returned and the events of the day seemed to be overtaking him. Already the summer day was drawing to a close, the sky darkening. Could it have really been only this morning that he had set out in a sailboat with Fidelma?

The small band of riders raced through the thick forests along the track which led across the peninsula from Brilhag directly to the abbey buildings. As they neared the abbey, the sound of raucous shouting could be clearly heard.

Bleidbara slowed the pace and the party trotted through outlying buildings into the quadrangle that lay before the chapel of the community.

The mob was not as big as Eadulf had expected, though it was big enough. There were some forty or fifty people gathered in front of the chapel steps, all of them men, waving an assortment of weapons, mainly agricultural implements, and burning torches. They were sturdy men who, from their appearance, laboured on the land. Around the front of the chapel, weapons at the ready, a few warriors stood facing them, obviously the men that Bleidbara had sent on before.

In front of them, hands held up in supplication, as if trying to quieten the mob, stood Brother Metellus. Some of the other religious of the community stood nervously by him.

Bleidbara, at a quick trot, swung his group of riders around the mob – who started to yowl with derision when they saw them. The warriors dismounted swiftly, one grabbing the horses and leading them to a secure place at a rail by the side of the chapel before rejoining his companions. They reinforced the line of stoic men facing the crowd. Bleidbara led Trifina, Fidelma and Eadulf behind to where an anxious Brother Metellus was standing.

'There will be no reasoning with this crowd much longer,' the Brother said.

'Tell us the story as quickly as you can,' Fidelma said. 'What has happened?'

'Macliau came running into the community. He was in a

bad condition – bleeding from some wounds, his clothes dishevelled. On his heels came some of these people.' He jerked his head towards the mob. 'They wanted to kill him. They accused him of being a murderer and thief, saying he is the leader of raiders who have been attacking their settlements for the last week. Macliau demanded sanctuary in our chapel and I took the decision to give it to him, now that the Abbot no longer lives.'

'Where is my brother?' Trifina demanded.

'In the chapel behind us,' replied Brother Metellus.

Without another word, Trifina turned and went inside.

Fidelma frowned as she surveyed the angry crowd.

'From half a dozen men, over the last few hours, the mob has grown,' Brother Metellus told her. 'Any moment, they will have gathered enough courage to brush us aside.'

'I am told someone called Barbatil leads this crowd. Who is he?'

Brother Metellus cast an eye towards the front of the mob.

'That man there.' He pointed to a middle-aged, stocky and muscular-looking man, with greying hair. He was weatherbeaten, though his cheeks showed a ruddy complexion. His garb and appearance clearly revealed him to be a farmer.

'I need you to come with me as interpreter,' said Fidelma. She glanced at Eadulf. 'Stay here. Only Brother Metellus and I will go forward.'

Then, without another word, Fidelma went down the few steps to the front of the crowd. Brother Metellus was clearly not happy, but dutifully followed at her shoulder.

The crowd grew silent and even fell back a little as she

came forward with apparent confidence. Fidelma went straight to the man Brother Metellus had pointed out.

'I am told that your name is Barbatil and that you accused Macliau, the son of the *mac'htiern* of Brilhag, of murder,' she said without preamble.

Brother Metellus duly translated this.

The stocky farmer's eyes narrowed. There was anger in every fibre of his body.

'I am Barbatil, and I accuse him. We will have vengeance!'

'If your accusation is proved, then you shall have justice,' replied Fidelma. 'But this is not the way to secure it.'

'What do foreigners know about the injustices that are happening here?' replied the farmer. He pointed to Brother Metellus. 'He is from Rome and God alone knows where *you* are from!'

Fidelma advised him that she was a lawyer in her own country of Hibernia and went on: 'It is the custom among all civilised countries to state your evidence when you accuse somebody.'

'You should know that during the last two weeks, warriors have been raiding our farms and settlements. They sail in a ship bearing the flag of the *mac'htiern* above it – the flag of our lord of Brilhag, who is supposed to be our protector – not our persecutor!'

'Anyone can raise a flag,' pointed out Fidelma. 'Is that your only evidence?'

The farmer seemed to grow even angrier.

'It is not. The young lord, Macliau,' he almost spat the name, 'has a reputation here. No man's daughter is safe. He takes his pleasures and we have to pay for them.'

Fidelma remembered Trifina's estimation of her brother. Then she recalled that Trifina had identified Barbatil as the father of Argantken, Macliau's companion at the fortress.

'A man's character as a womaniser does not make him a murderer,' she replied.

'No woman is safe from his lechery – and even the Church,' Barbatil gestured towards Brother Metellus, 'does not chide him for his debauchery – just because he is the son of the *mac'htiern* whose flag now inspires terror throughout this peninsula.'

'You say that men bearing the emblem of Brilhag made these raids. Did you ever go to demand an explanation from Brilhag?'

'At first we did,' blustered Barbatil. 'We saw the lady Trifina. She spoke in the absence of her father, Lord Canao. Macliau was not there. She claimed that no warriors of Brilhag were involved. She promised that she would take up our cause and find out who these people were. Nothing has been done.'

'I ask, yet again, where is your evidence that Macliau is responsible?' Fidelma demanded doggedly.

'Evidence? You ask for evidence?' Spittle edged the farmer's mouth. 'Did not this immoral libertine debauch my own daughter, Argantken! I accuse him of murder in her name!'

There was an angry murmur when the girl's name was pronounced.

'If Argantken is accusing him of murder, let her come forward and do so,' Fidelma said stubbornly.

The anger of the crowd seemed to increase.

'She cannot!' replied the farmer, barely keeping his temper. 'For *she* was his victim!'

Fidelma stared at Barbatil for a moment, taking in his words.

'Argantken, your daughter, has been murdered?'

'Have I not said as much?'

Fidelma's mind raced for a moment or two and then she faced the man with a softened expression.

'I am sorry for your trouble, my friend. But we must have some facts to work on, to resolve this matter. Rest assured, justice will be yours. But, I say again, it will be justice – *and not revenge*. Tell me the facts as you know them.'

The shoulders of the farmer, Barbatil, slumped a little as if there were a heavy weight on them.

'It was not long ago that Macliau turned his lustful attention on my daughter. She is . . . she was . . . attractive – the apple of her mother's eye and of mine too. She was a good daughter until he rode by our farmhouse one morning and coaxed her with honeyed words to ride away with him. She believed his promises of marriage and riches – as if the daughter of a poor farmer could ever become wife to the lord of Brilhag. She was too naïve and too trusting.'

'Go on,' coaxed Fidelma.

'I pleaded with her to return to the farm, but she would have none of it. She believed that scoundrel's lies and promises. Yesterday morning, word came to me that Argantken and Macliau had been seen riding along the coast at Kerignard, which is not far from my farm. I decided to make one last attempt to persuade my daughter to come back to her mother's home. But knowing that Macliau had some warriors with him, I asked some of my neighbours to go with me.'

'How many?' Fidelma interrupted.

'Two or three of those who are here with me now.' Barbatil gestured to those around him, who muttered in agreement.

'And then?'

'We went to Kerignard. I knew the little ruined oratory where Macliau had camped on other hunting trips. I suspected he would be there.'

'A ruined oratory?'

'It is an old stone oratory along that coast by Kerignard. There are cliffs all along that coast, and on the top of them is the oratory, which was built and deserted many years ago.'

'And was he there?'

'When we arrived we saw no sign of his warriors or huntsmen. I was not even going to look in the oratory until I realised that there was a loose horse wandering behind it. I went to the oratory – there was no door, it had rotted away years before, so the place was open – and the first thing I saw was Macliau, lying on the floor in a drunken stupor.'

'How did you know that he was drunk?'

'The smell of intoxicating liquor was strong. Macliau smelled as if he had just crawled out of a cider vat.'

'So he was lying there drunk. What then?' continued Fidelma, trying to keep the man calm.

'Beside him on the ground was . . . was my daughter! Argantken.' His voice caught. 'She was dead. There was blood all over the place. A dagger, Macliau's dagger, was buried in her lifeless form.'

'How do you know it was Macliau's dagger?'

'Everyone knows the emblem of the lords of Brilhag. It bore the emblem of the dove . . . the emblem of peace.'

His voice ended in a cry of almost physical pain. The crowd growled ominously and seemed to surge forward.

'Patience!' cried Fidelma, through the translation of Brother Metellus. 'I have promised this man justice but I need answers to more questions.'

She turned back to Barbatil.

'A few more questions,' she repeated softly. 'For your daughter will not rest quietly if the truth remains unknown.'

'What more do you want?' grunted the farmer, recovering his composure. 'The evidence explains itself.'

'Having come on this terrible scene, what did you do?'

'One of my neighbours took the dagger from her breast and covered her body.'

'Do you still have the dagger?'

'Coric, do you still have the dagger?' asked the farmer, turning to one of his companions.

A small man, whose short stature belied his thick, muscular body, came forward and held up a knife. Fidelma took it: it was exactly the same design as the one she had found in the body of Abbot Maelcar. The same emblem of a dove was engraved on it.

'I will keep this as evidence,' she said. 'And then . . . what of Macliau? What did you do then?'

The farmer scowled. 'He was drunk. We tried to rouse him. We hit him across the cheeks, but he was too far gone to respond. So we carried him outside and threw him in a stream. Even then it took us time to make the swine come to and comprehend his surroundings. Finally we told him that we were going to hang him for what he had done.'

The little man, the one who had been addressed as Coric, spoke for the first time.

'He started weeping like a child, pleading with us for his life, even claiming that he was not responsible and knew nothing of the killing. The lies that poured from his cowardly mouth made us sick.'

'We took Argantken's body back to my farm,' continued Barbatil, 'so that my wife and family could mourn her in the proper manner. And we took Macliau to my pigpen and locked him in. We decided that we would hang him after we had interred my daughter's body. That was to be midday today.'

'So what happened?'

'We buried my daughter. All these good folks came,' he encompassed his companions with a motion of his arm. 'Then we went to the pigpen. We found Macliau had managed to break free. We soon picked up his trail and it led us here. The coward has taken refuge in the chapel but we will drag him out like the animal he is and—'

'You will do no such thing. I have promised you justice and we,' Fidelma threw an arm towards the religious and the warriors, 'will not countenance vengeance. Vengeance only breeds more vengeance. Do you know what sanctuary is?'

Barbatil snorted derisively, replying, 'Just a cunning means to prevent the guilty from punishment.'

'No, my friend, it is a means to prevent injustice. The Church recognises the right of giving protection to all peoples.

Asylum is recognised by all civilised people, and rules and laws are devised to govern it. For a person to qualify for the protection of the Church there are rules, my friend. Rules not only for them to qualify, but rules as to how long that protection may be extended. So I tell you this: I must now hear what the accused has to say in his defence. When the evidence is heard, then – and only then – can a judgement be made.'

There was a muttering of discontent among the crowd.

Fidelma continued to speak directly to Barbatil through Brother Metellus.

'You hold the decision, my friend. You lead these people. Your word may stop your friends from pursuing a misguided course. Your word may even stop them squandering their blood needlessly for, make no mistake, the warriors you see before you will defend this right of sanctuary. Not to defend Macliau, but to defend a higher principle – the right of the Church to offer sanctuary. They will sell their lives dearly in this cause. Are you prepared for this unnecessary effusion of blood? Death of many for the pursuit of vengeance? Do you believe your daughter would rest happy in the knowledge that such injustice was carried out in her name?'

She saw the man wavering and she prayed that Brother Metellus was translating her words with the same eloquence as she was trying to give them.

'Send your friends away, so that they may not die this day. Remain here with me and hear the words of Macliau. Then you may see that I am not merely defending him for the sake of who he is, but rather to search for the truth. Out of this truth, justice will come to you.'

The farmer stood hesitantly. Then he sighed deeply and turned, handing his weapon to his companion Coric.

'I will go with the foreigner from Hibernia,' he said slowly. 'Wait for me here, Coric.' Then he turned to the rest and raised his voice. 'Friends, I thank you for what you have done. I am a man who believes in the Church and in the law. And I believe the law is for everyone, not only for our lords. I am going to give this foreign Sister of the Faith a chance to demonstrate that her words are not mere sounds that vanish on the air. I will go with her to see and hear what she intends, and how she will conjure this justice for my family and me. Indeed, justice for all of us who have suffered from the raids of this Dove of Death.'

'What do you want us to do, Barbatil?' cried a voice from the crowd.

'For the moment, disperse to your homes. Disperse, but hold yourselves ready, for if lies are being told here, then these lies must be met by a force that is born of our truth.'

There was a muttering among the crowd but then they slowly turned, in ones and twos, and began to remove from the buildings of the abbey, taking their weapons with them.

Brother Metellus had been sweating in his anxiety and now he almost physically collapsed.

Bleidbara moved in an aggressive manner towards Barbatil. Fidelma saw what was passing in his mind and spoke sharply.

'Bleidbara, I was not amusing myself with false words. Barbatil is under my protection and will not be harmed, for no one can condemn his actions entirely, given what he has suffered. He will come into the chapel and sit unharmed while we question Macliau. Do I make myself clear?'

Bleidbara reddened a little and then he bowed his head stiffly.

'You have made yourself clear, lady.'

Brother Metellus turned to her; the sweat stood out on his forehead and the relief was plain on his features.

'I can only commend your action, for I have never seen a woman stand up to an angry mob and turn their anger to a peaceful solution before. I was afraid for all of us.'

'Yet not so afraid that you were prevented from giving Macliau sanctuary and were prepared to defend your decision with your life,' smiled Fidelma. 'You did the right thing.'

'From time immemorial the right of protection on a holy spot has been inviolable. Of course I could not contemplate giving in before an armed mob,' replied Brother Metellus.

Fidelma glanced to where Coric had gone to sit on a stone wall nearby, still holding the weapons he and Barbatil had brought with them.

'There seem to be some essential witnesses missing,' she said, after a moment's thought.

'Essential witnesses?' queried Bleidbara, puzzled.

'Where are the companions of Macliau? He left Brilhag not only with Argantken but with two huntsmen and two warriors. Where are they?' She turned to Barbatil. 'Did you see any sign of the rest of Macliau's hunting-party when you found him?'

When Brother Metellus had translated this, the farmer shook his head.

'There was no sign of anyone else but the body of my daughter and her murderer.'

'That is a cause of worry,' Fidelma observed. 'Bleidbara, I suggest that you send out a couple of your men in search of these lost souls. You can spare them now. It is of concern that they have deserted Macliau.'

Bleidbara turned to his warriors and relayed the orders to two men, who immediately left on horseback. Meanwhile, Fidelma led her companions into the chapel, leaving the guards and most of the religious outside.

Macliau was slumped on the floor against the altar. He was in a pitiful condition. The stench of stale drink and the excrement of pigs was nauseous. There was blood on his face and clothing, and he was shivering as if with some ague. Trifina was standing over him and her angry voice faded as they entered.

Brother Metellus, hearing Fidelma's sharp intake of breath and the disgust on her face as she viewed Macliau, whispered: 'We have had no time to cleanse him or give him clean clothes.'

'At least give him a chair to sit on,' she instructed. 'By the altar, if he prefers not to leave it,' she added, for she knew that it was in the area of the altar that most churches placed their zone of sanctuary.

Trifina had turned as they approached. Her expression was anxious, but Bleidbara quickly told her what Fidelma had done. Fidelma, by unspoken agreement, took total charge of the situation.

'Barbatil shall sit there where he may observe,' she instructed. 'Brother Metellus, you will have to act as his interpreter for I shall speak to Macliau in Latin. Before you do so, Brother Metellus, send one of your brethren to bring water for Macliau to drink and a cloth to wipe the blood from his face. Bleidbara, help him into that chair.'

Someone had already brought a chair for the dishevelled young man and another for Fidelma. She seated herself opposite to him.

When Macliau, who had remained silent so far, had wiped his face and taken some water, he looked at her with a tearful expression, almost like a little boy lost.

'Why did they have to kill Albiorix, lady?' The words came out as a sob.

She stared, not understanding for a moment, and then she remembered his little terrier.

'Who killed your dog?'

'I don't know. Whoever killed Argantken, I suppose. Such a little dog . . . yet they killed him.'

Fidelma turned to Barbatil. 'You did not mention the dog.'

The farmer shifted uncomfortably on his chair. 'What was there to mention? It was only a dog.'

'It was Albiorix my dog!' wept Macliau.

'Did you kill it?' queried Fidelma sharply of Barbatil.

'Of course not, lady,' replied the farmer. 'We found the dog with its neck broken, lying at his feet. *He* must have killed it.' He jerked his head at Macliau.

'I did not kill him. I would never kill him,' snivelled the son of the lord of Brilhag.

Fidelma turned back, her voice unemotional and commanding.

'Pull yourself together, Macliau,' she remonstrated. 'You are the son of the Lord of Brilhag. Be a man and remember that your companion Argantken, this man's daughter, has died a most bloody and terrible death!'

Macliau blinked rapidly and looked round, as if seeing his surroundings for the first time. An apologetic expression crossed his face. He sniffed and wiped his face again.

'I regret you see me in this position, lady,' he muttered, licking his dry lips.

'And I regret to see any man in such a plight,' Fidelma replied, not unkindly. 'Perhaps you will tell us now what happened. You should start from when you left Brilhag.'

Macliau glanced nervously at Barbatil and then back to Fidelma. His eyes seemed to ask a question.

'It is Barbatil's right to hear what you have to say,' Fidelma said.

Macliau tried to gather his thoughts. 'I was going on a hunt,' he frowned, as if trying to remember.

'You left Brilhag with your companion Argantken,' prompted Fidelma. 'You also had four companions, two warriors and two huntsmen.'

He stared at the stone floor as if examining something there.

'I took my two huntsmen and two warriors,' he agreed slowly. 'I was hoping to return by nightfall.'

'But you did not. So what happened?' pressed Fidelma.

'The hunting was bad. Argantken was tired and so I took her to the old oratory where I thought we could rest and take refreshment. It was Argantken who suggested that while we . . . while we rested, the huntsmen and the others could go and try to track down a wild boar or a deer. So they left us there.'

'In the oratory?'

'Exactly. Night eventually came on and we had lit a fire. I wondered why our companions had not returned. Anyway, we had food that we had taken with us as well as drink, so we decided to remain there and not to attempt the ride back to Brilhag that night.'

'There was no sign of your companions at all?'

'None. I admit it was curious, but I assumed they might have lost the way back to the oratory.'

'Was that feasible? Had you been in this area before?'

Macliau frowned as if apparently thinking about the matter for the first time, before saying, 'It is true that we had hunted before in that very area.'

'So we can discount the idea that they could not find the way back to the oratory. Yet you were not so alarmed that you felt you should return at once to Brilhag?'

'Why would I be alarmed? Oh, you mean the brigands.' Macliau shook his head. 'But I am the son of the *mac'htiern*. Why should we be afraid of robbers?'

'Why, indeed?' Barbatil said loudly, when the remark was translated to him. 'He was one of them.'

Fidelma frowned warningly at the farmer before returning to Macliau.

'So you remained in the oratory that night?'

'Yes. We ate, drank and fell asleep. When I awoke, he,' he

pointed angrily to Barbatil, 'and his friends were throwing me into a stream. Me, the son of their lord!'

Fidelma looked at him closely. 'Are you telling me that you knew nothing between the time you went to sleep and being awoken by Barbatil?'

Macliau kept his eyes on the floor; it seemed as if he was trying to remember. Slowly, his eyes cleared and a look of horror came over his face.

'I was asleep,' he said slowly. 'And . . . and then I came awake and someone was holding me down. Yes, I remember that now. The fire had died and all I could see were shadows. Someone forced my mouth open and someone else was pouring strong drink into me. I thought I was going to drown – I choked and struggled to no avail, and I finally passed out. When I came to, someone was hitting me. Then I was thrown into a cold stream. People were yelling at me. Attacking me. They claimed that I had stabbed Argantken – that she was dead. They bound me and dragged me along. I was still only half-conscious but I saw some of them carrying a body. Argantken's body. Then I knew it was not a bad dream. It was true that the poor girl was dead. I remember that I had that one thought before I passed out again. I do not know how long I was unconscious.'

He paused. No one spoke.

Macliau rubbed a filthy hand across his face, streaked with tears. 'When I came to again, I was in a dark, muddy place. It stank; as I do now. I saw it was a pen, filled with pigs. Then I found the body of Albiorix. They had killed him and thrown his body into the pigsty with me.'

Fidelma held up her hand and addressed Barbatil. 'You did that?'

'I told you – *he* killed the animal. It was *his* dog. So after we have hanged him we shall bury him with the dog on top of him. That is an insult among our people.' The farmer showed no sign of guilt or remorse.

Fidelma exhaled softly and, with a shake of her head, turned back to Macliau again. She raised her hand before he could speak.

'I know you say that you could not kill your dog, but continue: what did you do next?'

'I tried to get out of the pigpen but someone had barred the means of exit. It took me all night, trying my strength against it. It was not long before daybreak that I managed to create a small burrow, whereby I crawled out. I managed to get into some nearby woods, and went through them, wondering where to make for. I had just realised that I was nearer to the abbey than Brilhag when I began to hear the cries of people whom I knew instinctively were my pursuers. I had to make it to the abbey. I ran. I ran as no one has ever had to run before. I nearly fell with exhaustion but then . . . then I saw the chapel and Brother Metellus, and I fell on my knees before him, begging him to shelter me from the fiends who were after me.'

'There were no fiends after you, Macliau,' Fidelma said quietly. 'It was a father who had lost his daughter, in a most violent and tragic way, and the friends and relatives of that father.' She was gazing into the face of the weak, indolent young man, trying to judge the honesty of his words. Finally she shrugged and rose to her feet.

'What of my brother?' Trifina demanded. 'We cannot leave him here in this state.' As much as she had criticised her brother, it seemed that the girl did have affection for her sibling.

'I agree,' Fidelma replied. 'However, as I see it, there is a case to be answered. Macliau must receive a fair hearing before one of your judges – a *bretat*, as you call them.'

'Iarnbud?' suggested Bleidbara.

Fidelma shook her head firmly. 'He is a friend of the lord of Brilhag. No, this judge has to be independent, someone who is beyond reproach. The people of this peninsula must be confident that the judge has no favouritism towards the family of the lord of Brilhag.'

'Then we must send for a judge from Bro-Gernev,' Brother Metellus suggested. 'That is the neighbouring kingdom.'

'Would that be acceptable to you, Barbatil?' asked Fidelma.

The farmer reluctantly indicated that if time was to be wasted in a legal hearing, then such a judge was better than one with a close association with Brilhag.

'Very well.' Fidelma glanced round at the company as they waited expectantly. 'I would suggest that we secure an agreement with Barbatil there. Macliau may return to Brilhag and give his word of honour, swearing as a sacred oath, to present himself before such a judge where this matter can be fairly heard. I presume that you have the same concept in your laws as we of Hibernia have in ours? A man is bound by his honour. He will make no attempt to escape or conceal himself from justice until the time comes for the hearing. And Barbatil must take a similar oath that he will not attempt to harm, or cause to be harmed, Macliau, while he resides at Brilhag awaiting this hearing. Can that be agreed?'

Macliau was hesitant about leaving the safety of what he saw as the sanctuary of the abbey but, if guarantees were given, he agreed to accompany warriors back to Brilhag – but on a curious condition. He demanded that someone went to the farm of Barbatil to recover the carcass of his dog so that he could bury it at Brilhag.

Barbatil took a little more persuading as he saw in the plan some plot to take Macliau to the safety of the fortress and deprive him and his family of justice. Fidelma argued long and ardently through Brother Metellus and finally the farmer agreed.

Brother Metellus immediately despatched a messenger to the neighbouring western kingdom of Bro-Gernev, to ask King Gradlon to send a judge to hear the accusation against Macliau.

'I suggest that we all return to Brilhag now, where we can await the coming of this *bretat* Bro-Gernev,' Fidelma concluded.

'It will probably take three or four days before the man can arrive here,' Brother Metellus warned them. 'Our messenger has to travel west to the city of Kemper, which lies at the junction of two rivers, a few days' ride from here.' He paused and then looked embarrassed. 'I nearly forgot – the Widow Aourken was here earlier and asking to see you.'

Fidelma was momentarily distracted because Trifina was still worried.

'Let us make sure the mob understands that it is to allow us safe passage back to Brilhag.' Trifina had swung round to

Barbatil, who reddened under the fire in her eyes and from the tone of the young woman's voice as she addressed him. Fidelma was not sure what she was telling the man. However, at the end of it, the farmer turned to Fidelma and spoke firmly and with dignity. Brother Metellus interpreted.

'He says that he has given his oath to you, Fidelma. He will abide by it and instruct his family, his neighbours and his friends to keep it.'

'Your word and honour is acceptable.' Fidelma smiled reassuringly at him. 'And Macliau will also keep his word.'

They left the chapel and saw Barbatil walk across to his friend Coric and begin speaking with him. The little man was shaking his head in apparent disagreement but finally he shrugged, shouldered his weapons and strode off into the gathering dusk with Barbatil.

Eadulf saw that Brother Metellus had been talking quietly to Fidelma and she turned to their companions.

'Eadulf and I have some business to discuss with Brother Metellus before we return to Brilhag.'

At once Bleidbara raised objections to leaving them alone there.

'Lady, night will soon be upon us and who knows that the mob may change its mood? It is dangerous to be abroad without escort.'

'I shall have Eadulf and Brother Metellus with me. And we shall not be long following you.'

When Bleidbara insisted, she finally agreed that he should leave one of his men as their escort.

When the rest of the party had left, she turned to Brother

Metellus with a query in her eyes. 'You say that Aourken wanted to see me?'

'She did,' he confirmed.

'Then let us see what it is she wants.'

Brother Metellus led the way along the path to the fishing village, the warrior walking a respectful distance behind. They went directly to Aourken's cottage and found the elderly woman sitting outside, obviously awaiting them. She rose with a smile of welcome.

'I have heard that much has happened since you left me,' she greeted them, and offered them refreshment. 'Biscam and his merchants dead, Abbot Maelcar murdered and Macliau, the son of the *mac'htiern*, accused of killing Argantken. I didn't know Argantken well but her father Barbatil is a good man, a farmer who is well respected on this peninsula.'

'Even good men can be mistaken,' replied Fidelma, after they had all declined the offer of refreshment. 'Brother Metellus tells me that you wanted to see me about something specific.'

The elderly woman nodded. 'You remember that you mentioned a black cat to me?'

When Fidelma indicated that she had, Aourken went to her door and beckoned Fidelma to follow. Then she pointed inside.

Before the hearth, in an old basket, a black cat was curled up. Fidelma took a pace towards it and the cat, hearing the noise, glanced up and gazed at her. Then it rose slowly and stretched on all four legs and let out a 'miaow'.

'Luchtigern!' breathed Fidelma, reaching down to stroke the animal. 'Is it you?'

The cat purred and stretched again. Fidelma checked carefully and felt the telltale lump of pitch still entangled in the fur on the back of its neck.

'It *is* the ship's cat from the *Barnacle Goose*. So it did manage to get to land. I was almost convinced that I was imagining it. That means the ship must have put in somewhere in this vicinity. Maybe the crew has survived as well.'

Eadulf silently wished that he had not been so ready to dismiss Fidelma's claim when they had first arrived at the abbey.

Fidelma turned to Aourken. 'Is it possible for you to keep hold of this cat until . . . until . . .' She was hoping that the young cabin boy, Wenbrit, who looked after the ship's cat, had survived.

Aourken gave her a sympathetic smile of understanding.

'Until it can be returned to its rightful home? Have no fear, I will keep it. I hope that you and Brother Eadulf will look after yourselves. It seems that these are dangerous times now. I disliked Abbot Maelcar, but no one deserves to be killed in such a fashion.'

'You heard how he was slain then?' Fidelma glanced at her in curiosity.

'Iuna told me.'

'When was this?' Fidelma asked quickly.

'This morning.'

'This morning? Where did you see her?'

Aourken was puzzled at the sharp interest that Fidelma was displaying.

'Is something wrong?' she countered.

'Nothing that need cause you alarm,' Fidelma replied with a tight smile.

'Well, I went to get some oysters with a few other women of the village. There is a bay to the north of here.'

'Facing the Little Sea, as you call it?'

'On the north side of the peninsula, yes. It is not a long walk from here. And the oysters are good.'

'And that is where you saw Iuna?'

'Indeed it was. She was there, choosing oysters for Brilhag. She likes to choose them herself.'

'At what part of the morning was this?'

'When was it that I saw her . . . about mid-morning, I suppose.'

Fidelma frowned, mentally calculating the time, and becoming aware that she had made a mistake. A bad one. Trifina had *not* been lying. Iuna could not have sailed to Govihan with Iarnbud, after all. However, she had no time to waste on rebuking herself.

'That is most helpful, Aourken. And you will look after the cat for a while?'

'I will. He is no trouble, but I think he is pining for his real owner.'

Fidelma was about to leave when she turned back.

'One more thing. You told me that you knew Abbot Maelcar when he was a young man here. Did he ever speak about his family?'

Aourken was surprised by the question.

'Not much. His parents had been killed in a Frankish raid when he was scarcely more than a baby. He was sent to be fostered at the abbey of Meven. Then he came here.'

'The abbey of Meven – where is that?'

'In the forests of Brekilien, north of here.'

'Did he have any siblings?'

The old woman frowned. 'I do not think so. He always spoke of himself as an only child.'

'I see.' Fidelma was thoughtful. 'That is very helpful. My thanks again.'

The small party left the old woman at her cottage door and walked back towards the abbey. They found their horses where they had left them and bade farewell to Brother Metellus before mounting and heading back to Brilhag.

CHAPTER FIFTEEN

❧

T hey had arrived back at Brilhag well after nightfall, and everyone was exhausted. Fidelma wanted to question Iuna immediately, but Eadulf persuaded her that the morning would be more appropriate. After a hurried evening meal, everyone went to their bedchamber.

When Fidelma and Eadulf descended to the great hall the next morning they found only Bleidbara standing moodily before the fire.

'Riwanon left the fortress early this morning,' he stated with a bleak expression. 'She decided that she wanted to pray at the oratory, just along the coast from here.'

'She has gone to do *what*?' demanded Fidelma in amazement. 'Why was she allowed to go outside the fortress when there is such danger abroad?'

'Who am I to dare question the decision of Riwanon?' Bleidbara answered dourly. 'Anyway, she has taken her maid Ceingar, and Budic with two of his men.'

'Better than nothing,' Fidelma replied but not with approval.

'Even so, she ought to be aware of the dangers hereabouts. When did she leave?'

'At first light.'

'And what is this oratory? I hope that it is not the same one in which Macliau was found?'

'No, it's on this side of the peninsula – a little chapel where it is said that one of the saints stayed during some pilgrimage.'

Fidelma shook her head in dissatisfaction. Then she glanced at the remains of the food on the table.

'It looks as though everyone else has been up before us.' Eadulf had sat down and was helping himself to bread and cold meats, but Fidelma excused herself. She did not feel at all hungry. Instead, she decided to go in search of Iuna. She found the girl in the kitchens.

'I was told that you met old Aourken from the village yesterday,' she opened immediately.

Iuna regarded her in surprise for a moment.

'You make that sound like an accusation of something,' she countered defensively. 'Yes, I did see her yesterday. We often meet when I go to buy oysters. She used to teach me when I was younger and when she was with the religious at the abbey. That was before—'

'Before Abbot Maelcar took over and changed the Rule at the abbey?'

'Just so. Abbot Maelcar changed so many good things.'

'I gather you did not like him?'

'How could anyone like him? He would insult me by calling me a provincial servant, when my family . . .' She took a deep breath. 'Maelcar was a lecherous old man who shrouded prurience in piety. He preferred to look at women from cracks in curtains. When I was at Brekilien recently, he—'

'Go on,' Fidelma invited when the girl suddenly stopped and a flush came to her cheeks.

'I hear stories, that's all,' Iuna muttered.

'And Iarnbud? I had the impression that you did not like him either.'

'Am I to take it that these questions have some relevance to the death of the Abbot?' Iuna said rudely.

Fidelma was unperturbed by the aggression in her tone.

'You may. You may also assume that I am still carrying out the commission Queen Riwanon gave me.'

'I was raised at Brilhag. The *mac'htiern* fostered me when my parents were killed in a Frankish raid. Iarnbud is always about the place.' She shuddered suddenly. 'He is a sinister old man, as far as I am concerned. Always creeping about the place, always peering and prying. No, I do not like him one little bit.'

'What was the nature of the argument that I saw you having with him yesterday?'

Again the girl looked at her in surprise and said nothing for a while. Fidelma decided to prompt her again.

'I was coming to speak with you when I saw you at the door which leads out to the path down to the small cove where some boats are moored,' she explained.

Iuna was still defensive. 'If you were that interested, why did you not come to speak to us and enquire then?'

'I had to fetch Eadulf, and by the time we came back, you had both vanished. We went down to the cove and saw a boat sailing towards Govihan.'

Iuna smiled grimly. 'That was Iarnbud.'

'But you had also vanished. I thought you might have gone with him?'

'I have my rowing boat there and was on my way to collect the oysters. So I left Iarnbud sailing to Govihan while I rowed along the coast to the oyster beds in the little bay beyond.'

Fidelma had already guessed as much after Aourken had told her of the meeting. She was still irritated that she had made a mistake in thinking Iuna and Iarnbud had sailed off together. So she and Eadulf had been on a wild-goose chase. She grimaced at the dark humour of the expression. They were, indeed, chasing the *Barnacle Goose*.

'And the argument between you?' she added.

'Iarnbud was asking too many personal questions.'

'Personal questions?'

'About Macliau, about Riwanon, even questions about you.'

'I don't understand. What sort of questions? For example, what would he want to know about Macliau? He has surely known him since birth.'

'He wanted to know about Macliau's friends. He was always going off hunting with them, even though there was no need for meat for the kitchens, and sometimes he would return without any game. Iarnbud seemed curious, for it was unlike Macliau to take an interest in hunting.'

'Why was this a subject of argument with Iarnbud?'

'I told him that there was a reason for Macliau's desire to hunt.'

'Which was?'

'Hunting was a euphemism used by Macliau. It disguised his pursuit of the local women. I am afraid my foster-brother is . . .' She finished with an eloquent gesture of her shoulders.

'You have heard the story of what happened yesterday. Do you think your brother murdered Argantken?'

Iuna's mouth became a stubborn line and she vehemently shook her head.

'Macliau is a fool, a profligate and reckless with women. He is also weak and he should never succeed his father as *mac'htiern*. That does not mean he is a killer. He has a horror of blood. Of course,' she added, 'there is no accounting what a weak man will do when there is a prospect of being denied the power he thinks he is entitled to.'

'You say he should not succeed as Lord of Brilhag. Who would become *mac'htiern* then?'

'When a suitable male is not available to become chieftain or king,' the girl replied, 'then it is time to stand aside for a woman to take over.'

'Meaning Trifina?'

Iuna's eyes flashed for a moment and then she seemed to catch herself and smiled without humour.

'Perhaps,' she replied shortly. 'She is the only other child of Lord Canao. One must not only be of the bloodline but be perceived as the best person for the task.'

'I presume Iarnbud was asking about me because he is suspicious of all foreigners?' continued Fidelma.

'He wanted to know if you had known Riwanon before you came here.'

This answer puzzled Fidelma. She asked: 'How did he think I would have known her?'

'Perhaps because your Cousin Bressal had been sent as envoy to King Alain and you were on your cousin's ship when it was attacked?'

'Why would that follow? Oh, he might not have realised that I only joined Bressal at Naoned. I suppose he thought that I had come to this kingdom with my cousin and had been at Alain's court?'

'Iarnbud is a strange man,' Iuna said, almost to herself. 'He has never liked Riwanon.'

'Any reason?'

'Only that he was once patronised by Riwanon's predecessor as Queen.'

Fidelma was trying to work that out.

'Do you mean that Riwanon is not the first wife of this King Alain?' she asked.

'Correct. She is his second wife. King Alain is twice her age, you see.'

'What happened to his first wife?'

'What happened to half of the population a few years ago? The Yellow Plague, alas.'

'And then Alain married Riwanon?'

'He did.'

'And where was she from? Domnonia?'

'No, she was of Bro-Waroch. Her father was Lord of Gwern Porc'hoed on the edge of the great forest of Brekilien.'

Brekilien again, thought Fidelma. This name cropped up so many times.

'So is Riwanon related to your foster-father's family?'

'The Lord of Gwern Porc'hoed was one of the chieftains who owed allegiance to the kings of Bro-Waroch, but he was not of the royal family.'

'And you think that Iarnbud dislikes Riwanon for no other reason than that she married Alain Hir?'

'He needs little excuse for his likes and dislikes,' the girl replied. 'And now I think I have gossiped enough. Excuse me – I have my duties to perform.'

With a quick jerk of her head to indicate that the conversation had ended, she turned and walked away, leaving Fidelma gazing thoughtfully after her. Perhaps, she thought, the family relationships were entirely irrelevant to the matter, but they were certainly complicated.

On her return to the great hall, Fidelma found that some of the others had arrived and were sitting morosely around the fire. Macliau was seated on one side of the hearth apparently recovering from his travails, while Trifina sat opposite him, both their gazes seemed concentrated on the flames. Brother Metellus had apparently made the early-morning journey to the fortress to report on conditions at the abbey after the near-riot. He sat near them, drumming his fingers uneasily on the wooden arm of his carved chair. Bleidbara was standing before the fire, hands clasped behind him, while Eadulf remained at the table, having finished breaking his fast. He raised his eyes in a meaningful expression as Fidelma entered, as if to indicate the awkward atmosphere that permeated the room.

Fidelma was just walking across to join her husband when the now-familiar warning blast on a trumpet at the gates of the fortress caused them all to start.

Bleidbara's head jerked up, his expression one of concern. He hurried to the doors and threw them open.

They could hear the sounds of horses arriving and Bleidbara's voice raised in question. It was not long before he came back. His expression was grim and foretold bad news.

'What is it?' demanded Trifina.

'My men have returned,' Bleidbara announced hollowly. 'They found the four men who accompanied Macliau.'

'Well, what do these men say? Why are they not brought before me?' snapped Trifina.

Bleidbara glanced at Macliau, who was waiting anxiously for his reply.

'They say nothing, lady, for they are all dead. They seem to have been shot at close range with arrows.'

There was a silence, broken only by a long shuddering breath from Macliau.

'I see,' said Fidelma slowly. 'And where were the bodies found? I mean, were they in the proximity of the ruined oratory?'

'Not far from it, but not close enough for any warning cry to be heard.'

'Did your men bring the arrows with them?'

Bleidbara gazed at her in surprise, then muttered something and disappeared. He had returned in a moment and held out one of the arrows to her.

She looked at it. 'Goose feather and three flights. A professional fletched arrow,' she said, glancing over at Eadulf.

He nodded slightly, to show he understood. Bleidbara opened his mouth as if to speak, but changed his mind.

Macliau raised his head again, his pleading eyes regarding them each in turn.

'They were my only witnesses that what I say is the truth,' he said. 'What trial shall I get now?'

Brother Metellus looked at him sorrowfully, saying, 'Dead men do not make good witnesses, Macliau.'

Macliau jumped up, his mouth working.

'*I* did not kill them!' he cried. 'Is that what you are implying, Brother Metellus? I did not kill anyone.' He turned and almost ran from the hall in the manner of a petulant child.

'This does not disprove Macliau's story,' Fidelma said. 'It could have happened in the way he described. His men were killed and then the killers could have waited until Macliau and the girl were both asleep, entered the oratory, made him so drunk he passed out, and then stabbed the girl. The story is still feasible.'

Bleidbara glanced at Trifina, who had resumed her gaze at the fire. Her jaw was clenched.

'There is one thing I should say,' he said quietly. 'Lady Trifina knows this.'

'What is it?'

'Our own fletcher made those arrows, which you remark on. There is a store of them in our armoury. Two weeks ago, the fletcher noticed that several bundles seemed to be missing. We could not account for their disappearance.'

'Well, we need proof one way or the other, if we are to satisfy Barbatil and the local men,' observed Brother Metellus.

Eadulf spoke up. 'The attackers could well have stabbed the girl – but as Macliau woke, when they poured strong liquor into him to dull his senses, it would surely not have had such a rapid effect?' he pointed out. 'You cannot pour liquid down someone's throat and expect them to become insensible with drink in so short a time.'

'Are you saying that Macliau is lying?' Trifina turned from the fireplace, her voice quiet but threatening.

'No, I am not,' Eadulf replied hurriedly. 'What I *am* saying is that I think he would have to have been drugged as well as having alcohol poured into him. If so, it would require someone with the skills of an apothecary.'

'But why not simply kill him?' Trifina demanded, and then added hastily, 'Thanks be to God that they did not. But I do not understand the logic of this.'

'I think the logic is easy to follow,' Fidelma intervened. 'Didn't you tell us that you thought this Dove of Death, as you call him, was trying to disgrace your family? To follow your logic, we have your brother accused of murder and nearly strung up by a mob for something he didn't do. Isn't that precisely what you claim this *Koulm ar Maro*'s purpose is?'

'So you believe Macliau is innocent?'

'I would add the word "probably" to "innocent". Having been too long in dealing with such matters, I cannot be dogmatic about anything until it is proven one way or the other,' Fidelma replied.

To their surprise, at that moment, another warning call of a trumpet was heard from the gates.

'That is a signal of approaching danger from the look-outs!' cried Trifina, her face white. 'The mob are coming for Macliau!'

'Calm yourself,' replied Bleidbara. 'The mob won't get into this fortress. Anyway, Barbatil has given his word.' The young warrior hurried from the great hall. He was back within minutes.

'It is Riwanon and Budic. They looked distressed.'

Within a short time, the Queen had entered, followed by Budic. Riwanon made for a chair and slumped into it, breathing heavily. She was dishevelled and covered in dust. There was a tear in Budic's cloak, blood on his face, although there did not seem to be an obvious wound. He, too, was covered in dust.

Fidelma immediately poured wine for them. All present waited in silence, no one asking the obvious question. Riwanon did not speak until she had gulped several mouth-fuls of wine.

'We were attacked,' she announced flatly.

'Attacked? What – by the mob?' demanded Trifina.

'Where and by whom?' asked Fidelma more cautiously.

'Make sure the gates of the fortress are secured,' Budic, having recovered himself, ordered Bleidbara. 'They were riding close after us.'

Bleidbara went to ensure that the gates were firmly shut and that a watch was kept on the highway.

By now, Riwanon had calmed down a little.

'We were nearing the little oratory, which I wanted to visit. I was riding in front with Budic, going through a stretch of forest. All I knew was that there was a cry and glancing behind I saw our two men had fallen with arrows in them. Dead, I think. I heard Ceingar give a scream. Budic whipped my horse and we bounded forward. Only Budic and I escaped. He saved my life, yelling for me to ride as I have never ridden before. I am sure that they are pursuing close behind.' She shuddered, before asking, 'Are the gates closed?'

'You are safe now in the fortress of Brilhag,' asserted Trifina coldly.

Riwanon ignored her, looking directly at Fidelma and saying, 'I need your assurance, Fidelma of Hibernia, that I am safe.'

Fidelma stared at her in astonishment, as there was a sharp intake of breath from Trifina.

'Do you doubt it?' Fidelma asked incredulously. For the implication was surely a direct insult to her hosts.

'I ask it because I glimpsed one of our attackers – and he held a banner in his hand,' said the Queen.

It was Budic who added grimly, 'The banner belonged to the *mac'htiern* of Brilhag. We cannot deny the evidence of our own eyes.'

Bleidbara had just returned and overheard what Budic had said.

'So you think that it was my men who attacked you?' he said quietly. 'We have had better things to do this day.'

'Riwanon, there seems some conspiracy to bring discredit on the family of the lord of Brilhag,' Fidelma intervened as

Budic was about to respond. 'We do not know the details, but we believe that whoever attacks under this flag is not connected with your husband's friend.' She turned to Budic. 'How many were in this attacking party?'

'Perhaps half-a-dozen, maybe even a dozen,' replied Budic hesitantly. 'We did not see them all.'

'And you had two warriors and yourself in the party?'

'The attack came by stealth. My men were shot down from behind the trees and bushes.'

'And yet one of the ambushers came forward with this banner, thus ensuring that they might be identified? Did you not think that strange?'

'Strange?' Budic frowned.

'To go to such lengths to ambush you, shooting from behind with the intention of killing you all, but then coming forward that you might identify them. I believe that is why you were allowed to survive.'

'I only glimpsed the banner over my shoulder as Budic whipped up my horse,' replied Riwanon thoughtfully. 'Perhaps they emerged to give chase to us?'

Fidelma turned to Trifina. 'I suggest that Bleidbara take some men and see if he can track these attackers. At least, he can recover the bodies of Riwanon's maid and guards.'

'You want Bleidbara and his men to leave the fortress now – when we might be attacked?' Trifina was astonished.

'But that will be dangerous!' cried Riwanon in agreement.

Fidelma smiled at them both.

'I am sure that these ruffians will not launch an attack here.' She turned to Eadulf with an apologetic smile. 'I would like you to accompany Bleidbara and his men. I need your expert eyes, for you know what it is I would like to see. However, I feel that I must remain here for the moment.'

Eadulf looked carefully at her. 'I do not understand,' he said. 'Why is it you want me to go?'

'*Stet pro ratione voluntas*,' she whispered, glancing at the company. Let my will stand as a reason. Then she added quickly in their common language: 'I don't want to prejudice you by saying what I think you will find – just observe and report directly back to me. I do not think you will be in any danger.'

'Very well,' he replied.

'I am willing to go, lady,' Bleidbara now stated. 'If it means finding out who is behind these attacks.'

'Bleidbara is a capable warrior,' Trifina said, 'but your request places him and your husband in danger.'

'I disagree, lady. The raiders only attack when the odds are in their favour. I am hoping that Bleidbara might be able to track them to their lair, wherever that is.'

'Then I should go with them,' Budic announced, apparently feeling that his reputation as a warrior was in question.

'As commander of the Queen's bodyguard, your place is here with her,' Fidelma pointed out.

'Where is it that this ambush took place?' asked Bleidbara.

Budic hesitated, as if trying to recall the exact location. 'It was along the track, just south of the oratory.'

'A good place for an ambush, as the road passes through a heavily wooded area. I know it well. We shall proceed carefully. I shall take six men, for it will be best to leave the others here, to prepare for all contingencies. I'll take Boric the Stout for he is not only a good warrior but the best tracker we have. I hope your optimism that the attackers have fled is not proved wrong, lady.'

'I would not like to be responsible for sending these men into danger unnecessarily,' Riwanon said, looking distraught.

'Be reassured, lady.' Fidelma's voice was earnest. 'There is necessity to this. And I do not believe there is any danger for them.'

Only Eadulf seemed to pick up a hidden meaning in her words.

Every so often, Boric halted the group of riders and slid from his horse, peering at the tracks that they were following. They were some way from Brilhag by now, and he had examined the tracks several times already.

'I can see signs of two horses heading for Brilhag, but no sign that they were being followed at this point, certainly not along this track,' he told Bleidbara.

Bleidbara glanced at Eadulf.

'So Riwanon was mistaken when she thought they were chased to the gates of Brilhag,' Eadulf said.

'There is one other thing,' Boric added. 'At this point, the tracks indicate that the two horses were proceeding at no more than a walking pace. So they must have realised, at this point, that they were *not* being followed.'

'Are you sure?' Bleidbara frowned. 'Maybe these are the wrong tracks. When they arrived at Brilhag, they came at a gallop.'

The stocky tracker shook his head. 'The horses were certainly not galloping here. I'd stake my sword on it.'

'We will continue – but with caution,' decided Bleidbara. 'Keep an eye on the tracks, Boric.'

'How far to this oratory?' asked Eadulf as they set off again.

'We are fairly close now. It is towards the north-east, along the shore of the Morbihan. There are some farmsteads in this area. They are well away from the main course of this track, more towards the south.'

'Then we should be coming to the bodies of Riwanon's companions soon,' Eadulf deduced.

From time to time, Boric had halted and dismounted to check the tracks but he had found no sign of anything untoward until they came to a track that intersected the one they were following. Here he reported that several horses had halted for a little while, for the ground was churned by their hooves.

'I can see that two horses have left the main group here. They are going back to Brilhag.'

'Are you sure?' Bleidbara asked.

'I can only report what I see on the ground,' replied Boric stoically. 'Shall we continue on?'

Bleidbara gestured assent.

Eadulf was thoughtful, still wondering why Fidelma had made him come along. Was there something she already knew or suspected?

After another period had passed, Bleidbara pointed through the trees on their left, north of their position.

'Those are the waters of Morbihan and the oratory is nearby.'

Eadulf followed his quick gesture and saw waters glistening beyond the trees.

'Well, one thing is for sure,' Bleidbara said. 'The raiders are long gone from this area and certainly did not maintain their pursuit of Riwanon and Budic after they had ambushed them.'

'That might be so,' Eadulf agreed as he looked around. 'However, we haven't yet come to the spot where the ambush took place.'

'True enough,' the other man agreed. 'We ought by now to have come across the bodies of those warriors who fell and, of course, the girl, Ceingar. The attack was probably closer to the oratory than Riwanon allowed. We'll continue on . . .'

He paused, for the stout tracker was standing still. He was sniffing the air suspiciously.

'I smell a fire,' he announced.

They could all smell it now. Boric silently pointed to the south, away from Morbihan. There was a gap in the canopy of leafy branches that showed clear sky and something else. A column of black smoke was rising and drifting against the blue.

'A forest fire?' demanded Eadulf, looking at it and then glancing at the tall trees on either side of the track that suddenly seemed to grow menacingly around them.

'I don't think so,' Bleidbara replied quietly. 'That is a man-made fire.'

Boric remounted. 'I'll ride on ahead,' he called over his shoulder as he urged his horse forward at a canter.

Bleidbara signalled his band to follow carefully. The smell of burning wood became stronger.

'There is a farmstead beyond that hill,' he said to Eadulf. 'Perhaps the farmer is burning his fields. It's that time of year.'

Eadulf vaguely knew that some farmers burned corn stubble in their fields on alternate years to ensure more fertile ground. It was a practice that, not being a farmer, he did not really understand.

'Why are you sure it is not a forest fire?' he enquired.

Bleidbara grinned. 'When you have lived in a forest you begin to develop a feeling, an instinct, and you also develop your eyes for such things.'

They found a small fork in the track that meandered off to the right and ascended a sloping area of ground. Boric was still ahead of them. The trees began to thin a little and suddenly they saw him halt his horse at the top of the rise. He did not turn round but held up his hand as if to stay their advance.

They came up carefully behind him and halted.

Some cultivated fields stretched before them, leading down to a stream, which ran snake-like through their middle. But it was not these that were on fire. On the far side of the fields were what seemed to have been a log-built farmhouse and some outbuildings. It was these that were on fire.

A group of people were milling about, some trying to form a human chain to the stream, along which they passed pails of water in a fruitless attempt to douse the flames. Some bodies were laid out nearby.

Eadulf tried to focus on the scene to discern its cause.

There was a sudden shout of warning from the people below. One of them was pointing up the hill towards them. Some grabbed for weapons. It was clear that their group had been spotted and identified as a potential threat.

Bleidbara began to ride slowly forward while Eadulf and the others followed a short distance behind.

As they grew close, Eadulf saw that those trying to put out the flames were reforming in defensive positions. They were those same sturdy farmers who had gathered to attack the abbey on the previous day. He could tell by their clothing and curious agricultural weaponry. He recognised the small man, what was his name? Coric! Coric – the friend of Barbatil, the father of the murdered Argantken.

They were halfway across the field when Bleidbara halted and called to Coric. It was in retrospect that Bleidbara interpreted the shouted conversation to Eadulf.

'Coric! It is I, Bleidbara. We are friends!' he cried.

'You come under the banner of Brilhag,' replied the little man. 'That is no sign of friendship – after this.' He gestured around him.

'What do you mean?'

'A group of your warriors attacked this farmstead, slaughtered old Goustan the farmer and his family and set fire to it. How should we welcome you as friends?'

'No warriors of mine did this, Coric. We have come from Brilhag in search of the brigands who ambushed Queen Riwanon this morning. Two of her warriors were slain, and her maid.'

Coric stood uncertainly. 'How can we know that you tell the truth?'

'I am Bleidbara. I grew up among you. My word is my honour.'

'I cannot accept the word of anyone who serves Brilhag after this day. Warriors have attacked us poor farmers too many times. But today, today marks an end of it. We will fight back. So I warn you, Bleidbara, stay back!'

'They may be using the banner of Brilhag, but that does not mean they are *of* Brilhag,' responded the warrior.

'So you say. We will choose our own counsel.'

Bleidbara was losing patience. 'Just tell us what happened and which way these raiders have gone?'

There was a pause, then Coric's surly voice answered, 'We saw smoke rising and, as several of our farmsteads had been attacked before, we came in a body to see what was happening. From the rise there, we saw half-a-dozen men loading booty on their horses. The cabin was already blazing. Old Goustan was still alive, we saw him arguing with the looters. Then one of them, perhaps the leader, simply drew his sword and cut him down. There was a scream and we saw Goustan's wife and child run from behind one of the huts. They did not reach him. Their bodies lie there.'

Again Coric gestured.

'We gave a shout of anger and all of us, as one man, raised what weapons we could and began to run down the hill. The attackers saw us. They had bows and might have cut down some of us. But their leader was wise, for he simply signalled his men to mount and they went riding away.'

'How long ago was this?' demanded Bleidbara sharply.

'An hour – perhaps more. The blaze was so strong here that we have not been able to quench it.'

'And which way did the attackers go?'

Coric pointed north but slightly to the east of the direction from which they had come.

'Once more, I assure you that this is no deed of Brilhag,' cried Bleidbara. 'I am going in pursuit of these raiders and will prove to you and your people that I am right.'

Coric and his fellows said nothing. Neither did they drop their weapons nor did they raise them. They stood unsmiling as Bleidbara turned his horse and signalled to his men to follow. As they rode quickly back across the hill in the direction Coric had indicated, Bleidbara quickly recounted the conversation to Eadulf.

'Then these must be the same men who attacked Riwanon,' Eadulf said unnecessarily. 'Where would they be heading to in this direction?'

'This way is the oratory.'

'Could they have landed from this ship you call *Koulm ar Maro*?'

'That is exactly what I fear,' agreed Bleidbara. 'They have such a head start on us that they may vanish out onto the waters of Morbihan again.'

'But they are on horseback,' objected Eadulf.

'Ah,' Bleidbara smiled brightly, 'that is true. I was almost forgetting. They must keep their horses somewhere if they are conducting raids like this.'

It seemed little time passed before they came within sight of the small stone oratory.

Immediately Bleidbara halted the band and, without any words being exchanged, Boric slid from his horse and moved quickly forward. It was obvious to Eadulf that these men had worked together before and did not have to waste time exchanging orders.

The first task was to ensure that no one was in hiding in or around the oratory, and when all was clear, Boric bent to the ground checking the area around the grey stone building. Then he moved towards the nearby shoreline and down to the embankment. While Eadulf was impatient, Bleidbara sat leaning forward, resting on the pommel of his saddle. It was almost as if he was nodding in a doze but the half-shut eyes were still bright, watchful and wary of their surroundings.

Boric reappeared and waved them forward.

As they dismounted, he spoke rapidly to Bleidbara.

'Several horses and riders have been here. It's difficult to tell how many. The most recent group halted and some men dismounted. Four riders took the riderless horses and moved on northwards.'

'How can you possibly know that?' wondered Eadulf.

Boric smiled patiently, then enlightened him. 'The earth always tells the story. Some horses came here; the depth of their imprint measures their weight. When they left, in that direction,' he pointed, 'only four of the horses impressed the ground with the same weight. The others were light. Then we found marks of boots, heavy shod of the type warriors wear. The wearers of these went down to the embankment and seem to have boarded a boat drawn up on the shore.'

'Probably they went to join their friends on the ship,' Bleidbara explained grimly.

Eadulf had to admit that the tracker knew his business well.

'And those that continued on?' he asked. 'Where would they go to?'

Boric shrugged. 'The only way to know that would be to follow them.'

Bleidbara was now all in favour of pushing on. He pointed out that Fidelma had wanted the attackers followed to their lair.

'What is the point of coming this far, only to turn back?' he pressed.

'But the sea raider, this *Koulm ar Maro*, is hiding somewhere out there.' Eadulf pointed to the Morbihan.

'It might be that in following those that continued on land, we will find out where their secret harbour is,' Bleidbara said.

'How so?'

'Why wouldn't they all try to escape to the sea, if escaping they were? I think they also have a camp on land and that is where they stable their horses for these attacks. In that place, we may also find the harbour that shelters their ship.'

Eadulf thought carefully. 'There is something in that logic,' he agreed.

'You sound doubtful?'

'It's just that I am wondering why we have not found the bodies of the slain bodyguards of Riwanon and her maidservant Ceingar?'

'Perhaps we missed them,' Bleidbara replied.

'Or they could have been made prisoners,' suggested Boric.

'The answer is to follow and find out for ourselves.' Bleidbara's tone was determined.

With a reluctant sigh, Eadulf conceded to the warrior. He still felt uneasy, however, and worse still, remained unsure what it was that Fidelma had expected him to see.

CHAPTER SIXTEEN

∽◉

There was an air of nervous expectation in the fortress of Brilhag. A warrior had retrieved the carcass of Macliau's little dog Albiorix from the pigpen at Barbatil's farmstead. Macliau, clearly stricken with a grief that Fidelma found surprising, had insisted on personally digging a little grave in the gardens of the fortress, observed only by Trifina and Fidelma. He had said nothing to them or they to him. After Macliau had interred his dog, he had retired to his chamber with a flagon of wine, moody and uncommunicative.

'Does Iuna know Budic?' Fidelma asked, as Trifina accompanied her slowly back to the great hall.

The other woman glanced at her in surprise. 'I don't think so. What makes you ask?'

'I just had a feeling,' Fidelma replied. 'Had Budic visited Brilhag before? I thought Riwanon said she had been to the Abbey of Gildas in the past. I thought they might have met then.'

Trifina shook her head. 'That was a long time ago, before

Riwanon married Alain. Budic has never been here. However . . .'

Fidelma raised an eyebrow. 'However?'

'Iuna has accompanied my father a few times to the court of Alain Hir in Brekilien.'

'I thought Brekilien was a forest?'

'So it is, but within it is the location of the royal court, near the Abbey Pempont, which King Judicael founded some years before his death. It is our great religious and royal centre.'

At this point, Trifina bade Fidelma farewell and retired to her own chamber. Fidelma herself went on to the great hall, but found only two occupants. At the far end of the hall, Riwanon and Budic were standing together before the fire locked in earnest conversation. What caused Fidelma to stop in surprise was the proximity of their bodies to one another; too close for the normal relationship between a Queen and the commander of her bodyguard. Budic was very close, staring down into the upturned face of Riwanon. Their voices were low and urgent.

Fidelma closed the door behind her, perhaps with a little more force than necessary, and the two sprang apart.

'Fidelma.' Riwanon forced a smile. 'Any news?'

'Bleidbara has not returned yet,' Fidelma said, moving forward to the fire. Although it was summer, the great hall seemed cold. 'And Macliau has just buried his dog.'

Budic sniffed disparagingly.

'Do you still think him innocent?' There was the familiar sneer in his voice.

'It matters not what I think,' replied Fidelma. 'It is what the *bretat* will judge when he hears the evidence.'

'It is no justice when one has to wait so long for it,' replied Budic. 'He should have been tried at once.'

'I did not think it was your law to try someone without a qualified judge present? No one, surely, should be tried by an emotional mob.'

Budic was about to respond but then he merely shrugged and moved away to sink in a chair before the fire. Riwanon looked at her guard commander with irritation at his rudeness.

'We are a little tense waiting for news . . . waiting for what might be an attack on this fortress by these brigands,' she said, almost in apology.

'Indeed,' agreed Fidelma. 'But we must all try to relax as best we can. From what I have seen of this fortress, we are well protected.'

'I hope your Saxon friend and Bleidbara can say the same,' muttered Budic from his chair.

Eadulf was seated on his horse, his heart pounding as Boric, the tracker and scout, came galloping back along the path to the clearing where he, Bleidbara and the others had halted.

'A horseman is coming!' He cried a warning in a low voice. 'A single rider, coming at the gallop!'

With one motion of his arm, Bleidbara signalled his men to take cover on either side of the forest path, ensuring that Eadulf followed him into the cover of the thick undergrowth.

Indeed, no time seemed to pass before they could hear the thudding of hooves along the muddy track. The rider was bent low over the straining neck of the beast. He was clearly in a hurry. Before he drew near, Eadulf saw that he was no ordinary warrior. He was well dressed with a multi-coloured cloak snapping in the air behind his shoulders. He had an ornate polished helmet, and a saffron-coloured tunic with designs that Eadulf could not clearly make out. The man wore a sword but carried neither shield nor spear.

As he drew near, Bleidbara urged his horse forward to block the rider's path while his comrades came up behind him. For a second or two, the rider's horse shied and kicked the air with its forehooves.

'Out of the way!' roared the rider angrily, his hand falling to his sword. 'In the name of the King, *out of the way*!'

'Who are you?' Bleidbara demanded.

'A messenger from King Alain on his business. Now move!'

'I am commander of the guard at the fortress of Brilhag,' replied Bleidbara. 'You ride in dangerous country, my friend.'

'Not if the *mac'htiern* of Brilhag is loyal to my King,' the man declared haughtily.

'Brilhag is loyal but there are enemies that lurk in these woods.'

'You do not have to tell me that. I was nearly caught by a band of cut-throats not far back along this track. They loosed some arrows at me but my horse was faster than they were. Are you seeking them?'

'You saw them?'

'Three men were all I saw.'

'We are in pursuit of them.'

'Then follow this path. I came on them making camp in a small clearing near a stream.'

Bleidbara was puzzled at the news. 'Camped already? But it is several hours until nightfall. Why, we could ride back to Brilhag from here and arrive before it grows dark.'

'And it is there that I have to go, on King Alain's business. Is the Queen Riwanon there?'

'She is,' asserted Bleidbara.

'Good. I am to inform her that her husband, Alain, will be at Brilhag by dusk tomorrow. He rides together with the lord of Brilhag and an escort of his warriors.'

'Then continue on your way, my friend,' Bleidbara said, moving his horse aside.

A short time later, Boric, who was scouting ahead again, returned.

'The messenger was right. There are three men camped in a small clearing ahead.'

'But why so early?' Bleidbara queried. 'That I really cannot understand. They could make more time before nightfall.'

Boric grimaced. 'I am afraid that they have their reasons,' he replied. 'The men have the female with them – the maid of Queen Riwanon.'

'Then Ceingar is still alive?' Eadulf's question was unnecessary.

The stout tracker nodded.

'It was my intention to just follow them until we find their lair,' Bleidbara said reflectively. 'Now I do not think we have a choice.'

'Agreed,' Eadulf said, 'there is no choice. We must rescue the girl.'

'How far ahead are they?' Bleidbara asked and, when the position was outlined, he turned to his men. 'We will leave the horses here and move quietly forward on foot. We will surround their camp and come on them suddenly. Hopefully, they will give up without a fight. But be careful – these men are ruthless and they kill.'

He glanced at Eadulf. 'Do you want to stay here to look after the horses?'

Eadulf shook his head firmly. 'I'll come with you, of course.'

They moved forward cautiously and, at a silent signal from Bleidbara, they spread out left and right to encircle the camp which announced itself by the sound of a crackling fire in the clearing ahead of them. As they drew near, Eadulf could see through the undergrowth the light of the blazing campfire. Two raiders were squatting before it, their weapons at their sides. There was no sign of the third man nor of the female prisoner. The two men were talking to one another in loud voices, and now and then glancing towards the far side of the small clearing and laughing lewdly. Eadulf raised his eyes and saw a movement from the bushes at which their glances were directed.

He reached forward, tapped Bleidbara on the arm and pointed.

The warrior nodded to indicate that he had understood. Then he held up his dagger, gesturing at himself and then at the bush. Bleidbara's men were highly trained. The young commander was already moving silently and rapidly, skirting the camp, making directly for his target. Eadulf kept close behind him.

They came on the scene that Eadulf had already suspected might meet their eyes. The girl, Ceingar, was stretched on the ground. Her dress was raised. She lay without struggling as the man panted and heaved on top of her.

In a couple of strides Bleidbara had moved across the intervening distance, grabbed the rapist by the hair and yanked him backwards. The man's reactions were quick. He gave a cry of alarm as he was wrenched off by Bleidbara's strong arm but, at the same time, he was grabbing for the dagger in his belt. Bleidbara had no choice but to use his own weapon, plunging it under the man's ribcage.

From the camp, Eadulf could hear the cries of alarm as Bleidbara's men closed with the other raiders. The inert form of the girl now came alive; screaming, she scrambled up, pulling down her dress and staring wildly about.

Eadulf moved forward.

'Have no fear!' he yelled. 'We are your rescuers. You are free!'

She was staring at him like one demented and, to his surprise, she lunged forward, clutching at the warrior's discarded knife and raising it. For a moment Eadulf froze. The girl would have struck home but Bleidbara, having dropped the dead form of the assailant, took a pace forward and grabbed the girl by the wrist, twisting it slightly so that she was forced to drop the knife.

He said something to her and she slumped forward as if in exhaustion and sank to the ground again.

'It's all right,' Bleidbara said to Eadulf. 'The girl did not know who we were and acted out of instinct. Let her sit still for a moment.'

Boric suddenly appeared. His face was grim with satisfaction.

'They are both dead,' he said, jerking his thumb across his shoulder.

'You killed them?' Eadulf felt disappointment. 'We could have questioned them.'

'I am afraid not, Brother Eadulf,' replied Boric without remorse. 'They fought like demons and had no intention of allowing themselves to become prisoners. They had the battle fever on them. There was nothing else we could do but meet their steel with our own.'

Eadulf glanced to where the girl, Ceingar, was huddled on a log, her knees drawn up to her chin, arms clasped around them, rocking back and forth. Her eyes were wide and bright, gazing in horror at the body of the man who had violated her.

'Does she know that she is safe?' he asked Bleidbara.

The warrior gave an affirmative gesture. He spoke to the girl and she eventually raised her head and stared from Bleidbara to Eadulf.

'She recognises us.'

'Ask her what happened,' Eadulf instructed.

'She says that they had been out riding, her mistress, Queen Riwanon, and her party. Suddenly, arrows flew. Two of the warriors were cut down. Riwanon and Budic galloped off but, as Ceingar made to follow them, one of the members of the ambush party leaped out and caught her horse's bridle and thus she was trapped.'

'What happened to the bodies of the warriors who were slain?'

There was some hesitation on the girl's face, a look of distaste before she spoke.

'The attackers put their bodies on one of the horses and took them away.'

'And what happened to her?'

'They told her that she was a prisoner and for a while they bound her wrists. They released her only when . . .' He gestured silently to the spot where they had found her.

'How many were there in this attacking party?'

'About half-a-dozen.'

'What happened after she was captured?'

'They rode along the track and over a hill until they saw a farmstead. The leader . . .'

'Who was the leader?' interrupted Eadulf. 'Did you recognise him?'

The girl pointed at her slain assailant. Eadulf was disappointed, as clearly this man was not the 'Dove of Death'.

'And what did he do at the farmstead?'

'They rode down on it and killed the farmer, then set fire to the buildings. Then a group of people appeared on the hill and came running towards them, bearing weapons. They were a large crowd, too large for them to fight off. So they rode away.'

'To the oratory?'

The girl frowned uncertainly.

'We saw your tracks there,' he explained. 'Was that where the ship was waiting?'

Again her eyes were wide. 'There are no tracks on water,' she said hoarsely, obviously still in shock. 'How did you know that?'

'A logical deduction – from the tracks,' Eadulf smiled. 'Three of your captors went on board the ship and then the other three took their horses with you and came here. Is that right?'

Ceingar sighed deeply. 'We came here and camped and . . .' She shivered violently.

'Well, it's all over now,' Eadulf said. 'Do you know where you were heading? Why did some of the attackers go aboard the vessel?'

As he expected, she did not know. 'They said nothing to me and I heard nothing of their plans,' she replied.

'We might as well take their horses and ride back to Brilhag,' Bleidbara said. He turned to the girl. 'Are you fit enough to travel?'

'I think so.'

Bleidbara was examining the sky. 'If we leave now, we should get to Brilhag by nightfall.'

At a signal, his men doused the fire, gathered the weapons of the raiders and some few items they found on their persons, and tied their horses together on a lead rope. Then they remounted and started back along the track at a swift canter.

'Bleidbara has returned,' Iuna announced as she moved to the doors of the great hall. Those gathered there had already heard the call of the trumpet from the main gates.

Even before Iuna spoke, the gates had swung open and the warriors, closely followed by Eadulf, came in. Behind them was the pale figure of Ceingar, looking dishevelled. She gazed quickly around, saw Riwanon and ran to her, casting herself on her knees before her and speaking rapidly, sobbing as she did so. Riwanon replied sternly and turned to Iuna, saying something. Iuna moved forward and helped the girl to her feet and, after a few words from Riwanon to Ceingar, led her away.

'The girl is distraught,' Riwanon told Fidelma, 'so I have sent her to clean herself and rest.'

'I would like to question her,' Fidelma said. 'We need to find out as much as we can about these attackers.'

'It will have to be later when she is more composed,' the Queen replied firmly.

'Very well.' Fidelma turned to Eadulf with a warning look to convey that she did not want him to discuss his observations in front of the others.

Bleidbara, however, recounted what had happened.

'Thanks be that you were able to save poor Ceingar.' Riwanon looked sad. 'I can only imagine the fate that those beasts had in store for her. But my warriors, ah . . . it distresses me. Both killed, you say?'

'We were unable to recover their bodies. Ceingar said that only she was taken alive in the ambush,' Bleidbara replied. 'She was not sure what the captors did with the bodies, but they took their horses. We have, of course, brought all the horses back to the fortress with us.'

'And you say that this attacking party split into two – that some of them went on shipboard while the others, together with the girl, rode towards the north-east?' asked Fidelma.

'That is so, lady,' Bleidbara agreed.

'It is a pity that you didn't take one of those men prisoner,' commented Trifina, 'then we should have found out the truth about this *Koulm ar Maro*.'

Bleidbara seemed a little irritated by the criticism.

'Lady, they did not want to surrender,' he replied stiffly. 'They fought to the death, with a fanatical zeal that I have not seen before.'

'You found that curious?' Fidelma was interested by the comment.

'It was unusual,' agreed the warrior. 'Our warriors might not contemplate surrender to the Franks, but with our own people, they know they would not be badly treated.'

'And you gave them the opportunity to surrender?'

'I am not in the habit of slaughtering men who would rather live, lady,' he replied firmly.

'Of course not. I just wanted to be sure that I had the facts.'

'But we are no further forward than before!' Trifina said petulantly. 'My brother still stands accused of murder. These brigands still attack unarmed farmsteads, kill merchants, even attack and capture foreign ships on the high seas – and we *still* do not know who they are or who is behind them.'

'We know one thing – that they do so under the flag of the *mac'htiern* of Brilhag,' pointed out Riwanon.

'That is just a ruse to mislead people,' snapped Trifina, colouring hotly.

Riwanon spread her hands and smiled.

'But it must be proved, must it not?' This last question was aimed at Fidelma.

'That is so,' agreed Fidelma. 'The people of this peninsula need to be shown, in a way that leaves little doubt, that these brigands and their leader are not connected with this household.'

'So it is a pity, Bleidbara, that you were not able to bring one of them here, even if they were wounded,' ended Riwanon.

Bleidbara coloured. 'I have already explained that we did not have the opportunity, lady.'

'But a pity, nevertheless,' she sighed.

Later, in their chamber after the evening meal, as Fidelma sat combing her long red tresses and preparing for bed, she was able to talk over the matter with Eadulf. She asked him to describe everything that had happened.

'And you are sure that Bleidbara gave every opportunity to the brigands to surrender so he could take one alive?'

Eadulf confirmed it.

'We were worried about the fate of the girl, Ceingar,' he explained. 'That was why we decided to attack the camp. Our original plan was simply to track them back to their lair. We thought that they would take the horses overland to some secret harbour where we might find the *Koulm ar Maro*, moored somewhere on the eastern side of the Morbihan.'

'It was certainly a logical plan,' agreed Fidelma.

'Then when we saw one of the brigands having his way with Ceingar . . .' Eadulf shrugged. 'Well, Bleidbara gave the signal to attack. I thought the other two, who were probably waiting their turn with her, poor girl, would surrender when they saw the odds were against them. But they refused and fought with such a fury that it could only have ended with their deaths or our own. *Deo adjuvante*, Bleidbara's men were good and the raiders paid the price for their sins.'

'It is a pity that I am not able to question Ceingar until tomorrow. She might have had some information about the leaders of this band by which we could track them.'

'She has suffered much, that one,' Eadulf reflected. 'Best that she have a good rest to recover from her ordeal. Then her mind will be clearer.'

'Yes, although sometimes a fresh remembrance of things is more helpful than letting a person rest on the memory. After a time, the mind begins to rationalise, make interpretations of the memory and thereby time distorts it.'

'It seems that we are no further forward to a solution to all this,' Eadulf said, rather wearily. 'We have been dragged into some local mystery not of our own choosing – and, to be honest, we don't understand the half of it. What makes it worse is that we know almost nothing of the language and have to rely on others for interpretation.'

'We know a little of the language of the Britons, thanks to our time in the Kingdom of Dyfed. So we have some idea of what is being said.'

Eadulf was moody.

'A little knowledge is dangerous,' he grumbled. 'The words might be similar here but we still have to look to others for detailed information. I do not think we should have become involved in this business. At least, I think Riwanon's commission to you was ill-advised.'

Fidelma's mouth tightened.

'We became involved when my Cousin Bressal was murdered, when our friend Murchad was cut down. We *are* involved and I will *stay* involved until I have resolved this mystery.'

Eadulf was about to respond but thought better of it. It was no use arguing when Fidelma was in this kind of mood.

'Well, I am for bed,' he said. 'It has been another long and tiring day, and I am exhausted.'

Annoyed at Eadulf's lack of understanding, Fidelma did not reply. She sat for a long time by the window looking out onto the shimmering moonlit waters of the Morbihan with its dark shadows of islands. Carefully, she turned over the events of the last few days in her mind. There was something there which nearly made sense . . . but not quite. She was sure that the answer was almost within her grasp; almost, but not quite. It needed something, some simple key, to make everything fit into place.

'There is no sign of the girl Iuna this morning,' remarked Riwanon. 'Do we have to fend for ourselves?'

Fidelma and Eadulf had come down that morning in a sombre mood to find Riwanon already seated at the table. Macliau was sitting in a corner by the hearth, staring with moody unseeing eyes at the embers of a fire that had not been attended to for some time. He neither raised his hand nor acknowledged anyone. Brother Metellus had returned to the abbey on the previous afternoon as matters there needed his attention. As they came down the stairway into the great hall, the door opened. Bleidbara entered and stood looking about uncertainly.

Fidelma noted the peevish tone in Riwanon's voice, but she understood that the Queen had been through much these recent days, with the attack on her and her entourage, and must be feeling the strain.

'Where's Budic?' asked Riwanon now. 'I seem deserted by my bodyguard, as well as my maidservant.'

'Budic is in the stables, practising his swordsmanship with Boric,' Bleidbara said.

'And Ceingar? Is she still abed?'

'I'll go to the kitchens to see if she is there with Iuna, shall I?' he suggested.

'It would be helpful,' Fidelma intervened, noting that Trifina was also missing. 'Meanwhile, I'll check that she is not in her room. There is an excuse for everyone to have overslept this morning.' She turned to Eadulf: 'Throw some logs on the fire before it goes out.' She raised her eyebrows, indicating Riwanon. From her expression, he understood that it fell to him to keep the company distracted in some way so that the heavy atmosphere could be lifted.

Fidelma ran lightly up the stairs. Instead of going straight to Ceingar's room, she made her way along the corridor to Iuna's chamber and knocked gently on the door. Iuna was always up early and her absence puzzled Fidelma even more than Ceingar's did. There was no answer. She knocked again, this time a little louder, then waited a moment before she tried the handle. The door swung open. The room was in semi-gloom but Fidelma saw that the bed was empty. The bedlinen was rumpled almost as if a struggle had taken place there. Then she noticed the pieces of a broken clay bowl on the floor beside the bed and a spoon, as if someone had been eating from the bowl and dropped it, breaking it. Certainly Iuna had left the room in a hurry.

Fidelma quickly examined the chamber. She noticed that the door to the adjoining chamber was slightly ajar and remembered that Iuna had said she slept in the room next to Trifina.

She walked across the chamber and pushed the door open. Again she saw that the bed was empty – but here the bedlinen had been pulled back as if in haste. A jug had been over-turned near the bed; it had fallen onto a thickly woven carpet, spilling some water, but obviously the carpet had cushioned it so that it had not broken, nor would it have created any noise as it fell.

Fidelma was about to walk out of the room when she noticed a dark stain on the linen sheet. She moved across and peered at it, wishing there was more light, then she put forward a finger and touched it. It was damp. She raised the finger, examined it and realised that it was blood.

She stood undecided for a moment or two before leaving through the main door into the corridor. She was about to go back to rejoin the others when she remembered the object of her mission – to locate Ceingar. Riwanon's maid had been allocated a nearby chamber.

Fidelma paused and knocked upon the door. She was not

expecting an answer and so, when none came, she merely opened the door and looked inside.

She was expecting another empty bed. In that expectation, she was unfulfilled. For Ceingar lay in the bed. She lay on her back, her white face turned to the ceiling, her mouth open slightly, and her eyes wide and staring. There was a knife buried in her chest and the dark stains of blood were all over her body and over the sheets.

Fidelma did not have to examine the knife too closely to see that it was a dagger – with the emblem of a dove on its handle.

There was a sense of shock in the fortress after Fidelma had told the others about her grim findings. Only her own quiet authority stemmed the mood of panic among them. There was much disquiet among the servants and the guards at the news. Macliau had retired to his chamber in his now usual uncommunicative mood. His dazed features seemed genuine enough, and Fidelma saw that he had taken a small amphora of wine with him. Only Riwanon and Budic remained in the great hall.

'I just pray that my husband, Alain, reaches here safely,' Riwanon confided to Fidelma. 'There is much evil here in Brilhag and I do not think we will be safe until he arrives.'

'I agree that there is much evil,' Fidelma replied quietly. 'And with your continued permission, I shall try to make what sense I can of these events.'

Riwanon made a small gesture with her hand.

'I am afraid, my Hibernian sister, there is little you can

do here. I was foolish to suggest that you could help. After all, you are in a foreign land and do not speak our language. Best stay here in safety and pray for the safe arrival of my husband. I was wondering if we should send a messenger to hasten him.'

'While it is wise to be cautious, his messenger said he would be here before dusk today. I feel I must do what I can, however limited my means of doing so,' insisted Fidelma. 'But, by all means, send one of your men to find your husband.'

Riwanon smiled softly.

'You have a good heart, Fidelma. If you feel you must persist in your enquiries, then carry on. You have my authority to do what you can to resolve the mysteries that beset this place.'

'Your authority?' pressed Fidelma.

'My full authority,' confirmed Riwanon. 'But I will remain here with Budic as my bodyguard until my husband comes.'

Outside the great hall, Eadulf said: 'I don't understand this. Is there a logic that Ceingar be killed and Trifina and Iuna abducted?'

'Even in the most bizarre set of circumstances you will find a logic, Eadulf,' Fidelma replied. 'From what you have told me of your finding of Ceingar, I think there is a reason why she was killed. But the abduction of both Trifina and Iuna is more puzzling. Let us see if we can trace how they were taken from their rooms and by what method transported.'

It was at that moment that Bleidbara approached them. His features were set hard.

'We've found another body,' he announced.

'Is it Trifina or Iuna?' asked Eadulf immediately.

'Neither. It is one of my men who was on watch at the small harbour below. His throat was cut. I think that Trifina and Iuna were removed by boat.'

'Kidnapped on the *Koulm ar Maro*?' Fidelma asked.

'Without question,' asserted Bleidbara. 'You know that I have been scouring these islands under the orders of Trifina for the last week, searching for this *Koulm ar Maro*? Yet I have not found its hiding-place. They must have raided the fortress last night.'

'But why kill Ceingar? Why abduct Iuna and Trifina?' Fidelma was thoughtful. 'It doesn't make sense unless . . .' She paused and then asked: 'What is the last place you would look for Trifina, if she was abducted?'

'The last place?' Bleidbara looked puzzled. 'I do not follow your logic, lady.'

Fidelma pointed across the headland, saying, 'You would not look for her in her own villa . . . on Govihan?'

'But there are servants on Govihan – Heraclius the apothecary and others. Why would she be taken there?'

'Because, as I have said, that is the last place they would think that we would look. Come on, let us sail for Govihan. You have your ship ready, it should not take long.'

Below, they could see the *Morvan*, still anchored in the bay.

Bleidbara looked undecided for a moment and then he shrugged.

'I suppose it is worth a try,' he admitted. 'I certainly have no better idea.'

On the quayside Boric joined them. He seemed excited.

'One of my men saw something, just before dawn,' he told them. 'He observed a man carrying the body of a woman on his shoulders, place her into a boat and sail off.'

Bleidbara stared at him, astounded. 'Then why didn't he report it immediately?' he almost shouted.

Boric spread his hands. 'The man was fearful lest he get into trouble. He shouted a challenge and when the man carrying the body did not stop, he loosed an arrow – which he was sure hit him. However, this man did not stop or release his burden. He climbed into the boat, hoisted sail, and away went the boat before the guard could reach it. It was then that the sentinel realised his mistake – and this is why he failed to report the matter.'

'Mistake?' Bleidbara stared at him. 'I don't understand.'

'The man he shot at was Iarnbud, and the orders of the lord of Brilhag are that Iarnbud is his *bretat* and has the right to come and go as he will. My guard only mentioned this to me just now when he heard the news of the disappearance of Trifina and Iuna. He is still afraid of being punished for shooting at the *bretat*.'

Bleidbara was angry. 'The man is an imbecile and shall answer to me when I return. He is sure that Iarnbud was carrying the body of a woman? In what direction did his boat go?'

'To the islands – he is not sure where.'

Fidelma looked grimly at Bleidbara. 'We will try Govihan first,' she said.

*　　*　　*

The young apothecary from Constantinopolis greeted them on the island of Govihan. He looked shocked when Fidelma told him the purpose of their visit.

'We have not seen Trifina since she returned to Brilhag with you, lady, the day before yesterday,' he said. 'As for the lady Iuna, she scarcely visits here.'

'I thought it was too simple,' Bleidbara said glumly, turning to Fidelma 'But we had better search the villa now we're here.'

'We will do what we can to find the lady Trifina,' Heraclius said, calling one of the maids to gather the servants together.

The search of the villa proved futile; even Heraclius, under Bleidbara's instruction, unlocked his stone-built hut so that they could look inside, but on condition that they touched nothing. As they came out, and Heraclius relocked it and disappeared through the walled garden to find out how the other members of the household were proceeding, Bleidbara, Fidelma and Eadulf stood on the clifftop, surveying the sea before them.

'There are a lot of islands out there,' Bleidbara said heavily. 'It's an impossible task to search them all.'

'If they were taken on board this sea raider – let's call it the *Koulm ar Maro* – from Brilhag, why did no one notice the ship in the bay?' demanded Eadulf. 'Surely you have lookouts on the *Morvran* who would have noticed such a large ship come into the inlet below the fortress – even at dead of night?'

Bleidbara was defensive.

'The *Morvran* was anchored in the bay under the fortress

walls,' he said. 'They would not see anything if the *Koulm ar Maro* came to anchor on the other side of the headland.'

Eadulf flushed a little at the rebuke because he had no sooner made his comment than he realised the answer.

'The question is – what now?' Bleidbara went on. 'I have sent men around the island to ensure that there is nowhere we have overlooked – caves or undergrowth, for instance. We have searched the villa, so there seems no way forward.'

Fidelma suddenly gave an exclamation of surprise.

She pointed downwards at the rocky coast below them. A little boat was bobbing on the water and a tiny figure was desperately trying to make it to shore. The surging waves brought the little boat tantalisingly close, but then pulled it back. The figure seemed to have no oar to guide the boat in. Then a larger wave than the rest suddenly propelled the boat right up the beach, and when the water receded, the boat remained there, held fast by the pebbles and rocks. The figure seemed to fall over the side of the boat into the still-frothing water and crawl using only one arm for a short distance before collapsing face down.

All those present on the clifftop shared the same thought: there was something very familiar about this lone sailor.

CHAPTER SEVENTEEN

❧

When Fidelma turned to speak to the others, she found Bleidbara and Eadulf already running down the grassy knoll which led to the shoreline below.

By the time they all reached the spot, one of Bleidbara's men was approaching, hurrying from the other direction. He, too, had seen the boat and its occupant.

Iarnbud lay face down in the shallows where he had fallen from the boat, trying to drag himself up above the tidemark. The shaft of an arrow was still embedded in him, close to his spine.

Bleidbara and his companion waded into the shallows, reached forward and dragged the *bretat* up beyond the clawing waves.

Iarnbud let out a pitiful groan.

'Mercy! He still lives,' muttered Eadulf, bending down to the man. But after examining the wounds, he rose and shook his head at his companions. The man was beyond help.

Iarnbud opened his glazing eyes, peered round and tried

to focus on Bleidbara. His mouth moved, but all that came from it was a dry rasping cough and a trickle of blood.

'What is it, Iarnbud?' Bleidbara encouraged softly.

The man spoke incoherently. They could discern the name 'Heraclius' repeated several times clearly, but the rest they could not understand.

'He wants the apothecary,' said Bleidbara. 'He asks for Heraclius.'

Then, with an apparent summoning of strength, Iarnbud grabbed hold of Bleidbara's shirt and dragged his head nearer. Of the words that poured forth from the thin, bloodstained lips, all they could distinguish were '*Koulm ar Maro*'.

'The ship?' demanded Fidelma quickly. 'What does he say about it?'

The warrior bent his ear to the man's lips. They moved feebly, whispering softly and then, without warning, in the middle of a word, Iarnbud's head fell back and he was dead.

Bleidbara gazed down at him for a long time and then exhaled softly.

'Well, he won't need Heraclius now.'

'What is it?' Fidelma asked urgently. 'What did he say?'

Bleidbara lowered the dead man's shoulders to the ground and looked at them. His expression seemed torn between sorrow and triumph.

'He found the ship, the *Koulm ar Maro*. He managed to overhear their plans. Apparently, those plans will come to fruition tomorrow.'

'Tomorrow? What happens then?' Fidelma wanted to know.

'The *Koulm ar Maro* is due to sail out into the Big Sea,

using the morning tide. It will then make a rendezvous off
the coast near the abbey, by which time the success of their
plan will be complete.'

'I don't understand,' Eadulf said.

Bleidbara shrugged. 'That's all he said. Apart from something about food and Heraclius, which made no sense at all.'

'Trifina said that Iarnbud was working for both of you. Is
that right?'

Bleidbara nodded, saying, 'He was loyal to the family of
Brilhag. During these last few weeks, he travelled around,
trying to pick up news of this *Koulm ar Maro*. Now he's
given his life for the little news that he could garner for us.'

'If only he could have told us what the completion of their
plan meant,' muttered Eadulf. Suddenly noticing that the small
boat was drifting, he waded into the sea to grab hold of the
gunwale and draw it back up on shore. As he did so, he
glanced inside and let out an exclamation.

'Quickly! I thought it was just a pile of cloth, a discarded
sail there – but look!'

Bleidbara tore aside the canvas.

The still figure of Iuna lay there. Her face was white and
she lay very still, as if in death.

Bleidbara reached into the boat and, with ease, the tall
warrior lifted the body of the girl in his arms. He walked the
few paces up the beach and laid her gently on the ground
beyond the waves.

Eadulf at once knelt to examine her.

'Still alive,' he said. 'Still alive, but unconscious and very
cold.'

He explored the girl's skull with his fingertips, and then he bent as if to smell her breath. 'She has not been hit on the head, but from the blue of the lips, I think she has taken a poison of some kind. I can smell it on her breath. But I'm afraid such a poison is beyond my powers to diagnose. We do need Heraclius, after all.'

Bleidbara swore softly under his breath and then, turning to his companion, issued a quick order. The man trotted away.

They stood anxiously round the unconscious form of Iuna, not knowing what to do, until the young apothecary arrived and made a swift examination.

'She has been poisoned,' Eadulf offered, feeling helpless. 'But I do not know with what substance.'

'You are right, Brother Eadulf,' Heraclius said, peering at the girl's blue lips. 'She has been poisoned. I believe that she has eaten the Death Cap fungi.' The seriousness of the situation showed in his features.

'Well? Can you help her?' pressed Fidelma.

'I cannot hold out any great chance of recovery. It depends when she ingested the poison. It is a potent one, usually fatal; just one of the fungi is enough to ensure that a full-grown man can suffer a painful death. It is usually terminal in two days.'

'You mean there is no antidote?' Fidelma said, shocked.

'No full antidote for the toxins. However, we will take her into the villa and give her an extract made from the ripe seeds of the Milk Thistle. There is hope, but only if she has not long ingested these toxins. If she is going to survive then we will know by tomorrow morning.'

He signalled to Bleidbara's man to lift the girl and carry

her up to the villa. Glancing at the body of Iarnbud, he said, 'I must tend to the living and leave the dead,' and turned after the warrior carrying the girl in his arms.

'I didn't warm to the man overmuch,' sighed Eadulf, 'but we can't let him give his life in vain.'

'Well, there is only one thing for me to do,' Bleidbara said determinedly. 'I will attempt to intercept the *Koulm ar Maro* as it makes a run for the Big Sea at dawn tomorrow.'

'How will you do that?' Fidelma asked.

'The *Morvran* stands ready. We will sail to the channel and await the *Koulm ar Maro* there. She has to pass through that narrow channel at the right time, when the tide is running from the Morbihan. My crew are men who are descended from the Veneti. We come from generations of sea-fighters.' His voice was rock-steady. 'We will be ready for them.'

'You might call this the Little Sea, Bleidbara, but it is still large enough to lose a ship in, and all these islands are easy hiding-places,' Eadulf commented.

'I am familiar with these waters, friend. Now I know where the raider is going to be and what it intends to do, I can deal with the *Koulm ar Maro*.'

'I want to come with you,' Eadulf announced firmly, without looking at Fidelma. The truth was that his prime concern was that she might insist on accompanying Bleidbara on the *Morvran* herself. If there was to be a sea battle, then he determined that she should be out of harm's way. 'I would be useful if any of the *Barnacle Goose* survivors are still prisoners with them,' he added, as if to find an excuse. 'I would be able to recognise them.'

Bleidbara was suddenly in a good humour. As a warrior, he understood action and was happy now that he had something to do that he could understand.

'You have courage, Eadulf,' he praised him. 'For a religious, you seem to have no qualms about throwing yourself into conflict.'

'If it means tracking down these murderers, then I can bear such discomfort,' Eadulf replied.

Fidelma reached out her hand and touched Eadulf on his arm, looking at him in silent approval. She understood why he had volunteered, and, if the truth were known, she felt he was right. Her place was to return to Brilhag, for that was where she knew she had to be, to resolve this mystery.

'I'll await your return at Brilhag,' she told him.'

'We will do our best to finally smoke out this evil among us,' Bleidbara said, and glanced at the sky. The journey to Govihan and the search of the island had taken them some time. It was well into the afternoon now. 'We have a long time to wait until dawn tomorrow. Let us return to the villa and see how Heraclius is proceeding. I will have need for him on board when we encounter the *Koulm ar Maro*. He will have to instruct someone who can nurse Iuna.'

Fidelma regarded him with surprise but he did not elucidate.

'There seems little to do until you sail out to intercept the *Koulm ar Maro* now. Even if Iuna recovers, she will not be able to tell us what happened for a while,' she said. 'One thing is certain, she was steward to the household at Brilhag and knowledgeable about all foods. She would not have eaten

Death Cap fungi in mistake for edible fungi. She was deliberately poisoned.' She paused. 'If my suspicion is correct, Brilhag is where we will find an answer to this mystery of the *Koulm ar Maro*. But you must bring me the final piece of this puzzle.'

'You know who is behind these raids?' Bleidbara asked.

'I now suspect who is behind them and why. I need only one more piece to settle the resolution. But before I do so, it would be good to know that the *Barnacle Goose* is safe with the survivors of the crew and, of course, that Trifina is with them.'

Eadulf was astonished at her confidence.

'If you already know who is behind the *Koulm ar Maro* and these raids and killings, don't you feel that you should share this knowledge?' he asked.

'I said that I suspect . . . suspicion, even based on circumstantial evidence, is not enough for an accusation to be proven.'

'Even so, a shared knowledge is a danger halved.'

'True, but a single whisper, or a glance might betray our thoughts, Eadulf, and if they *are* betrayed by as much as the blink of an eye, I may lose my quarry.'

'We can return you to Brilhag on the *Morvran*, lady,' Bleidbara offered. 'We will drop you off there tonight and then move on to an anchorage I know of, where we can wait until the hour before dawn. Then we can sail for the interception point to engage the raiders as they attempt to catch the tide out of Morbihan.'

'Excellent,' she approved. 'I feel things are drawing towards a conclusion.'

* * *

Dusk had fallen when the *Morvran* finally anchored in the bay under the headland on which the fortress of Brilhag rose. It had taken longer than they expected because Bleidbara had insisted on loading a number of curious-looking sections of wood, set into frames with ropes and wheels. Neither Fidelma nor Eadulf had ever seen such wooden constructions as were hoisted onto the deck, and had no idea what they were. Canvas sheeting covered them as they were set up in the bows of the vessel. Bleidbara had claimed that the equipment was necessary to his task, and that the presence of Heraclius was essential. Fidelma took the view that Bleidbara knew his business and so did not bother him or Heraclius with unnecessary questions. The young apothecary from Constantinopolis supervised the loading, paying particular care to a sealed wooden case as it was cautiously taken into the hold. Bleidbara saw their curiosity but did not explain.

Heraclius reported that Iuna had been given the treatment, but only the next twelve hours would show whether she would respond to it. He had left her in the care of one of the female servants at the villa, together with explicit instructions on how she should be treated. At Fidelma's insistence, a warrior was left with them for protection.

Now, as they dropped anchor before Brilhag, Bleidbara came to see Fidelma off in one of the ship's boats.

'We shall leave and anchor further down the coast so as to be ready just before dawn,' he said gravely. 'If all goes well, you will see our return here sometime tomorrow.'

'I'll be waiting,' smiled Fidelma. 'I wish you luck.'

'We all need luck, lady. These people, whoever they are, will be eager to destroy any that are in their way. If you need help, seek out Boric. He is a good man to have at your side in time of danger. Tell him that I have placed him under your orders.'

Fidelma turned to Eadulf. 'You look after yourself,' she instructed softly. Then she climbed over the side into the boat. She was ferried to the shore by one of the ship's company who left her on the quay and immediately rowed back to rejoin the *Morvran*.

Fidelma stood for a moment looking at the disappearing boat, heading out to the dark shape of Bleidbara's ship. Then she turned up the pathway that led to the fortress, trying to adjust her vision to the darkness. She wished that she had had the foresight to bring a lamp but, almost as she thought it, the moon suddenly appeared from the bank of clouds and cast its blue glow over the area, revealing the man standing blocking the path a few paces in front of her.

Even with the moonlight, she could not make out any more than a few details. He was holding a shield, and a sword hung at his side. He challenged her in Breton and she guessed rather than knew the meaning of his words.

When she responded, assuming he was one of Boric's guards, he moved forward and asked a further question, and this time she could not guess at its meaning.

'*Loquerisne linguam latinam?*' she asked hopefully,

The man shook his head, turned and shouted something. A moment later another man hurried down the path, surefooted in the darkness. The first man stiffened and spoke rapidly to him.

'Who are you?' demanded the second warrior in Latin.

Fidelma frowned. 'Fidelma of Hibernia,' she replied. This was probably the best form of announcing herself in a way that would be understood. 'Where is Boric?'

The man did not answer, but his eyes focused on the darkness behind her and widened a little. He obviously saw the outline of the *Morvran*.

'What ship is that?' he demanded before she could speak again.

'It is the *Morvran*, commanded by Bleidbara of—'

The man was already turning and shouting orders. Fidelma had an uneasy feeling.

'Who are you?' she asked. 'Where is Boric, who commands the guard here?'

'You will precede me to the fortress,' snapped the man, his hand resting lightly on his sword.

With a sinking heart she suddenly realised that these were not the guards that had been left behind by Bleidbara. And now there was no way to warn Bleidbara. With her thoughts racing, she was forced to walk on, the warrior two paces behind her, his hand ready on his sword. She followed the path up to the gate in the outer wall and through the door that eventually led into the kitchen area of the fortress. Guards were placed at all the entrances.

Fidelma asked herself how the fortress of Brilhag had managed to fall into the hands of these men. They were well-clothed, well-armed and seemed highly disciplined.

They were not as she had imagined the brigands of the *Koulm ar Maro*.

She was pushed firmly through the kitchens and finally into the familiar great hall.

Two men were standing before the fire, their features distorted by the flickering light. They looked up in surprise as Fidelma was ushered roughly into the room.

One of them – a tall, well-built man of over fifty, with long reddish hair and a beard, whose features seemed quite pleasant and handsome, took a step forward. His face seemed oddly familiar to Fidelma. His eyes were pale and she was not sure whether they were blue or grey. He was richly attired and wore a golden necklet and armbands.

'Who are you, lady?' he began.

Fidelma, angry with herself at being thus caught, replied angrily, 'Who are *you*? And by what right do your men hold me prisoner?'

The man's eyes widened in surprise for a moment at her fearless attitude. His companion, an elderly man with grey hair, chuckled as if witnessing a joke.

'Lady,' replied the tall man solemnly, 'I am called Alain of Domnonia and am King of the Bretons. By this right, do I do all things. And now, please answer me: who are you?'

Another figure emerged from the shadows at the end of the hall, saying, 'It is the stranger I told you of, Father. She is Fidelma of Hibernia.'

King Alain took a few rapid paces towards Fidelma with hands outstretched.

'Fidelma of Hibernia – welcome! Riwanon and Budic have

told me all about you, and how you came to be here. So I welcome you, but at the same time ask you to accept my sorrow for the suffering that you have been put through. Your Cousin Bressal had been an honoured guest at my court when we agreed a treaty between my people and your brother, the King of Muman. It grieves my heart to hear of his death and your distress. Where is your companion, Eadulf the Saxon?'

Instead of replying, Fidelma glanced towards Budic, who had perched himself with a grin on the table, with one leg swinging. It seemed his favourite posture. Then her eyes turned to the elderly man by the fire. His features, too, seemed familiar. Alain noticed her examination and smiled.

'I crave your indulgence for not making the introduction. This is the *mac'htiern* of Brilhag, Lord Canao.'

The elderly man came forward, and Fidelma now realised why his features were familiar. There was the reflection of Macliau and of Trifina on them. Whereas Macliau's features were weak, those of Canao, his father, were strong and held a quality of wisdom and maturity that seemed lacking in his son.

The lord of Brilhag held out his hand.

'I have heard how you saved my son from the mob that would have killed him, and how you set off to find my missing daughter. What news of her?'

'Alas, we have not found her,' admitted Fidelma. 'But we have some knowledge which might lead us to her.'

The warrior who had accompanied her now broke into a

quick speech to the King. King Alain turned to Fidelma: 'The captain of my guard says there is a ship in the inlet below and he is worried for our safety.'

'You need not worry. The ship is the *Morvran*. Bleidbara is the commander of it. I have just landed from her. My companion Eadulf is still on board and they expect to continue the search for Lord Canao's daughter at dawn. I also hope that they will be led to the survivors of the *Barnacle Goose*.'

Lord Canao nodded slowly in approval.

'Bleidbara is a good man. That's why I appointed him commander of my warriors. I am content, if he is in command still.'

Budic rose from his perch, saying, 'You must tell us all the details, lady. But I would like to be in at the kill, to take revenge for the deaths that have taken place here. I will get a man to row me out to the *Morvran*.'

King Alain glanced at the young man and held up his hand to stay him. 'Let us rather talk of the visitation of justice, my son, than of revenge.'

'Budic of Domnonia,' Fidelma whispered, gazing at the young man. 'Then he is the son of your first wife who died from the Yellow Plague?'

A pained expression crossed the King's features.

'You are well informed, lady. Budic is my only offspring. His mother was my great companion and partner. I thought that I would never survive the grief when she died of the Yellow Plague. Thanks be to God, I found solace with Riwanon. It is beyond man's expectation to find two great loves in one lifetime. But I have been truly blessed.'

'With your permission, father, I will join Bleidbara,' the young warrior requested.

King Alain shook his head. 'I need you here, Budic. Bleidbara and his men are capable enough. I must have my guard commander at my side.'

Budic looked unhappy, but then acknowledged his father's wish. King Alain spoke to Fidelma's escort and the warrior saluted and left. The King turned back to her with a smile.

'I have told him not to interfere with the *Morvran*.'

'So, tell us, Fidelma, what is the plan of Bleidbara?' Budic wanted to know.

Until her suspicions were confirmed, Fidelma felt it was best to say as little as possible. She chose her words carefully.

'Bleidbara believes he knows where the raider, the *Koulm ar Maro*, might be. I am not sure where, as I do not know these waters you call the Morbihan. I believe it might be some eastern islet.' She was deliberately misleading them.

'Well, let us provide you with refreshments,' announced King Alain. 'And you may give us an account of your adventures. It sounds as if this will be a story told by our bards for many years.'

'I would do so with pleasure, Alain. But the saga is not ended and I would advise you not to relax your guard too much.' Fidelma spoke in a serious tone. 'It is my belief that this mystery is quickly coming to its planned conclusion.'

'Its *planned conclusion*?' King Alain looked perplexed. 'What do you mean?'

'All I can say is that I will be able to tell you more tomorrow.'

'The lady is being dramatic,' Budic observed cynically. 'What mystery are we talking of?'

The King held her eyes in a thoughtful gaze.

'I have no need to ask if you are jesting, Fidelma. The gravity of what you say is in your expression. You suspect some conspiracy here?'

'I do. I suggest that you should continue to take a special care. As I said, I am hoping that by the end of tomorrow, we shall know enough to present you with all the facts. But tonight, with Lord Canao's permission – for I know of the proscription against weapons in this house – we should sleep *arrectis auribus*, with our bedchamber doors locked, and with trustworthy guards outside.'

'Fidelma!' At that moment, Riwanon came down the stairs and moved quickly towards her with a smile and both hands held out in welcome.

'I was so worried for you when you disappeared earlier today. After Ceingar's death and the disappearance of Trifina and Iuna, why, I was in great agitation. It is good to see you alive and safe. And now that Alain is here, all is well, is that not so?' Riwanon turned round as if searching for someone. 'But where are Eadulf and Bleidbara? Did you have any success in finding Trifina and the girl Iuna?'

Fidelma shook her head with a sad expression.

'No – but we have not given up,' she replied. 'We hope to have some news soon. Bleidbara is continuing the search. All we can do is get some rest tonight and await the coming of tomorrow.'

Lord Canao was looking glum.

'This is a strange homecoming for me. My son, Macliau, is accused of murder. My daughter, Trifina, and my foster-daughter, Iuna, are both missing. Abbot Maelcar and the queen's maid have been murdered under my roof. My people are now accusing me and mine of untold crimes. God alone knows what conspiracy is underway. I even find that a *bretat* from Bro-Gernev named Kaourentin has arrived here to judge my son.'

Fidelma was surprised at the news.

'Brother Metellus told me that it took at least four days to travel to Bro-Gernev and back,' she said. 'You mean the *bretat* is here already?'

'Apparently, Kaourentin was travelling from Bro-Gernev to Naoned and had arrived by chance at the Abbey of Gildas seeking hospitality,' replied Canao. 'Brother Metellus told me that it had been suggested a judge from Bro-Gernev should sit to hear my son's defence rather than my own *bretat*. Apparently, the people would not respect a judgement given by the *bretat* of Brilhag.'

'Is Brother Metellus here?' asked Fidelma.

'He came in company of this man Kaourentin. I would have preferred my *bretat*, Iarnbud, to be here to advise me.'

Fidelma looked at him levelly for a moment.

'I regret that Iarnbud is also dead,' she said. 'I will explain in a moment.'

'More deaths? Are we threatened in any way, Fidelma?' asked King Alain in a shocked voice.

Fidelma could not resist answering with dry humour.

'I think that we are threatened in every way,' she replied solemnly. 'As I said, we must be alert tonight.'

'But no one would dare break into this fortress.' Budic's chuckle was dismissive. 'We have guards enough.'

'Perhaps they don't have to break in,' replied Fidelma softly.

Riwanon shivered slightly, saying, 'You frighten me, Fidelma. What do you mean?'

'I simply mean that we all need to be vigilant, for tomorrow will be an important day.'

'Tomorrow?' queried King Alain. 'You keep saying that. Why tomorrow?'

'Because that is when this mystery will finally be unravelled.'

CHAPTER EIGHTEEN

❧

Like a swan gliding across the dark waters, the *Morvran* slid forward, her sails stirring at the first breaths of the pre-dawn breeze. Her rigging began to shake and whisper like the soft movement of fingers over the taut strings of a lyre. Bleidbara seemed relaxed as he instructed the man at the tiller, guiding the vessel into the westerly darkness with the first glimmerings of the light heralding a new day behind them. Not for the first time Eadulf reminded himself that these people were essentially a seagoing community whose ancestors, with their large ships and maritime dexterity, had nearly brought disaster to Julius Caesar's fleet centuries before.

Eadulf and Heraclius stood to one side of the raised deck at the stern of the vessel, near the tiller, where Bleidbara had planted himself, feet wide apart and hands before him, thumbs stuck into his belt. He glanced up at the moon that was still low in the western sky but so pale that it was almost indiscernible. The dawn atmosphere was chill.

'Do you think we will catch them?' Eadulf asked quietly,

breaking the silence that had descended since the order had
been given to hoist sail. 'There are so many islands for them
to hide behind in order to evade us, and once they are through
the channel into the great sea beyond . . .'

'You forget, Eadulf,' replied Bleidbara, 'the tide is now
flowing into Morbihan with a powerful surge. No ship can
move against that current in the channel. They are stuck here
until the tide turns and that will be well after dawn. It's a
very dangerous tide to face: the sea can rise up to four metres
here.'

Eadulf remembered what old Aourken had told them about
the passage into the Morbihan. As little as he knew the sea
and ships, he could still appreciate the dextrous way that
Bleidbara's crew handled the large vessel.

'What do you intend?' Heraclius asked Bleidbara.

'I intend to go to Er Lannig, an island called the Little
Heath, which guards the entrance to the channel. We won't
feel the strong pull of the incoming tide there. That would be
the closest point where the *Koulm ar Maro* can wait for the
turn of the tide. If they are not there, I'll start to weather up
to Gavrinis, the Isle of Goats, and then move up the channel,
keeping the Isle of Monks to our starboard. Unless I am a
bad sailor, we'll find our sea-raider somewhere in those waters.'

Bleidbara sounded confident enough.

'And when we do meet up with them, what then? What if
they want to fight?' asked Eadulf. 'I've never been in a real
sea battle before.'

Bleidbara smiled grimly in the semi-darkness and looked
towards Heraclius.

'We have the wild ass already in place at our bow. Then we will see if that little invention is what it claims to be. If it is not, it will be a contest to see if our bows are stronger than their bows, our arrows more powerful than their arrows.'

'The wild ass?' Eadulf peered at the bow, but in the darkness all he could see was the curious canvas-covered wooden frames that had been brought aboard the previous afternoon.

Heraclius touched him on the arm and pointed at the covering.

'The onager is a form of catapult used by the Roman legions. They called it the wild ass because, when the projectile is released, the engine that fires it kicks back like a mule,' he explained. 'I have trained some men to use it, and I'm hoping that we don't have to come to close quarters to fight the enemy ship. The range of the weapon is about three hundred to three hundred and fifty metres.'

'You hope to hole the ship by throwing rocks at it?' Eadulf had heard that the Romans had used such engines in siege war, but never on shipboard.

Heraclius just smiled mysteriously and shook his head.

Eadulf, during the period that followed, had cause to feel regret that he had come on such a voyage. He was not the best of sailors and now the excitement of the first part of the chase began to wear off, he realised the stark truth: he was on a vessel, ploughing across dark waters, en route to engage a ship that would obviously fight back. He was anxious but knew that showing anxiety would not be advisable; at this time he must feign the same indifference that Bleidbara and Heraclius appeared to be displaying. He had never seen two

ships engage one another on the sea before, and he antici-
pated that it would be fierce and bloody. His calling as a
religious would not protect him in this battle. He wondered
whether he should ask Bleidbara what he should do when
the attack began, but them compelled himself to refrain from
comment.

The vessel was moving along at a fast pace now as a south-
westerly wind, coming off the land, caught the sails. A white
ribbon of sea foam was spreading on either side of its bows,
almost phosphorescent and clearly visible in spite of the darkness. But the darkness was now vanishing. The moon was
still well above the horizon but had become a pallid white
orb, a wispy blob of sheep's wool in the pale sky. The coastline of the peninsula was close to their portside, a dark,
impenetrable line of trees and hills. To the starboard, the
humps of islands were now rising out of the early-morning
mist that hung across the Little Sea. The helmsman appeared
to know the waters well even in the darkness, skilfully moving
the helm a point or two to avoid submerged rocks, judging
his distance from points Eadulf could not even see.

Bleidbara suddenly shouted an order and one of the men
leaped agilely to the rigging and went up to the top of the
main mast. After a few moments he called down and
Bleidbara's mouth tightened a little at his words.

'The trouble is,' he confided to Eadulf, 'we have the dawn
rising at our backs. They will see us coming if they are directly
ahead of us – and before we ourselves get close enough to
see their sails. I have put a man up there to see if he can spot
any sign of them.'

Eadulf knew enough to realise that the height of the mast gave an advantage in sighting a vessel across the water that would otherwise be hidden from those on the deck.

They sailed on in silence for a while, the tension growing among the crew. There was a cry from the masthead.

'There's Er Lannig now,' grunted Bleidbara. 'We'll keep it to port and come north-west of it.' He gave a sharp order to the helmsman. 'We have to steer clear of the southern tip – there are submerged standing stones there.'

As the ship swung further north, Heraclius explained: 'The island seems to have been a centre of pagan worship. I have come exploring here before. There are the remains of two stone circles. Do you see them?'

Eadulf could just see the silhouettes of jagged stones, curving into the sea.

'One circle is entirely submerged, but one of the stones remains very dangerous. Local fishermen call it the blacksmith's stone,' Bleidbara went on. 'It could tear the bottom out of a ship like this.'

Now the dawn had become a reality, not with rich reds and golds but with a pale watery hue that seemed to fore-tell rain to come. The sun was well hidden behind a growing pack of pale clouds, but it was now clear enough to see for some distance – and all eyes swept the sea around them.

'We'll turn for the Island of Goats,' called Bleidbara, pointing ahead.

Another shout from the masthead made them all look up. Eadulf did not understand what the lookout was saying but his arm was thrust out more to the north of them. He looked but couldn't see anything.

Bleidbara slapped his thigh with a grin.

'There she is, just where I expected her to be. She is heading south towards us.' He glanced up at the sails. 'But we should have the wind with us. Take a care for yourselves, my friends, as we will soon be upon them.'

There was now a shout from the maindeck and Eadulf turned and saw a ship materialising across the water. Her sails were fully rigged but they hung almost useless in the prevailing wind. The ship was pitching and moving without elegance as it sought to make headway.

It seemed that they had been spotted, for there was move-ment on the oncoming ship. Its bows seemed to move as if it were trying to turn away.

'They are wearing ship,' muttered Heraclius. 'Trying to turn,' he added for Eadulf's sake.

Indeed, the ship was jerking idly backwards and forwards. It seemed that those on board had been surprised by the appearance of Bleidbara's vessel moving rapidly towards them, heaving and plunging as the wind grew stronger. The water was gushing under her bows; the plumes of white froth spreading more widely as she raced across the gap towards the sea-raider.

'Time to get ready!' Bleidbara shouted to Heraclius.

The young man nodded, and with a quick, 'Good luck,' to both Bleidbara and Eadulf, he made his way for'ard to where the wild ass was being uncovered by some of the crew.

Eadulf had never seen a machine like it before. At first it

seemed to consist of a triangular frame of dark oak whose base was fixed firmly on the deck. At the front end was a vertical frame of solid timber; through this frame, Eadulf noticed an axle that had a single stout upright spoke inserted through a skein of twisted rope. At the end of the spoke was a leather thong or sling. The axle or horizontal barrel was rotated by a crank which forced the vertical spoke backwards almost to a horizontal position. He had heard something about these Ancient Roman engines. A stone would be inserted into the sling and the vertical arm released, usually by the person in control, using a mallet to knock out the securing pin, which held the arm. Thus released, with such pressure provided by the tension of twisted rope, the arm went up and would throw the stone or rock for a considerable distance.

He could see Heraclius examining and checking the engine. Then he said something to one of his men. Two of them disappeared below decks and came back carrying the wooden box carefully between them. It was obviously heavy and they placed it cautiously by the engine. Heraclius bent down and opened it and extracted one of the large clay balls that Eadulf had seen in the apothecary's stone hut.

Bleidbara gave a warning shout to Heraclius and pointed to the oncoming ship.

Now, in the early-morning light, Eadulf could see archers lining the decks near the bows. He saw the familiar lines of the ship, the carved figure of the dove on its prow. It was, indeed, the *Koulm ar Maro*, The Dove of Death, that had attacked the *Barnacle Goose*. There was no disputing its lines as it turned for the attack. But Bleidbara was in charge of no undefended merchantman. His warriors were already lined up at the side with their own bows ready.

Nervously, Eadulf edged towards a position where a spar might afford him some protection from the onslaught of arrows that would undoubtedly fall on them. He had presumed that Bleidbara would run the ship alongside the *Koulm ar Maro*. Now he realised that Bleidbara was heading bow first towards the vessel as if to ram her. Heraclius and his companions had lifted one of the large clay balls into the sling and the young man seemed to be sighting his curious weapon as if measuring the decreasing distance between the two vessels.

'Heraclius won't knock a hole in that vessel with those clay balls,' Eadulf called to Bleidbara. 'Hasn't he got some heavy stones to inflict more damage?'

Bleidbara glanced at him and smiled reassuringly.

'Keep your head down, Brother Eadulf. We shall open the battle when we are three hundred metres from her.'

The *Koulm ar Maro* was no longer trying to turn but also coming bow first towards them in spite of the wind being entirely with Bleidbara's vessel. It was only now that Eadulf realised that the enemy's main deck was higher than their own, so the archers on the *Koulm ar Maro* had the advantage of shooting down while Bleidbara's men would have to shoot upwards. Eadulf knew enough about warfare to be aware that this was not the best position. With a dry mouth he watched the dark strip of water closing between the two vessels.

Suddenly Bleidbara shouted to Heraclius.

The young man bent forward. Eadulf saw the mallet in his

hand and heard it strike on the wooden peg. He could feel the vibration through the entire vessel as the pole with its sling released the projectile under extreme pressure. The clay ball arched upwards across the space between the two vessels, and Eadulf was bitterly disappointed to see it hit a jutting spar on the *Koulm ar Maro* and fall back into the sea, breaking into pieces as it did so. Then he gasped in astonishment, for even as it fragmented he saw a glint of fire – and next thing there was a patch of blazing water where the pieces of the ball had fallen in the sea. He could not believe his eyes. The seawater was on fire!

Heraclius and his team were already winching the pole back into position and another of the curious clay balls was being placed into the sling.

Bleidbara was grinning at him. 'Heraclius calls it *pyr thalassion* in his own language. He translates it as liquid fire. He says that his father Callinicus was developing it in Byzantium. It gives us more advantage against these sea-raiders now.'

Eadulf was speechless. Fire that could not be put out by water? It was terrifying. Barbaric. No wonder Heraclius had been guarding the secret so closely.

There was a strange whistling sound through the air as the enemy archers released their first salvo. The range was closing and several arrows embedded themselves into the ship.

Once more Eadulf heard the bang of the hammer striking the pin and felt the slight shudder of the ship beneath him as Heraclius' infernal weapon was released.

This time the clay ball fragmented on the forward deck of

the oncoming vessel, and it erupted in flame. He could hear the cries of alarm from the enemy, saw men running forward with buckets of water. But even as he watched, he saw how the water merely pushed the flame here and there, and made no impact on dousing it.

Bleidbara's crew let out a cheer. A sharp word from Bleidbara and they fell silent; another command and the archers lining the portside of the vessel took aim and, as one man, released their flight of arrows. Screams echoed across the water, showing that some of them had found targets.

For a third time Heraclius and his men made ready their onager and released it. This time, the terrible contents of the clay ball fell in the centre of the main deck and that was soon ablaze.

Six of the clay balls had been brought onto the deck and already Heraclius was superintending the loading of a fourth in his machine.

Bleidbara shouted to him: a call to pause. Stepping to the rail, and using his hands as a trumpet to project his voice, Bleidbara called across to the vessel where the flames were catching hold of the timbers. Eadulf presumed it was a call for the *Koulm ar Maro* to surrender. The answer came in a shower of arrows, one of which struck a crew member, and even as he fell, Eadulf saw he was beyond assistance.

Bleidbara signalled to Heraclius again. Once more came the ominous shudder and the projectile could be seen striking the stern of the vessel near the helm before the area erupted in flame.

Bleidbara was shouting to his own helmsman who pulled

the vessel over, edging it near the burning *Koulm ar Maro*.
Once again, he was calling on his enemy to surrender – without
response. Eadulf peered into the mass of flame now spreading
over its decks, trying to search out the slight figure in white
that he remembered so well. There was no sign of him among
those running to and fro on the deck, trying to put out the
flames that roared inexorably around them. There seemed to
be no one in command, for the enemy crew appeared in confusion. Some tried to put out the flames while others wielded
swords in futile gestures towards the closing vessel. Others
still tried to shoot their bows, seeming to get in each other's
way.

Eadulf was gazing in horror at the terrible inferno. Suddenly
an awesome thought came to his mind.

'Trifina! What if the lady Trifina is a prisoner on board?'

Bleidbara stared at him aghast, his face white despite the
reflected glow of the flames. In his battle fever, he had
forgotten about Trifina.

Bleidbara shouted again, yet another demand for surrender,
but an arrow whistled by his face and embedded itself into
a spar nearby. Had Eadulf been standing closer, it would have
found a target in him. Heraclius had released yet another of
his terrifying clay balls into the ship, where it burst against
the central mast, the flames roaring upwards as if racing to
get to the top of it.

The entire deck of the *Koulm ar Maro* was a hungry sea
of flames. Here and there, some men were jumping overboard, some with their clothes alight – which were not put
out even when the unfortunates struck the water.

Bleidbara turned to his helmsman with a swift order and the helm went over.

'We are hauling off from her,' he explained to Eadulf. 'This fire is too much. We must save ourselves from her flames.'

Eadulf could still see men jumping from the decks of the sea-raider. But he saw no sign of the slight figure in white that he was hoping to spot. He prayed that Trifina was not a prisoner on that dying ship. Some of Bleidbara's crew had brought out long wooden poles and were using them to push the ship away from the sides of the burning vessel. They swung free, their sails filling again as they clawed across the waves, distancing themselves from the blazing inferno. Within a few moments they could see little resemblance to the fighting ship that they had approached. The hungry flames were all-consuming; decks, bows and the entire hull of the vessel seemed to be one pyre of crackling flame.

Having secured the remaining clay balls below deck, Heraclius came trotting back along the deck to join Eadulf. There was a strange, rather sad expression on his face.

'So that was what you didn't want us to find?' Eadulf commented dryly.

'It is something my father developed for our emperor, Constantinos. It is something that I hope no one else discovers.'

'A terrible weapon,' Eadulf agreed heavily. 'No one could stand against that.'

Then: 'Look!' cried Heraclius. 'Look at that!'

Everyone stood watching in silence. There was a strange gurgling sound. As they stood, fascinated and unable to tear their eyes away, the gurgling grew louder and the flames suddenly ceased. Against the darkness of the island there was nothing to be seen, not even a glimmer of fire, just a pall of smoke rising above the waters and dispersing in the breeze. The sea-raider had sunk with such abruptness that it was as if the vessel, even blazing as it was, had simply vanished. Swallowed into the hungry maw of the sea.

Bleidbara was calling orders and the crew swarmed up the rigging to the sails while the helmsman put the tiller hard over.

'We are putting the ship about to see if there are any survivors,' Heraclius explained.

'From that?' Eadulf shook his head sadly. Surely there was little hope.

Amazingly, contrary to his expectation, some people had escaped unscathed; they were dragged from the water. Soaked and demoralised, they were brought aft to be questioned by Bleidbara.

'Ask them if the lady Trifina was on board,' Eadulf reminded him, although such a reminder was unnecessary.

Only one of the prisoners answered Bleidbara – and that only in monosyllables. Bleidbara struck him twice across the face, making Eadulf wince. He hated such brutality but had to admit that if it forced the man to speak, perhaps it was justified. Even so, the man was still defiant and his expression was one of hatred.

'He says there is a woman on the other ship,' Bleidbara interpreted.

'What other ship?' demanded Eadulf. 'The *Barnacle Goose*?'

The prisoner shrugged and Bleidbara was shouting at him again. Eadulf could not understand what was being said although a word that sounded like 'looverdee' was repeated several times.

In fact, Bleidbara grew quite violent with the man at this, grabbing him by the throat and thrusting his face within an inch of the prisoner's own. He shook him like a dog might shake a rabbit, and Eadulf could hear the man's teeth rattle.

The prisoner was still defiant but responded, repeating the word 'looverdee'. Bleidbara turned to Eadulf.

'He says the other ship is hidden on an island called Enez Lovrdi, which means the Leper's Island.'

'Do you know it?' asked Eadulf.

'I do. It is a small island not far from here – once used for lepers to dwell in, isolated from the rest of the communities. There is an old, grey-stone fortress there but it is no longer habitable.' Bleidbara seemed annoyed with himself. 'I had never thought to search there. People generally shun the island. So that is where the *Koulm ar Maro* was hidden all this time.'

'Well,' Eadulf said with grim satisfaction, 'let us go and collect the *Barnacle Goose*. Where is the young captain, the one in white? Did he perish with the ship?'

Bleidbara shook his head. 'It was hard to extract information from the man,' he said as he glared at the prisoner.

'So what is the plan? They might have left more men on this island to defend it in case of attack.'

Bleidbara rubbed his chin thoughtfully. 'I see your point. We need to make some plan of attack.'

'One that does not put our friends on the *Barnacle Goose* at risk,' Eadulf pointed out.

After a few moments, Bleidbara had decided on his next move. 'I am in favour of sailing the *Morvran* directly to the island and making an immediate attack. At least the *Koulm ar Maro* is sunk and they have no large ship to counter our attack now.'

'We should find out where it is anchored and how many men there are to defend it.'

Bleidbara grinned, saying, 'You have missed your calling, Brother Eadulf. You should have been a strategist.' Turning aside, he then whispered, 'This prisoner might speak Latin. Whatever I do, I want you to support me and not be shocked by anything.'

Bewildered, Eadulf nodded.

'If we can get the information we want, I will.'

Bleidbara turned to a couple of his crewmen and issued orders. One of them took a rope and threw it over a spar, then proceeded to tie one end into a noose. The prisoner watched wide-eyed as the task was quickly accomplished.

Bleidbara spoke to him harshly, then he turned to Eadulf and said in Latin: 'I have told him that he is a pirate, a murderer and thief, and he knows the consequences of his actions.'

The man began to tremble a little. And muttered something.

'It seems our pirate pleads for mercy,' interpreted Bleidbara.

'Mercy has to be earned,' Eadulf said, playing his part. 'I can only pray that he will find mercy in the next world.'

'You are right, Brother Eadulf. It is no use asking him for

information. I will tell my men to put the noose around his neck.'

The man's hands were secured behind his back and, with a struggle, the noose was put in place.

The man was sobbing now and talking almost incoherently. There was no need for Bleidbara to interpret. Eadulf's expression of disgust was genuine, for he was revolted by the whole spectacle.

However, Bleidbara was right. The man did speak some Latin and was straining towards Eadulf.

'Please, please, Brother. You are a man of God. You cannot let him do this.'

Eadulf turned to him with a severe expression, saying, 'The captain is within his rights. You are guilty of the things he charges. Why should I intervene?'

'I am entitled to a trial . . . I am—'

'You are entitled to nothing more than the lack of mercy you showed your victims,' interrupted Bleidbara harshly. He said something to his men and one of them tightened the rope so that the prisoner was forced up on tiptoe.

The man screamed as he found himself being hauled up.

'Stop!' Eadulf ordered. 'Lower him. Perhaps he could earn a hearing before one of your *bretats* – but only if he answers our questions.'

The man almost collapsed, coughing and sobbing. Bleidbara seemed to consider what Eadulf said for a moment.

'I might be lenient – if he tells me how many of his band are on Enez Lovrdi, exactly where they are placed, and where the prisoners are held.'

The words immediately came tumbling out of the man.

'There are only half a dozen fighting men on the merchant ship which we captured some days ago . . .'

'And the prisoners?'

'They are kept in the hold of the ship which is anchored in a creek on the north side of the island. It is deep water but surrounded by trees, so that it is hidden from casual observance.'

'Are there lookouts at the fortress?'

'Everyone who was left on the island is on the merchant ship.'

'And you say that the woman is aboard?'

'She is.'

'Where is your captain?'

The man gestured with the point of his chin towards the debris now floating on the waters.

'He was hit directly by one of those fireballs. So was the mate.'

'Was he a slight man dressed in white?' intervened Eadulf.

The prisoner looked at him blankly. 'Taran? He was a big man from Pou Kaer . . . Oh, you mean the man who gave Taran orders? He often came on our raids with us. No, he was not on board.'

'Who is he? Where is he? At this Enez Lovrdi?' demanded Bleidbara.

'Not on the island,' replied the man. 'As for who he is, I don't know. I presumed Taran knew. Whenever he came on board, he was dressed in white with a mask. A merciless man. You did not disobey him with impunity.'

'So where is he now?' demanded Eadulf sharply.

'Our captain said our orders were to head out to sea and then come along the Rhuis Peninsula on the seaward side tonight at dusk. We were to wait near the cliffs by the abbey. Then pick up the man in white and his companion.'

'At dusk?'

The prisoner nodded rapidly.

'And you swear that you do not know who this young man is, who has been giving you orders?' pressed Eadulf.

'I truly do not know who he is, Brother. Do not punish me for my ignorance. I have never seen him unmasked. I never saw his features, and if anyone dared disobey his orders then death was the immediate penalty. Even our captain, Taran, was in fear of him.'

'Were you ever told what cause you were fighting for?' intervened Bleidbara.

'For booty, for riches – that is all I know.'

Eadulf gazed down at the wretched man, who was now kneeling on the deck, hands still tied behind him and with the loosened rope still around his neck.

'One question more. Who supplied you with your arrows? They are all well made.'

The man hesitated a moment, as if surprised by the question, before replying, 'The man in white supplied them and told us to use them. Also to use the banner and to make sure it was seen when we carried out our attacks.'

'Did he explain the purpose?'

'Perhaps to Taran but not to us.'

'Let him be taken back to the other prisoners.' Eadulf sighed, feeling a little disgusted with himself at having to force the information out of him in such a manner.

Bleidbara gave the order but was gazing at Eadulf with something akin to admiration.

'Well, Brother Eadulf, I swear that you make a good conspirator. That man would not have spoken, had we not frightened him to extract the information.'

Eadulf's expression was one of repugnance.

'I did not enjoy the experience. What if he had refused to give the information?' he asked.

'Then we would have had to keep him a prisoner so that he could be tried,' shrugged Bleidbara.

Eadulf's eyes widened. 'You were just playing a game?'

'I did not think it was a game,' Bleidbara assured him. 'But we needed the information and quickly.'

'And now we have that information?' queried Heraclius, speaking for the first time since the scene was played out before him.

'I suggest that we sail directly for Enez Lovrdi, for this creek, and board the *Barnacle Goose*. While some of my men engage the guards, Eadulf will head for the hold and release the prisoners. He knows them, so he can reassure them about what is happening. Do we agree?'

'I should go with Eadulf,' Heraclius advised. 'He will need someone to watch his back.'

'Agreed,' replied Bleidbara. 'I'll instruct the men now, for we do not have much time before we are upon the island.'

* * *

It seemed only minutes later that the *Morvran* was bearing down on a heavily wooded island. Bleidbara was determined to lead the assault himself and passed over the handling of the ship to his first mate. Already the sails were coming down and two smaller boats were swung out and lowered even as the *Morvran* closed towards what at first seemed a wall of dark rocks and trees. But as they came nearer, Eadulf saw that the rocks parted into a passage. Edging closer still, he saw the stern end of a large ship and felt a sudden elation as, more by instinct than recollection, he recognised the *Barnacle Goose*.

He and Heraclius scrambled into one of the boats, joining Bleidbara and several of his men. Other warriors climbed into the second boat. Both small vessels were quickly propelled towards the creek in which the *Barnacle Goose* was moored.

A shout from the ship told them they had been spotted. Eadulf was surprised that they had not been seen long before. Perhaps the guards who had been left behind were lax in their watch or were more concerned with watching their prisoners than thinking of an external attack.

A few arrows flew harmlessly into the waters around them and then they were bumping against the side of the large seagoing vessel and Bleidbara's men were swarming up the sides. Yelling and the clash of metal, along with the occasional cry of pain, filled the air as Eadulf grasped the rope and hauled himself up on the familiar deck he had abandoned what seemed a lifetime ago. Was it really just a few days? Heraclius came quickly after him.

The deck was now a confusion of struggling bodies, men intent on killing each other. Eadulf dodged through them, the young Greek at his side, and headed towards the hold of the ship. It was no use trying to remove the deck hatches and so he led the way down beyond the stern cabins, for he knew that a small hatchway led from there into the cargo hold. They met with only one man, who seemed to be guarding the gangway; he lunged at Eadulf with his sword and, as Eadulf threw himself aside, Heraclius pressed forward and drove his weapon under the man's ribs. With a gurgling scream, the assailant sank to the ground.

Eadulf was at the hatch. He threw back the bolts and swung open the door. Inside was an evil-smelling darkness, relieved by a single candle. People were stirring there. A face appeared, familiar albeit bearded and haggard.

'Hoel?' frowned Eadulf, recognising the second mate of the *Barnacle Goose*. 'Is that you?'

The man's eyes widened. 'Brother Eadulf? Do you still live? We thought that you had drowned.'

Eadulf had no time to tell the story, merely saying: 'Get your people out and grab what weapons you can. You are being rescued.'

Hoel turned back and repeated Eadulf's words to those inside. There was a suppressed cheer and the next familiar figure that emerged was Wenbrit, the cabin boy.

'Is the lady Fidelma alive?' he asked wonderingly. 'We thought you had drowned.'

'We are both well,' replied Eadulf quickly. 'How many of you survived?'

'They killed no more of us after they murdered the captain, Gurvan and Menma, the crewman they shot when they first attacked the ship – and, of course, the lord Bressal.'

'And you have all been confined here in the hold?'

'We have.'

'Then we'll talk later. Let us make sure the ship is retaken.'

Heraclius led the way back to the deck and by the time they reached it, they found that the fighting was over. The followers of the 'Dove of Death' had paid a heavy price, for there was only one prisoner. The bodies of the others were strewn across the deck, their fighting days over.

The crew of the *Barnacle Goose* were confused after their long incarceration and by the bloody sights before them. Blinking in the daylight, and rubbing their eyes, they started to come to terms with the new situation.

Chapter Nineteen

〰️

Bleidbara strode forward across the deck and clapped Eadulf on the shoulder with a big smile of satisfaction.

'It was well done,' he said approvingly.

'Any casualties?'

'A few minor cuts and scratches, that's all. These scum are no match for real fighting men when it comes to a fair fight.'

Eadulf turned back to Hoel and Wenbrit and asked: 'Are all the prisoners safe?'

'We are,' Hoel confirmed. 'We were ordered to throw the bodies of Murchad and the others overboard while we were still at sea. We had to sail the ship here. Then we were placed in the hold. No one has harmed us since.'

Bleidbara was looking around with a frown.

'Where is the lady Trifina?' he asked.

Hoel looked blank.

'A female,' Eadulf said rather impatiently. 'A woman of this country. Was she not in the hold with you?'

Hoel shook his head. 'Since we were forced to enter this

creek we have been battened down below decks and have lost count of the day or night. We know of no other prisoners.'

Bleidbara was making for the stern cabin and Eadulf, seeing the expression on his face, went quickly after him.

The door of the cabin that had once been used by Murchad, the captain of the *Barnacle Goose*, was not secured. Bleidbara thrust it open unceremoniously. As he did so, a dagger embedded itself in the jamb of the door.

Bleidbara started back with a curse. Then, recovering himself, he pushed inside with Eadulf at his shoulder. Trifina was pressed back in a corner with an expression of fear on her face. This dissolved into one of incredulity and then of joy, and she came rushing across the cabin and threw herself into Bleidbara's arms.

'At last! At last! I thought rescue would never come.'

Bleidbara remained stiff and unresponsive. After a few moments, Trifina felt his coldness and drew back with a puzzled frown.

'What . . . what is it?' she asked uncertainly.

'Why aren't you a prisoner on this ship like the others?'

She did not understand the implication. 'But I am. I *was*.'

'The cabin door was unlocked.'

She smiled uncertainly, still not understanding his point.

'What matters? I could not leave the cabin and there were always guards outside to watch me.'

'Yet all the other prisoners were confined in the hold.'

'I could not help them. I was well treated, provided I kept to the cabin.'

'Lady Trifina.' It was Eadulf who spoke. 'The circumstances

look suspicious, especially when these cut-throats fight under the flag of your family.'

'But I explained that to Fidelma. These people are out to destroy my family,' protested the girl.

'They will destroy nothing now,' Bleidbara told her icily. 'The *Koulm ar Maro* lies at the bottom of the sea and we have slain most and captured the rest of their crew. Now all that remains for us to do is to identify their leader.'

When Trifina turned her gaze to Bleidbara, Eadulf thought he saw in it an expression of sadness, before her features hardened.

'Where is Fidelma?' she demanded. 'Am I now to be accused of being the leader of these raiders?'

It was Eadulf who answered.

'Fidelma is at Brilhag, so far as I know. That is where we are heading now, before . . .' He hesitated and then turned to the stone-faced Bleidbara.

'Then I demand to see her,' Trifina said. 'I was abducted and have been held a prisoner here.'

'And Iuna?' Bleidbara asked, his voice steady.

'Iuna?

'It was she who woke me and, with one of these ruffians, bound and gagged me and took me down to a boat. They killed one of the guards who saw us before he could raise the alarm. Iuna was in league with them all along.' Trifina sounded bitter.

'You ask us to believe that?' replied Bleidbara. 'How do you explain that Iuna was left poisoned in her chamber when you disappeared, while Ceingar was murdered? Yet you were abducted and put on this ship in comparative freedom.'

'Iuna poisoned? Dead?' Trifina cried, aghast.

'Pray God that she is not.'

'I do not know why you disbelieve me. I have spoken the truth. I *was* abducted by Iuna. I was placed on the boat and brought here, while she went back to the fortress.'

'Who do you claim is this *Koulm ar Maro* then?' demanded Bleidbara.

'I met only with a thuggish man called Taran. He was the captain of the ship, the *Koulm ar Maro*. I saw no one else.'

Eadulf turned to Bleidbara. He realised it was no use pressuring the girl any further. Fidelma would surely know what to do.

'We will leave things to Fidelma,' he told Bleidbara. 'Meanwhile, we'd best put one of your seamen on The *Barnacle Goose* to help the crew guide her through these unknown waters. I suggest we sail both ships back to Brilhag before we proceed further.'

Bleidbara turned without making any further acknowledgement of Trifina.

'I'll give the orders,' he said shortly, over his shoulder.

Alone for a moment, Trifina regarded Eadulf angrily, and then her expression softened.

'I am not the *Koulm ar Maro*,' she said, and she sighed deeply. 'I have told the truth.'

Eadulf had an instinct to believe, but then his instincts were sometimes wrong.

'I saw this person once, this Dove of Death,' he told her, 'dressed all in white and masked. He or she was of a slight build and had a high-pitched voice – a man trying to sound like a woman . . . or a woman trying to sound like a man. I do not know.'

'So you think it was me?' Her voice was resigned. 'Then the sooner we can get to Brilhag the better. Is it permitted that I go up on deck?'

Eadulf stood aside. 'Of course.'

On deck he met with Wenbrit again. The boy was physically none the worse for his experience, but he was clearly unhappy.

'What's the matter?' asked Eadulf, as he found the boy sitting disconsolately on a step by the stern deck.

'They killed Luchtigern.'

'Luchtigern? The cat?' Eadulf's memory stirred. 'No, they didn't. We saw him at the Abbey of Gildas. Or rather, Fidelma did. He obviously came ashore. Did the boat put in near there?'

'You saw him alive?' The boy looked incredulous.

'A lady called Aourken has been looking after him in the village near the Abbey of Gildas. The *Barnacle Goose* must have put in there.'

'I do not know the abbey,' the boy said. 'One of the men who held us captive threw him overboard. He must have swum to shore.'

'How was this? I thought cats didn't swim.'

'Luchtigern can. He's a ship's cat. But I didn't think he made it to the shore.'

'What happened exactly? Tell me from the moment the ship was captured.'

'After you and the lady Fidelma jumped in the sea?'

'Exactly so.'

'They sent a skiff out after you but we saw you picked up by a sailing boat, which took you quickly out of reach. The wind turned and that man in the white clothing recalled the skiff. He told us to work the ship, with his men watching us to make sure we obeyed. We were ordered to dump the bodies overboard . . . Murchad, Gurvan, Menma, Lord Bressal. The one in white remained on board with his men, while his own ship followed us closely.'

'Go on,' encouraged Eadulf, when the boy hesitated.

'The helmsman who took over headed for the coast. At least I thought so, but there was a wide gap between two headlands and suddenly we were in a strong current that propelled us at a fast speed between these two points of land. We were all surprised to find ourselves in a large inland sea dotted with islands. The *Barnacle Goose* was sailed round the eastern headland while the other ship held off. We were steered fairly close to shore and then the man in white and another man left our ship and rowed to the shore. That's when Luchtigern was thrown overboard. He scratched this man and the man simply picked up Luchtigern and threw him over the side. I was held back so I could not see what happened.'

'Well,' Eadulf reassured him, 'at least he managed to get ashore. That must have been on this peninsula they call Rhuis. What happened then?'

The boy shrugged. 'The man in white disappeared, while the other, who had rowed him ashore, returned to the ship and we sailed on again until we came to this creek – and then we were all forced into the hold. We must have been held there for many days before you came. How did you find us? How were you saved? What . . . ?'

Eadulf held up his hand to stem the flow of questions.

'All in good time. Did you see or hear anyone since you have been here? Did the man in white return?'

Wenbrit shook his head. 'No. They fed us once a day. Some of us could understand their speech for we have traded along these shores before, though no one knew of this inner sea – they call it the Little Sea, I am told. But even the knowledge of their speech did not help us because they refused to talk to us except to give us the food.'

'And you heard nothing of any other prisoner being brought to the ship?'

'As I say, Brother Eadulf, nothing did we hear until you came and opened the door to our prison. We did not even know there was a lady on board.'

Eadulf pursed his lips reflectively and glanced to where Trifina was standing by the railing, aloof and isolated. He then turned back reassuringly to the boy.

'Well, all will be sorted out soon. And your cat was fine and healthy, last time I saw it.'

'I suppose Hoel will be captain now that Murchad and Gurvan are dead?'

'I suppose so. That is the crew's decision. I think he was Gurvan's assistant.'

'Second mate,' corrected the boy gently.

'When we are ready, Hoel will have to sail us back to Aird Mhór.'

'He's a good seaman,' said the boy solemnly.

The crew of the *Barnacle Goose* had cleared the deck of the bodies of the dead and transferred the prisoner to join the others on the *Morvran*. Buckets of water had been hauled up to wash away the blood and remove all signs of the recent conflict. Under Hoel's instructions, the crew had also examined all the spars, sails and ropes to ensure that nothing had been tampered with and all was in working order.

Finally, Hoel came to inform them that the ship was ready.

Bleidbara smiled. 'Excellent. I am leaving a couple of my best seamen to guide you out of here, and we'll rendezvous off Brilhag.' He turned to Eadulf. 'I shall leave Trifina with you. Keep a careful watch on her . . . you know what I mean.'

He then addressed Hoel. 'Our rowing boats can tow your ship stern first out of the creek. Once you have room to manoeuvre, then we'll let you loose and it should be easy sailing.' He gestured at one of his men. 'This one is a good helmsman. You may put your trust in him to guide you through these waters to Brilhag.'

Bleidbara raised his hand, a quick gesture of farewell, and then followed Heraclius back over the side into the small boats.

The tow ropes were fixed and soon the ship, after the mooring ropes were cast off, was being pulled stern first into deep waters. Once clear of the shore they moved into a breeze that whispered against their sails. Ropes from the rowing boats were cast off and they could hear Hoel give the orders to hoist sail. With a crack of canvas they fell into place and the *Barnacle Goose* moved freely once again across the waters. Behind them, like a watchful guardian, came the sleek lines of the *Morvran*.

*　　*　　*

There had been consternation at Brilhag when the guards reported two ships moving into the bay below the fortress. But Fidelma recognised the first ship as the *Barnacle Goose* and her heart began to beat rapidly. Then she realised the escort was the *Morvran* and was filled with excitement and hope that Eadulf was alive and well. With a word of reassurance to King Alain, she raced headlong down to the small quay. Boric was about to launch a dinghy and readily agreed to take her out to the ships. She did not want anyone else from Brilhag to speak with Eadulf and Bleidbara before she had had a chance to hear their story.

Now, seated on the deck of the *Morvran*, where Eadulf had come to join her, she listened quietly to their story. At the end of it she peered across at the *Barnacle Goose*. She could see a boat being lowered.

'Trifina has persuaded them to take her ashore already,' she remarked. As Bleidbara stirred uncomfortably, she added: 'Don't worry. She will not be going anywhere other than Brilhag.'

'But I believe she is involved in this,' pointed out Bleidbara sadly. 'Nothing else makes sense. Yet I do not want to believe it, lady. However, she did not appear to be a prisoner on the ship. And she has always felt that she should be the successor to her father. It all seems to fit together and yet . . . and yet . . .'

'Yet you are in love with her,' Fidelma finished for him. 'Did she mention Iuna?'

'Only to claim that it was Iuna herself who had abducted her. Trifina says that once she was placed in the boat, Iuna returned to the fortress. She also claims that she knew nothing about Ceingar being killed.'

'How is Iuna – do we know?' Fidelma asked.

'When we passed Govihan, Heraclius went ashore to find out how she is, and promised to bring the news to Brilhag later.'

Fidelma stretched almost languidly, murmuring, 'Well, I think all falls into place.'

Bleidbara frowned, puzzled, but his anxiety overcame the questions that rose to his lips.

'We should be away soon, lady. We have to catch the tide to take us out into the Great Sea. We must get to the rendezvous at dusk to pick up the leader of the *Koulm ar Maro* – they will find the *Morvran* waiting for them instead.'

To their surprise, Fidelma gave a negative sign with her hand.

'They will not be at that rendezvous. So there is no need for you to go.'

'I don't understand, lady,' Bleidbara said. 'How do you know this? Do you mean that because we have captured Trifina . . . ?'

Fidelma rose and walked to the rail of the *Morvran*; she leaned forward, watching the dinghy bobbing on the waters away from the *Barnacle Goose*, making for the quayside below the fortress. They followed her gaze and could see the figure of Trifina in the stern.

'The leaders of this intricate plot are now at Brilhag,' Fidelma told them. 'The culmination of the plan was due to happen here, before dusk, before they left to escape on their ship.'

'Then you *do* know who they are?' demanded Eadulf in astonishment.

There was a smile at the corner of Fidelma's mouth.

'*Patientia vincit*,' she reproved with good humour. 'We will have patience and allow our conspirators a little more slack rope. Don't you agree, Bleidbara?'

The young warrior looked perplexed. 'Whatever you say, lady. I will follow your orders.'

'We will hold our investigation in the great hall at dusk. I have already asked permission of King Alain, who has now arrived. Also, the *bretat* that Brother Metellus sent for is here. Word has been delivered to those who need to attend, such as Barbatil. But now that the Dove of Death already realises that the plan is thwarted, that the ship is sunk and there is no escape, the next step is an uncertain one. Will they, at this late stage, attempt to carry out the final act to which these last two weeks have been leading?'

Bleidbara looked startled and Eadulf was just as bewildered.

'The final act? What is that?' he asked.

Her good humour banished, Fidelma looked grimly at each of them in turn.

'Why, the assassination of the King, Alain Hir, by the family of the *mac'htiern* of Bilhag. An attempt to put a new ruler on the throne of the Bretons.'

CHAPTER TWENTY

‿❧‿

The great hall of Brilhag was crowded. Dusk was gathering outside and numerous oil lamps, unglazed earthenware receptacles with a snout to support the wicks, had already been lit in the main body of the hall. Their flickering flames caused a smoky atmosphere to permeate the interior of the building, sending out a pungent aroma. With the people crowding into the hall, the place was warm, uncomfortably so. The ornate tables had been carried to one side, and chairs and benches placed for people to sit. Facing the main body of the hall, a small platform had been raised by the servants in front of the large fireplace. It was a wooden construction on which four wooden chairs had been placed. Behind each was a tall, wrought-metal candleholder in which beeswax candles were lit.

King Alain and Riwanon had seated themselves on the centre chairs. The red-haired ruler of the Bretons had a sombre expression. The attractive Riwanon was colourfully dressed, so that many an eye focused in her direction. On the King's right sat Lord Canao, the *mac'htiern* of Brilhag, Alain's close friend. He looked anxious, his forehead creased in a permanent frown. When he appeared, there had been many angry mutterings from the local people now pressed onto the benches to hear the judgement of Macliau by the King and his *bretat*. To Riwanon's left sat Budic, the handsome son of the King and commander of the bodyguard.

An elderly man with slightly stooped shoulders sat just in front and below King Alain. He was the *bretat* Kaourentin of Bro-Gernev who had arrived to be the impartial judge of the proceedings. He did not inspire confidence in Fidelma. He was a thin-faced man, with a pale complexion, a beak of a nose and a look of permanent disapproval on his features. His long, once-fair hair was a dirty white, tied at the back of his neck with a ribbon. Fidelma sat directly opposite him, with Brother Metellus at her side as translator. On Metellus' other side was Eadulf, then Bleidbara and Heraclius, their bench being slightly to the right of the elderly judge and thus opposite Riwanon and Budic. Facing Alain and Lord Canao, on the first bench sat Macliau, stubborn-looking, his chin held aggressively high, like a child about to be censured by its father. By his side was his sister Trifina, slouched on her seat with melancholy eyes downcast.

Behind them, all the other benches were filled. Among the people crowded there Fidelma had spotted Barbatil, the farmer and father of Argantken, Coric his friend, and the elderly Aourken. At the back was Hoel, now elevated to captain of the *Barnacle Goose*, with Wenbrit the cabin boy and other members of the crew. Fidelma presumed that the rest of the

crowd consisted of local people and members of the community of the abbey. At strategic points around the hall were
warriors of the King's bodyguard, together with some of the
warriors of Brilhag led by Boric.

There was a suppressed excitement in the great hall. The
murmurs rose and then gradually died as Alain Hir cleared
his throat. He opened with a few words in his native language,
phrasing them in a rich baritone that commanded people's
immediate attention. Then he switched easily into Latin.

'My friends, since the language common to most of us is
Latin then I enjoin you to use it. For those who do not possess
knowledge of it, your friends will know who you are. Please
will those friends go and sit beside you now – in order to
translate, so that you may understand what is being said. I
make this special concession in this hearing due to the fact
that we have a foreigner among us who will make a plea
before us, and, not being proficient in our language, will do
so in Latin.'

Fidelma was about to rise when the old judge, Kaourentin,
did so quickly and half-turned to acknowledge the King.

'I have to speak for the law we share among our kingdoms
and over which you, Alain Hir, preside.' His voice was dry
and rasping. 'It is a custom and has been observed from time
immemorial that *no* foreign person, especially one unable to
speak our language, may plead before our judges, let alone
in the capacity of a prosecutor. I raised this matter with you
last night when, after my arrival, the nature of this case was
explained,' he added reproachfully.

Alain the Tall gazed down at him.

'You made your point eloquently last night and I have weighed your words most carefully. However, I have decided, in the exceptional circumstances which face us, to allow Fidelma of Hibernia to state why she should be allowed to speak here.' He raised a hand to silence the judge, who was clearly about to make further objections.

Fidelma now rose and smiled quickly at the King. Then she took out the hazel wand of office, the wand of a *techtaire* or ambassador, that she had been carrying ever since she had picked it up from the deck of the *Barnacle Goose*, where it had fallen from Bressal's nerveless fingers.

'This is the symbol of office of an ambassador, which the people of Hibernia hold sacred, and which sacred office was violated. It fell from the hand of Bressal, who came to you in peace. He came to conclude a treaty with your kingdom and mine. As sister to my brother, Colgú, King of Muman in the land of Hibernia, I now pick it up and claim that role.'

'Your rank and position are recognised here,' conceded King Alain.

'Your courtesy is only exceeded by your wisdom, Alain, King of the Bretons,' she replied. 'I thank you. Let me make it plain that I am not here to prosecute in your court. I am an advocate of the laws of my country but that does not give me the knowledge to plead in your laws, which I freely admit remain unknown to me. What I would wish is to be allowed to present to those gathered here some facts. Should they be accepted and it is felt that there is a charge to be answered under your laws, I merely hand these facts to you. To *you*,

Kaourentin, so that you may pursue them to a logical conclusion within the constraints of your law.'

The elderly man gazed at her with his dark suspicious eyes.

'These facts that you have gathered by means of investigation – did this involve the questioning of people?'

'Yes, of course.'

'What authority had you to do so?' Kaourentin smiled thinly. 'Again, it is our law that no foreigner can come into our kingdoms and use subterfuge and guile to extract information to present for legal use.'

'Subterfuge and guile? That is a strange way of putting it,' Fidelma observed.

'A law nevertheless. So you admit that you have no authority to have made such an investigation?'

'I did not concede that I had no authority to do so.' Fidelma glanced meaningfully at Riwanon, who flushed slightly.

'She acted under my authority, I think,' the wife of Alain Hir announced.

Kaourentin, his brows drawn, turned to her. 'You say that you *think* she acted on your authority? How is this?'

'I told her to find out who killed Abbot Maelcar.'

'Hah!' Kaourentin exclaimed. 'May I remind you that the charge against Macliau, son of Lord Canao, is that he murdered the girl called Argantken?'

'The charge is further that he is the person behind the *Koulm ar Maro*, the sea raiders, and thereby responsible for all the deaths that occurred here,' Fidelma reminded him.

'The Queen has said that she told you only to find out who killed Abbot Maelcar,' quibbled the *bretat*.

'If it makes it clearer, Riwanon reiterated her authority on the very morning Ceingar was killed and when Trifina and Iuna were abducted, which authority included the other deaths,' Fidelma told the old judge calmly, but wondered whether he was being pedantic or obstructive. 'The words used in front of Budic and of Eadulf were that I had "complete authority" to do so.'

King Alain made an irritated sound and bent forward.

'My wife has explained this, Kaourentin. If that is not enough, then her authority is now confirmed by my own authority for, my wife in our law, always acts under my name.' He spoke sharply, clearly annoyed by this legal attempt to stop Fidelma speaking after he had given his permission for her to do so.

'Forgive me, sire.' Kaourentin was bowing to him. His voice was suave. 'It is my duty to instruct in the law and ensure that all is done according to its principles.'

'Having done so,' King Alain replied in a heavy tone, 'may we finally proceed?'

Kaourentin inclined his head and, sitting down, added: 'Speak, Fidelma of Hibernia. But remember that the primary reason we are gathered here is to hear the case against Macliau, son of Lord Canao, and consider his defence.'

Fidelma allowed the ripple of voices to spread through the great hall and eventually die away. She liked to concentrate her mind for a few moments when she was about to present a case before the Brehons of her own country. She realised that she would be limited in what she had to claim, since she had none of the legal supports of her own laws to back her.

She was not even sure that she would be able to cross-examine any of the people she wanted to. But for the sake of justice she had to pursue this course with all the eloquence that she could command. It was her duty.

'I did not come willingly to your country,' she began quietly but firmly.

She paused for a moment, as if gathering her thoughts again, but Fidelma had an advocate's sense of the dramatic.

'My companion, Eadulf, and I were returning to our own country of Hibernia on a ship called the *Barnacle Goose*. On board that ship was my cousin, a prince of my country, Bressal of Cashel, who had but lately conducted a treaty of trade with King Alain and was en route home with a cargo of salt from the salt pans at Gwenrann. An old friend of mine, Murchad of Aird Mhór, captained the ship. We were sailing near the island called Hoedig when we were attacked by another ship. That ship had a dove carved on its bow and flew a white banner from its stern, on which was the emblem of a dove. We were forced to surrender after one of the crew and the first mate were killed. After that surrender, the commander of this hostile vessel, a person dressed in white and masked, murdered my cousin in cold blood and then murdered the captain. Both of them were unarmed and were making verbal protest, my cousin showing the emblem of his office at the time.'

She paused once more.

'I shall not go into many details. Eadulf and I were about to be slaughtered so, to save our lives, we were forced to jump overboard. Brother Metellus, like a guardian angel, came sailing by and rescued us. Eventually he brought us to the Abbey of Gildas. There I saw evidence that our captured ship must have put in close to these shores.'

Aourken was nodding in her seat.

'I also learned that the emblem of a dove was known as the standard of the *mac'htiern* of Brilhag. Subsequently I discovered that there had been raids on farmsteads, an attack on merchants and several deaths attributed to these same pirates who acted under that flag. Both the ship and the leader of the raiders were referred to as the *Koulm ar Maro*, the Dove of Death.'

Canao now leaned forward in his seat. He spoke loudly and firmly.

'Let it be recorded that the *mac'htiern* of Brilhag clearly and completely denies that any of his followers have acted in the manner described, and that these deeds were *not* committed by anyone who was legally entitled to serve under the emblem of his family.'

Fidelma turned and inclined her head towards him as there came an outburst of angry murmuring from the direction of Barbatil, Coric and their friends.

'But let us agree that the pirates used the standard of Lord Canao of Brilhag during their raids,' she stated.

Barbatil rose to his feet and spoke rapidly, his words quickly translated.

'There are many of us,' he waved his hand to indicate his supporters in the hall, 'farmers, and others, who have witnessed attacks by warriors carrying that now accursed banner bearing a dove as its emblem. We should be protected

by the lord of Brilhag and yet, for these last two weeks, we
have been persecuted by him!'

'You are out of order!' shouted the rasping voice of
Kaourentin.

'Out of order?' cried the burly farmer, his anger bubbling
over. 'My daughter is dead. I am here not for order but for
vengeance! I am here to speak for the farmers who have
been killed, for our wives and daughters who have been
deprived of their husbands and fathers and sons. And for
those who have been violated by these vermin. I speak for
all the dead who have perished by the hand of this Dove of
Death!'

King Alain raised his strong baritone voice to suppress the
rising babble in the room.

'Let no one be under any illusion. This hearing will be
conducted in the name of justice, not of vengeance, and in
accordance with our traditions and spirit of our laws. The
guilty shall be punished. If they are guilty, they shall be
punished, even though they sit at my side.'

Lord Canao flushed but made no response, staring doggedly
ahead of him.

The King turned to Fidelma and motioned her to continue.

'Having landed here on this peninsula, we heard of these
attacks of which the farmer, Barbatil, has spoken. We found
the merchants of Biscam after they were attacked and slaughtered. My companion, Eadulf here, discovered this banner
clutched in the dead hands of one of them . . .'

Eadulf stood up, unfolded the silk banner he had brought
with him and held it up before the assembly, allowing them

to see it and recognise it before he sat down again. A ripple of voices spread through the great hall.

'The evidence is obvious,' shouted someone. Fidelma thought it was Coric, the friend of Barbatil. 'That is the flag of Lord Canao.'

King Alain was looking thoughtful.

'From what I have heard, these attacks began only two weeks ago. But for what purpose? They seem senseless, particularly so if they were being carried out on the orders of the lord of Brilhag – who, I have to say, for these last two weeks has been constantly in my company both at Naoned, Gwenrann and with me hunting along these shores.'

'I have said, and I say it again,' Lord Canao intervened. 'These attacks have *not* been ordered by me or the house of Brilhag.'

'Yet the act was done under your emblem,' Fidelma pointed out. 'We must, therefore, ask – why?'

The *mac'htiern* frowned in annoyance.

'Why would I, or any of my family, attack and despoil those very people who exist under the protection of Brilhag? I am their chieftain. They look to me and mine for their well-being. Our existence is symbiotic. I cannot exist without them nor they without me. Will there be honey if the queen bee should turn and kill the worker bees?'

As eloquent as this was, his words provoked some angry murmuring from Barbatil and his comrades.

'We are here to bring Macliau to justice,' cried Barbatil, 'not Lord Canao. If the father won't admit responsibility then his son must accept the evidence of his guilt.'

Fidelma ignored the cries of support for the farmer.

'Lord Canao has asked a good question. And now, I will answer it. These attacks started when those responsible for them learned that Alain Hir, King of the Bretons, was coming as guest to Brilhag. To what end were all these senseless attacks directed? The lady Trifina has provided the answer. Trifina, what was your response?'

Trifina hesitated and then rose uncertainly.

'I told you that someone was out to destroy the reputation of my family,' she said. 'I believed that the person using the banner of my family did so as a ruse, to bring disgrace on us.'

'Just so' agreed Fidelma mildly. 'But for what end? Just to bring disgrace on a family is not a strong enough motive in itself to go to such murderous lengths. Murder is not an end in itself. There must surely be something more.'

'What more could there be?' Lord Canao bent forward and asked. 'My daughter has given you good reason and has suffered because of it. Bleidbara has brought back half-a-dozen prisoners from his encounter with the *Koulm ar Maro* – they must be made to confess who their leader was. Confess if there was anyone else in conspiracy with them.'

'The truth is that they do not know,' Fidelma replied. 'They are mercenaries. Their captain, a man called Taran from Pou-Kaer, was the only one to have direct dealings with the person who organised them. They were paid from the booty they took, but they never saw their real leader unmasked. Perhaps Taran could have identified the real Dove of Death, but he lies at the bottom of the Morbihan.'

'It is true, Lord Canao,' called Bleidbara. 'They might be willing to talk to save their lives by confession, but they do not know what to confess.'

'I will come to the identity of the leader in a moment,' Fidelma said confidently. 'But firstly I will tell you the reason why this has taken place.' She allowed a few seconds to pass; the great hall was completely silent. 'The lady Trifina was right. This "Dove of Death" as this person became known, was using the emblem of Brilhag for a purpose. However, it was not merely to bring disgrace to this family – but to bring *blame.*'

'Blame?' enquired King Alain, showing bewilderment. 'Blame for what?'

'Your death.'

Fidelma waited until the wave of incredulous voices began to recede.

'These attacks started and built up so that people would already be in the frame of mind to hate and mistrust Brilhag. Who else would they blame if the King of the Bretons, arriving on a visit to Brilhag, were to be assassinated? Assassinated in such a way that the Dove of Death was blamed? The family are descended from the kings of Bro-Waroch, and some believe that they have long had a grudge against the house of Judicael, whose son is Alain Hir. Who would question their motive? Macliau, himself, bemoaned the loss of the kingship of Bro-Waroch to Domnonia, and boasted that he wanted to retrieve the ancient rights of his family.'

Lord Canao cast a look of dismay at his son. Macliau sat

white-faced, staring unseeingly at his feet. It was as if he had withdrawn into himself.

'So *he* is guilty! *He* is the Dove of Death!' shouted Barbatil. Alain Hir was grave and thoughtful.

'You seem to have gathered a lot of information in your investigation, Fidelma of Hibernia,' he said.

'My old mentor in law in Hibernia, the Brehon Morann, used to say that once you have a motive you will be led to the culprit. I am afraid that in this instance he was wrong. The motive was to kill you and place the blame on the family who might have claimed this kingdom on your death. But if that family were not guilty of the assassination . . . who else could possibly benefit from such events as have occurred here?'

'You mean, a beneficiary other than the house of Brilhag?'

'Exactly. As a Roman lawyer, Cicero, once argued before a judge – *cui bono*? Who stands to gain? That is the basis of this matter. Curiously enough, a short time before his death, my Cousin Bressal and I were speaking of the very motivation behind the assassination of a king or chieftain, and of our concerns for the well-being of our own High King. From the attack on our ship, we have made a long journey through many dark minds, but now all shall be revealed.'

'Let us confine ourselves to the accusation that Macliau killed his mistress Argantken and is, in fact, the Dove of Death,' demanded the *bretat* Kaourentin. 'That is why this hearing has been called and that should be the first thing we do.'

An expectant murmur ran through the audience.

411

'We cannot confine ourselves to that alone,' retorted Fidelma. 'However, let us put Macliau out of his misery. He was not guilty of Argantken's murder any more than he was responsible for the outrages that have been committed under the flag of Brilhag. He was a victim of the Dove of Death, a victim of another outrage which would make people think that Brilhag was responsible. And when the last of these actions, the assassination of the King and his replacement, would occur, everyone would blame the family of Brilhag, so that the person responsible could be swept to the kingship on an hysterical wave of support.'

It was some moments before the hubbub died away.

For the first time Macliau raised his head and an expression of hope crossed his features.

Fidelma glanced at him with a satisfied smile.

'I discounted Macliau's involvement on several grounds. Primarily, while, with the right motive, we are probably all capable of killing someone, what motive did he have for killing Argantken? Macliau loves the good life. He loves wine and women. He is no warrior. He confessed as much to us when we arrived here. Importantly, he would never have killed his dog Albiorix. I think he loved that dog perhaps more than he did the women in his life. No, it is impossible to see Macliau in the role of the *Koulm ar Maro*. The Dove of Death is vicious, a ruthless killer with a fixed ambition – not the sort of person who would fall into a drunken stupor next to their newly killed victim and their pet dog. Finally, how would Macliau have succeeded as King? Even his sister, Trifina, and others have pointed out that he did not have the support to succeed as lord of Brilhag, let alone King. I am told the Bretons still adhere to choosing the most capable member of the bloodline, male or even female.'

'If not Macliau then who . . . ?' began Lord Canao.

'I can now name the person who gave direct orders to Taran: the pirate who, dressed all in white and wearing a mask, even went on some of their murderous raids and enjoyed the killing as much as those they led. The person who killed my Cousin Bressal and the captain of the *Barnacle Goose* was – Iuna.'

There was a thunderous noise of incredulity and surprise through the hall. Trifina turned from her seat with shocked features.

'You must be jesting! Iuna, our stewardess?' she cried over the hubbub.

Fidelma was calm.

'Iuna was the person who actually led some of the raids. She is a ruthless and ambitious young woman. It was Aourken who first told me about that ambition. Her parents had been killed and she had been fostered by the Lord of Brilhag.'

'But she was content simply to be our domestic . . .' began Lord Canao. 'She was my foster-daughter. She had no ambition.'

'On the contrary, she had great ambition,' interrupted Fidelma. 'Iuna came from a noble family that dwelt in Brekilien. Iuna's parents had been slain. You knew that when you took her into your household.'

Lord Canao raised his arms in a helpless gesture. It was King Alain who, sitting back, was shaking his head with a sad smile.

'Unfortunately, Fidelma of Hibernia, in your accusation of Iuna, you are forgetting one thing. I knew Iuna's father, since he fought at my side against the Frankish incursions. He was a great noble and a great warrior. But he was not of the bloodline of Domnonia or Bro-Waroch. If the motive was to assassinate me and blame it on Lord Canao's family, in order that *she* could claim my throne, that would have been impossible.'

'True,' conceded Fidelma. 'But I did not say that she was aiming to be the direct beneficiary of these murderous acts. She was acting for someone else, someone who *would* be the beneficiary – *in the mistaken belief that she would then join him as his Queen.*'

'But,' replied King Alain, 'if I died now, there is only . . .'

There was a sudden silence and then Fidelma spoke slowly and distinctly.

'Yes. There is only your son by your first wife who is of the bloodline and would come to the throne without challenge. Budic would succeed you.'

Once again the rest of her words were drowned in the cacophony of voices throughout the great hall. Budic sat with a broad grin spreading over his features, shaking his head as if in disbelief.

Finally, Fidelma made herself heard again, speaking directly to King Alain.

'I did not know that Budic was your son and possible heir until you confirmed it last night. I should have realised it before, when Abbot Maelcar arrived in answer to what he believed was a command from you as King. Abbot Maelcar asked Budic if he had sent the message on behalf of his father. Of course, Abbot Maelcar knew you were Budic's father. Not recognising that fact was a serious error on my behalf.'

Budic was actually laughing now.

'And not the only one. You are accusing *me* of attempting to murder my own father?' He turned to King Alain. 'The woman is mad. When these attacks started to occur I can prove I was not even in this province.'

'I am sure you can because you were working with Iuna, the Dove of Death.'

Budic gazed at Fidelma with a cynical smile. 'You still have to prove all these accusations, and foreigner or not, a King's sister or not, you will have to account for them.' The vehemence in his voice belied the smile.

'Silence!' King Alain snapped. 'This is not the place to make threats. Fidelma of Hibernia is under my protection and may present her accusations here without fear. But I have to say that these same accusations are wild and unreasonable. You will have to present proof that Iuna and Budic are in such a conspiracy.'

'Indeed,' sneered Budic. 'And where is Iuna? Will she come forward to confess this? I think not. And for what reason am I supposed to have killed Abbot Maelgar, the girl found with Macliau and heaven knows who else?'

'Iuna killed Abbot Maelcar,' went on Fidelma confidently. 'The Abbot was from Brekilien and had been fostered in an abbey – I believe it is called Pempont. Next to it is the royal court. On a visit recently, he chanced on Iuna in a compromising position with Budic. He came back muttering about

loose morality at the court – about a provincial servant forni-
cating with the King's offspring. Aourken told me that. Alain
has only one offspring. Abbot Maelcar considered Iuna a
provincial servant. And Iuna let slip that Abbot Maelcar used
to call her that as an insult. She also said he was a man who
looked at women through cracks in curtains. She was about
to tell me what had happened at Brekilien when she realised
that it would incriminate her. Indeed, she realised that Abbot
Maelcar could be witness to her relationship with Budic. That
was why he was invited here and killed by her. She grew
more vicious as the time for the fruition of the conspiracy
grew close.'

During this recital, Riwanon had turned to regard Budic
with an expression of distaste, but the young man was still
sneering at Fidelma.

'But I am told that Budic himself was nearly slain in an
ambush by the followers of this Dove of Death,' King Alain
objected. 'They attacked Riwanon and killed members of
their escort. Budic saved her life.'

'Explain that, foreigner!' Budic taunted her.

'The ambush was faked,' answered Fidelma flatly.

Riwanon coloured and leaned forward, her cheeks aflame.

'But I was there,' she said. 'Bleidbara and your companion
went out after the attackers and found them, rescued my maid
while she was being raped, and killed them. How was that a
fake?'

'I'll tell you what really happened,' Fidelma said. 'Budic
and yourself rode out with Ceingar, your maid, and two
warriors. Budic needed such an event to enhance his

position when the time came to present himself as a hero who had escaped death from the evil machinations of Brilhag. Iuna had arranged for one of the raiding parties from the *Koulm ar Maro* to meet up with Budic and his party. In fact, I suspect the two warriors who accompanied Budic were either part of the conspiracy or mercenaries from the *Koulm ar Maro*. I found it curious that Budic and Riwanon had decided to go to the oratory that morning when the countryside was in such uproar. When they returned to Brilhag with the story of two warriors and their maid dead or captured and their own miraculous escape, I became very suspicious.

'What really happened was that the party had met up and then Riwanon and Budic had returned with their stories. Meanwhile, the two warriors and Ceingar had joined the others and even attacked a farmstead, killing a farmer and his family.

'Bleidbara and Boric, and Boric is a first-class tracker, could find no signs of any attack along the forest track where it was said to have happened. Nor could Boric find tracks of Riwanon and Budic's horses fleeing back to Brilhag, hotly pursued in the manner that had been claimed. Bleidbara and his men – Eadulf was with them – came across the camp of the raiders and Ceingar, the maid.'

'They arrived there as Ceingar was being raped,' Riwanon reminded her.

'Indeed, they did. Either Ceingar's lover was among these raiders or else she was a young lady of loose morals. From what Eadulf told me, she was not protesting against the man's amorous attentions. When she was returned to Brilhag, she was scared. In her hysteria the truth might have come out, but she was sent to her chamber before I could question her.

'Iuna realised the arrival of King Alain was imminent and nothing must go wrong with the plan. Perhaps even Budic gave the order. Ceingar had to be silenced. Iuna had already killed Maelcar and had no compunction about doing the same to Ceingar. Iuna is a cold-blooded killer.'

'Then why didn't she kill me?' demanded Trifina. 'Why did she simply kidnap me after she had killed Ceingar?'

'You were needed alive for the time being to mislead everyone into believing the Dove of Death was definitely a member of the house of Brilhag. King Alain was due to arrive: the conspiracy was about to come to fruition. Iuna and one of her followers from the *Koulm ar Maro* took you bound and gagged from your chamber down to a boat in the harbour. You were taken to The *Barnacle Goose* where you were placed as a prisoner, but were well treated and given free range of the captain's cabin. They needed to keep you in good health for when Budic made his accusation against the house of Brilhag.'

Bleidbara was clearly chastened and his face reddened as he realised that his suspicions about Trifina had not been justified.

'Iuna then returned to the fortress, perhaps to establish her own alibi. Budic was about to make his bid for power but Iuna, having set up the circumstances, was no longer needed. She had been useful to him and he had used her ambition to help his own cause. However, he also knew the dangers of that ambition and was determined that Iuna should never be his Queen. Indeed, while he had probably made all sorts of promises to her, such an outcome had never been his intention.

'His plan for her was quite horrible. On her return, after Trifina was abducted, he went to her room. Whether by guile or by force, he got her to eat mushrooms which contained a Death Cap fungus. Once prepared, it is hard to spot the differences in fungi, so perhaps it was by guile. Budic did not count on the fact that Trifina, aware that the *Koulm ar Maro* was trying to discredit Brilhag, had an able spy watching. That was Iarnbud.'

'How much more of this rubbish do I have to listen to?' Budic demanded, the smile now gone from his features.

'Iarnbud came ashore at Govihan alive and managed to tell us the story. He took Iuna from her chamber and carried her to his boat. His aim was to find Heraclius, Trifina's apothecary, as he knew that he might be the only one with the skills to find an antidote for her.'

'And did he?' enquired Lord Canao quietly. The great hall of Brilhag had fallen silent since Fidelma had begun her summary.

'A guard unfortunately saw Iarnbud as he carried Iuna to his boat. When challenged, he did not stop and therefore was shot at. An arrow found its mark but Iarnbud managed to get his boat out of the harbour. Unfortunately he was too weak – maybe he had passed out – and was unable to sail directly to Govihan. It was not until late the next day that he made landfall there, came ashore, told us the tale and then died.'

'So everything you have to say is pure conjecture,' observed the *bretat* Kaourentin, feeling it was about time he tried to take charge of the situation. 'You have no witnesses.'

'I am not given to making conjectures without means of supporting them,' replied Fidelma in a dangerously soft tone.

'Then where are your witnesses? Where is the evidence to—?'

Budic interrupted the *bretat*, full of arrogance again.

'Let her explain why I would poison Iuna if, as you say, she had helped me in this ridiculous plot and was my mistress? Your argument is full of flaws. You are better suited to take your place among the bards and storytellers, Sister Fidelma, than to plead before a court of law.'

'You wanted to be rid of Iuna so that, after King Alain's death, you could marry your real mistress, whose union with you would enhance your image when you claimed the kingship.'

'And do you name her?' demanded King Alain, in a terrible voice. It was now self-evident to most people where her logic led and whom she would name.

Fidelma raised her eyes to those of Riwanon.

'You are Budic's mistress, lady. It was a matter that puzzled me greatly. Why were you so keen to give me, a foreigner with a poor knowledge of your language, the responsibility of investigating the murder of Abbot Maelcar? With the murder committed under the same roof as where you were staying, as Queen, you had to be seen to be doing something. It would have otherwise been suspicious. Obviously, you did not expect me, with the disadvantages I have mentioned, to discover anything at all.'

Riwanon's jaw was thrust out defiantly but it was Budic who replied with a laugh.

'So where is your proof? Iarnbud died on the shore of Govihan – should we take the word of a dead man? This Taran of Pou-Kaer, the captain of the *Koulm ar Maro*, is at the bottom of Morbihan. The few survivors cannot identify the Dove of Death. So who else will support your fantasy?'

Fidelma turned towards him.

'You forget that Iarnbud had brought Iuna with him to find Heraclius the apothecary so that he might administer an antidote to the poison. Iuna was alive when she was brought ashore on Govihan.'

For a moment there was a deathly silence in the great hall, broken only by the crackle of flames from the fire.

Then Budic sprang up; his chair went over backwards and his sword appeared in his hand as if conjured there from nothing. With a terrible cry of rage, he leaped towards his shocked father. As quick as Budic was, Bleidbara was faster – for his dagger flew swiftly from his hand and embedded itself in Budic's sword wrist. The weapon dropped as he gave a scream of pain. Then the King's bodyguard came forward to restrain him. Another guard appeared quickly at the side of Riwanon. She had slumped in her chair, pale and shaking.

King Alain rose unsteadily.

'My son is condemned by his own actions.' His voice was thick with emotion. He glanced down at the *bretat* Kaourentin. 'I think the accusation against Macliau, son of Lord Canao, can now be dismissed. My son Budic will be punished under our laws for all the crimes he has committed against me and against my peoples.' He turned to Riwanon. 'Do you have anything to add to what we have heard?'

There was an imperceptible shake of the woman's head and a suppressed sob.

'Then know that you, too, must face the consequences for your part in this conspiracy.' King Alain turned his back on her.

After the guards had taken them away, King Alain addressed Fidelma, his face still bearing the marks of shock and sorrow.

'I am grateful to you, Fidelma of Hibernia. Thankfully, Iuna has survived to bear witness against my son, otherwise he might have continued to feign his innocence.'

Fidelma answered with a sad smile.

'I am afraid that I was being frugal with the facts,' she said in a tired voice. 'It is true that Iuna was alive when we brought her ashore in Govihan and Heraclius administered to her. But she was unable to speak and, indeed, she died before she could say anything to confess her guilt or to implicate Budic in her death. It was merely logical deduction that ensnared Budic and Riwanon. Their guilt produced their own confessions.'

King Alain gazed long and hard at her. For a moment he plucked at his lower lip. Then he sighed deeply.

'You are an ingenious woman, Fidelma of Hibernia. Riwanon's greatest mistake was in underestimating your ability and thinking you would be handicapped by a lack of knowledge of our language.'

Fidelma bowed slightly, a motion with her head only.

'I was always taught *vincit omnia veritas* – truth conquers all things.'

EPILOGUE

❧

All sails set, the *Barnacle Goose* was leaning into the wind, with the hum of the breeze in her rigging and the soft groaning of her wooden spars. Ribbons of cream-cap-waves spread from her plunging bow and trailed out at angles from either side of the large wooden vessel. It seemed odd to be back on the ship again. Everything seemed so familiar to Fidelma and Eadulf and yet, at the same time, so strangely alien. Instead of Murchad and Gulvan at the helm, there was the lean, fair-haired figure of Hoel the Briton. He stood easily balanced, with feet wide apart, his chin thrust forward into the gusting air, his keen eyes on the sails, noting every movement of the wind and adjusting the tiller accordingly.

Fidelma knew and trusted him as a capable seaman. She had no concern that the passage home would be anything but safe in his able hands. But the strangeness was due to the fact that she had been so used to Murchad's predictable mannerisms and Gulvan's stoic responses. They had been such an integral part of the ship, as much a part of it as the carved figure of the goose at her bows or the tall oak masts or beams. It was just hard to imagine that the *Barnacle Goose* could ever sail without them.

Yet everything else was the same. Or was it? Wenbrit seemed quieter, older, somehow not the same carefree child that he had once been, running eagerly to do her bidding. He had become – what was the word that she was looking for? – mature. That was it. He had become mature. And even Luchtigern, the Mouse Lord, the black cat that had been such an essential feature of the life on shipboard, had become more reclusive, preferring to stay in the dark shadows of the vessel rather than venturing out into the sunlight. Hoel too seemed taciturn and had taken refuge in his task of captain.

Once, the ship had been manned with a light-hearted quality among the crew. Sadly, there was no longer the occasional jest among them, the bluff, good-natured ripostes. All the crew had been marked by their recent experiences.

Fidelma leaned against the taffrail and stared solemnly at the receding headlands that marked the dangerous entrance to Morbihan. At her side, Eadulf seemed to read her mind.

'I shan't be sorry to see the last of that place,' he said tightly.

'It will be good to sight the coast of Muman again,' she agreed. 'Even better to see Cashel rising before us and to embrace our little Alchú again.' She suddenly gave a deep sigh. 'But there is also regret at leaving Brilhag. Travelling and meeting people, getting to know them, surely enhance one's experiences in life? Yet establishing such friendships also makes parting a sad experience when the time comes that we must travel on. Leaving such new friends behind is always a matter of regret. I hope things work out with Trifina and Bleidbara.'

'I am sure they will. Bleidbara's suspicion was natural. She will forgive him.'

'But he should have had more trust in her if he truly loved her,' Fidelma objected.

'It's hard to say. He is a man much concerned with duty. With some people, duty is often paramount rather than obedience to the heart.'

Fidelma looked at him closely, wondering if there was a hidden meaning somewhere.

'It seems that Brother Metellus will come well out of this,' went on Eadulf, apparently oblivious of her glance. 'He now stands to be elected Abbot of the community of Gildas. That was something he never expected.'

'And, perhaps, never wanted. Also, this adventure might be a means of making a man of Macliau.'

'Perhaps.' Eadulf did not seem sure. 'I gather he has left Brilhag to study poetry and music and, in that, he will have plenty of opportunity to pursue his libertine existence.'

'He was shocked by what occurred. He told me that he feels the need to redeem himself. I hope he succeeds.'

Eadulf sighed, then admitted, 'Well, I am quite happy to leave behind some of our new friends. Unfortunately, we always seem to get acquainted with the bad people of the world.' He glanced at her. 'I know, I know. It is your task in life to seek out the wrongdoer and secure their punishment. So it is inevitable that we must encounter such people as Iuna

– the Dove of Death.' He shivered suddenly. 'Such evil in a woman and in one so young.' Then he said awkwardly to Fidelma, 'Tell me, when you embarked on outlining the case against Budic and Riwanon, did you really do so knowing that you could not prove anything conclusively? That it was mostly circumstantial evidence?'

'You will find in the Law of the Fénechus that indirect evidence can be used to argue before a Brehon. You can present this circumstantial evidence, and if the accused has a physical reaction to the evidence, whether he may tremble, blush, turn pale, develop a dry throat or display any other symptoms of nervousness, then the suspicion of guilt is strong.'

'But not conclusive. Anyway, that may be so in Hibernia but what if Budic had not confessed?'

Fidelma smiled thinly, saying, 'I am a lawyer and have to use the tools that the law allows me. In these circumstances, my strategy worked.' She turned to regard Eadulf with her brows drawn together. 'I thought that the law was also the task *you* were born to,' she reproved softly. 'You were a *gerefa*, a magistrate of your people. You had to dispense the law among them. Remember that was how we first met? It was because you were a *gerefa* of your people and I a *dálaigh* of mine that we were brought together in Hilda's abbey.'

'I abandoned being a *gerefa* when your countryman, Fursa, converted me to the Faith and I went to study in Tuam Brecain. I am a member of the religious now.'

She hesitated, wondering whether Eadulf was implying a censure for, technically, she too was a religious. But she would always describe herself as an advocate of the laws of her country first. Indeed, that had been her inward struggle for many years. She had never ceased to ask herself whether she should give up the symbols of religious life. That would not be difficult for her, as she had never really been committed to them. She decided to ignore his remark and return to her previous point.

'Remember, in these travels, we meet not only the bad but also the good. We see not only the guilty but also the innocent.'

'What concerns me is that even the good can produce evil,' Eadulf announced reflectively, drawing himself up from the taffrail and staring towards the billowing sails above him.

'What are you thinking about?' she enquired, not sure of his meaning.

'I was thinking of young Heraclius.'

'Heraclius? I don't understand. I thought that he was a very moral young man.'

'But that invention of his, that thing that he calls the *pyr thalassion* or liquid fire – that is evil.'

'He told me that it was really the invention of his father, Callinicus of Constantinopolis. That he merely tried to remember the formula.'

'If an invention can be called evil, then this liquid fire is evil,' repeated Eadulf.

'It is not the invention that is evil, Eadulf, but merely the use men put it to.'

'I suppose that is a philosophical argument. Yet if it had not been invented, men would not use it. I will agree that we could argue that when the first stick was sharpened into a point to use as a weapon, that was an evil thing. But the idea of hurling fire onto a ship – well . . .' He shuddered. 'That must be the ultimate weapon.'

'But not a new one,' Fidelma replied. 'I had a long talk with Heraclius. While his weapon was more efficient, he told me that another countryman of his called Proclus Oneirocrites, set an entire fleet on fire when he was helping his King, Anastasius, to defeat a rebellion against him. It happened nearly a century and a half ago. Some say that he used the power of the sun, directed by mirrors, and some say that he used sulphur and hurled it burning onto the ships.'

'Well, this Greek Fire frightens me – the idea of the mass destruction that it can cause. Let us hope its knowledge will remain with those of good intent, for if it ever falls into evil hands . . .'

'There can never be a guarantee of that,' Fidelma replied. 'At least, it is not something we have to worry about in the Five Kingdoms. So let us relax and enjoy the voyage back to Aird Mhór.'

'And how long will it be before we have to start our travels again?'

Fidelma had the impression that Eadulf spoke the words without meaning to. They had come automatically to his lips.

She turned and placed a hand on his arm, saying, 'I am hoping that we shall be there a while. I know we have been a long time travelling, so long that I wonder if we will recognise little Alchú.'

Eadulf's voice held bitterness in its tone.

'It is not our recognition of the boy that concerns me,' he said. 'It is whether the boy will recognise us.'

Fidelma bit her lips. Eadulf was right, of course; she knew it and resented it. She was aware that she always placed her calling as an advocate of the laws of Éireann before all other considerations. But that had ever been, since she had left the school of the Brehon Morann to make her way in the world. Her cousin, Abbot Laisran, had persuaded her to join the religious at Cill Dara. Most of those who followed the professions had entered the religious, for they saw it as indispensable security to their callings – doctors, lawyers, chroniclers and so on. But when it came to a choice between obedience to the Abbess and obedience to the law, Fidelma chose the law. She was no religious at heart. She knew it. She even challenged some of the basic dogmas of the Faith where she felt they needed it.

So perhaps now was a time to cease this questioning of her motives? There was still a secular professional class among her people. She felt that her cousin Abbot Laisran had ill-advised her. Her life, she had discovered, did not rely on being protected by a religious community. She found the new ideas coming from Rome – that all should obey the set rules that most people felt alien to their philosophies – was not a path she wanted to continue on. Was it too late?

'You seem deep in thought.' Eadulf's voice awoke her from her reverie.

'I was thinking about what you said.'

'I just want our son to grow up knowing something of his parents.'

'Of course. I want the same.' Fidelma coloured a little. She had begun asking herself what her true ambition in life was, and had realised that her greatest joy was her pursuance of the law. The religious life counted as little compared with that.

'Perhaps, when we return to Cashel, we should spend time talking about the future?' ventured Eadulf.

He was a little surprised when she agreed readily. He gazed thoughtfully at her.

'That is good. We have travelled enough in one life. Now is the time to settle and become more reflective and, perhaps, find a retreat in that little mixed community at the Abbey of the Blessed Ruan, north of Cashel. What was it called? The oak-grove of . . . ?'

He broke off with a sigh when he realised that Fidelma was no longer listening. Her eyes seemed focused somewhere on the misty waters of the grey sea before her.

Had he but known, Fidelma's thoughts were actually running the opposite course to Eadulf's.

She was not thinking of settling down in a mixed religious community to reflect on the Faith. In fact, she was thinking about leaving the religious altogether and taking her place in the role that she had, unofficially, long since filled. That was the role as the legal advisor to her brother, Colgú, King of Cashel.

A smile crossed her features as she thought more about the idea. That would be her ambition fulfilled. She wanted to tell Eadulf immediately – but she hesitated. It would wait until they reached Cashel. It would wait until she had talked it over with her brother. Eadulf was not ready to consider the matter now. Best wait until they were home in Cashel. Everything would be all right in Cashel.

The Council of the Cursed

Peter Tremayne

It is AD 670, and Bishop Leodegar of Autun has called the church leaders together for an emergency meeting. But a fierce row breaks out and the assembly descends into chaos. Later that evening one of the delegates is discovered murdered, his skull brutally smashed.

Sister Fidelma and her companion, Brother Eadulf, unwittingly find themselves in the middle of a shocking murder investigation involving the most powerful religious leaders in the land. The disappearance of women and children and rumours of a slave trade indicate malevolent forces at work within the abbey walls.

To catch those responsible, Fidelma and Eadulf must challenge these fearsome individuals and, in doing so, risk their own lives . . .

Praise for the widely acclaimed SISTER FIDELMA MYSTERIES:

'The background detail is brilliantly defined . . . wonderfully evocative' *The Times*

'Tremayne's super-sleuth is a vibrant creation, a woman of wit and courage who would stand out in any era, but brings a special sparkle to the wild beauty of medieval Ireland' Morgan Llywelyn

'Definitely an Ellis Peters competitor' *Evening Standard*

978 0 7553 2841 3

headline

Dancing With Demons

Peter Tremayne

When Sechnussach, high king of Ireland is found dead in his bedchamber with his throat cut, all clues point to Dubh Duin, the chieftain of the clan Cinél Cairpre. But rather than surrender, or protest his innocence, Dubh Duin takes his own life.

The Chief Brehon of Ireland asks Sister Fidelma to find out what possible motives could have driven Dubh Duin to assassinate the High King. Fidelma, assisted by her trusted partner Brother Eadulf and accompanied by two Cashel warriors, sets out for the High King's palace at Tara.

Their investigation reveals an intricate web of conspiracy and deception. Is the true culprit still at large? If those responsible are not discovered in time, these intrigues threaten to send the five kingdoms spiralling into a bloody civil war . . .

Praise for the widely acclaimed Sister Fidelma mysteries:

'The background detail is brilliantly defined . . . wonderfully evocative' *The Times*

'Tremayne's super-sleuth is a vibrant creation, a woman of wit and courage who would be outstanding in any era, but brings a special sparkle to the wild beauty of medieval Ireland' Morgan Llywelyn

978 0 7553 2839 0

headline

Now you can buy any of these other bestselling books
by **Peter Tremayne** from your bookshop
or *direct from his publisher.*

FREE P&P AND UK DELIVERY
(Overseas and Ireland £3.50 per book)

The Subtle Serpent	£6.99
The Spider's Web	£6.99
Valley of the Shadow	£6.99
The Monk who Vanished	£6.99
Act of Mercy	£6.99
Hemlock at Vespers	£6.99
Our Lady of Darkness	£6.99
Smoke in the Wind	£6.99
The Haunted Abbot	£6.99
Badger's Moon	£6.99
Whispers of the Dead	£6.99
The Leper's Bell	£6.99
Master of Souls	£6.99
A Prayer for the Damned	£6.99
Dancing with Demons	£7.99
The Council of the Cursed	£7.99

TO ORDER SIMPLY CALL THIS NUMBER

01235 400 414

or visit our website: www.headline.co.uk

Prices and availability subject to change without notice.